CLEAR
FIRE

ALUN REYNOLDS

Copyright © Alun Reynolds 2023
Cleaning Fire

Editor: Will Rees
Cover by Martin Baines

Printed and bound in the UK by
Severn, Bristol Road, Gloucester, GL2 5EU

ISBN: 978-1-915439-84-0

Published by
Candy Jar Books
Mackintosh House
136 Newport Road, Cardiff, CF24 1DJ
www.candyjarbooks. co.uk

I fy nheulu

I

WE'D ONLY BEEN WAITING a few minutes when the Number 61 bus, which was fuller than usual that morning, arrived to take us down to Cathedral Road.

Both of us bespectacled, leaning on walking sticks. I'd forgotten to trim Gwyn's peppered goatie that day, a task which was now beyond him, and maybe beyond me as well. My previous expertise in Windsor knotting his St David-flagged tie was waning. His hair I swept back as it receded behind his creased and sun-spotted forehead.

Now and again I remember, or try to remember. All of it. The deference, the shame... My memory isn't what it was. The temptations, the innocence, the guilt, the depravity; it hadn't been bougainvillea all the way. But we won in the end, it was all worth it in the end.

Yet, I ended up here, in the cold wet November, shivering at the bus stop on Waungron Road, surrounded by castles. I emerged here, captured in my own snare, standing in a foreign land.

The Winchester 70, I insisted Gwyn give away. A parting gift to Adip Patel, a mark of their friendship.

At home in Broken Hill, Northern Rhodesia, Gwyn and I would get up early, at around the same time every morning, six o'clock, or thereabouts. We'd go to the veranda, share a Woodbine and listen, sometimes to the last musings of a nightjar, sometimes to the begin-

nings of the song of a rufous ant thrush, sometimes both, rarely
nothing. And that's how my story starts.

'You've begun to bite your fingernails again, Gwyn. Something
wrong?'

'Ain't much call for manicured nails out in the bush. All the boys
do it. Jabez will soon be here to pick me up.'

'Kapiri Mposhi, isn't it?'

'Yep, forty miles north of here, in the Mkushi Block. It ain't
Northern Rhodesia's finest. Not much to do in that place, that's for
sure.'

'When we going to talk, Gwyn?'

'Talk? About what?'

'Us, talk about us. It's been a couple of years now.'

Gwyn raised his eyebrows, opened his nostrils, and looked sideways.

'It's a small station. Its main purpose is as a cleaning fire installa-
tion, that's what we call it.'

'Gwyn—'

'All our trains need water, they're steam driven. Every seventy
miles or so they take on water. Cleaning fire, we call it. Without the
cleaning fire you'd have no trains. It's not easy, Daisy. People are
talking.'

'Does that bother you?

'We'll sort something out, Daisy.'

We were both like contortionists, trying to twist ourselves out of
a maze.

'Your chauffeur's arrived,' I said.

Shorts freshly pressed, khaki-shirted, Jabez Pugh, same as all
settler railway men, veneered by the weather, waited outside our
house in his old Land Rover Series I, the engine running. 06.20 sharp.
Jabez was a punctual man.

Like Gwyn, Jabez was in early middle age, but still sturdy and
powerful. He was average height with his shoulders back, but stooped
slightly now and again, especially when he was tired. An ageing
athlete whose prime had been and gone, but more than capable of

taking care of himself in a bar room brawl, if required, and more than capable of starting one. Dappled flecks of grey appeared here and there in his deep black hair, but peculiarly his moustache showed no such mottling; it was jet black, clipped neatly, a thin soldierly membrane above his top lip. His eyes bluish, one slightly out of alignment with the other. When calm he spoke with a hint of a Welsh accent, tempered and bevelled over many years by the savannah sun. In anger, the tempering and bevelling were gone. His face was overwhelmed by a deep diagonal grey-white scar.

Trouble in a tavern, Gwyn had told me once.

'Remember, Gwyn, we'll have to talk, I'm not prepared to go on with all this.'

'I'll think of something, leave it to me.'

I stepped in front of him, blocking his exit. 'There's nothing to think about!'

A pharaoh's mummy stared back at me.

'I've got to go, Jabez is waiting.'

Stepping around me, walking away, into the Land Rover.

'Ain't the colour of the sun beautiful today, Jab,' said Gwyn.

'Yeah, just like the colour of my piss. Come on, let's go.'

II

Site work was nomadic and this suited Gwyn well. He always liked moving on to somewhere new. A convenient piece of ground would be cleared of vegetation by cutting and burning, leaving a dry dustbowl for the construction of the navvies' huts, mostly made of wood and corrugated iron. Daytime ovens, nightime fridges. During this preparatory work any animals in the area either ran away or were burnt to death. On completion of each contract, the huts would be dismantled and moved to the next job, leaving the bush to recover as best it could. The dead wildlife cremated, a gust of wind would soon blow those ashes away. Following the clearing of Kapiri Mposhi, a couple of lifeless wattled lapwings, charred beyond recognition, save for their unmistakable long yellow legs, were the only cadavers found, but everyone knew there must have been numerous others. There were only two survivors, two injured birds, common tailed drongo. Gwyn had asked Foreman Daniel to arrange for the building of a small wooden pen for the birds to assist with their recovery. Daniel assigned young David to nurse them back to health. Chibwe was given the duty of constructing the cage.

'Why we bothering with such nonsense?' said Chibwe, gritting his teeth and staring back at Daniel. 'These birds are everywhere.'

'May as well try and do some good out here,' intervened David.

'That's right,' said Daniel. 'Mr Bowen wants you to make these drongo better, David. And, Chibwe, build that cage good.'

'They're almost half dead anyway, we should either kill 'em, or let 'em die. Food for the hyenas. The stupid always die,' said Chibwe.

'Just do as your told,' ordered Daniel.

Daniel was slightly stunned by Chibwe's arrogance. Maybe he had become too close to him. But Chibwe's haughty ease and assurance had always appealed to Daniel. The way Chibwe carried himself: boldly, confidently. Daniel liked Chibwe, and Chibwe knew it.

Chibwe sinewy, more than muscular, but he had a look; old man Mubanga called it 'the Chibwe look'. A sickliness in that arrogance. Chibwe thought of Mubanga as witless, too dull to bother with, which was his view of most people. Fools were only there to amuse him.

Behind the Kapiri Mposhi station platform, near the camp, the navvies had formed a circle. The men jostled for position. Gwyn ran towards the indistinct chanting rising into the heat-scarfed air. The savannah custard yellow, Rhodesia Railway issue boots dredging the dry sandy soil.

'What's going on, Daniel, what's all this noise?' shouted Gwyn, as he reached the throng.

Foreman Daniel shrugged his shoulders. 'It's Chibwe, found a boomslang in camp this morning, a tree snake. He was about to kill it when Mr Pugh stopped him.'

'Not like Jabez Pugh, he ain't no animal lover.'

'No, I know.'

Inside the dusty circle Chibwe and Chola had snared the snake, prodding it with sharp acacia sticks. The boomslang, five feet in length, light green, black-tipped scales, enormous pinpointing hunting eyes, an eater of nesting birds.

Jabez was also within the circle, carrying a small bird cage with two injured drongo inside. Pretty little birds, about seven inches in length, square tailed, their wings polished, glossy, parade-square black. Heavy billed, harsh voiced, red eyed.

'Boomslang, boomslang, boomslang!' shouted the navvies, rhythmical, atavistic, the off-sweet smell of their labourers' sweat hovering above the hiss of the boomslang and the squawking drongo.

Grabbing one of the drongo, Jabez held it aloft, trophy-like, waving the fluttering bird above his head. With a shout of 'Prepare to meet thy maker!' he threw it towards the snake as if throwing scraps to a pet dog. The bird was swallowed whole. The men roared again.

'Boomslang, boomslang, boomslang!'

Chibwe, Chola and Jabez, gladiators in the Coliseum, acknowledged the adulation. Da Vinci arms held straight outwards, shoulder height, palms at forty-five degrees. Jesus at his crucifixion.

Consumed by the moment, the three didn't see Gwyn advancing in silence into the ring, spade in hand, bringing it down two handed from a position far above his head, crushing the snake's skull with one heavy blow and immediately scraping away the brains of the boomslang from the spade with the toe of his boot.

'What the bloody hell are you doing!' shouted Jabez. 'Why did you do that, the boys and me were having fun. The drongos didn't have much life in them any case. You're getting soft, Gwyn!'

None of the men liked Jabez. They feared him, he was a bully with a hair trigger. But he knew better than most: it was not a good idea to deprive the men of their entertainment. Navvies had long memories.

'Break it up, men. Daniel, get the boys back to work!' yelled Gwyn.

Foreman Daniel did as he was told, the men dispersing in twos and threes, muttering, sulking.

'You know those shenanigans are bad for morale, don't you, Jabez?' said Gwyn.

'No, I don't, just the opposite,' Jabez replied.

'We're in the middle of the bush here, Jabez, a foreign army on expedition. The unquestioning requirement is discipline, unswerving obedience to civilised patterns of behaviour. I expect all of the men, and especially you, to uphold those rules.'

'All those graves along the line,' Jabez spat back, 'those poxy mounds of stone, a small knoll, a wooden cross, railwaymen who died from malaria, accidents, lions... Do you think they gave a monkey's about civilised patterns of behaviour? The railway don't stop for dying men and it sure as hell don't stop for a dying bloody drongo, who in case you've forgotten, we half killed anyway.'

'We cannot, *must not* descend to the level of the slaughterhouse. This is a magnificent country, and these are good people, but we must have discipline. This'll be their country, Bemba country, one day.'

'The future ain't pledged to anyone! Just what's happened to you, Gwyn? Do you think we're building these railways for the Bemba? We're building what Rhodes started, for Europeans, the settlers, the colonisers. Railways are for us, the oppressors, and you just can't handle that can you, Gwyn? Your beloved railways are a virus manacling Africa to foreign domination and you just can't cope! Psh, you can't even sing in tune, and when you do it's only those depressing Chapel songs. I'm going back to work.'

Jabez was of course right. Gwyn had no answers. There again, if a Bemba said in public what Jabez had just said...

'Jimmy, where's bloody Jimmy?' bawled Jabez, stalking away.

'Over there, boss,' answered Chibwe.

'Get over here, you bastard Chinaman, you're a mechanic, aren't you? The Bedford steering wheel's been playing up, get it fixed now! Be using her presently to take ballast up the track aways. It can't take much fixing, come back and tell me when it's done. I'll give you an hour. Well, what you waiting for? Skeedaddle!'

'Yes, boss, will do, boss,' replied Jimmy.

Jabez didn't say where the lorry was parked, and Jimmy knew not to ask. In this mood Jabez could have asked Jimmy to get two ounces of elbow grease from the throat of a black mamba, and he'd be off on the errand, no questions asked.

Gwyn left the dead snake where it lay. Shaking with rage he took the surviving drongo out of its cage, held its neck in his two hands and twisted, throwing the carcass into the long grass near the edge of camp. Stomping on the wooden cage several times, leaving the finely crafted pen wrecked on the sunburnt earth.

Thomas was the General Grade ticket clerk and storeman, and well regarded, not only for his tea-making skills, boiling water on a tiny cast iron stove, in a small tin shed at the southern end of the station. A dirty, moth-eaten cotton curtain scraggily sketched out his sleeping quarters, quarters which contained a considerable number of books, all of which he had read, many more than once. Some of them kept him awake, some of them sent him to sleep. He also possessed an antiquated heart-shaped Jtonia John Barker wind up gramophone, two of the original four tapering legs of which had long since disappeared. But their replacements, cut and chiselled miombo branches, functioned well enough. Thomas' record collection, of which he was very proud, was two in number: Chopin's cycle of 24 Preludes, played by Alfred Cortot, and Rachmaninov's piano concerto number 2 in C Minor opus 18, conductor and orchestra unknown. In his spare time he would listen to music or read his books, but never both at the same time; such mixing of energies was, in his view, clearly unacceptable. Whether listening or reading or speaking, he would frequently ruffle, sometimes caress his close-trimmed beard, these actions helping with his ruminations. Thoughts and images flitted about him like swallows over a pool of midges. He had tried to grow a moustache – he thought this would make him look older, more mature – but gave that over, not because he couldn't produce enough facial hair, but because the result he wanted was, in his eyes, inconclusive. The close-trimmed beard would do the trick.

The shed had one entrance, a rusty corrugated iron door hanging by one hinge. Thomas never locked the door; his world was open to everyone.

Thomas thought about winding up the gramophone. He would choose Chopin this time. Rachmaninov, it seemed to him, didn't fit the tempo of the moment. He always enjoyed comparing the two.

There were two raps on the shed door and in walked Gwyn, red-faced, in an upside down mood. Thomas spoke first.

'Cup of tea?'

'Thanks, Thomas,' Gwyn replied.

'Messy business with the boomslang.'

Gwyn didn't reply. Sitting down on a nearby chair, he lit a Woodbine, crossed his legs and pushed his chair back onto its two rear legs, finding the optimum balancing position. So poised, he watched his host work. Thomas, potentate of the tea shed, had an inelegant tendency of putting his right thumb in his back right-hand pocket, as if continually holding up his trousers, even though he had a first-rate leather belt wrapped tightly around his waist. He had been trying to rid himself of this habit for years.

In a few minutes Thomas sidled up to Gwyn, thumb in back pocket, left hand holding a hot steaming cup of Lipton's.

'Here you are, Gwyn. It's not just the best brew north of the Zambesi, it's the best brew north of the Limpopo!'

They both smiled, Gwyn accepting the offering with the dignity which he believed it demanded, his temper slowly subsiding like a window wasp finding escape.

Gwyn sipped the tea; it was too hot for the moment, and he placed it on a nearby table, thinking about the day's work ahead. Jabez and the boys would do general maintenance work on the track, and he'd take Foreman Daniel up to the dam, which had a tendency to silt up. He didn't want Rhodesia Railways running short of water for the cleaning fire. Locomotives like the larger Beyer Peacock Garrett guzzled up huge amounts of water; without water there would be no railway.

'How are those tobacco plants of yours coming along, Thomas?'

'Could be better. Seems to be a plague of vervet monkeys round here. They're always at those plants, munching away at my profits. General grade ticket clerk wages only go so far, and it pains me to see those animals devouring my supper.'

'Want to borrow my Winchester? That'll soon sort 'em out.'

'Don't think there's enough bullets in all of Africa for every one of those beasts,' replied Thomas, 'and my stomach couldn't stand all that killing anyhow.'

'Squeamish, eh? You're in the wrong place to be squeamish. The offer's there for you. Listen, let me talk to my brother. It'll be an excuse to speak, we were never close. He dabbles in the tobacco business, maybe he has an answer to your plague. Meantime, let me give you a few lessons on how to use the Winchester. Could come in handy one day, if not with those monkeys, then something bigger.'

'Thanks for the offer, I'm always up for learning new skills. Drink your tea before it gets cold.'

'I'll fix a lesson pretty soon.'

'Thanks, Gwyn.'

'You've got a fair collection of books here, Thomas. I've brought some of mine up from Broken Hill. I'll send some over, may be of interest to you.'

'Appreciate that. Come on, drink that tea of yours.'

Gwyn leant back against his wooden chair, balancing it again on the two back legs, sipping tea, smoking his Woodbine.

'Never see you with a cigarette, Thomas. Funny with you growing the stuff.'

'Don't like the taste, makes me feel sick. As long as folks buy it I'll keep growing it.'

'Your old man smoke?'

'Never knew him, he started off as a labourer in one of your farms, then worked in the asbestos mines. Died when I was a baby. I was an only child. Mother never remarried, brought me up on her own. Big Catholic, Jesuit, taught me and all the children in the village the Truth. We lived a frugal, a goodly life, making no enemies, doffing the cap as required. Time came for me to grow up. Village had become a hearth where the fire had long burnt out, a cold empty bowl. My mother a Christian, but I was Bemba, the two ain't the same. Spoke to my uncle Mubanga, he's out here with you. Didn't tell my mother, told uncle I wanted to go on the railways, so little by little here I am today.'

'Old man Mubanga, he's your uncle! Never knew that. He give you any advice?'

'Asked me if I knew what the railways were like. Told me it wasn't pretty trains choo chooin' across the veldt. It's settler folk telling you what to do, when to eat, when to go for a crap. Told him that happens to us anyway, at least I'd be paid for going for a crap!'

' "Sassy little kid ain't you," Mubanga said. "I hope your mother doesn't hear you talk like that." Took me years before I talked railway talk.'

'And your mother, what did she tell you?'

'Don't start on the wrong ladder, the Devil's ladder, she said, that only leads one way. And be pleasant to people. Can't be pleasant all our lives though, can we, Gwyn? Only fools are always pleasant.'

'Your different to the others, ain't you, Thomas?'

'Maybe, but being different means being alone.'

Gwyn finished his tea in three whale gulps, stubbed his cigarette on the table, threw the butt on the floor and walked outside to the Land Rover. Foreman Daniel was already sitting in the passenger seat, ready to head out to the dam.

'Why did you stop the boys having their bit of fun, Gwyn?' asked Daniel. 'It didn't harm anyone, it was only a couple of animals. You didn't have to kill that drongo neither. I thought you liked birdlife? You got plenty of books on the subject, that's for sure.'

Foreman Daniel's hair, such as he had left, clipped curtly around his ears, ears which on close inspection protruded slightly more than normal, but only a mother or lover would ever notice such things.

It was mid-morning, all the windows of the Land Rover lowered, the breeze through the vehicle like the baking gush from opening an oven of cooked scones.

'Jabez thinks I've gone soft,' said Gwyn. 'Maybe he's right. But sometimes... Sometimes when I'm here out on site, I want to stay forever. I don't want to go home. Everything is uncomplicated, no compromises, no bullshit. The bush is honest. We're all comrades.'

'We're all supposed to be comrades, that's for sure,' replied Daniel.

'It's as if I'm carrying a rugby ball. I've run past every man on the field, dodged all the tacklers, I'm going to score the try that wins the match... then I trip over myself and knock the ball on, out of my grasp.'

Gwyn turned on the wipers, not a drop of rain in sight. Midges and mosquitoes, the adversaries this time, took flight or were smeared across the screen. For a few moments, the sound of rubber scraping over glass, chafing like an incontinent warthog.

'Men seem to be a good bunch. I know most of the Bemba. Where did you get the Indians and the Chinamen?' asked Gwyn.

'They come highly recommended. Friend of mine up in Ndola in the Copperbelt told me about them. Best of the lot is Jimmy. He's a good mechanic and he can cook.'

'Useful qualities out here. You killed two birds with one stone there.'

'Just like you and the drongo, eh, Gwyn?'

'Yeah, very funny, Daniel.'

They passed close to a herd of buffalo.

'Look, Gwyn, over there, about fifty yards on the right. There's a buffalo giving birth. See the calf's head, see it just beginning to appear?'

Gwyn drove on. Soon they passed a pack of wild dogs, heading in the opposite direction. They had picked up the scent of the birthing buffalo. There would only be one outcome.

'There's talk coming down from head office that they want to strengthen the track, build more sleepers, up from nineteen hundred per mile to over two thousand two hundred. That should see you and me through, boss.'

'It might see me through. Jabez says you want my job, to be the top man. I want you to know, Daniel, I don't mind that. It's your country after all. We've been lording it here for far too long.'

'So this isn't your home, Gwyn?'

'Oh God, there's a question.'

'If this isn't your home, where is it? Some rain-soaked village on a marshy hillside in Europe? You'll have to decide, and sooner than you think. I know where my home is, where my country is, and it's right here. You feel the change happening, Gwyn? Maybe it ain't happening quickly enough, but it's happening all right. Like that buffalo, new life. Then we'll be the chiefs, not people like Jabez.'

'Or people like me? Am I Jabez?'

'To my people you're all Jabez, but don't worry, Mr Bowen, calamity won't befall you yet. We're still learning your rules. There are numberless tomorrows, too many to count. In one I might be your friend and in another one, well, who knows. But we're not there yet.'

'Do you ever have doubts, Daniel?'

'About the way the country is headed, you mean?'

'No, more than that. Doubts about who you are, how you want to live, who you want to be.'

'You talking religion and stuff?'

'No, much more than that, much deeper than that. Who... *what* you really are.'

'I don't fuss about such matters. I only fuss about how much pay I get from being out here, that's the only thing you need to fuss about.'

'This last year or so…. I have doubts, Daniel. Being with Daisy, I've never been with a woman for so long before.'

'I'd keep that secret if I was you. I know it's the 1950s not the 1850s, but best to hide these things.'

'That's what I'm talking about, Dan. The hiding, the fighting. Trying to hide me, who I am, subduing feelings, not just feelings about Daisy, but… Not living the truth.'

A few drops of rain fell from somewhere in the sky that seemed cloudless, enough for Gwyn to engage the wipers a few seconds, the rubber fanning the windscreen, raspily scouring the guts of dead insects over the glass.

Daniel lifted his right hand and with the outside of his fingers caressed Gwyn's face, up and down, up and down.

'Is this what you mean, Gwyn?'

Gwyn tamely pushed his hand away.

'Leave it, Daniel, leave it for now.'

Thomas watched from his shed as a few hours later the Land Rover and its occupants returned, exiting from opposite doors, going their different ways.

III

THE FIRST DAY ON SITE was a settling in day, and Gwyn always insisted on Daniel introducing him to all the labourers. Jabez, as second site engineer, subordinate only to Gwyn, thought such sensitivities stupid. But without fail, Gwyn made sure that, before anything else, all the men sang a few songs together. Said it helped with harmony and team bonding. Usually the songs were the hymns Gwyn had learnt at Moriah Congregational Chapel in Broken Hill: 'How Great Thou Art' or 'Cwm Rhondda'. The Indians and Chinese were perplexed, mouthing along as best they could. But both Daniel and another of the Bemba, a man called Kabwe, had fine baritone voices, and most of the Bemba knew the hymns, having been taught by missionaries as children.

Gwyn would have liked if all the nationalities could have sung together, but the singing Bemba were sufficient. Gwyn always sang out of tune, but no one ever told him, except Jabez, whose acquaintance with diplomacy was cursory. Jabez, on the other hand, sang in a mellifluous tenor voice; a true lover of music, the scarfaced crooner.

Foreman Daniel's English was excellent, and he mustered the men in front of Gwyn and Jabez as he had done on all previous assignments.

'Right, Bemba, form a line and shout out your names, beginning over here.'

'David.'

'Chibwe.'

'Chola.'

'Ephraim.'

'Kabwe.'

'George.'

'Mubanga.'

Gwyn scanned the men as they spoke.

'Thank you, Daniel,' said Gwyn, stiffly. 'Mubanga, my old friend, how have you been? You've worked on the railways more years than everyone here, more than the lifetimes of some of these youngsters. Rhodesia Railways draws you back like the rest of us.

'Bemba! Here is a man you should respect, an older man, a wise man. Follow his path and you will not go wrong, isn't that right, Mubanga?'

'If you say so, Mr Bowen, it must be right,' replied Mubanga.

'Careful with that tongue, Mubanga!' shouted Foreman Daniel.

Old man Mubanga had seen and heard it all before. In his early sixties, his demeanour neither timid nor submissive, a tall column of a man. His say-what-you-want eyes were well known to Gwyn, eyes which surveyed the muster and wandered in such directions as he fancied.

David, the youngest, his whole body communicating a zealous intentness, a tense expectancy as to what railway life would be like. Displaced, like all the others, where the sweet wafts of bougainvillea were replaced by darker odours, he'd had enough hunger. He loved his fellow man; he was too young to have enemies.

'That's ok, Daniel. You never were one to soft soap, were you, Mubanga. The railways haven't crushed that out of you yet, you should be grateful.'

Windblown dust eddied, encircled them all. They were gnawed and bitten by the unbaptised.

Turning to the six other navvies. 'Right, Daniel, who have we got here, shout them out.'.

'This is your boss, Mr Bowen,' Daniel barked at the men. 'Give your names.'

The three Chinamen looked to their leader for guidance.

'Jimmy...' one spoke hesitantly, and the others followed.

'Lee...'

'John...'

Jimmy, a small tree trunk of a man, was shorter than both Lee and John. Jimmy had a sunless bearing which sucked his two compatriots into its orbit; there was obviously only one leader amongst them. His cratered face, the result of childhood chicken pox, added to the piece: a thirty-year-old whose depth was impossible to fathom. Like Jabez, his face did not make him easy to love.

Immediately the three Gujuratis followed and called out.

'Chowdhury.'

'Desai.'

'Kumar.'

What on earth is the point of this gathering, thought Chowdhury. *Is this the way the railways work, a singsong and some kind words? Didn't they have anything sensible to say? Where do we eat, where do we sleep, when do we have breaks?* The heat, he was suddenly aware of the heat. A small bead of sweat escaped down his forehead on to his nose and stuck on his top lip. Chowdhury tasted it. Warm salty water infused with dust and some of the grease with which he coddled his hair every morning.

Kumar clutched a mosquito struggling to enter his left nostril. He put it into his mouth and ate it. No one noticed. He laughed to himself. He was no politician, he had no ulterior motives. He was the smallest in stature of all the navvies, thin legged and narrow shouldered. Just by looking at him Gwyn could tell that he was someone who Jabez would take, above all others, a liking to bullying.

Walking amongst, inspecting the men in spasms – two steps, stop, two steps, stop, shoulders back, head held high – Jabez looked downwards, sometimes upwards into their eyes, as if judging stock in an agricultural show. He would have looked at their teeth if he could. They all dropped their eyes save for Ephraim, Kabwe, George and old man Mubanga. When Jabez came to little Kumar's place in the line, little Kumar, with his comrades Chowdhury and Desai flanking him, Jabez stopped, stooped open mouthed, and looked down on him. Jabez had a protruding Adam's apple and with his open mouth he looked like a pelican about to devour a tasty tilapia. He let the seconds tick, said nothing.

'Who cuts your hair then?' Jabez asked eventually.

'I do, sir,' replied Kumar, his head bent meekly.

'Not a very good job, is it,' Jabez answered, and with those few words walked off. Time had, however, stood still for Kumar. He would have liked to cough, to bring the remains of the mosquito stuck in his gullet up into his mouth and spit it out, but he decided that choking in silence was by far the better option.

Gwyn, losing interest in the standoff, looked out towards an acacia tree, trying to count how many plump, heavy billed Chaplin's barbets he could see cackling away at each other. But he knew he must speak. The pulpit was now his.

'You all have the proud honour of working for Rhodesia Railways,' he said eventually. 'This is not a mere job, it's a calling. You all follow in the footsteps of Cecil Rhodes and of hundreds of men before you, men who were proud to call themselves Rhodesia Railwaymen. Not all of them came home. Many are buried along these iron lines. They gave their lives, that is true, but they gave them for a noble cause, to bring civilization and Christianity to this continent. And you have the signal honour of following in their footsteps.'

'Three cheers for Rhodesia Railways!' shouted Daniel.

'Hip, hip!'

Silence.

'When Daniel says hip hip, you blockheads, you shout back, hurrah!'

'Alright, Jabez, that's enough,' said Gwyn. 'Once again, Daniel.'

'Three cheers for Rhodesia Railways, hip hip...'

'Hurrah,' came the muted response from the Bemba.

'Hip hip.'

'Hurrah!' This response from Bemba and Gujurati.

'Once again, come on, all of you. Hip hip...'

'Hurrah!' Bemba, Gujurati and Chinamen answered as one.

'Thanks, Daniel,' said Gwyn, 'Have the men got everything they want? Are they all aboard?'

'Yes, Mr Bowen, they have everything, we're all ready for work, we're all aboard.'

'Right then, Jab, I think it's time for a song, don't you? What do you think it should be, what about "Cwm Rhondda", that'll get them going. Will you pitch it? Men, Mr Pugh will lead us in a hymn. You, Bemba, will know it, "Cwm Rhondda". The rest join in as best you can, ready Jab.'

Clearing his throat, Jabez placed his right index finger to his right ear, and off he went.

'*Guide me, oh thou great Jehovah,*
'*Pilgrim through this barren land.*'

By the time he arrived at the third line, '*I am weak, but thou art mighty,*' Daniel, David, Chibwe and Chola were with him, all perfectly in tune. Jimmy, Lee, John, Chowdhury, Desai and Kumar stood bewildered. Gwyn as usual a very flat second bass. But the chorus went exceptionally well, the top tenors ringing out, '*Feed me till I want no more.*' Ephraim, George and Mubanga knew the words but stood unmoving, choosing not to sing. Kabwe mouthed along, pretending.

'We could start a choir out here, Jab,' Gwyn declared, after the declamatory final notes, 'we could call it Rhodesia Railways Male Voice Choir. It would do wonders for community harmony.'

'As long as they can sing, I don't give a shit about community harmony.'

The crowd dispersed, Daniel ordering, cajoling, directing the men to their stations. Jabez walked closer to Gwyn, and in a low whisper, devoid of the richness of his singing voice, he said, 'What was that speech all about? "A noble cause, a calling." These ain't the crusades. We're just different grades of labourers, hired hands working for a wage. Some of us get paid better than others, but we're still labourers. You're getting too sentimental about the navvies. Sentimental leads to sloppy, they'll all sense that. None of these boys are stupid.'

'We all need encouragement, a gee up.'

'These boys come here for a wage, we all do. We don't come here for the singing, for camaraderie, and certainly not for community harmony. It's not a calling. Only thing you got right is that there'll be burials, there'll be accidents, happens every time we're out here.'

'Must the railways forever be about brutality, Jab? Isn't there room for flights of fancy. You've got your singing, I've got my words.'

'And you be extra wary of that Daniel and some of his pretty Bemba boys. He's a maverick, thinks he's better than all of us. Thinks he's *clever*. But clever gets you killed out here. If you're not careful, he'll be in control soon, and we'll be taking orders from him. I've seen how he sidles up to the top brass. Cleverley, the chief engineer. You be careful, Gwyn. Don't like the look of that Jimmy neither.'

'Daniel's been with me for years. He's a good man. Everyone should have a chance to improve themselves.'

'What, even Bemba?'

'Why not, it's their country, they were here before we were. They're people, aren't they? With homes, families—'

'Christ, Gwyn, you're living in a dream sometimes, you really are. You know the story about the stationmaster down at Chisamba, what was his name now? Lane, yeah that's it, Lane.'

'What about him.'

'Blackwater malaria got his wife, left him with a seven-year-old daughter, the apple of his eye. The girl was a mess after her mother died, we can all understand that. Chisamba was a lonely outpost in those days. The little girl had no one to talk to, no one to play with.

'Out on the savannah one day, Lane saw and shot a leopard.'

'What kind of rifle did he have? A Winchester 70? Damn fine piece of kit.'

'That ain't important. Lane shot the leopard plumb dead. He walks up to the kill pronto like, pulls his knife out to skin the cat before too many flies and sundry third parties start appearing.'

'That'd be a fine trophy, a leopard pelt. Hang it on the wall or suchlike, could even use it as a carpet. It'd make a dainty rug, that it would.'

'Stop interrupting! Lane walks up to the kill, has to work fast on the skinning, there being so much heat and all. As he gets close he hears a smooth purring sound in the long grass. Cocks his rifle again, lifts it to his shoulder ready to shoot, when a delicate little cub appears in front of him.'

'Lane had shot its mother.'

'He sure had.'

'Did he shoot the cub as well? Mother and cub would have made a nice pair of trophies on his living room wall.'

'He thought about it, all right. In fact he thought too much about it. See, he became sentimental. Pretty little cub, beautiful wee animal. And he'd killed his mother. Hundred and fifty yards away, that adult leopard was just another wild beast, but when he got within a spit of the offspring, his Christian spirit got the better of him. Lane didn't have the heart to shoot the cub as well. That was his first mistake.

'Lane did the skinning there and then. He thought more than once about ending that cub's life. He had to push the cub away regular so he could finish his work. Closest he came to it was when that cat bit him on his hand while he was labouring on its mother's underbelly. Punched the little runt hard on the chin. Seemed to do the trick, cos he finished the job uninterrupted.'

'Rifle would have been no good for that task. Lane was too close, the cartridge would have smashed the body to kingdom come, ruining the pelt. Used his knife, on the cub did he, so he could get a clean cut?'

'None of those things. Like I told you, he became too sentimental. Lane wrapped up the mother's hide in a bundle, dragged it behind him, and the cub followed, its mother's scent leading him back to Chisamba station. That was his second mistake. Wild animals' sense of smell is strong, their memory of what's gone on, what they are, where they should be, all those things go deep in 'em. Lane thought this little pet was the answer to his prayers, a lovely present for his lonely daughter. So that's what he did, came home and gave the cub as a pet to the young un. The cub bounded towards the girl like a lap dog to its master. That was his third mistake. His daughter and the cub became best pals, pretty soon they were inseparable, going on walks together, she even fed it five times a day with cow's milk which Lane bought from one of the local settler farmers. Without that milk the cat would have perished. Her love kept that animal alive, and it thrived.

'Now what was the girl's name... Polly, yeah, Polly that was it. As the cub grew, Lane, a wonderful carver, crafted a pretty leather leash made of cape buffalo hide so that Polly could lead the cat on their wanderings round and about Chisamba station.

'Lane had married Polly's mother, sure enough, and he loved both his wife and Polly dearly, but he was also married to Rhodesia Railways. You know what it's like on the railways, Gwyn. Loyalty, duty, all these fancy words you're so good at using. Some cleave to them so close they make them true – for themselves, anyway. Gradually, as time passed, Lane slowly came to forget about the loss of his dear wife, so blinded was he by Polly's happiness with the cub. Trouble was, he couldn't see the cub growing into maturity, becoming the savage beast that nature had ordained.

'As misfortune would have it, one day after breakfast, Lane was up the line about a hundred yards, inspecting some girders, taking his rifle with him as he always did, when he heard the screams, Polly's screams. He ran back down the track, and from what he could glean from Polly's wailing, she'd accidently cut her hand on the leather leash, the leopard had licked the blood, a taste was enough, and in a frenzy it pounced on her throat. Hysterical, she tried to fight him off but the cat was too strong. It was born to be a killer no matter how much care and attention the girl had given it. The injuries were catastrophic. Lane shot the leopard then and there, splattering the poor girl with the brute's blood in the process. Throwing his rifle to the ground, Lane cradled Polly, hugging her as close as he could to his body. She died a few minutes later, in her father's arms.

'After that Lane became something of a hermit. Best thing for him, the bone headed idiot! He hadn't stowed away enough common sense not to trust the animal, any animal.'

'That's a sad story, Jab. I suppose you think I'm Lane?'

'You're getting far too close to these people, to Daniel, to Mubanga, to that shopkeeper Patel. There's even talk from some folks that housekeeper of yours...'

'Talk of what, Jabez?'

'Talk that she's more than a housekeeper. Listen, Gwyn, no one gives a cuss if you meet a Bemba woman in Murphy's, so long as you pay for her, that's fine, but not, well, you know... Your goings on with that housekeeper, treating her as if she's your common law partner, your equal and all. Ain't right. For Christ sakes, she's a Bemba! You'll lose settler respect and you'll lose Bemba respect, and once you lose

Bemba respect your finished on the railways.'

'And if I lose settler respect, what happens then?'

'Mixing ain't natural, even the Bemba agree with that. One day something will happen, you know it will, and then you'll have to make a decision, you'll have to decide which side to come down on. That's the way it is, that's the deal. Decisions have no friends. And by the way, all them Bemba speak and understand English. I hear them. Daniel wants to be top dog. And that Kabwe ain't far behind. I ain't a thinker like you, all I know your walking down a dangerous path. Just be careful, that's all.'

With these words, Jabez held Gwyn's gaze, not with the steely, dispassionate aggression so familiar to Gwyn. No, there was something imploring in his expression now, even pleading.

Then he turned and walked away towards the navvies, jamming his right forefinger firmly against the right side of his nose, expelling with gusto all the irritating contents of his left nostril. Doing the same on the opposite side, then rubbing his hands clean on his trousers. Shouting as he did, 'Daniel, Daniel, make sure the boys set up the WC away from those bushes. I don't want to be some big cat's dinner whilst I'm having a crap.'

'Yes, sir, directly, sir.'

'And start clearing this site, there's enough vegetation here to hide a pack of hyenas. We want plenty of veranda room for our palaces.

'Kabwe! Take Ephraim and David, hand out the machetes. George and Chibwe on the brush hooks, start cutting these trees down, rest of you boys dump the arisings yonder. We'll have a good old bonfire tonight, they might even see it in Broken Hill! It'll frighten all the veldt! We'll show them creatures who's boss around here.'

'Sure thing, boss,' replied Kabwe. 'Let's go, boys. Watch out for snakes, don't want anyone dying too soon, do we? There'll be plenty of time for that'.

'Chola, George, Mubanga with me,' said Jabez. 'We'll burn some of this heathen land back to the bare earth. God and good luck'll look after whatever gets in the way, and if they ain't got them two on their side, they deserve to burn.'

*

Gwyn went about his own business as the dry grass started to smoke, the flames to catch. The cries of birds and beasts filled the air, and not long after it, the familiar smell – like overcooked offal, a smell which clung to your clothes no matter how often you rinsed them. He'd never truly got used to it. Maybe he'd visit Thomas in his shed for a cup of tea.

And that's how Gwyn operated. Would you say that's a strange companion for me, a Bemba woman to have? I think you'd be right.

IV

THERE WERE FOUR CLASSROOMS in the main school building, forming two sides of what Mr Bennett, the headmaster, called the playground. His interactions with pupils and teachers were as symmetrical as the length of his watery white cotton trousers: short, shabby, blemished. An awkward man, both physically and emotionally, as irritable as an unconsummated bridegroom, a man, in his opinion, of towering ability, although it must be said, incapable of accepting that anyone had suffered as much misfortune as he. Delyth had no idea, and had no desire to know, what that suffering had been; after all, it was nothing to do with her. A man who liked to be miserable all the year round, even on his birthday.

Holding Delyth tightly by her left elbow, Bennett brought her forth into the classroom as if she were a child being taken to the dentist. Letting Delyth go, he swayed back and forth, heel to toe, toe to heel, then tapped the back of his left hand twice with his righthand fingers, his signal that the class should come to attention. The sound from the signal was barely audible, but the rigmarole was of course not required. The way Bennett opened the door was sufficient for class to know Bennett was present.

'Good morning, children.'

'Good morning, Mr Bennett.'

'This is your new teacher, Miss Jenkins. Say good morning to Miss Jenkins.'

'Good morning, Miss Jenkins.'

'Good morning, children,' replied Delyth.

'We have the cream of settler society here, don't we, children?' said Bennett. 'Each one a budding Rhodes. Well I'll leave you to it, I am sure we will all value your long, and no doubt successful sojourn with us. Good day, children.'

'Good day, Mr Bennett.'

Delyth's first assignment was a quick dash to the outside tap. Bennett's initial, overlong handshake had been sticky, and heaven knows where his mits had been.

It was just after nine in the morning, the day already warm, early in the day for Delyth but not for most of the pupils, sons and daughters of farmers, small businessmen and miscellaneous lower ranking government officials.

'Mr Bennett tells me you like arithmetic,' she announced upon returning to the classroom, 'so we'll do some of that today.'

It was as if Delyth had suggested a session on Kierkergaard. A soft, almost noiseless communal groan shuffled from the class.

'Right, textbooks out.'

A hand was raised. The urchin, for so he seemed to Delyth, looked young, at least twelve months younger than the other ten-year-olds under her tutelage. Underfed, pasty, skinny, with overlarge brown eyes which appeared, because of their size, to destabilise the rest of his face. His hair short, prickles of hazel barely noticeable. Such a small lad, but still he had outgrown his green woollen jumper, threadbare at the elbow, ribs like a tinker's greyhound pressing at the weft.

'Yes? Your name?'

'Paul, miss.'

'Well, you have a question, Paul?'

Hesitatingly Paul answered, 'Who are you, miss?'

'Didn't you hear Mr Bennett? I'm Miss Jenkins, the new teacher.'

'What happened to Miss Edwards, is she ill?'

'No, of course not.'

Bennett had told Delyth that the position had become available due to Miss Edwards' promotion to deputy headmistress in a school near Livingstone, adding that he could not wish her well on her promotion as she had only given him the contractual two weeks' notice, which was bad form on her part. He had therefore had little time to make enquiries for a suitable replacement. Delyth had been the only decent candidate, indeed the only candidate available. All this had been made known to Delyth by Bennett in his own unique, tactless, way.

'She's gone to a better place,' said Delyth.

'You mean she's dead,' the young Paul answered.

'No, she most certainly isn't dead. She's gone to Livingstone, to another school. Sit down, Paul, and open up your notebook. That goes for all of you. We'll start with the eight times table.'

Whilst the class copied the eight times table, which Delyth had written on the blackboard, she noticed a number of stained circles on her desk, marks left by glasses of water, cups of tea. They looked to her like celestial orbs circling a mottled brown universe.

'Miss, miss, Margaret's thrown her pencil sharpener at me, hit me in the face! Look, I'm bleeding!'

The class sniggered.

'I can't do this, miss, we only did up to four times table with Miss Edwards.'

'That's because your stupid, that's why,' someone answered.

'Can I go to the toilet, miss?'

'He's pinched me, miss, he's pinched me!'

'I can't read your writing, miss, what does eight times seven say?'

'Are you from here, miss?

'Could we open the window, please?'

And so the day wore on. Aimless, fruitless notions wormed their way into Delyth's head. She made a bicycle out of one of the celestial orbs, and a nose, moustache and spectacles from another. Who knows how much time had elapsed when the door opened again, and the class fell silent. Bennett was standing in the doorway.

'Just passing, Miss Jenkins. Wondering how you're getting on. Have the children behaved?'

Shuffling some papers to hide her doodling, she replied, 'Very well, it's gone very well, Mr Bennett. The children have been lovely, all of them.'

Little Paul looked bemused. Was this what adults were like, he thought, lying all the time. He wished that Miss Edwards was still there.

'Excuse us, class, I need to speak to Miss Jenkins in my office for a few minutes. I want you all to write out the four times table by the time we come back. Come, Miss Jenkins.'

They left the classroom and walked along the corridor to Bennett's office.

'I have the contract ready for you to sign, Miss Jenkins. Four weeks, that's what we agreed. We'll soon see if you're up to the task. Eight times table is far too advanced for that lot. Keep things simple, keep things ticking over, that's all you need to do. We don't know how long your services will be required. We want dutiful minds in this school, not enquiring ones.'

'Can I take the class out, Mr Bennett?'

'Out? Out where?'

'For a walk. Not far, not into the bush. Give them a bit of fresh air. We won't go looking for wild animals, I can assure you. The classroom is stuffy, musty, some of the windows don't open. It would do them good.'

'Your expectations are somewhat ambitious, Miss Jenkins. School is a classroom with four walls and a ceiling. The outdoors does not count.'

'These children are in this beautiful country, shouldn't they be able to see some of it, enjoy what it has to offer?'

As if stomping his little foot, Bennett replied, 'Miss Jenkins, let me remind you we have a lot of farmers' children here. They see enough of the country every day, don't you worry!'

'One of them, little Paul, looks as if he hasn't seen the sun ever.'

'Ah, poor Paul, from one of the less advantaged families in our community. Some say that his mother is closely related to the high commissioner himself, but that's idle gossip as far as I'm concerned. Providence has not been kind to the Delaneys, let's leave it at that.'

A pleasant breeze stirred through Bennett's office, from two half-opened sash windows, bringing with it the hint of bougainvillea, which mostly swallowed up the heavy staleness in the room. A framed print of a suburban setting hung above Bennett's desk. It didn't warrant further inspection. Unusually, there was a sofa, some cushions and an elegant flowerless vase just to the side of the window, resting on a small mahogany table.

'Here it is, Miss Jenkins. I've drafted the contract myself, you'll find everything in order. Pen. You don't mind using a fountain pen, do you? A noble implement.'

'I'd like to read it first,' said Delyth.

'Read it. Good Lord, how disrespectful! I've drawn up dozens of these over the years, dozens. My word is my bond. I find your attitude very unbecoming. You don't want to start off in this untoward manner!'

'Read it I will, Mr Bennett. You must excuse me, I have to return to my class. The eight times table waits for no one. I'll consider the contract tonight.'

And with that, Delyth walked back to her noisy classroom, curbing her twitching cheeks, suppressing a smile. She wondered what else she could do with the celestial orbs.

V

EVERY MORNING, a very pleasant early light would stream through the window to the left of Delyth's desk, but as the school day progressed, pleasant turned into harsh as the afternoon sun spotlighted two desks, one unoccupied, the other where Paul sat, banished to that unpleasant spot by his classmates. The air that afternoon was particularly sluggish, the subject at hand spelling.

'I'm going to write three words on the blackboard, all beginning with the letter Z. I want you all to copy those words into your notebooks, and then we'll discuss what they mean,' said Delyth.

The three words Delyth chose were zenith, zephyr and zigzag. Paul wasn't much interested in zeniths, zephyrs or zigzags, but he did open his notebook at the centre page, and whilst Delyth's back was turned to the class, he detached as silently as he could one of those pages, tore it quickly in half, scrunched it into a ball, put it into his mouth, chewed two or three times and then swallowed. He then did the same with the other half page. For a moment, sitting there chewing, Paul was happy. The next thing he heard was the swishing of a skirt. It was Delyth, and she was right next to him.

'What are you doing? What have you got in your mouth?'

'He's eating his notebook, miss, does it all the time. It's his breakfast, they don't feed him at home.'

'Back to your work, Ruth, I'll deal with this.'

'I'm only saying, miss.'

'That's enough!'

Paul was pretending that he was eating mutton pie – a bit chewy, but mutton pie it was. He stored up his thoughts before coming to school, to decide what he would be eating that day. It wasn't always mutton pie; sometimes he'd have cabbage, or potatoes; other days it would be three dollops of ice cream, usually vanilla, that was his favourite flavour. He'd never had any other flavours. He'd never had any ice cream either for that matter, apart from the notebook variety.

Paul rested his chin on his open hand, elbow on his desk, the strong sun in his eyes.

'Well?' asked Delyth.

'Well what, miss?' replied Paul, holding up his palm to shade his eyes from the swelling sun.

'Don't you "well what, miss?" me, young man! What are you doing with your notebook, why are all those pages missing?'

'What does zephyr mean, miss?' asked Sara.

'What does zenith mean, miss?' asked Jim.

'Quiet!' shouted Delyth. 'You're coming with me to the headmaster!'

By this time, the mutton pie gratefully consumed, Paul had no further interest in his notebook, save that he might take a snack later on in the day – apple sponge with custard, he hadn't had any in quite some time. He did, however, feel slightly dyspeptic at his upcoming audience with Headmaster Bennett. This was never good for the digestion.

Delyth knocked briskly on Bennett's office door and entered unbeckoned, clasping Paul by the shoulder. The headmaster, sitting on his swivel chair behind his desk, had to negotiate a quick fumbled adjustment to his clothing. He was quite pink in the face. She'd smelt a trace of fustiness in his room before, but it was far more noticeable this time. Matters weren't helped by the windows being closed and the blinds down. She supposed supplicants usually waited to hear 'Come!' before entering.

'Mr Bennett, this is Paul,' said Delyth, as if announcing the next competitor in an Eisteddfod. 'What's your surname again, Paul?'

'Delaney, miss.'

'This is Paul Delaney, Mr Bennett, I caught him eating his note-book this morning, and by the looks of things this isn't his first time.'

Bennett had indeed been flustered, flushed from rind to innards, which hadn't helped with his humour. Rotating his chair some ninety degrees, he leapt panther-like up from a seating position, and with three timely leaps had grabbed the miscreant scholar by an ear, dragged, pulled him to the desk and smashed Paul's head, once, twice, three times against it. Bennett would have continued the assault but he was concerned at the damage it might cause, not just to the veneer on the mahogany, but to the wood itself. Desks such as these were, in his opinion, works of art.

'How many times have I told you, you're not to do this!'

Paul shrieking, crying, wasn't able to make a coherent answer. Bennett whacked him again but, on this occasion, with his hand. 'How many times! I don't know why I allow a Delaney to stay in this school, I really don't!'

'Don't you think that's enough, headmaster?' Delyth interjected.

Paul's nose was now bleeding, he had a thumping headache and one of his teeth felt looser than it should do.

'Here, Paul, take this,' said Delyth, handing over her white cotton handkerchief with embroidered corners, one of her mother's, Sunday best from the old country.

'Squeeze your nose with it, it will help stop the bleeding.'

'Get out, Delaney, and if you do this again, you'll be out of this school. Do you understand?'

'Yes, sir.'

'Not even a sorry from you. Get out!'

Paul did as he was told, trying desperately to stop crying before he had to return to his classmates. He was a boy used to violence. He knew how to put on a brave face.

'Miss Jenkins, would you remain, please? I'd like to have a private word with you.'

'Did you have to hit him so hard,' Delyth protested. 'You could have fractured his skull! All I wanted was for you to admonish him, not to almost kill him!'

'That's all these people understand, Miss Jenkins. Discipline, it's what keeps this whole place going. Come, let's forget about this irrelevancy. Let's both sit down over here on the sofa. I'll plump up the cushions, make yourself comfortable. Let's talk about your future.'

Bennett was a man of moles, many moles in fact, dotted around his face like pieces of brown congealed fat on an old cold blancmange. There was one mole in particular, King Mole, just to the left of the cleft at the bottom of his left nostril, a mole bigger than the others, from which protruded a wizened and wobbly single hair, trembling even when Bennett's face was rigid. Bennett was black haired, but the hair from King Mole was newspaper white, soiled and grubby, much like Bennett himself. This was the first time that Delyth had noticed the hair, and it repelled her.

'Some sherry? Would you like a glass?' proffered Bennett.

'No, thank you, it's classtime.'

'Of course, you're right, Miss Jenkins. You know, I used to have many discussions on how to educate our young people with your predecessor, Miss Edwards, here, right here on this sofa.'

So that's why she left, thought Delyth. Bennett the brutal, Bennett the fumbler, Bennett the grabber.

'Well I'm not Miss Edwards, I can assure you of that!'

'Indeed, I can see that, you're a much different proposition to Miss Edwards.'

Delyth made a movement to leave but Bennett interjected, 'And by the way, do not contradict me in front of the children. Moreover, the contract, where is the contract, have you signed it yet? This is my school, I have rules in my school and those rules have to be kept.'

'I'm still thinking on the matter, Mr Bennett, and frankly after seeing you assault little Paul, I'm not so sure.'

'This isn't a monastery, Miss Jenkins. There is only one rule, and it is that my rules have to be obeyed! And furthermore, no one enters my study unless I specifically tell them. Next time you should wait for my permission to enter!'

'I'm no lapdog, Mr Bennett, I'll decide what is good for me and no one else. Now if you will excuse me, I'll go back to my classroom and see how Paul is doing. Good day!'

'I'd take him to a vet if I was you,' Mr Bennet called after her. 'A doctor is too good!'

Back in class Paul still held the handkerchief tightly against his nose; every time he let it go blood started dripping. His head throbbed.

'Come, Paul, let's get you home. Ruth, go to the headmaster's study. Tell him I've taken Paul home, he'll have to take class himself. Knock on his door and go straight in.'

Balancing her cotton holdall over one shoulder, and holding Paul's free hand, Delyth led the boy outside. It smelt of late morning to Delyth, the heat plunging the day into a lazy, syrupy stupor. Paul, of course, smelt nothing, only congealing blood and the weeks of dirt on his unwashed hand.

'Where do you live, Paul?'

'Over there, miss.' Paul pointed with his free hand, still clutching the soaking handkerchief, which was now all but drenched, although he did notice a fairly insignificant island of white remaining. He adjusted his tourniquet accordingly.

'They won't be happy to see me, I should be in school. Please don't tell them what happened.'

'Let me worry about all that,' replied Delyth. 'You just keep that handkerchief tight.'

She didn't know the area around the school that well, so she followed the lead of the urchin with the bloody nose, loosened tooth and headache. The piloting only took about five minutes. The house was brick built, one storey, the door open. Dollops of hardened cement flopped between each course of brickwork, like too much cream on a Victoria sponge, each course skipping-rope crooked. The windows were thick plastic sheets held down by bent nails, tacks, staples and conveniently shaped pieces of wood and stone. The wind buffeted them, hollow-sounding tambourines in the wind, a breezy percussion. Uncleanable spots of sand and dirt dotted everywhere, inside and outside the windows; to try to clean the sheets would be to destroy them.

'Mam, it's me, I'm home!'

'Who's that?'

'It's me, Paul. I'm home early from school. Miss Jenkins has brought me.'

'Who the Christ is Miss Jenkins? What the hell have you done now!'

A moment passed.

'Hello, hello, Mrs Delaney,' interjected Delyth. 'It's me, Miss Jenkins, Paul's teacher, can I come in?'

'Miss Jenkins? I thought it was Miss Edmonds or something. But come on, come in if that's what you want.'

Mrs Delaney – she couldn't be anybody else, could she – tiny, barely up to Delyth's shoulder, ruddy faced. She smelt, the whole room smelt, a mixture of stale breath, rotting food, stale kitchen smell, stale everything. A cross between a Labrador, sheepdog and something unnamed, with most of its left ear missing, half dozed in one corner, chewing on a silver white bone of a beast unfamiliar to Delyth, a coating of stench all of its own. There was only one room, more like an open space, in the entire house, where Delyth could see a stove, pieces of firewood, a miscellany of pots and pans, a few chairs, a table and a pot. Some dry bullrushes were spread near the stove, but the dog dozed somewhere else. Delyth realised she was looking at her pupil's bed.

Mrs Delaney was peeling potatoes, her thick hair unwashed, half covered by a blue, now blue-black Sunday chapel bonnet which had seen many resurrections.

'Paul's had an accident at school, Mrs Delaney. He fell in the schoolyard, his nose is bleeding a bit, his teeth aren't too good either.'

'His teeth are bloody rotten, they've never been any good. He'll lose all of them soon like me, see.'

Mrs Delaney opened her mouth as wide as she could and pulled each side of her lips apart, gums pink-red, top and bottom. They were hardly visible, as the only daylight entering the room was as brown as an empty bottle of stout.

'That's why we always have broth in this house. Easier to eat, no need for chewing. And spuds, mashed spuds, bit of butter with them if we're lucky. No one can say that the Delaneys don't eat well. So he fell? Looks fine to me. You look fine don't you, shorty? He'll be all right.'

'Yes, Mam, I'm fine,' replied Paul.

'There you are. Take him back, Miss Edmonds, there's nothing for him to do here.'

'I'll stay with him if you'd like, Mrs Delaney, and you can go on preparing the broth.'

'Suit yourself, I don't give a cuss what you do. I've got potatoes to peel, always plenty to eat in this house.'

Delyth led Paul outside on to a mud-baked yard.

'Thank you, miss, for not telling Mam what happened.'

Suddenly Paul started crying, his body rickety. Delyth had saved him from another beating.

'No need to cry, Paul. I'm sure there'll be no need for you to see Mr Bennett in his study ever again.'

Paul nodded. His body was wracked with sobs; it was like a full body convulsion.

'Here you are, miss, your handkerchief,' he stuttered.

'You keep it, Paul, just in case you start bleeding again. Ask your mam to give it a good wash, and it'll come back right as rain. In fact why don't you keep it, it'll come in handy for you, I'm sure. Look, I've got some ham sandwiches here in my bag. They were my lunch, but I don't feel hungry anymore. Here, have them.'

'Sure, miss?'

'Go on, take them.'

Bad teeth, loosened teeth, none of those impediments mattered: Delyth's lunch was gone in minutes. A passing fly showed an interest, Paul tried to eat that as well.

'Sorry Mam got your name wrong, miss. She's just forgetful that's all.'

'Don't worry, I'll see you in school tomorrow. Do you like cheese sandwiches?'

'Cheese, lovely,' replied Paul, through a mouthful of bread and ham.

VI

DELYTH WAS NOT TO KNOW that this would be her last day at school, but perhaps, somewhere in her subconscious, she sensed it. She was never normally hungry first thing in the morning, a cup of tea and a little weak watery porridge was all she needed, but today she'd eaten a whole avocado, with scrambled eggs, and to finish a mug of tea with two rounds of toast with honey. For lunch she packed an apple and a round of corned beef sandwiches for herself, plus, as she always did now, lunch for Paul, which today would be two rounds of Fray Bentos, an apple and two shortbread biscuits. Delyth always put a little more salt on Paul's sandwiches, hoping that it would help to bring out the taste of the meat. She reminded herself to buy a loaf of bread on the way home from school; all week she'd made sure that Paul's sandwiches were thick cut and hearty, so that today she had to make do with corned beef between the last two crusts of the loaf. Paul's teeth and crusts were not a good match.

Tranquil was the best way to describe Delyth that morning. Her hunger was unusual, but her feast of a breakfast had never tasted better. She was looking forward to class, and while she thought briefly about signing Bennett's contract, that could wait a few more days. He had said it himself: she had been the only candidate, and she saw no point in giving in quickly to his demands.

Leaving the house laden with her provisions, she returned almost immediately, having forgotten her umbrella; it might rain later on, you never knew in this country. Opening the front door again, she could just about detect a mustiness in the house, ever so slight, nothing significant. A task for after school, a bit of bleach and housework; her home was always clean. And off she went again, smiling, skimming over the streets of Broken Hill. It was a clear day, a great-to-be-alive day; the young morning sun was a balm, its middle-aged lethargy still hours away. A heavy truck laden with ore dieseled its way past her, and even the stench it trailed did not detract from her humour. Delyth hadn't decided what she'd be teaching in class today: something uncomplicated, not too taxing – perhaps simple long division would do. There was a slight breeze in the air, not enough to cause too much dust to rise, just enough to cool the skin and make the walk pleasant.

Bennett was outside on the playground, red faced, an unfeathered old cockerel ready for a fight.

'Miss Jenkins!' His eyes narrowing, his king mole quivering.

No plucked blusterer would get the better of Delyth. 'Morning, Mr Bennett. What seems to be the problem?'

'Come this way, to my office. Follow me immediately!'

'If it's the contract, don't worry, I've left it at home, but I'll sign it tonight, rest assured.'

'Contract? *Contract*? You can forget about that piece of paper, Miss Jenkins.' Bennett opened his office door and pointed into his sanctum, the path to perdition. 'In you go!' he barked. Even an executioner addressing the condemned would have shown more politeness.

'There she is, there's the bitch!' a voice came from behind Delyth. 'That bloody woman! What have you got to say for yourself, you brazen hag, ruddy harridan!'

'Calm down now, Mrs Delaney, please calm down,' said Bennett.

'What's this all about?' asked Delyth, standing her ground as best she could, ambushed between them.

'What's it all about? You've been feeding my little Paul, feeding him sandwiches and the like. You saying I don't feed him at home? Told you before us Delaneys eat well.' Mrs Delaney could shout and adjust her Sunday chapel meeting hat simultaneously.

'Is this true, Miss Jenkins?' The prickly Bennett, the principal conductor, as zealously domineering as a child pulling legs off a fly.

'Of course it's true. You've seen how Paul is. You tug his jumper and there's nothing there, only skin and bone. He's so desperate for food he even eats his own notebook! You do feed him, don't you, Mrs Delaney?'

'How dare you! Mr Bennett, what are you going to do with this teacher? I don't want our family name trashed all over town. We've been here longer than this woman and her family, they're bloody newcomers!'

Bennett's face was motionless, save for the single hair trembling from king mole. He looked at Delyth like a zookeeper about to humiliate a caged animal for the benefit of paying customers. He could never let any moment to torment pass.

'You have exceeded your duties, Miss Jenkins. There is no place in my school for fifth columnists, staff or scholars who undermine the rules of this establishment. You're a teacher, madam, not a purveyor of foodstuffs!'

'Paul's half starving! He's not fed properly, and you know that, headmaster, you know it very well!'

'Is this true, Mr Bennett?'

'Calm down, Mrs Delaney, I'll deal with this.'

'Everyone in school knows about Paul, everyone in Broken Hill knows about the Delaneys. It's so well known that no one is shocked anymore. I only want to help your son, Mrs Delaney, that's all I'm trying to do,' said Delyth.

'Enough,' hissed Mr Bennett, 'that's enough, Miss Jenkins. You will leave this school with immediate effect. Collect any belongings you have and do not come back, do not dare ask for a reference, and never ever return again. Is that clear?'

'Shove it up your arse, Bennett, shove the whole school up your arse!' Delyth's face shook, electrified with rage; she stared at Bennett, who took one step back from the confrontation.

Trying to calm herself, Delyth took Paul's lunch, wrapped neatly in a muslin bag, out of her holdall. The sandwiches, the apple, the two shortbread biscuits, she held them out to Mrs Delaney.

'It's Paul's lunch,' Delyth told her, handing the muslin bag to Mrs Delaney, who snatched at the offering greedily. Delyth wondered who had humiliated the woman so deeply that now the smallest of gestures caused such resentment. Delyth pulled a second muslin bag, containing her own lunch, from the holdall, and offered it to Mrs Delaney.

'Here's my lunch.'

Mrs Delaney grasped the second offering, looked at Delyth, looked at the floor.

And that's how Delyth operated. Could you say that she would make a strange companion for Daisy the Bemba woman and Gwyn the railwayman? I don't know the answer to that one.

VII

A FEW WEEKS BEFORE the boomslang incident, the courtship had begun.

'I've just bought a new pair of Zeiss binoculars, Delyth, would you like to try them out? We could go in the Land Rover for a picnic outside of town near the river. I'll bring my rifle with me, just in case.'

Gwyn had been surprised by his own directness. He had never felt comfortable in the company of women, was never an instant friend with anyone, man, woman nor beast.

'I'd love to, I'll prepare a picnic.'

'I suppose there'll be no Fray Bentos!' Gwyn grinned.

Later they both stood on a small kopje overlooking the plain and the banks of a slow-moving river. Carmine bee eaters rested, impala herds neatly trimmed the savannah, giraffes nibbled acacia, bathing hippos snorted in the sunshine.

A picnic of cold ham and tomatoes, made into sandwiches with white bread and goat's milk butter, followed by a jam sponge, the cream congealing in the African sun, and a flask of tea.

'What do you think of the binoculars? Pretty good, aren't they?' said Gwyn.

'Let me have a try then, and I'll let you know.'

Gwyn put the binocular straps around Delyth's neck, looked at her face, her honest eyes, her hair, how it was tied neatly, smoothly in a bun, strands dislodging in the slight breeze. Her fingers slid into his. She touched him and he touched her back.

'I want you to know that you can count on me,' said Gwyn. 'I know you've lost all your family, but hopefully you've found a new one.'

Delyth upright, legs apart within her linen skirt.

'We'll have so many things to look forward to. I'll bring you out here in the evening on moonless nights to see the stars, the Southern Cross. You don't get that at home, did you know that?'

'Even the heavens are different here,' she said.

'Everything is different,' he sighed.

Delyth gazed out across the plain. She focussed on the bee eaters along the riverbank. Then a blur of movement caught her eye. She scanned, refocusing. A vulture was arcing towards the ground.

'What's that down there,' she said. 'It looks like... Yes, there must be dozens and dozens of bloated carcasses, I can see hyenas as well.'

'Let me have a look, said Gwyn, taking the offered binoculars, and focussing where she directed. 'Dead buffalo, most likely a herd trying to cross the river. The banks are steep around here. Stampede probably. It's a death trap, especially for the weak and the young. The place will be teeming with flies. There's some crocodiles down there as well. When they clear off, those vultures will move in. They'll gorge themselves fit to bursting. If you look closely you'll be able to see their crops bulging out like balloons.'

'Everything is cruel here, isn't it?'

'Perhaps it wasn't such a good idea to come out so far,' Gwyn said.

'No, no, it's ok, I'm doing my best to get used to it.'

The sound of cackling guinea fowl, mellowed by time and distance, floating on the updrafts from the valley below.

'You know I'm friendly with Adip Patel, Patel Grocery Store in town?' said Gwyn.

'No, I didn't know that. I didn't even know his first name. I've always thought of him as Patel. My parents were recent incomers, I don't think they ever really settled down. I definitely haven't. We didn't get to know many people, certainly not the Patel Grocery Store man. My father always said that the settlers who'd been here for

generations looked down their noses at newcomers like us, said we
were second class.'

'We're not all like that, Delyth.'

'I miss my parents. Now all my choices are my own. Pass me the
binoculars again, would you?'

Delyth scoured the scene again. A crocodile spun, white watering
the river, its teeth implanted in the bloated remains of a dead buffalo.

'Adip told me a story once from an Indian book he'd read,'
Gwyn continued, 'about a student in Bombay, a law student, I
think he said. The student's parents, all his family were Muslims,
but he had abandoned the faith. One day the student happens
upon a street riot between Muslims and Hindus. A rioter is
stabbed, and in the chaos the injured man is trampled to death.
Hindu, Muslim, no one knows. The army and police arrive to
restore order, the law student escapes, believing he may have
trampled the man to death himself. His mind is numb, he's confused, he climbs the high wall of a suburban garden, which has a
tall ring-shaped tower in one corner. He climbs a ladder up to the
tower searching for sanctuary, and at the top he meets a grimy,
unwashed man, a common thief who steals gold teeth from the
corpses brought by priests to the tower, where in accordance with
their religion, the corpses are consumed by vultures.

'The law student falls asleep, and wakes up with the dawn. A
silvery dimness cloaks his surroundings, soundless, save for a
crowing cockerel and the sounds of the community waking, readying
themselves for another day. The thief had gone, stealing what little
money the student had with him.'

Gwyn could never talk about love, about emotions. Zoroastrian
priests and their burial practices would have to do.

'Do you want me to stop, Delyth?'

'No, please, keep going,' said Delyth, adjusting the focus on the
binoculars, waving away an irritating insect. 'I wonder how they
managed to carry the poor man up the tower. He must have been
pretty heavy.'

The question bewildered Gwyn, so he carried on.

'Penniless, and believing himself to be a fugitive from justice, the student decides to hide, to bury himself in India, and rely on charity to survive. He may have killed a believer, but he does not know which religion possesses truth. There was no Moriah Chapel in those days, Delyth!'

'Well there wouldn't be, would there? Come on, get to the point!'

'He vows to search for Truth, and is told during his wanderings that there is a Prophet, a man who knows it. The Truth. The student acts like a detective. One witness leads to another, and the closer he gets to finding the Prophet, the closer he is to finding Truth. Each witness has a portion, a fragment left behind by the Prophet, who alone in all the world, knows how to fit these pieces together.'

Delyth followed the crocodile through the water. She found this far more engaging than Gwyn's story, but there was no point letting on, she would leave him his dignity.

'Does he find the Prophet? Does he find Truth?' she asked, brushing away another insect, one she knew this time, a passing mosquito.

'Do you want to know the answer, do you really want to know?'

'Come on, tell me.'

'It's in himself, Delyth. Truth is in himself. This is what Adip told me.'

A large piece of the buffalo's torso was now in the crocodile's mouth, the rest of the carcass floating downstream. The crocodile swam upstream to the closest sandbank to digest his picnic in the sun.

Delyth had seen enough. She turned to Gwyn. 'You've still got to find it, though, haven't you? Whether it's in you, or in a prophet.'

'We've all got to find it, but it's within us nonetheless. You don't need prophets or religion for that.'

Did Gwyn even believe in what he was saying? Because Delyth didn't. She was worrying that the process was taking so long, as was Gwyn. Both would take some time to discover their own vested interest in the rapidity of the love affair.

'I wonder what Minister Roberts would think of Mr Adip Patel?' Delyth mused.

'They'd probably go back and fore till their minds were numb, have a cup of tea to finish, and agree on nothing! Ashamed to say I don't think I've been to Moriah much since my Sunday School days. What about you, Delyth?'

'Now and again, I go there now and again. It was a great help when my parents passed away, but other than that, well, I don't know. It's like they're offering you emeralds and diamonds on a beautiful island, far from everywhere, but you have to die before you can get your hands on them.'

'And you want that treasure now?' said Gwyn.

'Yes, why not, why wait for something when you don't know what it is you're waiting for? At least the thief got the gold teeth, they were no use to the dead man after all.'

'Look around you, Delyth, it's all here, the treasure is all here, now. And it's for you, it's for both of us to enjoy.'

Gwyn dribbled a chewed tomato down his chin. The goat's milk butter was going off. He would decline the jam sponge.

'Here have the binoculars back,' Delyth said, 'and wipe that tomato from your face, you look like Bela Lugosi.'

'Bela who?'

'Never mind, Gwyn.'

A train tooted tunefully in the valley below, puffs of smoke unspooling, rising sightless into the heavens above.

Advancing towards Gwyn, Delyth kissed him lightly on his lips. He did not reciprocate, glowing reddish pink from the neck up. Delyth knew she was cleverer than Gwyn, and she could see that Gwyn was falling in love with her. He would have to do the deferring, the complying, but there was no need to talk about such things; clever people didn't have to speak to show how clever they were. She was sure that in time Gwyn would understand all this; he seemed to be a sensible man, if slightly dull, but that was all right. She might, one day, be able to fall in love with him. But that was no reason not to be with him, not for now. Love was such a messy business anyway.

'I'm not used to this Delyth, I'm—'

'Shush now...' She kissed him again, fully, pulling his head towards hers.

'This hasn't got to be complicated, Gwyn. We both know what we want, there's no need to ask anyone for permission. You know that, don't you?'

Both lips sunburnt, dry, but only for a few moments. She tasted curdled goat's butter, they both did.

VIII

GWYN TOLD ME about Delyth. Told me that people, not just settler people, were talking about the two of us, called us the Daisy and Gwyn household. Told me there were 'family reasons' forcing his hand, that he had no choice in the matter. We were on the veranda one evening after supper, when he said there was something we needed to discuss. And high time too, I thought. It had been raining, there was mud everywhere, pools of water here and there; still, it kept the dust down.

'You have to understand, Daisy, I've got to marry her.'

'Understand? It's been almost two years, I thought I'd become more than just your housekeeper. You promise so much, but your words and your actions never meet up. You're a liar, just like all the other Europeans round here.'

It was true, Gwyn was different in his actions to the other settlers; he treated all people the same. But I wasn't 'all people'. What could this girl, Delyth, give him which I couldn't? Why was she so special?

'I can't tell you the full story yet. I want to, but I can't.'

'Just tell the truth, why don't you? It's simple, truth is simple, it's straightforward. If she's coming, I'm going. Do I not stir you?'

'You'd break my heart if you went, you know that.'

'What are you settlers like! White boy marries white girl and both come back to live with Bemba housekeeper happily ever after. And I'm supposed to be the guilty one!'

'I'm confused about lots of things at the minute, Daisy.'

'The only confusion I see here is where I'm going to put all my things when I move out.'

'Please don't leave me.'

'You want me to stay! It's you that's leaving me. Have you settlers told your lies for so long that you no longer know what truth is?'

'Truth? I've been grappling with that for a long time, believe you me. It won't be forever with Delyth, it's a temporary accommodation.'

'And does she know about this temporary accommodation?'

'Not exactly.'

'So you'll be lying to two women. At least there's equality to be found there!'

'You'll soon see the reason I'm marrying her, it'll be impossible to hide.'

'She's pregnant, is that it?'

Gwyn nodded. 'But I ain't the father.'

'Then who is?'

'Can't tell you that for now. And Daisy,' he added, looking at me seriously. 'She cannot know that I know about the baby. It's... difficult to explain, but I'm only trying to do right by my family.'

'So family honour trumps poor old Daisy. Respectability to the white girl, what about respectability for the Bemba woman?'

'You're the one I want to be with, you know that. Without you I'm nothing.'

I'd heard enough soft-soaping to last me a lifetime, but who was the fool here, the real fool? Gwyn for marrying pregnant Delyth when he wasn't even the father - and I believed him on that - or me, relegated to the shadows, where I was to tend to my lover's wife and fetch him a cold beer now and again. But what was the alternative? This was Northern Rhodesia, not Shangri-La. Betrayal and jealousy were comrades in this part of the world.

'I wasn't the one that created this problem, Daisy, I'm just a scapegoat, clearing up the mess. Please will you accept this? We'll find a way through, I'm sure we will.'

We'll find a way through. As if such things are left to our choosing. What is life but a series of events out of our control? Thinking otherwise would make someone the real fool.

*

Gwyn had broached the subject of Delyth with Daisy, and having stumbled over that hurdle, it was time to broach the subject of Daisy with Delyth. Again it was nightime, the wind was picking up, as Delyth and Gwyn walked together through the empty streets of Broken Hill.

'She'll make you feel right at home,' he explained. 'Good company for you. I'll be away with work pretty often, remember.'

'Strange that she lives in the house with you, don't you think? A Bemba.'

'She doesn't live with me. Someone needs to be there whilst I'm away, to look after the place and things.'

Delyth thought of the three of them sharing the same house. What would Broken Hill think of that? Once upon a time Delyth would have been troubled by the notion of shame and dishonour, but those days were gone. Her greatest need was to marry, and marry quickly; this swallowed up all the shame and all the dishonour in all the world. There could have been a hundred Daisys, and she wouldn't have cared.

Within a few weeks of their meeting, Moriah Congregational Chapel, Broken Hill, Northern Rhodesia bore witness to the wedding of Miss Delyth Esther Jenkins and Mr Gwyn Mordecai Bowen. Minister Cadwaladr Roberts officiating. It was a small affair. Mr and Mrs Bowen were very happy.

There were mutterings from some in the congregation. Regular three-times-on-a-Sunday devotee Mrs Amber Thorpe was surprised at the speed of events. Her daughter had had to wait a good eight weeks for her nuptials, and Mrs Thorpe had hardly seen Gwyn in Moriah, not since his time in Sunday School. Delyth only came for funerals. They must have paid the minister extra, or made a substantial contribution to the roof renovation appeal. Well, Mrs Thorpe knew the whole story would come out sooner or later.

Delyth was dressed in her mother's wedding dress, save a few alterations here and there. Delyth commissioned the excellent Mrs Kowalski to undertake the work. Delyth declined Gwyn's offer of payment for the seamstress' labours. The ceremony was functional, if somewhat glacial, Mrs Thorpe thought. Delyth was content.

As for Gwyn he wondered how he was going to keep everybody happy.

The marital residence was to be the old Bowen family home, set in a garden impregnated with memories of Gwyn's long dead relatives, mixed with much more recent remembrances. A large and powerful looking baobab tree, planted by Gwyn's father, dominated the shrubbery, obstructing the sun in the early morning.

A new world for Delyth.

This is how Gwyn presented me to Delyth.

'My Bemba housekeeper, Daisy. She's been with me for years. Useful to have someone round the house, as I'm away a lot. I'm sure you'll get on. She lives in the kia at the back of the house, you can't miss it. She'll be very helpful, won't you, Daisy?'

'Pleased to meet you, Mrs Bowen, I've heard so much about you from Gwyn.' I think I may have even curtsied. I could see that Delyth was surprised by my use of Gwyn's Christian name.

'Don't worry, it's always been Gwyn and Daisy here, no formalities,' said Gwyn.

'I think we can start off by calling me Mrs Bowen, and see how we go from there.'

I looked at Gwyn and then at Delyth.

'Of course, Mrs Bowen, I understand completely.' I felt there was no need for me to be prickly; Delyth already seemed ill at ease.

Gwyn, as usual, was not home for long. There was no time for a honeymoon; a trip down the Zambesi in a cruise ship would have to wait. His leave had come to an end. Rhodesia Railways waited for no one.

'I'll only be away for a few weeks,' he said. 'Daisy will settle you in; anything you need, just ask Daisy. I don't think staying with me on site in the bush would be suitable, it's much more comfortable here. This is your new life, Delyth, we'll all be very happy here together.'

Like a passing raindrop, he pecked her on the cheek, said goodbye, and with that he was gone, leaving the two of us alone together.

'Please, Mrs Bowen, let me show you round the garden,' I said eventually. 'Gwyn takes great pride in it. The house and garden were built by his father. Mr Bowen senior chose the location himself for the wonderful views. He wanted to make sure the building fitted neatly into the natural beauty of this place. I don't think the house has changed much since his father's time, save for the swimming pool. That pool is Gwyn's offering to the Bowen dominion over Africa. It's just a hole in the ground at the moment. He hopes to start spraying concrete for the sides when he's back next. Everything takes its own time here.'

'I'm sure the garden's beautiful, Daisy, but if there's one thing I've found out about Africa is that there's danger and savagery everywhere; there's a harshness to this place.'

It was a settler response, the coloniser's slant. I was disappointed in Gwyn. Why on earth had he chosen such a woman?

'There's savagery in all kinds of places, not just here. As long as you know where not to go you won't find it,' I said.

'And you'll be my guide, my local Bemba guide, my good and faithful servant?'

'I'll do my best, Mrs Bowen. Gwyn and I will do our best. Do you like the veranda? Gwyn got the bench from an old railway station near Ndola he was working on, and the two chairs were salvaged when upgrades were carried out at Mufulira station a few years ago.'

'It still looks pretty industrial to me. I like the nice cushions though.'

Thank God something pleased her.

'Glad you like them, Mrs Bowen, I embroidered them myself. I agree bits of railway furniture aren't the most pleasing on the eye, and they can be very uncomfortable. But that's Gwyn, he's never home long enough to feel uncomfortable. He enjoys the freedom of the savannah, working on one site, finishing the job and moving on to somewhere else, that's his life really.'

'And you don't think I'll change him, do you?'

'We can all change, Mrs Bowen, if we want to.'

Delyth sat on the bench, adjusting the cushions.

'Like chapel pews, terrible for the buttocks and back. The cushions are a delightful touch nonetheless, the Bemba civilising the civilisers.'

I didn't know whether Delyth was trying to be funny or whether she really believed what she was saying. I tried to change the subject.

'Gwyn and I built this lattice to support the granadilla creeper.'

'Teak, is it?'

'No, acacia, Gwyn thought that acacia would be more suitable.'

How could anyone mistake teak for acacia.

'The granadilla grows well here and it shades us in the afternoon hours. Gwyn likes to take a nap here after we have our lunch.'

'You do a lot together, don't you?'

'I think he likes female company after being out in the bush with those navvies. They're a pretty brutal bunch, there'll be no feminine touches out there. I mean, no refinement.'

'I think I know what you mean, Daisy.'

We walked further into the garden, midges and dust cradled in the breeze.

'Tell me, Daisy, why is there a long pole each side of the house? I can't see any wires coming from them. Are they flagpoles or something?'

'Gwyn calls them Faraday poles. He spent days with some of his railway friends, digging holes into the ground, so that they would be secure. Got it done, nonetheless it was hard work. Most of the ground around here is solid rock.'

'What are they used for then, putting up flags?'

'There's so much lightning around here, the poles attract the lightning, draws it safely into the ground, keeps the house safe.'

'Gwyn thinks of everything, doesn't he, Daisy?'

'He's a practical man, he is a son of the Railways. That's him and he treats me well. He treats all Bemba well.'

'Not like some of the other settlers, is that what you're saying?'

'I wouldn't know anything about that, Mrs Bowen.'

I had to tread carefully here.

'It's the middle of the twentieth century, Daisy, you can say what you want these days. Well, almost. No spies from the High Commissioner's office in the neighbourhood, are there? I need to know what you think if we're to strike up a relationship. Gwyn being away so much, we'll need to get along in as much a business-like way as possible.'

'The sun plays hide and seek with the sisal when the jacaranda trees are in blossom,' I said. I was uncomfortable, the whole conversation made me feel uncomfortable. 'It truly can be paradise here, it truly can.'

'You two are very close, aren't you?'

'For a Bemba and a European?'

'For a man and a woman,' said Delyth.

'There are no secrets in this house, Mrs Bowen.'

'And there'll be no secrets between us, Daisy, is that clear?'

'Would you like to inspect the kitchen?' I said.

The bungalow was not supplied by mains electricity. A paraffin powered cooker was the centrepiece of the windowless kitchen, which comprised an oven and two Bunsen burner type contraptions on the top. It suited me well.

'Everything works, Mrs Bowen. There's a pantry through here which Gwyn and I find very useful, it stays cool all the year round.'

'Probably attracts vermin, does it? Those little field mice get everywhere. As long as there are no rats coming in here, I'll be all right. Can't stand those buggers.'

'There have never been any rats, not since I've been in this house. I keep this place spotlessly clean. Gwyn will tell you that.'

How much of this was I supposed to bear?

'Not much of a kitchen, is it, no natural light coming in? We'll have to change that.'

'The room's a nice hideaway if you want some peace and quiet, Mrs Bowen.'

'What's that smell, Daisy?'

'Smell?'

'Yes, that smell... stale smell.'

'It's nothing, probably just the spices I use for Gwyn's curries. He adores his curries. There are no windows to let some fresh air in, so there are always lingering smells in here, I'm sure you'll get used to them in time.'

'No, no, it's not spices, I know what they smell like. It's more musty. It's coming from this floor.'

'The linoleum is perfectly clean, Mrs Bowen. I wash it every morning. As I've told you I pride myself on my cleanliness. This house is spick and span. Gwyn can't stand a dirty house or a dirty kitchen, he'd sack me on the spot if this house was filthy.'

This was all getting too much for me.

'Well he's not here now. I'm in charge, and I say there's a smell!'

Delyth dropped down to her knees and started tearing at the linoleum.

'What are you doing? You can't just come here and rip up Gwyn's house! That lino's been here for years, leave it alone!'

I clamped my hand against Delyth's right wrist without thinking.

'Don't touch me, how dare you touch me, get your hands off me! This is my house now, not yours!'

Delyth yanked a segment of the yellow floral linoleum from its fastenings. Immediately a pungent stink swelled into our nostrils, the floor under the lino shifting in countless directions. Moist, clammy, climbing, scrambling, squinting. Delyth shrieked. Hundreds of writhing maggots feasted on the remains of a dead squirrel who'd wandered underneath the floorboards to die. I was horrified.

'Oh, Mrs Bowen! I'm so sorry, leave it to me, I'll clean this up, I'm so sorry!'

I rushed out of the kitchen panic-stricken returning within moments with all the implements and liquids required for an exhumation and annihilation.

'You see, I knew there was something wrong, you should have listened! shouted Delyth.

I was about to lift the carcass, maggots and all.

'Daisy! Daisy! Stop! Get some gloves first, the two of us together can get this done far quicker, I don't want my house stinking like a pig sty! You're lucky I won't tell Gwyn about this!'

'I'm so sorry, I am so very sorry.' I was sobbing. 'Please don't tell, Gwyn, Mrs Bowen, please don't tell him!'

And that was my first introduction to Delyth, or should I say Mrs Bowen. Not the best, was it? It was clear to me that the marital bed would trough on each far side of the mattress, not in the middle.

IX

GWYN DECIDED TO DRIVE this time to Kapiri Mposhi. Both knew the hierarchy. And so it was after the nuptials with Delyth. The railway stretching northeastwards from Kapiri Mposhi, on to Nakonde on the border with Tanganyiika, and then on to the Indian Ocean. Mostly farming country where travelling salesmen plied their trade, emissaries from the world beyond.

'Bad luck, Gwyn,' said Jabez.

'What do you mean?'

'You just got married, didn't you? Can't be pleasant leaving your new bride and all. She promise you undying love? And you her? Taking comfort from that? A cageful of affection. Bet she won't love you like the Railways loves you. Still, you'll have an extra apron around the house, what with her and your Bemba. Twice the house-wifery.'

'You been drinking again, Jab?'

'You know what I mean. Are you all going to be peacefully happy together, are you all going to love one another forever?'

'Well, Jab, it's a bright morning, and I love bright mornings.'

The sun was giving the slip to fragmenting high clouds.

The roads in Broken Hill were composed of two strips of cement, or sometimes tar, about two feet wide, either side of gravel or mud running down the centre. Driving could get hairy; facing oncoming traffic, each vehicle would have to veer left and leave only their right-side tyres on the strip. As the left side dirt was below the level of the strip, getting back on was like riding a dodgem in a fair. Jabez, being Jabez, would attack this re-entry full on, like an angry rhino. He enjoyed seeing how close an approaching vehicle would come before veering to the left; Jabez would never be the first to undertake this manoeuvre. Progress on strip roads was satisfactory, but outside town they would be on dirt tracks, and it would take a good few hours to reach Kapiri Mposhi.

'What you got in your skoff box then?'

'Oh I don't know, Daisy puts stuff in the night before.'

'That'll all have to change, there's a new mistress in your house now. That Bemba woman'll have to learn taking orders from Mrs Bowen.'

Gwyn asked Jabez to steer whilst he peered into the stout galvanized metal container.

'The usual stuff, four or five tins of Fray Bentos.'

'Steak and kidney?'

'Yeah, steak and kidney, and steak and onions. Got some corned beef, some vegetables. Tea, sugar.'

'You're lucky to have her, Gwyn. You've got Daisy and now you've got Delyth. I'm sure they'll get on like two pigeons in a coop. Me, I've got Murphy's, that's all I need.'

The day was warming up. Gwyn was biting his nails, trying not to touch the slivers of irritatingly painful skin on each side, working methodically from one finger to the next, spitting the clippings out of the Land Rover window.

'Remember Marco Schillacci?' he said. 'Not someone you'd want to come across after he'd had a few drinks. Remember him, Jabez?'

'Remember him? Of course I remember him. How do you think I got this dainty little line across my face?'

'That was Marco?'

'Pulled a knife on me in Murphy's a few years back, said he'd paid for the companionship of one of the girls I'd had. Jane, I think her name was. Can't remember all of them fillies! There was no debating with him, an' things got messy. Lucky I had some of the boys with me, or I'd have snuffed it there and then. Dead in the Smoke Room at Murphy's, what a story that would have been, might even have made the front page of the *Bulawayo Chronicle*. A bit of an inconvenience in a whorehouse, that's all it was.'

'And Marco, what happened to him?'

'He didn't leave that Smoke Room with a pretty face either, after we all got the better of him. The boys had to hold me back else I would have nailed him good and proper there and then. Once my goat's up, look out.'

'Well had he?'

'Had he what?'

'Paid for the girl before you.'

'None of your business, Gwyn. Who knows, who cares. All I know is he's buried at Peg 240 up near Chambisi. Labouring for the Railways in them parts, sleeper fell on his leg, turned septic and that was him done for. He didn't like my singing much neither, dumb bloody Italian.'

'He must have had a tin ear, everyone likes your singing, Jab.'

'Nothing wrong, mind, in going to Murphy's. Got to spend my money somehow, don't want to be the richest navvy in the graveyard. Get a cooked meal, ok it usually ain't the best, leastways it's hot. Then the whisky, then the company… It's got the lot. They're providing a service, much like us on the Railways. Nothing different in it as far as I can see. No settler can survive out here without an establishment like Murphy's. That includes the married ones too, plenty of those in Murphy's. Besides, puts money in them women's purses, they need work like the rest of us.'

'Save you don't risk the pox in our line of work,' said Gwyn, avoiding another pothole on the trail. 'Or the clap.'

'Touch wood, never happened to me yet. Anyway, railways are dangerous too, you know that. Government can't expect us to conquer Africa without a Murphy's in every town, the two go together like sun and heatstroke. It's natural, that's all, its pleasure not procreation.'

'Some folk call Murphy's a cesspool of vice,' said Gwyn.

'An' I call it my second home. As long as I've got money in my pocket, I'm welcome. It's good to see what a girl has up her skirt. Dainty and gifted, not coarse, that's me'.

'What sort of creature works there, Jab?'

'Amenable ones, ready to oblige. Don't have to own a jerkin to keep warm, a cadged one will do. I'm contributing to the needy, helping 'em to stand up on their scraggy legs. You should partake, Gwyn, I'm sure God will forgive you. Nothing like a hot girl in Murphy's on a cold night. Blinds drawn, stuck frozen to the window, the Murphy girls doing their work, masters of their craft...'

'Once your money runs out though, they won't want to know you.'

'Once my money runs out I'll be dead. You're more than welcome to come to my funeral. Just make sure there's some singing, proper tuneful singing alongside the open grave, and when they lower me down I want you all to be wailing, crying your hearts out for the dearly departed Jabez Pugh! Don't want no laughter and merriment when I'm buried, that clear? In the meantime, it's Murphy's for me.'

'It's has a bit of a chequered history, Jab.'

'What do you mean?'

'You know, a girl got murdered there a few years back. Can't remember her name. An off-duty policeman walking home one quiet night, not even a frisky tomcat about, saw three men coming out the back door, carrying what looked like a hefty carpet. It was a carpet all right, save there was a naked woman inside. Heavily bruised, bloodied nose, and very dead. Turns out she was one of the prostitutes. Tried to escape a number of times, but they always caught her, brought her back. Every time she was beaten, some say stoned and burned, but on this last occasion, she was hurt so bad, especially round the face, that none of the paying customers wanted her company.'

'I can understand that,' said Jabez. 'Carved women don't pull in the shillings. That's what's good about Murphy's, you can do pretty much whatever you want with them girls, and there ain't no come-backs.'

'She was, how shall I say this, she was no longer of productive use, and because of that she was killed. As you say, a bruised and battered girl is no good to a brothel. Turns out she had no kin, so that helped smooth things a bit. I mean with the disposal of the remains and such like.'

'Can't call me a man of God, Gwyn, because I ain't, but you trying to make me feel guilty here? Had no part in what happened. Unfortunate business, I got a temper, there's no denying, but I don't batter no whores. We're giving these women work. Someone's got to do it. It's not going to go away, it's been around forever. There's white girls there too, so there's no argument on that front, is there? Ain't nothing immoral in sex.'

'Not saying there is, Jabez.'

'What happened to the killers, they get justice?'

'Police said they couldn't prove who'd done the actual killing, everyone blamed everyone else.'

'All native Bemba, eh, Gwyn?'

'Yep, everyone save for the owners. The place closed down for a few days, that's all. New coat of paint, a good clean, reopened as if nothing had happened.'

'Seems to me nothing happened because the police and their government friends didn't want anything to happen. They're Murphy's best customers, see them there all the time, flashing their money, most of it taxpayer coin. That's you and me, we're being jacked off by them so's they can get jacked off by them whores.'

'Not like you to be so poetic, Jab!'

'Gets me riled that's all. And another thing, that off duty officer should have kept his trap shut. His days of promotion are over, that's bloody well sure. He won't be able to afford Murphy's for the duration. Won't know what he's missing, ruddy idiot.'

'*The Northern News* kept bleating on about the story, about the injustice...'

'Never read newspapers, got no interest in what's going on, and I don't trust what's in 'em. They kept bleating on cos it was good for circulation, Gwyn, helped them sell more advertising space for tractor parts!'

'All the religious crowd were up in arms about it too, but it all went away in time. The power people didn't want to know. New owners came along in a few months, that seemed to help quieten things as well, together with some free samples for the high ups of course.'

'They're the worst. Not too long ago saw the chief of police himself take three girls with him upstairs, at the same time! Didn't pay for one of them. Two, I can understand, but three!'

'Did it because he could, no doubt,' said Gwyn.

'Ups the price for the others. Too much demand, too little supply.'

'You should have been an economist, Jab, not an engineer. Or a poet. Or a singer!'

'What about Fat Theo the Turk then? He was a one.'

'Greek, wasn't he?'

'Greeks, Turks, all the same, ain't they. Went fishing one Saturday near Bancroft, took some dynamite and his wife with him, too much heat and too much beer, blew his right foot clean off. Fat Theo was too fat for his wife to move. By the time she got help it was feeding time for the hyenas and vultures.'

'Hyenas couldn't open his skoff box though, not one to share his tucker was Fat Theo!'

'Never found his head did they – that's the lightest Fat Theo ever was. I mean at his funeral.'

'Helped to keep the cost down. Those teak caskets don't come cheap, the big ones always cost more than the small ones.'

Gwyn engaged third gear, then second gear, fording a drowsing stream of rank water, accelerating away. Billowing pillars of dry, orange red dust followed Jabez, Gwyn and the Land Rover. The noise spooked a solitary serval, spotted and striped, sending it speeding into the bush for cover.

'The old days were great, weren't they, Jab? Out on site, no one bothering us save for the chief engineer poking his nose in now and again. Taking pot shots at passing zebra or a giraffe. I hit a buffalo calf once, when we were repairing a bridge over the Mulungushi. Bullet entered just below its right eye, stumbled into the river. Crocs got him, didn't last more than a minute.'

'Winchester 70, ain't it? Never had much time for guns, me. Give me a knife anytime. It's more personal, you can smell a man,' said Jabez.

'Another time, working on some rail tracks near Lukanga swamp, winged a zebra on its left thigh. Wanted to start tracking, but the bloody chief engineer was expected on site that morning so I let it go. It would bleed to death anyway.'

'There's plenty of them zebra on the veldt anyhow.'

'A few weeks later I was working one of them tough cuttings up in the granite hill country in Chifunkunya, and my foreman, Daniel, told me the trail of the injured Lukanga zebra was picked up by a pack of wild dogs. Daniel said no one saw the kill, but knowing the injury and the tenacity of those dogs, he reckoned that zebra would have been dead within twenty minutes of their first sighting.'

'Not like you to miss out on two clean kills, Gwyn. You and that Winchester are usually pretty deadly.'

'It got me worried, sure enough. Both them shots should have been clean kills. There must have been something wrong with the rifle, maybe the sight needed adjusting. Mind you the Winchester's at least fifteen years old, and nothing lasts forever out here. First chance I could, took it for a full service to Faulkener's gunshop in Ndola.'

'That do the job?'

'Sure did. Front sight was out, rifle's good as gold now. When I pull that trigger, I kill, no messing. Tom Faulkener isn't cheap but that rifle's worth persevering with, it's that good.'

'That's what's first rate about this place, Gwyn. You can do what you want here. This locale is still big enough, you know, still big enough to dodge 'em, dodge people, dodge them civilisers.'

'But nothing lasts forever, Jab.'

As I told you, I didn't like Jabez. There were too many Jabezes about the place, in the shops, on the streets, in their chapels and churches. But there was one place, their natural habitat, where they bloomed like viruses, and that was Murphy's.

X

THAT FIRST NIGHT on site, Daniel, Mubanga and Jabez knew Gwyn would insist that all the men eat together around a single campfire, made up of the arisings left from clearing the site.

'It's good for morale, Jabez,' said Gwyn.

'All I can see is it helps to remove all the tinder and the like, reduces the fire hazard. This job's dangerous enough as it is.'

Sixteen men, at least five languages, hundreds of darting fireflies and a million stars. Sounds of crackling acacia, nightjars, night owls, bitterns. Men slurping, swearing, belching, farting, smoking, singing; most had been decent and honourable until the savannah sucked them in.

They all ate Bemba food for that first supper, as insisted upon by Gwyn, nshima and chibabwa.

'I'm not bloody eating porridge and pumpkin leaves, give me Fray Bentos any time!'

'I don't expect you to, Jabez. You eat what you want.'

'You're too kind, Gwyn. But see, you expect the Indian and those rice-eating Chinamen to eat the stuff. I notice you haven't given them a choice.'

'I'm trying to create a team here. We'll need it when we hit problems,' replied Gwyn.

*

'Why are we eating this mush?' asked Desai, another young man in his mid-twenties, of medium height, lean with dark, hollow eyes, argumentative and prone to excitement.

'Shut up, Desai, just bloody eat,' replied Chowdhury. 'You're always looking for problems.'

David noticed, some way off, a grey duiker running for cover into a dense thicket of acacia trees. He hadn't seen many of these small brown antelopes in his young life, and no one else had seen what he had seen.

'Look, Chibwe, a duiker!' David said, excitedly.

'Duiker, spiker, you want to be a wildlife expert or something? This is the Railways not a safari adventure!' replied Chibwe.

Chola came over to sit with Chibwe, and David moved away to sit with Mubanga. Chibwe was in his late teens, a year or so older than Chola. They were always together. Chola thought they were friends and equals. Chibwe thought of him as someone who worked on the Railways, and that was all they shared, and definitely not as equals, but he never let on. Chibwe wanted to be far distant from the Railways, to escape to some place where he was not known, to start again, a rebirth, a pure beginning. To be rid of the clutches of Daniel. If he could leave he would be revived; a new location would make everything better. But Daniel was always there, Daniel and his weird ears, Daniel and his friends... He reeked of them. How he craved to be free, for liberty, for a limitless expanse without people.

'You ever been with a woman, Chibwe?' asked Chola, finishing off the last of his nshima.

'Course I have, and you?'

'Not yet, but I'm aiming to once I get my pay. They say you should start with an ugly woman.'

'There's something pleasing in every woman. No woman is all ugly, they're all beautiful somewhere. Men too, there's beauty there as well.'

'Come on! You don't mean that, that's crazy talk. We're not supposed to think like that,' said Chola.

'Who says so?' asked Chibwe.

'Everyone. Old man Mubanga for one.'

'Christ, old man Mubanga thinks just because he's old, he must be wise. He's in the waiting room to go and see his maker, and he'll be there pretty soon. You want to finish this?' Chibwe handed his bowl to Chola. 'I'm going to bed.'

Daniel and Gwyn were together, and on their own, as they often were.

'Congratulations on your wedding, Gwyn. It's going to be difficult to, I don't know, "love" two women.'

'Love, Daniel? Things are a bit confusing on that front.'

'Don't you love 'em?'

'Well, I wonder how they're getting on together. That's something, isn't it? Caring.' Strangling his hands as he spoke. 'I think I admire both in different ways. They both have graceful silky skins, the kind that shimmers in the morning light. Their hair, they both have beautiful hair, distinctive, strong. You could tie a bundle of firewood with that hair of theirs, it's so robust. And their eyes... stop you in the street eyes.'

'You speak as if you're describing a painting in an art gallery, portraits from an artist's oil brush, from the imagination. Do you talk with them, do you go on walks with them, do you make love with them? Do you touch each other in the nights?'

'I watch them undressing, at dusk, when the moon shines through one of the bedroom windows. No one speaks. The curtains are never closed... The room becomes part of the garden. We're with all the other creatures of the outside, we become no different to them.'

'Which one we talking about here? They both love you?'

'Is love important, Daniel? There are too many bad people around, too many people with smooth tongues, who praise without meaning, who smile without passion.'

'You saved them from those bad people? Why did you do that? Why was it your responsibility, why did the burden fall on you?'

'It was my choice, sure enough. Call it my contribution to loyalty and duty.'

'But not to love, Gwyn?'

'No, not love, Daniel.' Gwyn stared straight ahead. 'Do you think

I'd allow anyone else to speak to me the way you're speaking to me now? I let you because I respect you.'

'Respect? Is it more than respect?'

Gwyn wasn't prepared to give an answer. Shadows were the places he liked to live in, hidden from all those prying, gossipy eyes.

XI

THE LAST GLOW of light from the setting sun had long gone, shapes fading peacefully into the night. A shooting star blazed above them, but no one saw it; the wind rose a little, the stars appeared, but Jimmy, Lee and John were not tired, squatting, clutching their blankets, seeking comfort from the cold. They had no problem with the food, unfussy eaters save that they were still getting used to knives and forks. But they got on with things as they always did. At best they were treated with condescension by the other navvies, at worst a kick here, a bloodied nose there, but they had been warned by their family and friends at home that it would be so – foreigners were wicked people.

'It's a cold one,' said John, grasping his blanket ever tighter. John was the youngest of the three, just out of his teens. He had known Lee since childhood. They had been brought up in the same village. John wasn't very tall, and he often stood on the tips of his toes when speaking, for greater effect.

Lee had an uncomplicated manner, unlike the self-important Jimmy. Lee liked to tease John, even though he was only a few years older, but Lee felt his seniority merited such merriment. Those few years had given Lee the wisdom which John, excitable John, lacked. Jimmy was new to both of them.

Lee was sometimes referred to as 'Three Sweaters' by the other navvies. Prone to shivering in the cold evenings and early mornings, he always wore three layers of sweaters; the first was too tight, the second just right and the third a floppy and shapeless overgarment. All to keep him warm. Only on the hottest days would he take the two outer sweaters off, and the innermost never.

'My father liked to gamble,' said John.

'It's in our blood, rice and gambling,' replied Lee.

'And fighting,' answered Jimmy.

'And working,' said John.

'Rice growers, fighters, workers and gamblers, that's what we are. Our contribution to the world. We built the Great Wall, we fight each other, we gamble on crickets and we eat rice!' said Lee, laughing.

'We'll get the Mahjong out tonight, boys,' said Jimmy, 'have a game before bed.'

'That's if I've still got the strength. This work, this heat, this cold – it's tough,' replied Lee.

'Good fortune follows us,' said Jimmy. 'To come here, to find work, to get paid, that's good fortune. We'd all be dead if we'd stayed at home, either from a Chinese bullet or a Japanese bullet, makes no difference, we'd still be dead. Only thing that can kill you here are the animals.'

'And Jabez, and Daniel. Are they animals too, Jimmy?'

'The worst kind, the kind that don't think twice about whether three Chinamen are alive or dead. All laowai are animals.'

'Long as we do our work we get paid, stay away from trouble we'll be fine, won't we? asked John, looking at Jimmy. 'That's right, isn't it?'

'It's been right up to now. All we got to do is keep it that way. Anyone up for a small wager?' asked Jimmy. 'Who remembers the Sanxing, the three stars, and whose got any money?'

'I've got a farthing,' said Jimmy.

'Me too,' said Lee.

'I ain't got nothing,' said John.

'I'll lend you a farthing, pay me back a ha'penny on pay day,' said Jimmy.

'What's this all about?' Lee asked.

'It's the stake, the farthing's the stake,' said Jimmy.

'What's the bet?' enquired Lee.

'The bet's the three star gods, Sanxing. Come on, you remember. The gods of these three stars Fu, Lu and Shou, the lucky symbols,' said Jimmy.

'This going to take long, Jimmy?' said John. 'A warm bed is what I want, it's freezing out here.'

'John, you first, who was the star of Fu?'

'Didn't get as much education as you, Jimmy.'

'Come on, we all know about Fu, just a few words that's all. Lee and me will do the other two, we say the stories, and I'll tell you the bet.'

'OK then, but no one makes fun of me if I get it wrong,' said John.

'Jabez ain't around. Come on, let's hear it,' said Lee, sensing a bit of sport at John's expense.

'The star of Fu is Fuxing, the big planet, the biggest planet,' replied John.

'Jupiter,' declared Lee.

'Thank you, Lee, Jupiter the star of Fu.' Jimmy firmly had the floor.

'And what else, Joe.'

'What else?'

'Ever heard of Xang Chen?'

'Go on, finish the story off for him, Lee,' said Jimmy, more as command than request.

'Xang Cheng was a governor of a big province during the Tang Dynasty. He lived in a little town where all the people were short. The emperor, who was also a short man, felt powerful when visiting the town. He could look down on them and not up, as he usually had to do. On returning to his palace the emperor decreed that the town was to send fifty of its citizens to him every year as slaves. This troubled the townspeople greatly, and as a result the population declined every year and, with it, the town's prosperity. The governor Xang Cheng took pity on the townspeople. At great peril to himself he wrote a petition to the emperor and pleaded with him in person to end this barbaric act. The emperor was moved by Xang Cheng's words and agreed to end the taking of slaves. By the vigour of his words, Xang Cheng had persuaded the most powerful man in the whole world to change his actions. His pleas had saved the town from poverty and extinction. Xang Cheng then became known as Fu Ching. Fu had brought good luck and prosperity to all the townspeople. He was loved by the people, and he is the god of wealth and prosperity'.

'Excellent, Lee, now it's your turn proper,' said Jimmy.

'Which one you want, Jimmy, you've got Lu or Shou?' asked Lee.

'I think you should do, Lu,' he replied.

'Fine, Lu is the god of importance, his star is Luxing. You're the top Chinaman in Africa Jimmy. Luxing is your star.'

Lee knew it paid to be on the right side of Jimmy; his pockmarked face, the full and broken nose, the dense folds which surfaced on his forehead in moments of anger did not make for a soothing companion.

'Enough of that,' said Jimmy. 'The last star is Shou, his star is Shouxing, the star of the South Pole, the star of long life. Shou grew in his mother's womb for ten whole years and was already ancient when he was eventually born. He was always happy, always friendly.'

'But what's the bet, Jimmy, what's the bet?' asked John.

'In a minute. Shouxing, we all recognize him, even you, John. He's the old man with the big brow, carries the peach of long life and a staff.'

'Not sure if I remember him, Jimmy. Like I said, I ain't had an education like you two,' said John.

'There's something else about him, John, something Jimmy hasn't said,' declared Lee.

'What's that then, oh great storyteller of Cathay?' asked John.

'Shou has the power to decide how many years any person can live, save that the numerical figures for the years can be switched around.'

'I don't understand what you mean. Let's get to the bet.'

'Shut up, John. Tell the story, Lee,' ordered Jimmy.

'There was a young boy called Zao Yan who lived in a remote village in a clearing in a great forest. One day a fortune teller came to Zao Yan's village, and the young boy, being curious, went to see the fortune teller, who said that the god Shou had told him that the boy would die when he reached the age of nineteen. Zao Yan was broken hearted. However, the fortune teller told him to take the best food and wine that he possessed into the dark forest. He was to offer the food and wine to two ancient white-bearded men who he would find playing chess in the forest, but he was not to say one word to them until after they had consumed his gifts. Zao Yan, in a state of great distress, did as he was told. Off he went into the forest, where he found the two old men playing chess. He presented them with the food and wine, but as instructed said nothing. The two old men accepted the gifts and enjoyed them immensely. One of them was the old man of the South Pole and the other the old man of the North Pole. Seeing that the boy was troubled, they asked him the cause. Zao Yan told them how many years of life the god Shou had granted him. The old men discussed his plight and decided the best way to repay Zao Yan's hospitality would be to reverse the numbers granted by the god Shou. They changed the figure nineteen to ninety-one. Zao Yan thanked them profusely. As bestowed, Zao Yan lived until he was ninety-one years old and died peacefully in his bed at home, quietly in his sleep.'

Well,' said Lee, 'remember the story now, John?

'Very nice, but what's the bet?'

'Ah, young people, they have no money and they have no patience,' said Jimmy. 'The bet, for a one farthing stake from each of us is this: I will write on three separate pieces of paper the name of the three gods, one god per paper. I will then scrunch up the papers and place them into my hat, the first hat. Each of us then writes our name, and the name of our favourite god on one paper each, and those three papers, separately scrunched up as before, will be placed in John's hat, which I will call the second hat. You, John, will have the honour of pulling the papers out of the hat.'

'I still don't understand how this is going to work, Jimmy.'

'Calmness is required here, John. Now listen, from the first hat you will choose one paper and announce to us the name of the god written on it. From the second hat you will, in turn, pick out a paper and tell us which one of our names is written on it, and the name of the god which that person has chosen as his favourite god. Whichever one of us chooses the same god as the one you picked initially from the first hat wins. Who knows, we may all share the spoils. Remember, Fu prosperity, Lu importance, Shou long life. You have a minute to decide.'

Within seconds Lee and John had made their decisions. Writing their name together with the name of their favourite god on the second scraps of paper, scrunching up the papers and placing these second sets in into John's hat, Jimmy having already placed three papers in the first hat.

'What the hell have you done with your paper, John?' asked Lee.

'Jimmy said scrunch it up, and scrunched it up I did.'

'There's scrunching and scrunching, boy, you'll need a pickaxe to open that paper. It's folded as tight as the emperor's wallet.'

'Shut up, let's get on with the bet,' commanded Jimmy. 'Wait for me, almost done. Right we're all in, ready. John over to you. Here's my hat, the first hat. Pick one of the papers, name the god who will decide the fate of our farthings. May we all have good fortune.'

'Shouldn't we pick from John's hat first, the one with our names and the names of each of our favourite gods? Then pick the winning god last. Makes it more exciting that way, doesn't it?' said Lee.

'Good idea, Lee. Here's your hat then, John. Open each of the three papers, one at a time now, reveal all,' said Jimmy.

'Come on, John, start picking.'

'Stop bullying me, Lee, will you.' Unfolding the paper. 'The choice of Lee is the god Lu.'

'The god of importance, wise choice,' said Jimmy.

'Your picking's hopeless, John, let me do the next one,' said Lee.

Choosing one of the folded papers. 'What kind of writing is this?' asked Lee.

John peered over Lee's shoulder.

'It's me, it's my writing.'

'Call this writing?'

'Stop making fun of me.'

'What's John's choice then, Lee?'

'Fu, the choice for John is Fu, prosperity and wealth.'

'Another excellent choice. Come on, John, pick the last one, pick mine,' said Jimmy.

'I don't want to, Lee's making fun of me all the time.'

'Lee'll keep quiet, won't you, Lee? Come on, John, pick the paper. Which god have I chosen.'

Putting his hand in his cap, John pulled out the third paper.

'Don't tell me, don't tell me, Jimmy's written Shou, the god of long life,' said Lee.

John held the paper close to his chest.

'Yes, he has, we've all chosen different gods.'

'What were the odds on that happening? Let me see, runt,' said Lee.

'Well, well, well, this makes it interesting,' said Jimmy. 'We've all chosen different gods, which means there will only be one winner. On whom will good fortune smile today? John, here's my hat. Three pieces of paper, three different gods, Fu, Lu and Shou. Come on, John, pick one, and one only, mind.'

Fumbling in the hat, Joe pulled out one crumpled piece of paper.

'Come on, open it up, let's see who won,' said Lee impatiently.

'I see John wants to keep us in suspense, Lee.'

'Shou, it's Shou, the god of long life!' said John. 'You've lost a farthing, you've lost a farthing, Lee's lost a farthing!'

'Hell, you're so stupid, you've lost as well, you stench-ridden horsefly,' said Lee.

'Right, that's a farthing you owe me, Lee. And John, it'll be a ha' penny from you come pay day'.

Reluctantly Lee scrabbled into his trouser pocket, produced his farthing and handed it to Jimmy.

'A stupid bet, that was,' the farthingless Lee said.

'We, all had the same choices, boys. Next time luck will be with one of you,' declared Jimmy. 'Tell you what, why don't we make things more interesting? What was that you said about the god Shou, something about predicting life?'

'Yeah, how long someone's going to live.'

'Seeing as we're out here, working in this wilderness far from home, wild animals, wild men everywhere, what if we bet on who will be the first to die on site. There's always been deaths on the Railway,' said Jimmy. 'Every time we've been on site something happens.'

'That ain't a comforting thought, Jimmy,' said Lee.

'Tell you what, what if we say we can't place a bet on one of us, that's to say, one of us dying. Wouldn't be seemly. We each choose one person. Granted, only one choice each means there's less chance of us winning the bet, 'cos there's about sixteen of us out here. But that means the stake is practically risk free, and it'll still be a bet, and that's what's most important, right, Joe? It's the bet not the winning.'

'Means we have a chance of winning as well,' said John.

'I hear you. That being the case let's raise the stake.'

'How much?' asked Lee.

'Yeah, how much, Jimmy?' asked John.

'All our wages from this site work. Low chance of anyone winning means low chance of anyone losing. That's right, ain't it, John?' said Jimmy.

'That's right, Jimmy,' agreed John.

'All our wages? That's just crazy, Jimmy', said Lee.

'What you say, John? You get a chance of doubling those wages of yours, or more likely not losing anything. What you say?' asked Jimmy.

'We get to choose any one of the boys?' asked John.

'Anyone, save us three here, of course. That wouldn't be decent,' said Jimmy.

'Don't do it, John, just don't do it, risk is too great.'

'Don't listen to Lee, he's just worn out and grumpy. Tell you what, I'll let you off that ha'penny you owe me, how does that sound? Might give you good luck. You did choose Fu the god of prosperity, bet he's looking down on you now, bet he'll reward you with riches for choosing him.'

'But I get to choose first, I mean the navvy who's going to die first, I get to choose before you do.'

'No problem, of course you choose first, John. You're the youngest, you deserve the honour. Give me your hand.'

And with that Jimmy and John shook on it. The only shaking Lee did was with his head.

'Right, John, who's it going to be.'

'Old man Mubanga.'

'Old man Mubanga, excellent choice. He's the oldest one here, who knows, his heart may go pop at any moment, in this heat and with all this heavy work. Could be a snake gets him in his sleep, blackwater fever... difficult to tell. Good choice anyway. That's exactly who I would have chosen. I think Fu has given you wisdom in your choice of death,' said Jimmy.

'Speaking of snakes, who are you going to settle on, Jimmy?' enquired Lee.

'It's potluck from here. Oh, I don't know, I think I'll choose... I'll choose one of them Indians. Kumar. I select Kumar for an early death.'

'Why him, Jimmy?'

'No reason, John. Your choice was the best one. The chance of me winning after your decision is pretty remote, but I gave my word. You can start counting that money now, young man, because if one of us is going to win, don't look like it's going to be me. But a bet's a bet.'

'Absolutely correct, Jimmy,' replied John triumphantly.

'Let's get some sleep, boys. Jabez or Daniel will be on our backs first thing tomorrow,' said Lee.

'You two go ahead, I need to go to the craphouse on urgent business,' said Jimmy.

Jimmy walked towards the latrine and threw the two remaining crumpled pieces of paper out of his hat, the god Shou written in his hand on both. Jimmy was not a man to lose a farthing in a bet with anyone, and never a man to lose all his site wages on a wager; there was always more than one way to win a bet.

There was no moon that night. The gloom had tiptoed into every cranny. Jimmy had to have his wits about him if he was to find the privy and win the bet.

XII

GWYN HAD SINCE EARLY ADOLESCENCE framed the photographs of assorted locomotives, which he'd cut out of various magazines and periodicals. The SAR7955 and the SAR8B1126 from the Zambezi Sawmills Railway handbook, the 16A class used on the line running southeast from Bulawayo to West Nicholson, which he found in the *Chronicle*. One of his special favourites were the industrial locos used up at the Selebe-Pikwe copper mine.

The framed photographs were placed on the top row of the grand bookcase built against the northern wall of the lounge, distempered in pure white. Constructed from Zambezi redwood – or Rhodesian teak, as it was also designated at Richardson's sawmill, and as Gwyn liked to call it – the same wood as used for railway sleepers by Rhodesia Railways. The sawmill manager always allowed the Railway engineers a chance to pick and choose teak off cuts in the yard, for construction of furniture and miscellaneous household requirements.

'I didn't know Gwyn was such a reader,' Delyth said, surveying the shelves.

'He's a private man, Mrs Bowen,' I replied.

'That means he's a lonely man. All readers and all authors are lonely men. Beautiful colour, isn't it, Daisy?'

'It's redwood, very easy to clean, one wipe with a shammy and it's done. Gwyn made it himself, said it was difficult to work with, but termites or rot doesn't seem to bother it none. It'll be here long after we're all gone.'

'I've read some of these books. *Animal Farm*, *The Little Prince*, oh I do love that one. *Death of a Salesman*, haven't read that. They all smell of stale bread and old pockets.'

I'd also read most of the books myself, all white, all foreign. Still it was useful to know what the other side thought. I can't say I enjoyed all of them. Seemed to me Europeans could only have excitement if they had a pen or a rifle in their hands.

'He comes in here on his own to try and find sense in things. I tell him the more books he reads, the more rubbish and confusion gets into that head of his. It's as peculiar as someone trying to find answers in dreams or palm reading.'

'Gwyn's told me about truth before, says it's in all of us. That's what Adip Patel told him anyway, that's where the answer is,' said Delyth.

Feeling more comfortable in Delyth's presence, I ventured, 'Well he won't find no answers in books that's for sure. And you Europeans think we're the primitive ones.'

'Europeans, some Europeans, think Africans are poor and ignorant, but if that's the case why do our men love your women so much?'

'Don't know about that. All these books could burn to ashes as far as I'm concerned, they could all be replaced. There's nothing new in books, there just can't be. Everything has always been the same, everyone has said the same things as everyone else before them. Mind you, that's me. Gwyn doesn't think like that. Gwyn thinks too much.'

'Does he have a favourite book? What is his book, *the* book?'

'He's still on that quest, still on that journey to find the complete book, the pure book,' I replied.

'Surely that must be the Holy Bible, that's the Lord's book, the perfect book. It's a catalogue for all the books that will ever be written.'

'Those are lots of big words, Mrs Bowen, and I'm sure lots of folks agree with you, but Gwyn is still searching, like the hundreds of thousands before him.'

'And where will he find that book, is there some shelf somewhere in a far off library, where he'll find what he's looking for? Is the library in Africa? Is that why he's here?'

'Settlers wouldn't like it if that library was here. Reckon they'd say it's somewhere in Europe, but in one of the warm parts, not the rainy parts.'

'And what if he found that book, Daisy, what then? Would Gwyn be content just to read it, or would it become so precious to him that he'd dare not leave it out of his sight? Would he die to protect what he'd found? Humiliate himself, do anything for this book? And whilst he's searching, would he notice that he's getting older? The creaking bones, the rotting teeth, the failing eyesight. All that's lost while searching, would he even see it go?'

'Gwyn will put off any issues that can be put off, to search knowing that he will never find. It's a mirror opposite another mirror. If I found that book, I'd burn it straight away, get rid of it, and I'd tell the world so that everyone could be at peace with themselves. Why doesn't he write his own book for heaven's sake?'

'He speaks a lot with Mr Patel, the grocer, doesn't he? Does Patel talk sense, does he speak truth?'

'Who knows, Mrs Bowen. You'll be lucky to find the truth anywhere, and I certainly don't think you'll find it in a redwood bookcase.'

'Look,' observed Delyth, 'all the authors are in alphabetical order, everything is so... orderly, eternally orderly.'

'Gwyn's an orderly man all right. Helps me take the washing off the line, he makes sure that when every peg is put back they can all slide along the line. Me I put 'em back higgledy piggledy, slide or no slide.'

'Everything seems to be in its rightful place. Am I in my rightful place here, Daisy? It's stuffy here as well, isn't it, all these old books. Gwyn should have spent more time finishing off that swimming pool in the garden and left the bookcase alone. We could have had a good old cool down. This heat is unbearable.'

'There's a stream flows near the back of the garden, used to be crocs there in times gone by, but they were shot and killed by settlers years ago. My people used to go swimming there after the killings.'

'Well, at least that's one good thing Europeans have brought to this country. You can't argue with that, can you, Daisy? Why don't we go there for a dip, ten minutes or so, just to cool down.'

'The stream's ok for us Bemba, but I'm not sure about Europeans. I wouldn't like you picking up any ailments in that water, Mrs Bowen.'

'It's not stagnant, is it?'

'No, it's quite free flowing and the current isn't too strong.'

'That's the test, isn't it? If it's stagnant, don't go in; if it's free flowing, it's fine, sweeps the nasties away. That's what my teachers in school told me.'

'That would be settler teachers, Mrs Bowen, would it?'

'I'm sure some of those teachers were born here, on the law of averages they must have been. Wisdom isn't only confined to Bemba, there are other views out there in the big wide world.'

'I'm not sure, Mrs Bowen, I'm really not. What would Gwyn think?'

'Oh come on, Daisy, don't be such a baby. Gwyn won't know, and after all I'm the mistress, and you're supposed to be the housekeeper, remember? Who is giving the orders here anyway?'

Two rayon jerseyed swimmers. I was in red, Delyth in blue, both of us with knit cotton linings standing on the banks of the rippling stream. The mauve-flowered jacarandas were beginning to lose their petals, falling like confetti onto the ground.

'Looks good to me,' said Delyth, dipping her feet into the water. 'Come on, after three. One, two, three!' And in she rushed, diving, laughing into the coolness. Swimming under the water, a shoal of small cichlids shuddering out of her way.

'No crocs here! Come on, it's gorgeous, Daisy, it's gorgeous! Come on, you baby, come on! It's an order!'

Reluctantly I went in, swimming towards Delyth. This was a mistake, but what could I do about it? I was only the maid.

'This is the life! The water's a shot in the arm, it really is.'

Delyth laughed, a peculiar laugh, a nervous laugh, an insecure, jittery laugh.

Both out of our depth, treading water, we swam slightly upriver to maintain our place opposite the sandbank where we'd left our towels.

'Who needs a pick me up before dinner when you can have this? Gwyn never told me about this place. He must have been saving it for a special occasion. How long can you hold your breath underwater? I'll go first, and you can do the counting.'

She didn't wait for an answer. Holding her nose with her right hand, into the water she dived, just a foot or so below the surface, waving her left hand at me. I was more a lookout than a timekeeper. Back up she came, like a breaching whale.

'How long, how long was I down there, what's my time?'

'Thirty-two seconds, almost thirty-three.'

'You were counting, weren't you? No fibs now!'

'Thirty- two seconds, Mrs Bowen.'

'Your turn now, in you go, let's see whose got the biggest lungs, the local or the foreigner.'

I dived in. The cichlids had long disappeared. I counted to twenty-five and resurfaced.

'Twenty-eight, I win, I win! See, I knew I was a good swimmer, told you, told you! Let's see if we can reach the opposite bank. It's not too far for you, Daisy, is it? No need to hold your breath, just do some gentle breaststroke, you'll be ok.'

'We'd better stay on this side. All those miombo trees on the opposite bank could be hiding some nasty creatures, hyenas and such like.'

'What a baby you are, where's the warrior African spirit in you? I'm going anyway, last to the other side's a baby!'

Off she went, her energetic front crawl splashing water into my eyes. I followed quickly, easily catching her up. We both reached the far side in less than half a minute.

'Can't see any hyenas, can you? They've all left with the crocodiles. What are you worried about?'

I saw movement, two eyes looking at us from the miombo trees. A sable antelope, male, about four feet at the shoulder, thick necked, rich chestnut in colour, probably wandering down to the river to slake its thirst, waiting for us impostors to leave. I don't think Delyth noticed anything. She was too busy practicing holding her breath underwater.

'Forty-five seconds, forty-five seconds... That's my best ever, must be close to a world record. Hip hip hurrah!'

'I think we've had our ten minutes, Mrs Bowen, best not to push our luck too much out here.'

'Oh what a spoilsport you are! Come on then, let's go in.'

The antelope left, disturbed by the scent of a pack of wild dogs on the breeze; it receded further into the forest out of sight, leaving the river to us foolhardy day trippers.

As we swam and then waded up towards the bank, Delyth's feet gave way underneath her, and she stumbled on some shiny pebbles a few feet from the shore. Instinctively I held out my hand to lead her out of the river. My hand was declined.

'Think I grazed my ankle a bit there,' she said. 'It was worth it though, for the swim. It's quite slippy here with all these pebbles. I'll know better next time.'

I passed one of the white cotton towels to Delyth, noticing the slight grazing on the left ankle.

'I'll dry you,' she said. 'You can do the same for me.'

She put her hands either side of my hips and pushed me back slightly. A woman stands here, settler.

'Head down, let me give your hair a good seeing to. Come on, arms next, now your legs.'

Grasping my shoulders, she swung me around; she didn't speak until she had finished.

'It's my turn next.'

I stroked Delyth's hair with her towel, I dried Delyth's legs and knees, and then the rest of her body, all but caressing it. I did not feel ashamed. We were both quiet, happy to be out of the water, sunning on the riverbank.

'You enjoyed the swim, Mrs Bowen?'

'It was great, don't you agree? Great to be away from that musty old house, all those books and that dead squirrel.'

'There'll be no dead squirrels from now on, Mrs Bowen. I can assure you of that. I'm truly sorry for what happened. It was my fault. I should have smelt the problem earlier. I'll make sure to check underneath the house more often in the future. Don't want anything else creeping under there.'

'Don't worry, it's done now. Gwyn's got so many herbs and spices in that kitchen, it's like an Arabian bazaar. No wonder you didn't smell anything.'

We changed out of the swimming costumes into our day clothes. We looked at each other's bodies. I looked at her long lean legs, her slightly masculine hands, her breasts, her reddish-brown hair, her square swimmer shoulders, her creaseless face.

'Everything ok, Mrs Bowen?' I asked.' You look as if there's something on your mind.'

'I'm just thinking, Daisy, looking at your beautiful body, I can see now why European men love your women so much. Let's go before the crocodiles arrive.'

I could also now see why European men could also love Delyth. Why confine emotions to Europeans and to men?

XIII

THE NEXT MORNING was another glorious sunny day in Broken Hill.

'Morning, Daisy. Can't say I feel on top form today, must've caught some sort of cold from the swim yesterday. There's some blotches on my arm as well, which are terribly itchy.'

'Let me have a look, Mrs Bowen.'

I could see there were five small, distinct red blisters running up Delyth's forearm.

'I've seen these before, nothing to worry about,' I said reassuringly.

'What do you mean, Daisy, what are they?'

'It's called bilharzia. It sounds worse than it is.'

'Bill what? What part of this frightful country did Bill come from?'

I looked at her without answering.

'Not from the stream? We were only there for a few minutes. There was no stagnant water, all the crocodiles were long gone. What are these, is it a mosquito or something? Have you had this before?'

'Bemba are more used to these streams than Europeans. It's nothing to worry about. All you need is a few injections from Doctor Cosgrove, and you'll be right as rain. Let's go and see him tomorrow. I'll go with you.'

'I can't wait for tomorrow, I'll go and see him now. You can come with me to the surgery if you want, but I'll see him on my own, not in front of an audience. This should be a private consultation, not a committee meeting, thank you very much.'

Gwyn's parents had shown a lot of foresight when building the bungalow, not only for its pleasant location, but because it was only a brisk twenty-minute walk to what had been Doctor Alderman's surgery. One of the early settlers in Broken Hill, Doctor Alderman had died in his mid-sixties, in a riding accident during the dry season, near a famous local beauty spot.

His horse Bonny snagging its foot in a dried elephant footprint, sending both the doctor and Bonny hurtling onto the rock-hard ground, the doctor dying immediately from a fractured neck. Bonny broke her left front forelock and was discovered hobbling in great pain by a group of schoolchildren and their teacher on a nature walk. The teacher raised the alarm, ensuring that Doctor Alderman's face was covered by his jacket before the deceased's family and Johnson the undertaker arrived. As for Bonny, she was humanely dispatched by one rifle shot to the head, administered by a neighbour of Doctor Alderman, one Sam Edgar, but only after the school party, the deceased's family and undertaker Johnson had left the scene.

Bonny's carcass was left to the scavengers, the family having decided the cost of transporting the dead horse back to the knacker's yard in town as prohibitive. Naturally the fine leather saddle and all tack were salvaged and entered into the probate sale some months later. Due to the visitation of numerous vultures, hyenas, wild dogs and the occasional lion, the beauty spot was out of bounds to the local citizenry for a number of weeks. The location to this day is known as Edgar's Shot, its previous Bemba name being unknown to the settlers, as no one had cared to ask us.

Doctor Alderman's practice was now run by Doctor Cosgrove, a recent arrival from Sligo in Ireland. Doctor Cosgrove had seen the post advertised in the *Journal of the Medical Association of Ireland*, and thought he might as well give it a go, due to the unhappy ending of his long-standing courtship with a nurse in Oughterard, County Galway. If he had to forget his lost love, it would be better to do so as far away from Connacht as possible.

'It can get terribly stuffy in the surgery waiting room, Mrs Bowen,' I said as we walked. 'There's only one overhead fan, and it breaks down all the time. You can't book an appointment either; Doctor Cosgrove's one of the modern types. Europeans, Bemba, Indian, even Chinese, they're all the same to him. No jumping of queues except for an emergency.'

'I've obviously got an emergency. He'll see me immediately, you can be sure of that. He's one of us after all.'

The walk to the surgery from the bungalow involved passing the railway cattle loading pens, never a pleasant place. Although this was the quickest route, I was in two minds whether to take Delyth by another way.

Lowing, bleating, whistling, shouting, clouded by ascending dust, disturbed earth risen by the hooves of hundreds of impounded, unruly livestock on their way to a soundless cessation in the slaughterhouse. Seven pens conveniently constructed as an appendage to the railway line. Built of galvanized metal up to shoulder height. Cattle and sheep guided up ramps, loaded on to railway tracks, abattoir bound. Wooden sticks thrashing flesh, shrill whistles and the 'Cattle Prodder', a two-foot electric rod bringing its own pain to the endeavours.

'Look at those poor beasts, packed like tinned sardines. How on earth can they breathe?'

'They are animals, Mrs Bowen, and Gwyn does like his steak and kidney pie.'

'What's Gwyn's stomach got to do with all this cruelty?'

The last pen contained about fifty sheep with their lambs. A short section of thick wire had been placed in every lamb's nostril, with the two ends pointing away from the nose. We could not but see the result.

'The lambs are hurting their own mothers! Look, they want to suckle but they can't get close enough because of those things in their noses. The sheep are bleeding from their udders! What kind of country is this?'

'Come on, Mrs Bowen, don't look, let me hold your hand. A brisk walk and we'll soon be at Doctor Cosgrove's. We'll leave this all behind.'

*

As I'd expected, the surgery reception was fusty, full of crying babies, tearful mothers, old men on crutches. All of humanity was welcome at Doctor Cosgrove's surgery, but everyone had to wait their turn. The settlers' clothing trumpeted their prosperity, their self-proclaimed superior standing. Sunday best in the doctor's surgery, under an overhead fan recycling only hot air. It was another two hours before Delyth was seen. She told me to stay in reception.

'Mrs Bowen, isn't it? What can I do for you.'

Doctor Cosgrove was remarkably well groomed considering the conditions under which he laboured. A striking tweed waistcoat barely visible, protruding behind his white cotton medical coat. He must have been very hot. He had a full moustache, with just a hint of unkemptness; he was a man who contrived at being in control.

'It's my arm, doctor. I've got this itchy rash running along it. My housekeeper says it's bilharzia.'

'That's a big word for a housekeeper, and which medical school did she qualify from? Please, let me have a look.'

Dutifully Delyth rolled up her sleeve.

'Have you been swimming recently?'

'Yes, we went, Daisy and I, that's my housekeeper, we went yesterday in the stream behind our house. I thought it'd be ok, thought it would be safe.'

'This is Africa, Mrs Bowen, nothing is safe in Africa. You should know that by now.'

'Will I be ok, doctor?'

'Calm yourself, Mrs Bowen, this is quite common for Europeans, especially Europeans who go swimming in infected waters, full of infectious snails. Good that you came to see me so quickly, and yes, your housekeeper was right, it is bilharzia. She must be a bit of an expert on the condition. But don't worry, this is the twentieth century. I'll give you a series of injections over the next twelve months which should clear it all up, and you'll be fine. Just don't go swimming in streams again, leave it to the crocodiles. Best advice I can give you is ask your husband to build you a swimming pool and tell him to put lots of chlorine in it.'

Doctor Cosgrove's efforts at jollity were not well received. Delyth crossed her legs, grasped each side of her chair and blurted out, 'Doctor, I think I'm pregnant, will this affect my baby?'

Doctor Cosgrove's demeanour did not change; he was as constant as an unused piano in an unused room. 'Are you sure you're pregnant, Mrs Bowen?'

'Of course I'm sure, I'm a woman, aren't I?' Delyth started to cry.

'I'll need to monitor you as we go along. We've got to keep you healthy, that's our first priority. Get rid of the infection, give the baby its best chance.'

'But will the injections, or the infection, affect the baby? You're not answering my question.'

Doctor Cosgrove looked back at Delyth, mumbled something about bilharzia and Sligo, then looked at his notes.

'You don't know, do you, doctor? You don't know whether the baby will be affected. You're more of a newcomer here than I am, what do you know about African diseases? I should have gone to the native witch doctor, I'm sure he's more of an expert than you are! God, why did I ever come to this place!'

'Compose yourself, Mrs Bowen. The mother in these instances must come first. Everything will be fine. We'll just need to monitor you. You'll get the best care that Broken Hill can provide.'

'That's what's worrying me. Broken Hill, more like broken bloody down!'

'If we do nothing, the infection could harm your liver and kidneys, and we don't want that. Tell that housekeeper of yours that you're not to do anything strenuous from now on. And no more swimming in streams! Don't worry, I've had years of experience as a doctor.'

'But I haven't had years of experience as a patient!'

XIV

'HOW ARE YOU TODAY, Auntie Maisie?'

Auntie Maisie, an old bone weary, spent woman, age-condensed, ferried past her allotted time, ferried beyond the meadows of childhood, ferried past all companions and clan, save for Jabez, still liked hot soup and an argument.

'Why haven't you come to see me, Jabez? No one ever comes to see me. I'm here on my own. Where have you been?'

'No need to worry about that, I'm here now. I come as often as I can. It's not easy with me working away so often. How are they treating you here since I saw you last?'

'You saw me last? You've never seen me.'

'I was here ten days ago, brought you some pink roses. They were in this vase by your bed. Look what I've brought you today, some bougainvillea. I'll ask the nurse to put them in some water for you. Don't you think they're nice? You always liked bougainvillea. You used to have them in your garden, remember?'

'Where's John? He never comes to see me neither, just like you.'

'John's passed away, Auntie Maisie.'

'Passed away where?'

'He passed four years ago, had a heart attack. You always said he should lose weight. I've been looking after you since then. Have you been eating well?'

'Plenty of food here. The nurses work so hard, always busy. I used to be a nurse, did you know that? Where's John, why doesn't he come to see me?'

'Soup, Mrs Evans? Some nice vegetable soup for you.'

'Let me, nurse. I'll help her.'

'Your nephew will help you with the soup, Mrs Evans, is that all right?'

Auntie Maisie nodded.

'Let me taste it first.' Jabez took a small spoonful. 'Just right, not too hot, not too cold. Come on, let me puff up those pillows, lift you up a bit. Here we go, one, two, three, up! That's better. I'll tie this napkin round you, don't want that pretty nightdress spoiled with soup stains.'

Jabez sat on the side of the bed, spoonfeeding his aunt.

'Nice soup, Auntie Maisie?'

'Yes, very nice. Someone's trying to kill me.'

'Pardon?'

'Someone's trying to kill me. They come from Livingstone every Thursday and try to kill me. I know who they are, but I'm going to escape tonight, through that window over there. I'll be gone before they turn up.'

'Stop being silly. No one's trying to kill you, everyone loves you, Auntie Maisie.'

'I see them. They walk in here, nobody's supposed to be walking around here. They're supposed to close the doors. They come up to my bed, but I'm too strong for them. But they'll be back. They always come back. Thursday comes around every week and those murderers come with it. I'm sure I've seen those young ruffians before, but I can't be sure of it. Any more soup? I adore vegetable soup. I get so hungry here.'

'You're eating well. Let me see if nurse can get us an extra portion. Excuse me, nurse, sorry to bother you, but is there any chance of some more soup for Mrs Evans?'

'Of course there is. Let me go down to the kitchen.'

'How has she been? She says that someone is trying to kill her.'

'The dementia is getting worse, Mr Pugh. It canters quickly. You've probably seen the change since you were here last. But she eats well. Physically she's remarkably strong for her age. Her heart is weakening, certainly, there's some swelling in her legs, but it's the mind that's waning fastest. She's one of the oldest here.'

'Does anyone else come to see her?'

'No one, apart from the minister from Moriah Congregational, Mr Roberts. He comes round every Thursday like clockwork. He's a good shepherd to his flock. Apart from Mr Roberts it's only you, Mr Pugh. She's lucky to have you. You've been wonderful to her. Before her mind went she always spoke about you, and always in the most glowing terms. How you've helped her since her husband died. She's been with us for almost three years now, and forgive me for speaking out of turn, but it must be a heavy financial burden for you.'

'It's the least I can do. My uncle John, her husband, my late mother's brother, died far too early. No pension in those days. Auntie Maisie spent her life caring for others, now she deserves the same. She used to be a nursing sister in Lusaka Infirmary. She's always been very proud of that fact.'

'Well I never, I didn't know that.'

'She was the midwife who brought me into the world, the first human being ever to set eyes on me. I looked a bit prettier then, I daresay. Mam said if it wasn't for Auntie Maisie, I would have died there and then. 'Cause of the complications with my birth, Mam couldn't have any more children. She died of smallpox when I just turned nine, 'n' my old man couldn't take things no more. He up and left, leaving me parentless. Auntie Maisie brought me up as her own son. She and Uncle John had always desperately wanted kids. So you see, I owe everything to her. She's the reason I'm here at all. She'll get the best whatever the cost. I really don't know what I'd do if something happened to her, I really don't.'

'Don't you worry, Mr Pugh, she'll be well looked after here. All the staff love her to bits.'

'Thanks, nurse, that's very comforting.'

'I'd almost forgotten, matron asked whether you could call into the bursar's office when you leave. Mr Ballard needs to talk to you about the fees. His office is directly next to the entrance.'

'I know where it is. Institutions like these ain't cut price.'

'Afraid they aren't, Mr Pugh. If only Mrs Evans knew what you've been doing for her, that would give you great comfort, I'm sure. You've had to make sacrifices, and I hope you don't mind me saying, you're only on Railway pay. The clientele here is, how shall I say, rather select.'

'No sacrifice is big enough for my aunt. I suppose the clientele don't like the look of a knife-scarred Railway navvy, do they? More used to double-talking lawyers and colonial civil servants.'

Well, there we are, let me get some more soup.'

'What was the nurse telling you, Jab? Does she know who those Thursday people are, those murderers? What day is it today, it can't be Thursday, please say it isn't Thursday!'

'Calm down, Auntie Maisie, it's Sunday, it's Sunday. There'll be no murderers coming to see you today.'

'Thank God for that!'

'Has Mr Roberts from Moriah been to see you?'

'Mr Roberts?'

'Mr Roberts, the minister.'

'Do I know a Mr Roberts?'

'Never mind, Auntie Maisie, never mind. Remember when we used to sing in the choir? You were contralto, weren't you, and I was tenor. And those duets we used to perform in the vestry for the Saint David's Day concert... Everybody loved our duets, do you remember?'

'Is John here yet, where is he? He never comes to see me. He's never here. Tell him, Jab, tell him when you see him next, tell him to come to see me, would you, please? It's not like him to forget. I'm sure he's got a good reason, I'm sure he has.'

'Do you like the flowers, Auntie Maisie?'

'John brought them. John and I always like flowers. Bougainvilleas are our favourites. We've got a garden full of them, pink ones, white ones. They flower for months on end. All the neighbours say how nice they are. When am I going home, so I can see John, give him a piece of my mind for not visiting me? It's not like him, it's not like him at all, no it isn't. Plenty of food here. The food's wonderful.

'John thinks the world of me, he brought these flowers, always looks after me. He's the best husband in the world, I couldn't be without him. He brought these flowers, aren't they nice?'

'They're very nice, Auntie Maisie.'

'You've seen the fly, haven't you, buzzing away in this room day after day? I tell the nurse about it, but whenever she comes over to me that dang fly is gone. Must be a very bright fly. Hear it now?'

The room was silent, save for the chirring of the overhead fans and the occasional cough from slumbering patients.

'Yes, Auntie Maisie, I hear it.'

'Bring me a fly swat, would you? That fly and me are going to have a powerful coming together. I'm going to show that insect who's boss. No one gets the better of Maisie Evans.'

'Here you are, Mrs Evans, some more vegetable soup.'

'Soup?'

'Yes, some beautiful vegetable soup.'

'I can't stand vegetable soup, I never have, take it away, take it away! Did you ask for vegetable soup, Jabez? I hate it, John would never have ordered vegetable soup. He knows me so well, much better than you do.

'Some people from Livingstone are trying to kill me. Every Thursday, they try and kill me every Thursday, did you know that? I'll tell John, he'll sort them out. Why can't you be like John? He always looks after me. See, he brought me these pretty flowers, aren't they nice?'

'They're glorious, Auntie Maisie. John is so good to you, he really is.'

'Did you enter the Ministry like I told you? Did you go to Theology College, learn the Bible, brush up on that voice of yours?'

'I'm giving it some serious thought, Auntie Maisie. Got the application forms just the other week. I'll bring them with me next time I see you.'

'I need to take a nap now, Jab. Have to look my best when John comes to see me on Thursday. Need to do my hair. I'll phone the hairdresser, put some makeup on for John.'

'I'll be off then.'

'What day is it?'

'It's Sunday.'

'It's not Thursday, is it?'

'No, it's not Thursday, Auntie Maisie.'

Auntie Maisie's eyes had closed before Jabez had finished his sentence. Jabez waited a few minutes and walked away from the bed, passing the nurse again.

'Remember to go and see the bursar now, Mr Pugh. Matron would kill me if I hadn't told you.'

In the bursar's office there was an inner office and an outer office, the waiting room a softwood bench in the outer office, next to the entrance door off the corridor. A Mrs Harrison and a Miss Jacobs toiled in the outer office, working away at two well used Imperial Typewriters. Being an accountant by profession, porky, icily smug Ballard ruminated in algorithms, save when he was dreaming of Mrs Harrison and Miss Jacobs naked, beavering away on their typewriters, taking the occasional shorthand. And yet there was hardly more distress or more sorrow and humiliation for Ballard than to daily look upon what he considered two delightful and radiant secretaries, beautiful and efficient, with a yearning that was never, ever reciprocated.

Ballard believed that he was more than able enough to keep both Mrs Harrison and Miss Jacobs fully employed. He gave dictation on maintenance of patient records, both the confidential and non confidential type; schedules of supplier ledgers (ingoing and outgoing); details of staff matters; and most importantly the financials, or balancing the books, as he used to say.

Mr Ballard had to produce the latter on a quarterly basis to the care home trustees. The meeting was always held in Mr Ballard's office, a meeting which Mrs Harrison and Miss Jacobs knew that they should on no account disturb. The session usually lasted a good hour, after which the parties would adjourn for a long and agreeable luncheon convening at the Great Northern. Initially, sherry would be taken in the guest lounge of the hotel, and the meal itself partaken in one of the private dining rooms which seemed to litter the Great Northern. There had been rumours that certain of the hostesses from Murphy's had been seen coming in and out of that private dining

room, but Mrs Harrison put this down to malicious gossip instigated
by some of the care home's bad debtors, and Miss Jacobs wholeheart-
edly agreed.

All the expenses for the convivialities, naturally being tax
deductible as a cost of doing business, would be paid for by donations from the voluntary contributions box in the main entrance
foyer, and topped up by petty cash, which Mr Ballard ensured was
in rude health prior to every quarterly meeting. The walk from the
care home to the Great Northern was something of a procession, a
ritual almost: the four trustees in the van, with each one jostling to
be out in the front, and therefore to appear to the ratepayers of
Broken Hill to be the one in charge, and Mr Ballard bringing up the
rear, both hands held firmly behind his back, anticipating that first
dry sherry followed by both the usual and exotic prandial and
post-prandial indulgences.

Ballard was just noting with gratitude that once again the quarterly meeting had passed smoothly, without anything untoward
coming to light, when Jabez marched into the outer office without
knocking.

'I've been told Ballard wants to see me.'

'Have you received our letters, Mr Pugh?' enquired Mrs Harrison.
'We've sent quite a few to you recently.' She was about forty years of
age, tall, some would say even of an elegant bearing, walking as if
trained in one of the best of St Petersburg's ballet conservatoires, her
neat auburn hair always swept back in an orderly bun, accentuating
her high cheek bones and light blue eyes.

'I've been up country. I'm away a lot, work with Rhodesia Railways,' replied Jabez with irritation.

'I'm sure you've received our letters. I've hand delivered some
myself through your letterbox,' came the brusque response from
Miss Jacobs. She was Mrs Harrison's second in command, and as
there were only two in this particular platoon, there was no one at
all she could look down upon. Her nickname at school had been
'little pullet' due to her thin, unusually long nose, which turned up
slightly at the tip. The nose counterbalanced well with her thin,
bloodless lips and her habit when walking of looking straight down

like a hen searching for seeds on the ground. This caused her shoulders to round in on themselves, which would cause her severe backache in years to come.

'How do you know you've got the right address? I might have moved.'

'What is your address then, Mr Pugh?' asked Mrs Harrison.

'I may have seen something on the floor.'

'That would be our letters,' responded Miss Jacobs.

'Haven't had time to read them. Tell Ballard I'm here, will you, haven't got all day.'

Mrs Harrison knocked on Mr Ballard's door. Miss Jacobs glanced occasionally at Jabez but kept on typing, sucking at a Fox's glacier mint through the few teeth that still lingered in her mouth; hens, as we know, have no teeth.

'What you looking at? Ain't you seen a scar before, ain't you got enough typing to do?'

'Mr Ballard will see you now,' said Mrs Harrison.

'Ah, Pugh, come in, have a seat. Tell me, how is your aunt? Mrs Evans, isn't it?' said Ballard, slimily like a recently serviced crankshaft.

Ballard's face was round, stitched and saddled with a lifetime of lines, of currying favour with his betters, of poring over profit and loss accounts, of chasing debtors, of covering tracks, of thinking about Mrs Harrison and Miss Jacobs. Eyes piggy, deeply submerged, eyes which he closed when he spoke. Ballard sweated. Ballard never liked the heat.

'What do you want, Ballard?'

'Very well, let me be candid with you. It's about the arrears on your aunt's fees. I can't run this care home from the donations in the voluntary contributions box. Nurses and doctors have to be paid, medicines procured, the building has to be maintained. I really must insist. The trustees want to know what I'm doing to collect these arrears.'

'I can't be the only bad payer.'

'There are others certainly, but you're by far the worst offender, and some of the others are, well, of exceptional antecedence, pillars of the community.'

'None of 'em are lowly Railway engineers like me, that's what you're saying, ain't it, Ballard?'

'I know you're not from around this neck of the woods. A bit rough round the edges, maybe, a newcomer amongst us, but this isn't the way we do things out here. Debts are debts, and debts must be paid.'

'You'll get your money, Ballard, you'll get all of it.'

'Can I speak frankly, Pugh? The question is *when* will the money be forthcoming. That's the question my trustees want the answer to. Haven't you had my letters? This establishment has been more than patient. I believe your last payment was four months ago, a cheque drawn on the Standard Bank of South Africa, Broken Hill branch. Can I suggest you discuss your financial position with Mr Wilson, the bank manager there? He is well disposed towards this institution and is highly respected by the trustees.'

'Trouble is, Mr Wilson ain't well disposed to me.'

'What about family, can't they help?'

'Only family I got left is staying in your care home, Ballard.'

'Friends, work colleagues? I hear you railway people have a strong sense of camaraderie. There must be someone there you can ask, surely there must be someone?'

'I ain't no beggar, Ballard. I make my own way in this world. I never been beholding to anyone, never. Auntie Maisie looked after me as a kid and I've looked after Auntie Maisie since I became a man. And I'll keep on looking after her until she's buried in Moriah Congregational Chapel cemetery, Broken Hill, that you can be certain of. There'll be four black stallions pulling her hearse right through the middle of this town, ain't no one gonna forget Auntie Maisie, not whilst I'm around, that clear?'

'Your devotion to your aunt is indeed admirable and to be commended, but it butters no parsnips with my trustees.'

'Don't talk high falutin gibberish to me, Ballard, just keep it plain and simple. After all, I'm only a lowly railway man.'

'The fees must be paid. Is that plain and simple enough for you?'

'How long you think she has to live. Weeks, couple of months maybe?

'All the management and staff wish your aunt long life, but her fees must be paid. You know how much they are.'

'I know all right.'

'Well?'

'Give me a couple more weeks. Got some irons in the fire, should be able to clear everything in that time.'

'Fairy godmother?'

'Something like that.'

'Very well, one month! Four weeks from today. Unless all the arrears are paid by that time, together, I might add, with a further four weeks fees in advance, your aunt will be removed, forcibly if necessary, and taken to the Government Hospital in town. I'm sure I need not remind you that the care she'll receive there will be far below the excellent standards which she has experienced hitherto. No doubt you've heard of the increased incidence of malaria in that hospital? The usual precautions, functioning mosquito nets, daily dose of quinine, are not so rigorously maintained over there. I would even go so far as to say that the epithet "hospital" to describe that shower over on the Kingsway stretches the language almost to breaking point. The annual subsidy from the government can only go so far. Enteric is also on the rise, I hear.'

'Enteric, what the hell is that?'

'Typhoid, Pugh. The drinking water is sometimes not of the best quality, and for someone of your aunt's age and infirmity, well, need I go on? The director of Sanitation Services is I'm sure doing his utmost to reduce the problem, but he can only work with what he is given. We are proud in our institution that the medical staff, nurses, doctors, one and all, are European. Regrettably that is something which you will not find in the Government Hospital. I hear that a scheme is being drawn up for an African Subordinate Medical Service to train the natives, but I can assure you that, whilst I am bursar in this care home, we will not be availing ourselves of their graduates.'

'You've put the squeeze on me well and good, Ballard. I hear what you're saying, fancy words and all. You'll get your blood money just like I promised, so you can tell those two scragends outside to stop delivering their letters. Neighbours are thinking I've got something going with them. Even railwaymen have standards!'

'You'll never amount to anything, you know that, don't you? You're a fiscal illiterate! Now good day to you, Pugh.'

'Good day to you, Ballard.'

XV

IT WAS QUIET in Murphy's mid-morning. Three of the girls sat at one of the corner tables chatting, combing each other's hair. All the bar stools were empty. About fifty empty, recently washed whisky glasses, half pint and pint glasses, even some champagne flutes, were waiting to be dried and put back neatly on the shelves under the bar, ready for next time. Joe stood behind the bar, clean cotton cloth in his hand, his biggest distinguishing feature a mole with a rounded scab at the intersection of his nose and forehead and between his eyebrows. The scab never healed and now and again would dribble. Joe believed people saw the scab before they saw him, which was of course true. Otherwise his face was bright, enquiring, intelligent, and he was shrewd enough to adopt his tone to the uttermost degree of sycophancy when required.

'Hello, Joe,' said Jabez.

'Morning, Mr Pugh. Bit early for you, isn't it? I only just finished cleaning up after last night.'

'Had a busy one?'

'Big wig politicians up from Livingstone and Lusaka looking for votes and contributions from some rich farmers and mine owners. Those politicians sure know how to enjoy themselves, especially when someone else is paying. Seen pictures of some of 'em in the papers, can't say I could put a name to 'em.'

'They were all settlers, right?'

'Course they were.'

Murphy's catered for all types – well, all white types. Not just politicians, but railwaymen of all descriptions; miners of copper, cobalt and diamonds; plumbers, carpenters and stonemasons; painters and decorators; journalists, gossip columnists and editors; bookkeepers and accountants; haberdashers, drapers and grocers; travelling salesmen and teachers; lawyers and doctors; vicars, preachers and ministers; farmers, ranchers and cattlemen (from smallholdings to bigholdings); boozed up and teetotal; sniggering, tittering, giggling, blubbering, snivelling, sobbing; longfaced, poker faced; in a bevy or all alone. Barman Joe was the only Bemba allowed in Murphy's – or more precisely, the only male Bemba allowed in the establishment.

'What would you like to drink, Mr Pugh?'

'Whisky, double.'

'Any water, ice, soda?'

'Just as it is.'

'Bad morning, huh?'

'You try to do what's right, help others. It ain't easy.'

'Doing right always the most difficult thing. You got to take the lead, but it's the lead horse gets whipped the most, Mr Pugh.'

'How much do you get paid here, Joe? Tips must be good. One of the girls give you a free when all the johns have gone home, must be worth something, right?'

'Boss man keeps an eye on all of us. House gets to keep all the tips, save when he ain't looking, that is. And all the girls only do tricks with the johns, no frees in this house.'

'You've been here a long time now, haven't you? Must be five, six years? Ever since I've been here you've been behind that bar.'

'Seven years this year. I've seen it all, believe me.'

'And still just a lowly barman.'

'Barman, bouncer, medic, marriage counsellor, wages clerk, security guard...'

'Boss man lets you deal with the wages but doesn't allow you to keep the tips? Even have a free?'

'Boss man say I've got it easy here. Out there up in the Copperbelt or on the Railways, says I could get blackwater or die in an accident. Says I've got it cushy here.'

'I'm surprised he allows you do the wages, Joe, I really am.'

'Been doing them for over two years. Every last Friday morning in the month. Boss man asks me into his office, he opens the safe, and we both add up the month's takings. Put 'em all in tidy packets wrapped up like birthday presents, fivers, one pound notes, ten bob notes, loose change in a bag.'

'Sounds like a lot of responsibility to me.'

'It sure is. We talking thousands of pounds here, month after month after month.'

'He trusts you with all that money? He must have great faith in you, that's for sure.'

'Great faith, Mr Pugh, but regrettably not great reward.'

'How does he know you ain't on the fiddle?'

'Boss man knows everything. We both count the takings, not once, not twice, three times or more until we both agree the same total, down to the last farthing. He writes down that total on a piece of paper and we both sign that piece of paper. Boss man calls it the document of record. Then we do the wages. He tells me how much I'm to pay each of the girls. The new ones, country girls, they stupid, know no different, get a couple of shillings. Figure goes up for the more experienced ladies. They the top of the tree. Ain't there for long though, this a savage business. That's when the bitchin starts.'

'Some of the girls give you trouble, do they?'

'There's a tipping point. Those girls who were top, once they see too much action, all them tricks leaves a mark. They get sloppy, get too sassy, think they queens of the whorehouse. That's where boss man's good. He knows when they're on the slide. He sees the little things, them signs that their time here is coming to an end, and that's when their wages start going down. And that's when the fighting and crying start. Course, only one winner. Before they know it, they back on the street, risky place to be for a woman. Then the cycle starts again. Young girls come in, get popular, all the johns want to be with them, swarm around 'em like ants, but the more johns they have the more overcooked they get. They become less popular, fewer Johns want to be with them, that ain't good for bossman, means he reduces their wages. Then the ructions begin again. Like I say, a girl could once have been the highest paid filly in the whole whorehouse gets a pay cut, sooner or later sees the door. All the girls know it. They know it's a business better than anyone.'

'Fact you know how things work don't make it any easier to accept. You know how this place works better than anybody, Joe. Know how it operates. You've got the inside knowledge. You could be bossman, run your own place, ever thought of that?'

'Settler folk ain't going to go to a whorehouse run by a Bemba. Them people have their queer outsider standards. They don't mind taking turns with a Bemba woman, but they ain't gonna pay a Bemba bossman for the privilege.'

'I'm not talking about settlers. We're all human, ain't we? Same needs apply to native men as to settler men.'

'Run a Bemba whorehouse for Bemba men, is that what you're saying?'

'Yeah, why not? You've learnt all the knowledge here, you've done your apprenticeship. Time you became your own master. You know enough of the top men in the local villages, I'm sure. They could supply the raw material, that shouldn't be a problem.'

'Do that already, means I get first tastings! Boss man don't know that.'

'Yet another task you carry out for the boss man. So what's the problem with my suggestion? I can see it now... Big sign outside, Joe's Palace or Club Joe... You could be calling the shots, why not? Boss man's getting lazy.'

'The problem is, Mr Pugh, the money. Boss man calls it capital investment. Murphy's is well established, almost runs on its own. Long as boss man freshens up the offering on a regular basis, those settlers'll keep on coming through that door. Ain't no competition either, nearest one is over in Ndola.'

'Yeah, Gordon's Bar. Been there a few times, ain't a scratch on this place. They keep the girls on for too long, they become too rough even for my industrial leanings. They don't smell too good neither, all sweat and beer.'

'Boss man calls Gordon's the offal emporium. He ain't afraid of no competition from that particular quarter.'

'Then come on, Joe. Make a name for yourself. Join the masters, don't stay as a servant.'

'But it's the money, the capital investment. Where's that gonna come from?'

'Let me think. Maybe there's a way we can both find answers to our difficulties.'

'How's that?'

'What happens after you and boss man agree and sign the document of record?'

'Then we do the wages. Boss man knows how much each girl gets. Ain't written down anywhere, he tells me the amount. It's the way I told you, varies depending on the usefulness of the girl to the business, where she is on the graph. Gives me the wages and tells me to pay each of 'em.'

'Doesn't he do that himself?'

'He used to, but since he's got to calling himself an entrepreneur, says its beneath him. Doesn't want to get his hands dirty, as he calls it.'

'So he trusts you to do the right thing, give the girls the correct amount of money?'

'Hey, Mr Pugh, a few pennies here or there don't go amiss, he knows that. The girls know not to mess with me neither, else I'll cut their wages. All helps to run a smooth business, boss man knows that as well. Those girls wouldn't dare step out of line with me or the boss man, their tantrums only passing.'

'Unless they're on the skids?'

'Yeah, that's different. They all know when their time's coming to an end, but the ones who ain't on the way down yet don't usually cause problems.'

'What about the balance? Wages can't account for that much, the takings must far exceed the wages.'

'Of course they do. For about six months now, boss man allows me to take the money to the bank in town.'

'Which bank is that?'

'Barclays. He makes sure I bring back the bank deposit slip. That slip's got to be stamped Barclays, and it's got to tally with the figure we both agreed before I leave his office. And it always tallies, so he know I ain't cheating on him. And that's it, that's how Murphy's works.'

'Another whisky, Joe. Double again, straight up.'

'Sure thing, Mr Pugh.'

'You know you've got your future in your hands, don't you? The money you need for your own future, for your own bar, you're carrying it every month to the bank. We've got to bust some rules here.'

'There's some stupid settlers come into Murphy's, Mr Pugh, didn't think you were one of them. Thought you were a bright man. You think boss man'll allow me to just walk off into the bush with all his money, just like some wild dog walking away with a dead monkey?'

'No, no, I know that. You've got to make it look bad, make it look like you've been robbed. You've got to get roughed up a bit. He'll need to see blood, plenty of it, and bruises, black eye, broken nose, that type of thing.'

'Who'll do the roughing up? Don't want someone to get overexcited. Some men get carried away when their blood's up, can't stop kickin' and punchin', you know what I mean.'

'I'll be that man. A few clouts round the head should do it. Your bonce'll be thumping for a few days, but it'll all be worth it. In a week or so you'll be just dandy and a very rich man. Make sure you go back to work when you're better, but tell boss man you don't want to do the bank run anymore, tell him you're too frightened. Tell him you don't want to do the wages either, because the girls vexing you so much. In fact, tell him you don't want anything to do with handling money. He'll see you for a plucked rooster, and them things ain't no use in a whorehouse. He'll either sack you or you can leave quietly in a few weeks. Once it's done you can open that bar. you'll be the boss. Don't open up in Broken Hill, mind, go somewhere else, somewhere that don't compete with here, somewhere far away.'

'And you, Mr Pugh, what do you get?'

'Fifty-fifty, we split the takings fifty-fifty.'

'Ain't my risk bigger than yours? This is my job here, this is my bread and butter. I'm the one who's going to get hurt, and pretty bad by the way you're talking. I'm the one boss man will suspect of faking all this. And you still get half the money, you got no risk at all.'

'Joe, if we get found out we'll both be in trouble, only difference being I'll be defending myself in the High Court of Rhodesia and you'll be in front of the Native Commissioners Court. But whichever court we're in will make no difference, we'll both be in Broken Hill Central Prison for a very long time. Come on, what do you say, you in or not? I've given you a choice, a prospect outside the dreams of all Bemba. You want to stay as boss man's lackey, a settler servant for ever, or do you want freedom? Picture it, the proud proprietor of Joe's Palace, the first Bemba owned whorehouse in Northern Rhodesia. Play your cards right you could become a man of standing, politician or such like. Things are changing fast in this country, Joe, and you should be part of it, get in on the ground floor.'

'Let me think some more on your proposition, ain't no need to hurry when it comes to big decisions. You settlers don't like change anyhow. You stamp on things as soon as you can. You see a pretty animal, first thing you want to do is to shoot it, cut its head off, stuff it and mount it on your wall.'

Joe rubbed the mole between his eyebrows as if to polish a magic lantern, waiting for a genie to arrive. The scab was oozing again. The cotton cloth would come in handy.

'If you don't take the leap, Joe, then sure as hell someone else will. If you don't do something, nothing happens.'

Jabez walked out into the street. The day had not yet become drowsy. A bluish-purple turaco perched on a nearby tree. The hour was majestically clear, save for a puff of cloud on the hills. The whisky aglow in his belly.

Joe went back to drying the glasses, mulling over Jabez's proposal. He was tempted, he surely was, but wasn't Jabez just another john? He'd seen plenty of those halfwits over the years. What if things went wrong? It would be too late to turn back the clock then; not even all the takings of all the whorehouses in all the world would be enough to even buy one second back.

I was no real friend of Joe, but if I'd known any of these plans, I would have told him to keep well away from that scar-faced ruffian. No good would come of it. Jabez would crap on Joe like he did with all people. But who was I to pontificate? Shouldn't everyone have a chance to better themselves? As long as no one got hurt. And as for bossman, well, he deserved a comeuppance.

XVI

DELYTH AND I walked out of the surgery together. Pushed by a gust of curiosity, I asked the inevitable question.

'Do you mind if I ask you what Doctor Cosgrove told you, Mrs Bowen? Just a few injections, isn't it? They'll sort you out, won't they?'

'It was bilharzia all right, but Daisy... I'm pregnant,' replied Delyth tearfully.

I feigned surprise. 'That's great news, Gwyn will be thrilled!' Truth at times like these was, for me, inconsequential.

'You don't understand, I'm pregnant but I've got this horrible infection, this bilharzia. I've got to be injected every few months with some poison that kills my disease, but how will it affect my baby?'

'What did Doctor Cosgrove say.'

'He doesn't know. I don't think he's got a clue. He's probably only dealt with coughs, sore throats and broken bones. How I wish I wasn't expecting!'

'That's enough now, that's enough.'

'What am I going to tell Gwyn? Should I tell him I've got bilharzia? Should I even have the baby? All my plans have turned upside down.'

'What plans, what do you mean?'

Delyth tried to compose herself. 'Just plans. Plans I had for Gwyn and me, Gwyn and me and the baby.'

'Bilharzia and Daisy got in the way, did we?'

That was cruel of me. I might not have liked our three-way household –who on earth would have – and I didn't care what other people thought, but this poor girl was in trouble. Those doctors called the bad effects of their cures 'side effects', but that was just fancy words; if the baby might suffer, to me that was an 'effect', pure and simple.

'I don't mean that, Daisy,' Delyth said tearfully. 'I don't mean that at all. I know that Gwyn has plonked me on you, but have some pity for me, please. You could just have easily been the one pregnant and contracting this awful illness. I don't blame you, Daisy, I really don't.'

She was half right. I could well have been bitten by one of those infected snails, but being pregnant... That was something I could never, ever be, and oh, how I regretted that.

'You're overwhelmed by this place, aren't you?' I said gently.

Delyth started to tremble. 'Yes, I am, Daisy, yes, I am. Everything here's a fantasy, unreal. All that's important now is the baby.'

'And Gwyn? What about Gwyn?'

'Of course Gwyn, you and Gwyn.'

'Come on, let's go home. We'll avoid the cattle pens and those bogie wagons this time.'

I held her hand and led the way. She needed calming; public emotion and Broken Hill were two unacceptable bedfellows. I led the way and talked. I talked about anything that crossed my mind – anything to keep Delyth from disappearing into her own thoughts again.

'Before I became Gwyn's housekeeper, my mother sent me to domestic science classes. Said she thought it might be useful to help me get a job in service. She knew how much Europeans loved their stomachs. I learnt all about your food. Boiled cabbage, roast potatoes, treacle pudding...'

'You're funny, Daisy. Thank you for being here.'

'We can do some cooking when we get home. Bake a cake or something.'

'You're not just the housekeeper, are you? I've seen the way you look at one another.'

'Gwyn is very very fond of curries, a real Indian curry. Coriander, turmeric, garlic, cumin, fenugreek, chilli, we've got all the ingredients. Before Adip Patel expanded his shop in town, Gwyn had to have most of the spices delivered from Livingstone. There was an Indian business there, import-export. The delivery was usually once every two months or so. One day a delivery arrived, Gwyn was away with work and I went to the door to collect the goods. The delivery driver was Indian, apologising, he said they'd run out of turmeric in the store. He said they expected to have it in stock within the next few weeks, and he told me to apologise to my "Madam" and explain that he'd bring a double portion with his next round. Out of devilment I told him I was the "Madam" of the house. The poor man looked horrified, dumped all the spices in my arms, turned round, scuttled back to his truck, didn't even ask for payment. And he was an Indian. Can you imagine what would have happened if the driver had been European?'

I wondered what Delyth really knew about Gwyn. He'd been a bachelor by choice, he had feelings which weren't exactly... How shall I say this, weren't exactly commonplace in Broken Hill.

'They tell me the district commissioner himself is permanently vexed by people from one ethnicity fraternising with people from others.'

'I wouldn't know anything about that, Mrs Bowen. I haven't had the pleasure of having been introduced to the district commissioner. Do you know who the Kalwena are?'

'Not acquainted with them, no. Is this another African tradition I've never heard of?'

'They're from Portugese West Africa. They're the excrement removers of Broken Hill. They work exclusively in the early hours of the morning when everyone else is asleep. The Kalwena carry out one of the most unpleasant jobs in this pretty little town of ours. The Bemba don't do the work, wouldn't dirty their hands. It's the work of the Kalwena. There's a hierarchy here, Mrs Bowen. We all know where we stand, we all know our place. Save for Gwyn. He says Darwin should be the patron saint of the savannah, and he didn't mean just for the wild animals.'

'Do you know where you stand, Daisy, do you know your place? Do I know mine?'

It was a muggy early evening. An unwholesome slate-stained storm screened the sky. Vultures surfed on the updraught. The gentle breeze turned stronger, transporting the fragrance of bougainvillea through the air. The breeze freshened, lifting dust particles skyward into the narrowed eyes of pavement walkers cursing the dirt. The wind hardened, thrashing the jacarandas ferociously.

'Quick,' I said, 'we need to hurry. We don't want to be caught out in this. Those Faraday poles will soon get a battering.'

As we got indoors, single droplets of water turned into a cloudburst, shifting up into a storm of heavy hailstones that pummelled the windows.

'Look, Daisy, look, it's raining fish! Fish are falling from the sky. And frogs, there's frogs there as well. Where's Moses, where's Pharaoh, we're in Ancient Egypt, for God's sakes! What else can happen in this place!'

'Shh now, calm down, come away from the window. Let's go to the kitchen. We can hide there, away from all this hullaballoo. Come on.'

As I piloted Delyth through the corridors to the kitchen, I realized she existed on a tipping point, balancing unsteadily between level-headedness and, well, tumbling, tumbling, tumbling...

'What about making some Welsh cakes? I'd never heard of them in Domestic Science class. It was Gwyn told me about them.'

The new bright-yellow flowered linoleum kitchen floor wasn't that much different to the old one, save that the flowers this time were roses and not carnations. I was thankful that the kitchen was windowless, as it moderated the sound of the hailstones and heavy rain outside.

'Right,' I said, 'let me see. We'll need eight ounces of self-raising flour, pinch of salt, four ounces of butter, four ounces of caster sugar, two ounces of currants, half teaspoonful of mixed spice, one egg and some milk. That should do it. You want to do the mixing?'

'No, not really.'

'Oh come on, we've braved the cattle pens, we've braved the storm, we've even braved frogs and fish falling from the sky. We deserve a treat. Once we've baked the Welsh cakes, we'll eat them whilst they're still warm. They're fantastic, they really are, but you know that anyway.'

My positivity was the fruit of long practice with Gwyn, but Delyth was unmoved.

'I'll do the mixing then, and you can crack the egg and add the milk. You've got to do something for your tea, I'm not your skivvy, you know.' I said this lightly, smiling, trying to coax some life into this dying butterfly.

I put all the ingredients into the mixing bowl, melding them together with my hands.

'Right, it's your turn. Get one of those eggs from over there and crack it into the bowl, then add some milk. We'll soon have ourselves a nice little treat. We can have some tea with the Welsh cakes as well. Come on, come on now.'

Reluctantly, randomly, Delyth picked an egg from the half dozen or so nestling in the cardboard container near the cooker.

'Knife,' she said. 'I need a knife to crack the egg. I was never any good at cracking them open on the side of the bowl.'

'Under there.' I pointed with my head to the cutlery drawer. This was my kitchen after all, my hands still inside the mixing bowl, covered in the sweet, buttered flour.

'Ok, watch out then.' Holding an egg in her left hand, Delyth gave the shell a sharp rap from a heavy serrated knife in her right. Part of the shell fell into the bowl, followed by a large-eyed chicken embryo, neck totally severed from the body.

Delyth instinctively half dropped, half threw the knife and the remaining portion of the shell into the mixing bowl, the knife barely missing my hands, now covered both in buttered flour and the fetid viscera of the dead embryo. She screamed.

'I can't take it anymore! I just can't take it anymore! I wish I'd never come here, I wish my parents had never come to Africa!'

Her body heaving up and down uncontrollably, tear-tightening eyes.

'I wish I wasn't me!'

Tenderly but firmly I enveloped Delyth in my arms.

'Quiet, quiet now, everything's all right, everything will be fine....'

'Why did I pick up the egg, why that egg, I picked the wrong egg, I picked it. It's all my fault!'

'There's nothing to worry about, Delyth, these things happen.'

I swelled around her, holding her even closer in an effort to calm her hysterical convulsions, to draw her into a Bemba calmness. Sugary flour and the entrails of the dead foetus tainted our two pretty summer dresses.

The dark storm clouds shadowed the house. I wiped my hands on a kitchen cloth and lit a candle, held it in one hand and put my other hand in Delyth's.

'Come on, Mrs Bowen, follow me.'

Delyth followed the candle. I'm not sure she knew I was there. Through the kitchen and the lounge to the back of the house, I opened the door to the second bedroom. Gwyn had insisted that I should sleep closer to the main bedroom; lodging in the kia in the garden was too far away if ever there were any complications, whatever the nature of those complications might be.

'Sleep with me tonight,' I said.

'But—'

'Please.' I blew out the flame, my bedroom now in a half light. 'Shall I help you.'

'No, no, I'm all right. I'll rest on top of the bed just for a few minutes, before I go to mine.'

I cleaned Delyth's hands as best I could. Her face was moist. I left her tears alone.

She spoke then, flatly. As if her mind was elsewhere, her words slipped out rote-like.

'My father was a weaver back in the old country, Daisy,' she said. 'He was always neat and tidy. He had one of those little beards. You know, a small beard that covers the chin only.'

'A goatee, you mean.'

'That's it, trimming it every day with his little scissors. Mam was his second wife, his first died of TB. They had two sons, my stepbrothers. Mam was much younger than Dad. In fact, my stepbrothers were older than my mother. I've still got a lock of Dad's hair somewhere, we were very close. Dad's business failed, he lost everything. The five of us had to live in lodgings. My two stepbrothers shared one bedroom. I slept in the same bedroom as Mam and Dad. I had my own little bed, but sometimes Dad would invite me to join him and Mam in bed. It felt safe there. We had one kitchen-cum-dining room. That was us.

'Dad said we should try for a new start, a simple life. That's why we came out here. He borrowed heavily from family, sold what little he had just to get here. His sons wouldn't hear about moving. They stayed behind. Dad never saw them again. Mam and Dad didn't really settle down here. Mam soon became unwell. She said that she could see things – you know, hallucinations. She told me she tried so hard to dream pretty dreams, beautiful dreams, but they just wouldn't come. Only things she could dream about were frightening dreams, ugly dreams. She could only see bad.'

'What kind of things did she see, Delyth?' I asked her.

'She said she could snakes moving on her bed, and then a large buzzard would fly into the bedroom, clasp the snakes in its talons and fly away with them through the walls. She'd be walking down the street and say that Dad's old weaving machinery was blocking the road. When she hallucinated, she would sometimes mutter a few words in English, a language which she hardly knew. Dad even took her to a hypnotist in Johannesburg, anything to try to help her. I found out later that the hypnotist had given Mam morphine to calm her down. She took small doses regularly after that.'

'We can't control our own dreams, Delyth. They're who we truly are. Who knows what's seen or heard alone in darkness.'

'But Mam was ok before we came here, even when we were living in the lodgings she was fine. We weren't here long before they both contracted malaria. I remember their fevers, their tiredness, their vomiting. It was horrible. Dad went on frequent trips to Johannesburg, said he was going to buy top quality quinine. In fact he was going there to buy more morphine for Mam.'

'Did they ever think of going back?'

'They couldn't, the humiliation would have killed Dad. Although malaria got him anyway. Then Mam passed too. We were crossing the street, just by the Great Northern Hotel of all places. Mam told me to meet her there in the lobby after school one day. She was friendly with the receptionist or something. She was holding my hand. She was going to buy me some ice cream. I remember she was flustered. Whether she was hallucinating or whether it was the morphine, I don't know. She walked off the pavement onto the road without looking. I tried to pull her back. I shouted, I shouted as loudly as I could. "Look out, Mam, look out!" I tried to pull her back, but she let go of my hand. She let me go. She was hit by one of those big mining lorries and died instantly. I just stood there, on the pavement, shaking, crying. I should have held her harder, I should have shouted louder. I was nothing.'

I turned Delyth on her side and faced her. I held her hand, kissed her on the cheek, quietly, softly like a falling snowflake.

'That's enough now,' I said. 'Enough for today.'

Delyth moved her body closer, placed her arm around my waist. Our legs touched; our faces were within inches of one another. The meeting of two breaths. We drifted quietly to sleep and wandered into our own separate dreams.

XVII

THE RAILWAY DAM, built of concrete between sandstone outcrops, had a capacity of approximately six million gallons. A pipeline took the water down into the station at Kapiri Mposhi.

Hand on his hips, looking down at clouding water, Gwyn shook his head. 'It's like Thomas said, dam's silting up pretty bad. This place will be just sand and gravel before we know it. The outlet system's going to be clogged well before we put our tools on the bar for the last time. Still, water looks inviting, Daniel.'

'That it does. Fancy a dip to cool down?'

'That'd be crazy, wouldn't it?'

'Only some brainless halfwit would do that, don't know what's sneaking in them depths.'

'Halfwit or a settler, eh, Daniel?'

'Or a settler, Gwyn.'

Getting out of the Land Rover they both checked the dam wall for any signs of cracking and erosion. The water smooth as whisky in a glass.

'Don't think we need spend much more time here, these dams were built to last. Come on we've chewed the cud enough for one day. Let's go back to site.'

*

'You plan to stay on the Railways rest of your life,' Gwyn asked, as they drove back to camp. 'Man like you could do much better for himself. Ever think of going into the army?'

'My father joined your British Army. Fought your so called Great War. They told him he'd be fighting for king and country against the wicked Hun. Can't say he'd ever seen one of those before. Off he went with his backpack and his rifle to fight the nasty Germans in Tanganiyka. He never came back, was killed over there. I never even met him, I was born when he was away. But at least he died for your country all right, expect he was proud of that? You people think that dying for your country is painless, is painless slaughter. It means only tears for us.'

'And that wasn't the end of it. British troops came to our village, took all our cattle and grain, said they were impounded for the war effort, on orders from your king. So I lost my father, and my family lost everything else. Big wigs get to do the winning, soldiers get to do the losing. So, no, to answer your question, I won't be joining the occupation army. I don't want to be fighting someone else's war. Ask Ephraim what he thinks of the army, he was away helping your lot on the last one just gone. Once copper was discovered, you know what happened?'

'I suppose I do.'

'It bears repeating. Your government set aside so much land for the settlers that us Bemba were left short, not enough land to farm and live on, to pay settler taxes, so now we've become your paid labourers. No dignity in that is there?'

'What about going up to the copper mines to work?'

'Those riots a few years back, how many were killed, seventeen was it? Hear talk of a trade union for Africans, that's what we need on the Railways.'

'The powers that be ain't going to like that, Daniel, you know that.'

'What do you suggest? We just good enough to fight your wars? You can have our cattle, our grain, hell, you've had our women for years, and we always just gonna be labourers, one step up from the dirt?'

'Why don't you become a teacher? Missionaries and the government are providing more education now. You're bright enough, and it's much safer than the Railways. Join one of those new welfare associations, campaign for your people, get justice for them.'

'That's what I've got in mind, Gwyn. That'll be my future. Once I'm finished here, I'll be away. Next time you see me, you better doff that hat and you better be calling me sir.'

After the boomslang bravado, Jabez and the men had got right back to work. The foundations for part of the track about a mile from the station had been washed away by flash flooding, and new ballast of crushed stone had to be laid as replacement. Most of the men were experienced, knew their jobs, Kabwe having taken over as site foreman in the temporary absence of Daniel.

'Well, did you fix it, Chinaman?' asked Jabez.

'Yes, boss,' replied Jimmy, squinting up at him. 'The universal joint needed seeing to. The steering wheel right as rain now. I'm sure you'll be well pleased with it, sir,' His hands and forearms were covered in black grease and oil. There must have been something similar in his lungs.

The small lorry carried the crushed stone chippings stockpiled outside the station up to the repair site. Jabez the driver, Ephraim and George sitting in the trailer with the crushed stone. The hydraulic mechanism to lift the trailer and disgorge its contents had broken some time ago, which meant that Ephraim and George were tasked with loading and unloading the stone. Ephraim wasn't one to take the lead, George even less so, neither one a leader, but neither a hapless follower either.

Jabez had not calmed down since his bust up with Gwyn over the tree snake. All the men were conscious of his foul mood, and all the men were wary. They did not wish to agitate Jabez even further and tried to hide themselves in back-breaking labour, the harder they worked the more invisible they would become.

'Wish Mr Bowen and Daniel hadn't gone to the dam today, George,' said Ephraim. 'They the only ones can control Jabez. We don't want to cross him, now more than ever.'

'Come on, you two, enough of your mumblings,' barked Jabez.

'That's enough ballast. Jump on the back, we'll squeeze another load before tucker.'

The truck was a Bedford QL which had been used in the war, with the driver's cab directly above the engine and four-wheel drive. The men called it Queen Lizzie, but the dear old Queen had seen better days. The passenger door was long gone, together with both side rearview mirrors. But Jabez knew Queen Lizzie well, from the gearbox to the brakes. He knew how to handle her.

The trailer was loaded to capacity, Jabez depending on Ephraim and George to direct his reversing. The crushed stone was usually limestone, light blue chippings. The chippings were so small that they provided a comfortable place to lie down, to take a breather or have a quiet nap.

Few people had ever seen George smile; maybe his mother, or maybe he'd been breaking wind. The other navvies took bets on who could make him crack; they made jokes, pulled silly faces, took their trousers down. No one ever won the bet. His nickname was Smiler.

Unlike the other men, George was clean; he believed in God, he believed in cleanliness. Every night, literally every night, he'd wash his clothes, put them out to dry before going to bed, and they'd be good as new the following morning. The rainy season posed a problem, but George got by. And on occasions that the work took him to a river where the water was very hard, it might be difficult to get any lather for his soap, but a little added baking soda helped.

George wanted to get married one day. That's why he kept himself clean; no woman would look at a dirty man. George was even fastidious in the crapper; he'd hold his trousers up around his ankles when seated - no need to get clothes dirty if it could be avoided. He was also particularly pernickety about the smell caused by his bodily movements; what would a potential wife say about a smelly potential husband? He would therefore make sure that he would never be caught short whilst courting; things would surely end badly if that happened.

Both Ephraim and George sat as best they could on the crushed stone when the QL was fully loaded. Their work clothes talcum-powdered from the chippings, some particles too small to see, they coughed now and again, bringing up the lathered dust, spitting it out through their mouths or ejecting it from their noses as the need arose. They were always thirsty; water was a godsend, there was never enough of it. The beauty of the veldt not for them. The fragrance of the savannah was the exhaust fumes from the Bedford.

Jabez on the third full load of the morning, speeding towards the repair site, still agitated, jamming the accelerator dead to the floor, daydreaming, picturing himself at Murphy's, by the bar with one of the girls, maybe Meg, maybe Holly, maybe both. Double whiskys, all round, strong and stinging, with a fat cigar smooth and sweet for himself. Money in his pocket, women, alcohol and tobacco, and a tuneful song. Perfect.

He thought he heard a tiny thud. Possibly he'd driven over a small pothole nothing more. Then Ephraim started screaming.

'Stop, stop! Stop Lizzie, Mr Pugh! Stop the lorry!'

Jabez didn't react immediately, surprised at the assertiveness of the command; after all, Gwyn wasn't there, so he was boss. Taking his foot off the accelerator, easing the footbrake gently to the floor to avoid destabilizing the load, downshifting gears, he brought Queen Lizzie to a complete stop within forty yards, the lorry masked by rising savannah dust.

'What's the bloody problem, Eph? It better be good, I don't want to lose time this morning.'

'It's Kumar, you've hit Kumar!'

'What, I didn't see anything! Where is he?'

Ephraim and George had by now leapt off the trailer and were looking back down the dirt road, eyes squinting to avoid the dust.

'Back there, Mr Pugh!' Pointing sixty or seventy yards to the rear.

Ephraim and George sprinted down the road, Jabez following at a brisk walk.

Kumar was lying face up just to the side of the road, next to two empty jerry cans, as if in a deep stupor, his apricot-coloured work trousers blending with the dry orangey clay of his resting place. George knelt by the body, a bead of sweat running down Kumar's cheek the only movement he could discern. Both Kumar's eyes were open. George gently moved his hand down over Kumar's eyebrows towards his nose, closing the eyes as he did so.

'There's not a mark on him, Ephraim,' remarked George.

'Let me see, out of the way, give me some room for Christ's sake!' Jabez moved his hands roughly over the corpse, looking for signs of injury, but he could find none.

'I must've hit his head, poor sod, I didn't see anything. He must have slipped hit his head against the QL. Can't be helped, it's done now. George, run to the boys, tell 'em what's happened, and tell Chowdhury and Desai to come here. They're curry eaters, his people. Can't have him lying here all day. There'll be all sorts of pests around the body soon, what with the heat and all.'

Within minutes George, Chowdhury and Desai were running over, accompanied by Jimmy.

'I said just the two Indians, don't want a Chinaman as well.'

'Only want to help boss,' said Jimmy, who showed an interest in anything that might be turned to his advantage.

George, Chowdhury, Desai and Jimmy lifted the body on to the top of the ballast in the QL.

'Rest of you go back to work. As you're here, Chinaman, make sure the body don't fall off. We'll drop it at the station, return for the Indians when we dump the load. Expect they'll be wanting to do some strange religious things with the body.'

'What about the jerry cans, boss?' asked George.

'Leave the bloody jerry cans. You boys got to work for your water.'

Alone with Kumar atop the QL, Jimmy rifled through the dead man's pockets, such as they were. He found Kumar's farthing, looked at it, and kept it.

After their shift had finished, Chowdhury and Desai carried Kumar's body and placed it behind the railway station, out of sight of everyone. News of the tragedy had already reached the tin shed. Death travelled quickly on the Railways.

Thomas stood and watched for a few minutes from his rear window as Chowdhury and Desai carefully stripped Kumar of his grimy railway clothes, which were placed to one side. They emptied his pockets. Nothing was in them save for a dirty red cotton handkerchief and savannah dust. Using the same two jerry cans as had been carried by their friend, now filled with water, they washed Kumar, cleaning him of all the stains and all the foulness of Africa, of the QL, of Jabez. Desai started to cry. Chowdhury was composed. They both worked slowly.

A dead friend naked before them, his suffering over, Chowdhury and Desai remembered the better days, the good days, the days of happiness. But all their many thoughts ended with Jabez. Jabez the killer. The three had also experienced demanding times together, and one of them was now demandingly dead.

They both turned away from the body as they saw Thomas approaching. Thomas' duty was before him: to comfort as best he could.

'Please, let me help you,' he asked, coughing.

He coughed regularly; he didn't have a cold or influenza, it's just that he coughed. Gwyn had suggested he visit Dr Cosgrove in Broken Hill, who had diagnosed something called globus hystericus, incurable, but nothing to worry about. The usual diagnosis.

'I know he has to be wrapped for cremation. Will this Rhodesia Railways cotton bedding do?'

Thomas looked at dead Kumar, a static, lifeless navvy, spread out on the veldt, straightened, tidy, ready for cremation. Thomas had never spoken to Kumar, had never heard him speak; he wasn't a friend, he did not know him. But there Thomas was, standing above the dead man, holding his Rhodesia Railways cotton bedding, his innards moving like waves on a beach.

'What are you doing here, Thomas?' asked Desai.

'Pass the stuff to me,' said Chowdhury, taking out his knife, cutting and tearing the bedding. 'Lift his shoulders, Desai, and we'll start. You can help too, Thomas, if you want.'

Kumar seemed to Thomas as if he had a smile on his face, untroubled.

The process moved forward calmly, Chowdhury wrapping the cotton around the body, Desai reacting rhythmically without guidance or direction, moving the body as required. Thomas looked on, helping as best he could. Once the body was enveloped, Chowdhury tied both Kumar's big toes together with string and placed a red ochre tilak mark on the deceased's forehead.

'Sorry for the sobbing, Chowdhury,' said Desai. 'I just can't stop.'

'I'm not going to tell you not to shed tears, there's no cruelty in crying,' replied Chowdhury.

Chowdhury was a smallish man, his ears had no lobes, prone to sweating, and was, because of the heat which veiled the navvies daily like a shroud, prone to smelling. Although he greased his jet-black hair profusely, not a sliver touched his thick goatee, a graveyard for mosquitoes and miscellaneous other small peregrinating, flying or perambulating insects. He was not a pernickety eater, which probably explained the preponderance of living creatures on his chin. His bright brown eyes had narrowed and darkened, a legacy of his sorrow for Kumar. Chowdhury walked bowlegged; the men nicknamed him Cowboy.

'My condolences to you both,' Thomas said. 'What a sad affair this is. What do your gods say about death, Chowdhury?'

'We call this Antyesti, the last sacrifice, our funeral rites. Why have you come out here, ticket clerk? Bemba have never taken an interest in us before.'

'We should show more of an interest. We share the same land. Even in troubled times, you will find brothers.'

'Well, if you must, life and death to us is part of something called Samsara. You would call it rebirth. God is in us all, and the purpose of life is to become aware of God.'

'That means God is in Jabez? Or is this for Hindu people only?'

'Why do you mock us now, Bemba?' Desai said. 'These are our beliefs, accept them or ignore them as you please.'

'I'm not mocking, Desai. I only want to help and to learn. I want to see how we can understand one another. Come on, let me help you. Bring Kumar inside, into the office. He'll be safe there until the ceremony this evening.'

Chowdhury had asked David and Chibwe to prepare the funeral pyre whilst he and Desai were attending to the corpse. After obtaining consent from Daniel, and to Chowdhury's specification, David and Chibwe constructed a pyre of dry acacia wood and brush, side by side with cast off softwood sleepers from broken railtrack.

Thomas watched the three Chinamen, Jimmy, Lee and Joe, together with Desai, carry Kumar on an old Rhodesia Railways stretcher and place him carefully on the pyre. It was a marker for Thomas, a proof. They could all be comrades for what was to come. Every one of the navvies was present. Gwyn had insisted on this. As Kumar's eyes had closed, Thomas' were opening to what they might achieve if they all stood together.

Chowdhury walked around the pyre.

'Kumar came here, like all Gujurati, to look for a better life. He was a happy man, he loved his family, he was a good worker, a good Hindu. He never forgot his parents in India, sending back what money he could to help them in their old age. I am proud to call him my brother. Young men vanish, and the old loiter, dry out and wither. I will not forget him, his name will not be lost. A price always has to be paid.'

Chowdhury placed rice in Kumar's mouth, sprinkled the body with clarified butter and drew three lines in the earth near the pyre.

Thomas was curious. Jabez was bored. George didn't want to get any smoke-filled fumes on his clothes. He'd already completed his day's end ablutions; his god was not Kumar's god. Kabwe thought what advantage he might make of the chaos. Mubanga stared sternly and soberly at the fire, as shrouded Kumar disappeared into the dusk to meet the stars. Chibwe didn't give a toss either way.

'What's he doing, Desai?' Thomas asked as reverentially as possible.

'One line is Yama, god of the dead, another line is Kala, the god of cremation, and the third line is Kumar himself.'

Chowdhury lit the pyre, and this time accompanied by Desai, they both walked round the pyre twice again.

'I can't believe it! Kumar's dead! That's an impossible bet, Jimmy,' said Lee.

'The god Shou had foretold how many years he had on this earth. Nothing to do with me. Thank my good fortune to Shou,' answered Jimmy.

'And thank my bad fortune to Shou,' said the downhearted John.

'How's it gonna feel, John?' said Lee. 'You working in this heat all day, the sweating, the back breaking, and for what? For absolutely nothing. You're working for nothing. No, hang on, that ain't true, you'll be working for Jimmy here. Just like those slaves that Xang Cheng freed way back in the Tang dynasty, save we ain't in the Tang dynasty now and there ain't no Xang Cheng. Stupid maggot, more fool you for taking the bet. Thought you could outfox Jimmy, didn't you? No one outfoxes Jimmy, he always wins. And what you going to tell your family? They relying on your wages to eat, pay the rent, what they going to do now? Jimmy wasn't the man you thought he was, was he?'

'Jimmy?'

'I'm sorry, John, I truly am sorry. How on earth could I have known that poor little Kumar would be first to die. Old man Mubanga was the banker, not some random Indian.'

'But Jimmy, my family'll starve without my wages.'

'Forgive me, John, but we all have to live by our rules, the rules we like and the rules we don't like, else we'd be no better than wild animals and savages. How could we ever trust one another again? We shake hands, we give our word. We are brothers in spirit after all.'

'Brothers in spirit, my ass, Jimmy!' said Lee. 'You don't feel pity, do you, you only feel money.'

'A wager is a wager, Lee.'

'So you won't change your mind then, Jimmy?' begged John.

'I can't, you must see that. Those are the rules, those are the rules of Chinamen.'

'Fuck you then, fuck all Chinamen!' yelled John.

'Quiet over there!' shouted Chowdhury, his face illuminated by Kumar and his burning body, the flames blowing stench and heat upwards and outwards. 'Give our friend Kumar peace on his last night with us.'

Gwyn beckoned Ephraim and George to join him and Jabez. Gwyn was the boss on site, and some kind of report would have to be written for the company. He'd done this before: a few words on a piece of paper, a couple of paragraphs would usually suffice.

'What happened?' he asked.

'Damn fool tripped, fell right into the path of the QL. He should've been more careful. There was nothing I could do,' said Jabez.

'Ephraim, George, did you see anything?'

'No, Mr Bowen, we saw nothing. It's just like Mr Pugh said,' answered Ephraim.

'George?'

'Exactly like Mr Pugh said.'

Gwyn, Jabez, Ephraim, George all knew, all the men on site knew: the matter would not go further. This was the way, this was the Railway.

After some time, when the heat was at its most intense, Chowdhury took a long teak stave sharpened into a point and drove it into Kumar's burning skull.

'What the hell you doing, Chowdhury?' shouted Jabez. 'Thought he was your butty? Leave him some dignity, will you, for Christ sake!'

'He's releasing Kumar's spirit, Mr Pugh, from his dead body. That body is now finished but his spirit lives on,' said Desai.

'Bloody heathens!'

'Chowdhury, did he have any family?' asked Gwyn.

'Yes, Mr Bowen, a wife, and a boy aged three, and a daughter about twelve months old. They live in Broken Hill. We are all Gujurati, we are all Hindu. His widow will be looked after.'

'We can't do much more about this, Chowdhury,' said Gwyn. 'You know that, don't you? At least no one will steal any gold teeth from this funeral pyre tonight.'

'Excuse me, Mr Bowen? I don't understand.'

'Nothing, Chowdhury, nothing.'

Ephraim and George drifted away from the others round the pyre.

'What did you see, Ephraim?'

'Same as you, George, nothing. And we don't want to see nothing.'

'But that ain't right, is it? Jabez was driving like a madman.'

'He's the boss. Boss can do whatever he likes.'

'Someone died, Ephraim. Kumar died. No fault of his own, far as I could see. Man, I holding on to the side of the trailer just to keep from falling off, Jabez driving so fast. Both of us could have died if we'd fallen.'

'But we didn't fall, did we? What you expect, a seat in the cab with Jabez? You got to know your place, boy. Only way you'll get along out here. You being so precious, why didn't you ask him? "Please, kind Mr Pugh, you mind if I sit with you in the cab?" He'd spit in your face and start cussing. Besides, only room for two in that cab. Where would I go, back outside on top in the trailer with the ballast? That'd make you better than me. We all gotta suffer the same. Once you start picking and choosing who goes in the cab, they got us. One day it'd be me, next day you, never ever both of us at the same time. It's called divide and rule, George. That's how they keep us where we are. One Daniel's worth a thousand Georges.'

'I ain't talking your politics here, Ephraim,' replied George. 'I'm talking about staying alive on this Railway. Jabez, he a loose cannon, he liable to hurt someone without thinking. He's the law out here, no one to hold him back save for Bowen, and he got his mind filled with Daniel and Thomas most days. Rest of the time he's dreaming on being Bemba.'

'We ain't got no cards to play with. Either we stay out here, work for the Railways, get paid by the Railways, or what? What else is there, what you suggesting?'

'I ain't suggesting anything,' said Ephraim. 'We gotta be careful, that's all. Stay on his right side, get out of his way, laugh at his jokes.'

'I'm all for laughing, man, I can do that all right. But there's some others here that can't, and that's when things gonna get messy.'

It was about this time that Thomas started to talk to me about things. Always on my own, and never when anyone else was around. About settlers, about Bemba, about why everything was so unfair, but hell, we all knew that anyway. But it was more than that, more than discussing the problem - it was what we could do about it. I'd known Thomas forever; we'd grown up in the same village. It was always Daisy and Thomas or Thomas and Daisy. He had a bit of a name for himself as, how shall I put this, a thinker. All those books and that queer European music... He was different and deserved attention when he spoke.

XVIII

GWYN AND JABEZ had very little to do with the arrangements, remaining in the shadows and deferring to Chowdhury. Gwyn's shoulders were hunched, his head stooped. Jabez stood, hands behind his back, staring straight at the funeral pyre.

'Got to say it's all pretty impressive. Pretty exotic for two chapel boys like you and me, Jab.'

The pyre spat hot acacia outwards and upwards, creating a circle of smouldering black around the base of the fire. Dying insects tried to escape, living moths tried to get closer.

'This cremation thing, it's just mumbo jumbo, Gwyn, some stupid Indian superstition. Ruddy Hindus. We can't civilise these people. Why can't we just bury the guy and be done with it? We can't even have a drink to send him off, and we're not to wear black neither. You're giving in to these people again. Why do you always give in to them? It'll do you, do us, no good in the end.'

'Do you believe in anything, Jab?'

'I believe in Murphy's.'

'No, I mean believe. Believe in another world. God, the Almighty, whatever you want to call him. You know, more joy in heaven over one repentant sinner than over ten righteous men...'

'I ain't godly. I don't believe and I ain't going to show respect to something I don't believe in. That's two-faced, and that just ain't me.'

'But you sing hymns, don't you, Jab?'

'That's different. That's music, exercising the vocal cords, trying to have a good time. That's what we always used to do at home, no? For Christ's sake, come on, we've done the right thing, Gwyn, paid our respects, we ain't doing nothing by hanging around this fireball.'

'We'll slip away quietly in a minute. We've got to be seen doing the done thing. Death and sentimentality are two chums, ain't they.'

'Death? Death means no whisky, no women, no Murphy's. It got nothing to do with sentimentality.'

Gwyn and Jabez wouldn't linger alongside the fire for longer than Gwyn's sense of duty and dignity demanded. It was many hours later before the cremation fire turned wan and ashen. All the others remained save for Chibwe and Chola.

'Tell me the truth, Ephraim. Tell me the truth, George. How did he die?' Daniel pointed his right thumb towards the cremation.

'He must have slipped,' said Ephraim, 'tripped against the QL. George and me were sitting up top with our eyes to the rear, Kumar was on his way to the station with the empty jerry cans to collect water for us, for Jabez as well. He'd asked Jabez for a lift back to the station in the QL. Two jerry cans are mighty heavy when full, but Jabez refused, said Kumar in the trailer would mean less room for the ballast.'

'Ballast before a navvy. That's the nice Mr Pugh all right,' said Desai, part speaking, part singing through his few remaining teeth.

'Quiet, Desai!' intervened Ephraim. 'Don't get involved, it won't bring Kumar back.'

'Jabez didn't give Kumar a lift 'cause he wanted to see him suffer in the heat.'

'Is that so, Desai?' quizzed Daniel.

'Yes, it is. Jabez was in a hell of a mood this morning on account of Mr Bowen stopping the tree snake show. Can't say I was too happy either. Jabez wanted to pick on somebody, anybody. All of us kept our distance from him. Could have been me, could have been Kabwe. Chola and Chibwe, can't do no wrong with him, so they were in the clear. Could have been you, Daniel, save you weren't here. You were in the embrace of Mr Bowen, weren't you?' replied Desai.

'What do you mean embrace, curry man!'

'You know what I mean!' screamed Desai. He'd had retribution on his mind for some time, and his nature would not let the occasion pass. He could not hold himself back. 'We all know what it means, you're eyeless with arrogance! You're his favourite, just like Chola and Chibwe with Jabez. You're Mr Bowen's lackey and more! Gwyn this, Gwyn that. You think you're his equal? You're no better than any of us! Bemba, Gujurati, Chinamen... we're just navvies. One of us dies, there'll always be a replacement, a cheap replacement. We all live on our knees!'

'Shut up, Desai!'

'Don't need your help, Chowdhury. And what kind of name is Daniel anyway?' Desai was unrelenting. 'Don't you have a proper Bemba name like Mubanga or Chola or Chibwe, or do you prefer a nice pretty European name, so Mr Bowen can rouse you faster? Daniel, oh Daniel!' Desai sang wildly, his arms swinging in the air, a vaudeville actor playing the drunken fool. 'Does he speak some fluffy, tender words to you, get you in the mood quicker. That's what you are, Mr Foreman, licking the hands of the noble European! Hey, boys, we know it's more than that, don't we? It's more than hands that Uncle Daniel licks! Oh, Daniel, get me my tea. Oh, Daniel, get me my supper. Oh, Daniel, I love you!'

'Shut up, Desai!' yelled Daniel, yanking a knife from his belt. 'Shut up.' His voice now calmer, colder, his stare cemented on to Desai's face, his teeth tightened.

'Leave him be, Daniel,' said Chowdury, 'he's just a fool. He's unarmed, and he's upset 'cause of Kumar's death.'

'That's his problem, Chowd,' replied Daniel. 'Should've kept quiet. Should've stopped his taunting. I'm boss man here. He needs to learn respect.'

A dagger landed at Desai's feet, thrown there by one of the navvies. In the rumpus neither Desai, Daniel nor most of the others saw where it came from, but the meaning was obvious to all. Desai would have to pick the dagger up and fight.

'Pick it up, Desai! Shouted Daniel. 'Pick that knife up. Seems like you got a friend here somewhere, could even be a Bemba, wants to even up the stakes. Go on, pick it up, you arsehole. You want to be head man? All you'll get is your guts in the mud!'

'Leave him be, Daniel,' pleaded Chowdhury. 'He's got no idea how to use it. Come on, leave him be!'

'Teach him a lesson, boss!'

'Shut it, Chibwe, don't need no one's advice here. Pick it up, you bastard, take a shot!'

'Pick it up! Pick it up!' The braying navvies shouted in unison.

'Pick it up, Desai! You started it!' Chibwe shouted. 'Go on, Dan, show him who's boss.'

'Think, Daniel, think!' shouted Chowdhury.' What's Bowen going to say if he finds Desai dead tomorrow? Do you think you'll be able to cover it up? Someone's bound to talk. Do you think I'll stay silent? I'm Gujurati too. Or the Chinese boys, will they keep quiet? Are you going to kill us all? And the Bemba, do you trust them? What's on the other side of their smiles?'

Daniel advanced towards Desai, eyes narrowing, black, icy and insistent, a hateful peering plunging deep into Desai, the homeless dagger still untouched. Desai felt a sharp pain just below his left cheekbone and fell heavily to the savannah floor, blood dripping from the cut left by Daniel's knife.

'Enough, that's enough!' shouted Chowdhury. Daniel turned his back, walked away, surrounded by an entourage of braying parasites.

'You all right, Desai?'

'Get away from me, Chowdhury. I'm fine!'

'You need to think,' said Chowdhury. 'Take that cut as fair warning and think. What are you going to do, take on half the camp over an accident? And it could have been an accident, Desai. Kumar's death could have been an accident.'

'They don't care,' Mubanga stepped in. 'Accident or not, they don't care.'

'What do you know, old man?' replied Desai, his eyes narrowing with pain. 'You're too old for the railway. Am I the only man here with blood in his veins?'

'Not just Bowen and Jabez,' Mubanga continued. 'Daniel as well. Wants to be like them settler bosses. Rigged out like something he ain't. Looking like a prime cut of steak, but once you open the tin he's just chitterlings. Navvies dying all the time on the railway, no verdict's ever returned out here. You've got to remember that.'

'I'll make them care,' Desai with his hands and knees on the ground, blood still dripping, his head bowed in pain, silhouetted like a wild dog before a hunt.

'Jimmy, Chinaman, what do you think? You've kept quiet, what should we do?' asked Chowdhury.

'What do you mean, what should we do? We can't do anything. Do you want to fight them? You may as well try and reclaim Africa for the Africans. And you, Mubanga, you think you're the saviour of your people? We all do what we're told, we turn up for work, we hopefully survive, we get paid and then we go home to our families, that's what we do. Go back to India, both of you, if you want. There are thousands more of your brothers, cousins, family who'll come here and take your place. There's nothing at all we can do, this is the way it is!'

Chowdhury was left to tend Desai's wound, the others sulking into small huddles. The night swelled around the cremated body of Kumar.

'What we going to say to Bowen tomorrow, Chowdhury? About tonight? This face of mine isn't going to be better by the morning,' said Desai.

'All you got to do is say the right thing. No knife, no Daniel. Blame Africa. You fell against a sharp thorn or something.'

'They're not going to believe that. We all know what a knife cut looks like.'

'You blame a thorn tree and they'll believe you all right.'

'And Kumar, what do we do about him?'

'I'll collect his ashes, take them home. See his widow and a holy man, if we can find one. We'll scatter the ashes into the river in Broken Hill. There are no crocodiles there anymore, should be safe enough.'

'Is that it? Where does his soul go?'

With that Daniel reappeared from the gloom.

'How's the face, Desai? It could have been worse, much worse. Lucky I felt sorry for you, with your loss and all.'

Desai didn't answer, holding a cotton rag to his face, not a white patch on it.

'Desai was asking what's happened to Kumar's soul,' retorted Chowdhury.

'Soul, Chowdhury, soul? Lifetimes follow lifetimes, we only events happening to one another. You ask your priests for an answer, priests got answers for everything.'

'Is that what you really think, Daniel?'

'Me?' Daniel sighed. 'My soul an echo of others, reflections of you. My knife in Desai's face, I've left my mark. We all leave our mark on each other, means we live forever. That's what my grandpa told me. But now I'm a Christian, a good Christian. Makes me eyeless with arrogance, ain't that so, Desai?'

A few hours had passed since the fight. The camp was quiet, peaceful embers burning. In the light of a half-moon, Kabwe appeared, smirking, like Lucifer from the bush, returning for his knife.

navvy, a knifed navvy is nothing to them. Jabez, Daniel, can do what they want as long as the boss says nothing. They'll do whatever they want and get away with it.'

'I need this job, Desai,' replied Chowdhury. 'I need the money. There are piles of earth all along this line with dead bodies in them, dead navvies. The work never stopped for them. There were no investigations, no grand official inquests. They get killed, they get buried, but there will come a time, a time of reckoning, and we'll both know when that time comes.'

'So that's it then?'

'Yeah, that's it. For now.'

That lunchtime Kabwe sat with old Mubanga, the young David and George. Chibwe and Chola, the sugary two, as Mubanga called them, were as usual with Foreman Daniel.

'You boys heard of someone called Dixon Konkola?' asked Kabwe.

'He work on the Railways?' enquired George.

'I heard of him,' responded old man Mubanga, 'he's some jumped up teacher from around Mporokoso in the north, says he linked to a Bemba royal family. Some say he related to the Chitimukulu himself. Just another one who wants to rule over us, if you ask me.'

'Someone's got to give the orders, haven't they? asked David.

David was by far the youngest of all the navvies. His face had not yet acquired the coarseness which befell all navvies, working outside in the bush for years on end. It had an alluring feminine attractiveness, the whole in proportion to each of the parts, unwrinkled, unblemished. A quick learner and someone who wanted to learn quickly, he spoke with a very slight stammer, which he snuggled away by speaking slow, measuring before communicating.

'Men like Bowen and Jabez,' said George, 'and anyway, what do you know? How old you, boy? Sixteen, seventeen? Hear you more interested in animals and flowers than anything else. What kind of a navvy is that?'

'Shut up, George,' said Kabwe. 'Young David's a quick learner. Took courage for him to leave home, him being just a lad. Strong too, ot the heart of a bloodhound. A fine carpenter as well. He should

XIX

THE NEXT MORNING'S DAWN waxed and the early mist waned, revealing the awakening veldt, and with it Desai's cut face, as conspicuous as a hyena in a hen house.

'What's happened to your face, Desai?'

'Nothing, Mr Bowen. It was so dark last night, I stumbled, scratched my face on a thorn bush. It'll be gone in a few days.'

'We're doing important work here, Desai. It's your responsibility to look after yourself. I don't want any more people getting hurt."

'Yes, Mr Bowen, of course, Mr Bowen.' His face burning, Desa scuttled away.

'What did the boss want, Desai?' asked Chowdhury.

'Just asking about this.'

'What you tell him?'

'Told him what he wanted to hear, tripped and fell on some th

'Did he believe you?'

'I don't think so, said we were doing important work.'

'Much more important than a knifed Gujurati.'

'Even if I'd told him the truth, that his beautiful Daniel had me, would he have believed me? They didn't even stop for We had to wait until evening time before we could have th tion. Can't be no delay to the important work we're doin have built that wooden cage for the drongo, not Chibwe, save Bowen couldn't see that, he's too stuck in his ways. And why should things stay the same? That's what Konkola says.'

'Because it's always been that way, that's right, Kabwe, ain't it?' said George.

'Why should it always be like that, Smiler? Been malaria here forever, doesn't say it's right. Doesn't say it's got to last forever,' responded Kabwe.

'And this Konkola of yours is going to get rid of all those wicked bosses that give us a bad time? And how he going to do that? He going to put on a nice three piece tweed suit, fine silk tie, crisp white shirt and all, walk up to the high commissioner and say, "Excuse me, your excellency, I think it's time you and your types left our beautiful country, and allow us to take control?'

Both George and David smiled as Mubanga put on his best settler accent.

'Don't take no heed of him, boys,' said Kibwe. 'Obvious why you called "Old", Mubanga, you're stuck in the old times. Cecil Rhodes is still alive for you, old man.'

'So how we going to change things, Kabwe? What's this Konkola man saying? How we gonna get our wages paid when the settlers got all the money?'

'We all work for the railways, right? Mostly pick and shovel work, lucky ones do some plate-laying, get paid extra, nothing wrong with that. We do the work, we do the hard work.'

'And them Indians and Chinamen, don't leave them out,' interrupted David.

'And Indians and Chinamen, ok, them too. Without the hard work there'd be no Railway. We do the labouring but not the ordering. That's down to Bowen and Jabez.'

'And their little Daniel,' said Mubanga, 'don't forget him. He's Bemba, ain't he, Kabwe? He one of us. How does the deep thinker from the northlands factor the likes of Daniel into his little account of liberation. He's as trapped as we are, powerless and helpless. Soon as we tumble out from underneath our mothers' thighs, the road is set for us. We all feel humiliated, but you here to preen your intelligence before us.'

'Daniel ain't the same as us,' said George. 'Not in every way. Gets paid more, works half as hard as we do, always with Bowen, riding around in that Land Rover of his,' said George.

'I suppose you're going to tell me next, Kabwe, that poor old Daniel don't know he's trapped. He's like them drongos in the cage, get food and water every day, protected from boomslangs and hyenas, but can't fly,' said Mubanga.

'It's still a cage, ain't it? He ain't free just like the rest of us,' said Kabwe.

'We sure as hell don't want to be thrown as tidbits to no boomslang,' said George.

'What the hell's wrong with all of you?' said Kabwe. 'You saying you don't want to change all this? Bet none of you spends two minutes thinking about things. Don't you see through their card game chicanery, or do you just gawp at it? We're paupers at our own doorstep!'

'Money here's better than most places, Kabwe, you got to admit that,' said George. 'Mr Bowen, he a good man, and Jabez, well, nothing can be done there, but Mr Bowen keeps him under control.'

'Under control! Someone should have told dead man Kumar that! There's no peace when Jabez is around. He always out of control. Only peace from Jabez is the peace that Kumar found.'

'But that was an accident, right?' came the response from young David. 'The Indiaman just stumbled into the QL. Jabez could do nothing about it, that's what Jabez said.'

'Ask Ephraim, ask George. Ask them, David, they were on the QL,' said Kabwe.

'Save those two were looking backwards. That's what you said, George, ain't it?' asked Mubanga.

'Backwards, forwards, it ain't important now. Kumar's dead. His ghost's probably whispering to Chowdhury right now, planning things. That Indian's got a funny look about him,' said George.

'Which way were you looking?' asked Mubanga.

'Forget about Kumar,' cried Kabwe. 'Let's talk about the living, let's talk about us. We do the hard work, we do the hard work on our own land, in our country. The wages we get goes in rent and food to

European settlers, and them Indians with their grocery stores, and what we got left? Tell me, what we got left? What do we do with our flotilla of farthings? A day trip to the Falls on the bloody Railway, that's what we do. And then we start all over again and again and again. You think there's dignity in that? Ain't you heard of the colour bar? You all make me sick!'

'Perhaps these boys don't want to be saved, Kabwe. Perhaps they don't want your freedom,' said Mubanga.

'Perhaps they're stupid!'

'Shut up, Kabwe,' said George. 'Just shut up. Don't want you spoiling our living here. All we'll be doing is changing one set of bosses for another. Can't see that doing anything for us. When the house of a big boss caves in, the hired hands inside get killed too. Do you want us to be free so we can have the right to starve to death?'

'Are you all blind? You've doffed your caps so long you think it's normal. Like some performing lion in a zoo who's had his balls cut off!'

'Nothing wrong with my balls, ask around town about that, Kabwe!' laughed George.

'That's enough,' said Mubanga. 'We've got to get back to work. They'll agree with you one day, Kabwe. Tide's moving in your direction. But today we've got wages to earn.'

Mubanga knew in himself that he had been living up to his Old Man name for some time, but he was doing his best to hide it. What he really should have had were a pair of slippers, a warm fire and a fine single malt whisky, but he was a labourer on Rhodesia Railways, not the master of the line. His hands had become increasingly arthritic, his lower back ached constantly. He hobbled when walking, the result of two rheumatic knees, and varicose lumpen clusters speckled both his calves. But his strength was still there, and he was determined that no one would get the better of him.

'What's going on here, boys?' asked Ephraim. 'Some kind of private gathering or is it open to everyone?'

Ephraim was in his late thirties but looked well into middle age. Black folded pouches underneath his eyes, some so thick that they looked they would fall like overripe peaches to the ground. His ears

neatly lobed, his face wreathed in wrinkles, twisting this way and
that, coiling like the toing and froings of a moist slug on a dewy
morning on a garden path. His hairline retreating; soon it would have
nowhere left to go. All the navvies liked to, had to, spit, but Ephraim
was the master in that department; the more he spat the less likely
he was to drizzle others whilst talking.

'Sit down, Ephraim, join us. This ain't no secret society,' replied
Kabwe.

'Kabwe talking politics again,' George explained. 'You a man of
the world, Ephraim. You been fighting abroad, you killed foreigners.
What do you think?'

'All I know we was told we were on the right side of right, we
fighting to free nations from strangers. I hadn't even heard of no
Burma or Japan, and no one asked this Bemba if he wanted freedom
for his own country. It was the first time I had a piece of paper with
my name on it, and they couldn't even spell it the right way. I machine
gunned a Jap, feet away from me, bullets tore his uniform to shreds.
Face, what was left of it, drenched with his own blood. I shot him so
fast he was still holding his rifle when he fell. What was the Jap's
name? Which village did he come from? Was he a bad man? What
lies or strong arming brought him so far from his home?'

'But you made sergeant, right? They must've thought well of you?'

Ephraim gave a derisive snort. 'Thought well of me? Let me tell
you, when we all came back from the killing, the settler soldiers got
a new suit, shoes, tie and all. Me, I got a bowl of chisamba! On our last
ever parade in Livingstone, the officer say the king thanked us from
the bottom of his heart. He even read out words from the *Bulawayo
Chronicle*.'

'You know what that is, don't you, David?' asked Kabwe.

'No, I don't.'

'It's a settler newspaper, boy. The officer read from the newspaper,
shouts it out top of his voice so we all could hear. "Men," he says,
"you've all returned as heroes, you've freed the world from tyranny,
and look in my hand, the front page of the *Chronicle*. 'Men, Women
and Africans played their part in Winning Victory!' " They don't even
think of us as men or women, we something other! We just ain't

proper people to them. We can kill for 'em, die in their wars, but when we home, we ain't nothing. You a wise man, Mubanga. How much the cheapest maize meal gone up in the last few years, about a third? Sugar, meat, tinned milk they all more expensive.'

Kabwe took up the theme. 'And what about cloth, boys, blankets? They double the price they used to be, and quality half as good. They pay us minimum pay of twenty-six shillings a month, and then deduct eight shillings for rations. You get ill, go to the Native Hospital, man, that's even worse than the Government Hospital. Ill folks sleeping on beds, under beds, between beds, people starving everywhere.'

'You talking like a politician, now, Kabwe. We know the problems, tell us what the answers are,' said Mubanga.

'We got to strike, demand better wages, better conditions, the right to peace and quiet. Not kneeling and not in poverty, and not have tomorrow the same as yesterday,' continued Kabwe.

'And you expect the settlers to open their Christian arms to you?' said Mubanga. 'To help their fellow man? You heard Ephraim, didn't you? Ain't you been listening to him? We ain't people to them. They ain't going to budge. They'll send in police, start cracking a few heads. And most of them police will be Bemba too, Bemba who need the work same as us.'

'What you suggest, old man, wait for Jehovah to come down from on high, save his suffering children here on earth? Religion's for the weak, for stupid fools that know no better. Missionaries promise you paradise in the hereafter just to stop you tryin' for fairness in the here and now. Just another settler story to keep us quiet!' said Kabwe.

'I ain't got the answers, Kabwe,' said Mubanga, 'but I know one thing, when Judgement Day comes, and it comes to us all, including you, you'll see the face of God, and you'll ask forgiveness for your sins, 'cause you and all of us will be screaming to go to Heaven. Only fools don't believe in God. We all got a price. You'll have yours, Kabwe, no different. You'll double cross yourself, then when you look in a mirror you'll be looking at a liar. You boys mark Thomas over in his shed, I know he ain't much older than young David, but he the future. Listening to that crazy European music, he the future!'

'He's soft in the head, that's what he is,' said George.

David listened like a cat in a rhododendron bush. He believed in what Kabwe was saying, he believed in what Ephraim was saying, but most of all he believed in what old man Mubanga was saying, save for the God part. But one thing he knew above all was that strength and right were nothing without a bullet.

XX

I DON'T KNOW when it really started for me, the dream to retake our land from the settlers. Maybe that was the type of question a settler would ask. Maybe for me, Daisy, it was always there: like having two hands or two ears, I was born that way. Doesn't everyone feel the same for the land where they were born? I was all for sharing it, but we should all get to decide on the sharing, and the sharing should be done fairly. I never knew my father, and hardly knew my mother either, but they, I'm sure, would have had the same views. All our people, to various degrees, thought this way, just like Thomas did, save he was more combative.

I was told that my mother died when I was about five years old, but I still have memories of her, little sparks here and there. Sitting on her lap in front of the fire, mother laughing, cuddles before bedtime... I knew mother loved me.

I was clear the settlers would not give up power voluntarily; we would have to seize it, and as far as I could see only violence would bring this end about. Which brings me on to Gwyn. How could I justify living with a man who logically was my enemy? I was not a philosopher, I'd had no education; I had no need to tie myself up in dizzying arguments about the situation. Everyone must live their life as they see fit, with all contradictions included. Gwyn was sympathetic, after all, but his timeframe was longer and more peaceful. How our goal would be arrived at in the way he wanted wasn't clear, neither to him nor to me. I thought his idea of doing things, of allowing things to happen over time, was total pie in the sky. As for Delyth, what she believed, I was sure I'd soon find out.

Thomas was in his shed listening to Rachmaninoff, sitting eyes closed as if in prayer. Two taps on the door and in came Gwyn.

'What the hell is that racket?' he said.

Thomas opened his eyes and reluctantly lifted the stylus from the record. He wasn't that delighted to see Gwyn. His mind had been far away. He had set aside the next half hour for music. But Thomas had always been polite to Gwyn. Thomas was polite with most people.

'Right, Thomas,' Gwyn declared, 'it's time for your lesson on the rifle like I promised. We'll go behind the station, it'll be safe there. Come on, let's go.'

It was a windless day. The sun, close to midday, had cleared away every shadow, the world now unveiled, graphic, delineated.

The training ground was a flat clearing leading down to a transparent stream, with a modest but steep hill on the opposite side. Miombo and waterberry trees grew close to the water – a perfect place, said Gwyn, for target practice.

'First things first, always point the muzzle in a safe direction. Always assume the rifle is loaded, even though you just checked that it's not.'

'That's common sense, no problem with that,' Thomas replied.

'It's easy to forget, Thomas. I've seen people get shot when their minds are not on the job. Go on, hold the rifle, have a feel for it.'

'Heavier than I thought.'

Why did Thomas have to do this? Why did he agree to it? It didn't really interest him. He had no interest in killing vervet monkeys; that was just cruel. Not to mention, the sight of blood usually made him nauseous. What good was a Winchester to him?

'It's about seven pounds in weight, slightly more if you've got a full fifteen rounds in the magazine. This is a dangerous tool, Thomas. One round is enough to kill. To open the breech, pull this bolt up and back as far as you can. Go on, try it.'

He did as he was instructed and had no difficulty in carrying out the command.

'Now push the bolt forward as far as you can and close it.'

'Done.'

'That action you've carried out strips a bullet from the magazine. The rifle is now ready to fire. What shall we aim at? I know, see that waterberry tree over there, near the stream, about a hundred yards away?'

'Yeah, I see it. Bemba have many uses for this tree, from fish poison to a cure for stomach ache. I used to climb them trees as a child and eat the berries.'

'You know it well then. It's about thirty feet high. Aim for the main trunk about five to six feet from the ground.'

'That's a man's height, Gwyn. Am I practicing for any particular man today?'

'Your mind's racing too far ahead. It's a waterberry tree. You're right handed, put that hand around the grip. And keep your index finger outside this bit, that's the trigger guard. Do not place your finger on the trigger for the moment. Hold the front of the rifle with your left hand but don't touch the barrel, hold the rifle tightly into your shoulder. You should be in command of this piece of equipment, not the other way round. You're the boss. And don't prize the contraption too highly, do that and you'll be in chains.'

'That makes a change!'

'This is no time for fooling around, keep your wits about you. I like to wrap the rifle sling tightly round my left arm, gives me better control, helps me to cradle the rifle more securely. It's a personal preference. More you use it more you find the best way for you. Now comes the moment of truth. See this button here? It's called the safety. Click it on to fire. Put your right index finger on the trigger. Now, I've calibrated the trigger for my own personal use. It's quite sensitive, doesn't need much pressure to pull it back. Look through the scope and place the crosshairs on the target. Ready?'

From Thomas' slight head motion, Gwyn could see that he was.

'Take a deep breath, like a predator before it pounces on its prey. Then let half of your breath out, wait, then squeeze the trigger. Once you're done, breathe fully out and remove your finger from the trigger. Immediately put the safety back on.'

The shot rang out. Six hooded vultures sprang up from a wild pepper tree some fifty yards distant, spotted hyenas yelped in the miombo.

'That's a lot of power in one little finger,' said Thomas.

'Let's go over there, see if you've hit the tree.'

'Want the rifle back?'

'No, that's fine,' said Gwyn, as they set off towards the waterberry tree. 'Sling it over your shoulder, get to know it. Safety on?'

'Safety on,' echoed Thomas.

'Can't see you've hit anything, probably off target. My old man brought me up on guns. His eyesight was razor sharp, even into middle age. Claimed he could tell a helmeted guinea fowl from a crested guinea fowl a ways off. Never got to telling me what "a ways off" actually meant. Still, it impressed me as a kid.'

'Can't see anything neither.'

'Let's try again.'

Thomas as disinterested in the mechanics as a eunuch in the functions of a bordello.

'Practice makes perfect. Once you've mastered the Winchester you'll find it a great piece of kit. Zebra, wild dogs, you name it, this rifle will sort them out.'

'What else is it good for, Gwyn?'

'Whatever use you want for it. Remember, you're the master, not the other way round.'

'As I'm the master, that mean I can go Faulkener's in Ndola, put my Railway wages on the counter and ask Mr Faulkener to sell me a Winchester just like this one?'

'You know those days are not here yet, but they're on their way, be in no doubt of that.'

'A thousand Bemba with a thousand Winchesters could be mighty powerful, don't you agree? I can think of a lot of people warrant the touch of a Winchester, some of 'em not far from here.'

'All people want to live, Thomas, are you the one to decide who lives and who dies?'

'Begging your pardon, Mr Bowen, right now, I ain't got no say in the matter.'

As they walked back for the second shot a headless spotted hyena floated downstream, the first victim of the new warrior.

XXI

LATER THAT SAME AFTERNOON, Thomas was back in his office when he heard three timid knocks on his front door.

Thomas coughed. 'Come!' he answered mechanically.

'Afternoon, Thomas,' said David, a slightly overlong gap between his first and second word, his voice, soft as overripe avocado, tottering into a stammer. 'Mr Bowen...'

'Yes, David, Mr Bowen?' Thomas asked curiously.

'Mr Bowen, he asked me to bring you these.'

'Ah, the books. Come in, come in, have a seat. Move the cat, it won't mind.'

A stray cat had found its way to Thomas' shed, a black and white straggler, sex unknown, two white streaks down both its front legs, balding slightly over its right shoulder. It purred a sigh as David did as he was told, hesitatingly nudging it off the chair. Smoothly, silkily, it floated towards Thomas and eased itself under his chair, where it closed its eyes and went to sleep.

'Can't wait too long. Jabez and Daniel will be asking where I am.'

'Tell them you're on important educational business, teaching Bemba about superior culture.'

'Not sure I understand that, Thomas.'

'Tell them you were on Mr Bowen's business. Been an eventful time in Kapiri Mposhi of late, ain't it, what with one Indian dying and the other meeting up with Daniel's knife. Makes you think whether someone up there's got a masterplan for their kind.'

'Too many of 'em on the Railways anyhow, that's what Daniel thinks.'

'Is that right, and what does young David think?'

'Me, I go along with what those that do the thinking think, people like Ephraim, Kabwe, old Mubanga and the like.'

'Ain't you got a mind of your own? Old enough to be a navvy, old enough to think.'

'Muscle and brain two different things. Muscle grow first, the brain grows after.'

'That sounds to me like Mubanga talking, old man talk. Don't pay no heed to others, pay heed to yourself. You give the orders to yourself first, everything else comes second.'

'He your uncle, ain't he? Besides, easy for you to say. No bosses in this office, far as I can see, excepting yourself. Different out there, got bosses comin' out of my ears. I'm only a runt bantam, and Railways full of punchy roosters.'

'Won't always be like this, David.'

'What you got in mind? Where will I find the grit, the guts?'

'Guts? For guts, main thing is strength, and you got that. Second essential is a gun. Time we looked after ourselves, no settler folk to tell us what's what. Bust ups began the moment they dipped in here.'

'If you don't mind me saying so, that's fairy tale talk. You got an army hidden out here in the bush somewhere, awaitin' your orders? Gonna rise up, sweep those settlers back where they come from? You die a glorious death on the field of battle, resurrect like Jesus and be a hero to all Bemba? Everyone keep telling me you're the genius round here, but who's the stupid one now?'

'There's new ideas all around us. You can coop yourself in like a chicken ready for the pot, or get out there and grasp the new possibilities.'

'You think I'm empty headed, don't you? The usual slow, half-witted Bemba. Man, you're no better than the settlers!'

'How many Bemba you think there are, David? Ten thousand, twenty thousand?'

'More than that, must be at least a hundred thousand of us.'

'More like hundreds of thousands. Way more than a million, maybe even two million. Bemba, Bantu, kin like us, all living in this land.'

'Yeah, that sounds right.'

'And how many settlers, David, how many settlers are there?'

'Couldn't help you there. Hundreds of 'em in and around Broken Hill, they got farms everywhere. Lot of 'em up in the Copperbelt and down in Livingstone too.'

'But there ain't millions of 'em, are there?'

'No, there ain't.'

'Let's say there's twenty thousand. No, let's say there's thirty thousand. That's still short of the millions of us. But the thirty thousand call the shots over the millions.'

'They got the guns, the money, the power, Thomas, nothing to do with the numbers. One thing bargaining over the cost of maize with someone in the market, different thing if that someone's got a gun. You pay the price the man with the gun asks. Ain't no haggling with a bullet.'

'They've turned up here and command us, but they don't want to learn from us, you think that's fair?' asked Thomas.

'Not saying it's nothing, but that's the way it is. If the chief of the clan says we go to war, we go to war. No point in arguing, do as we're told.'

'So if the chief of your clan says fight the settlers, you'd do that?'

'He ain't gonna, is he? Those white folks got him in their pocket. Gets let off paying taxes, gets to keep his land, gets the best cattle brought him every year. He paid off. There ain't no chief that ain't paid off. They all got a price. Best ones hold out for more, stupid ones get the least.'

'And you ok with that?'

'I ain't got your brain, Thomas. What you asking here?'

'Change, we have to change the way things are. It ain't fair, we all know that. We've got to fight, else we'll be taking orders for ever. I don't like the gun or the soldier, David, only what they can bring.'

David looked at Thomas, studied him. Thomas thought David was a reasonable, fair-minded young man, like thousands of others in the country. He deserved so much better. They all did.

'What if we fail, what happens then?' asked David.

'Failing is part of trying, ain't it? If it was easy, everyone hereabouts would try it. The contented man is the man who lives with the least pain. Without pain, you don't succeed. Look for greatness, David. That'll be my contentment.'

David plunged headfirst into the deep.

'Get me the gun then, and I'll be the soldier. I'll be the muscle and you be the brain.'

'But remember one thing, David. Once you rebel there'll be no second way. You'll be hunted by day and by night. Jackals never tire, the slaughterhouse never closes. You prepared for that?'

Before he could answer, another visitor appeared, Foreman Daniel.

'What you idling here for, boy, ain't you got no work to do?'

'Sorry, Daniel, just delivering some books from Mr Bowen to Thomas here,' replied young David.

'How long does it take to deliver books, boy? Get back out there, 'fore I tell Jabez 'bout you. Don't want no mommy's boy out in the bush!'

'Thank you, David, remember to call again,' said Thomas calmly, as David scurried away to the accompaniment of low mutterings from Daniel.

Just outside the shed, David retched three times, vomiting. He shuffled his feet on the savannah dust to cover his bile, then looked around, saw no one and went on his way.

'What the hell was he doing here?'

'As the young man said, Daniel, he was delivering some books from Bowen. It's good to know what the occupiers read, what they think, don't you agree? Hear you vented your anger on Desai real good, why did you do that?'

'Didn't like the way he talked to me, that's all.'

'So you cut him?'

'Yeah, I cut him, what of it?'

'If ever those settlers are to go, we'll need everyone on our side when the time comes.'

'Even Indians and Chinamen?'

'Everyone. Them Europeans never leave anywhere of their own accord, takes a powerful amount of pushing and shoving. Need to let them think they're safely in charge.'

'Don't aim to get rid of Europeans, only to get a bunch of Asians ruling the roost.'

'They're just like us, Daniel.'

'No they ain't! I'm with you only so far. Bemba? Yes. Indians and Chinamen? No.'

'We'll talk about this later when you've calmed down some. I'm in no hurry to see that knife of yours myself. You started talking to the men? You getting a feel of where we're at?'

'Some are ready, some are not. This ain't going to be a quick conclusion. More like a wild dog hunt than a mamba kill.'

'Same result, ain't it? We've got all the patience required. After all, the wild dog does eat eventually.'

'Don't want to wait forever, Thomas. Working on the Railways, tomorrow's not your own. It ain't guaranteed.'

'Make sure you're safe, that's all. Take all necessary precautions, and don't let that temper of yours defeat you. A dead Daniel ain't good for no one, and sure as hell ain't good for me.'

'Ain't good for me neither! What young David think? He one of us, or is he just another arsehole?'

'He's a good man. We got plenty of time for tuition. More books Bowen asks him to deliver, more chance I've got for guidance and schooling. Now get out there, Mr Preacher. Us missionaries need all the converts we can get. And one more thing, you be careful what you get up to with those two boys of yours, Chibwe and Chola. Bowen is one thing, do what you like with him, he's only a settler after all . Just don't do it with a Bemba. We do not want to bring them kind of practices among our people. Is that clear, boss man?'

Daniel did not respond, stalking out the room in a huff, leaving Thomas on his own with his books, his stove, his tea leaves and his gramophone. As for the cat, it had gone its own way, slithering out through the open door, like lubricant oil in a piston.

Thomas decided it was time for Chopin. He chose to start on the twenty-third prelude, the moderato in F major. He closed his eyes and soon nodded off to sleep.

XXII

FOLLOWING THE DAY of the egg, Delyth and I didn't talk much. We kept our own company until early evening. I felt guilty. I didn't want her to think that I was washing my hands of her situation. I wanted to keep her close to my heart, to bring her some joy.

'Gwyn told me you used to help out at the local school?'

'Only for a short while, and that was weeks before Gwyn and I started going out together. They were settler children, Daisy, aged five to fifteen. Parents were farmers, railway and mining people mostly. It wasn't long before I understood the rules there.'

'What do you mean?'

'Not to hope for anything from the quiet ones. The pupils who said nothing, the pupils who accepted everything you taught them without a response, without a second thought. They gave nothing back to me so I gave them nothing in return.'

'They may just have been shy, that's all.'

'Do you think there's a place for shy in Africa? The only students I made an effort with were the ones who complained, or who questioned my teaching, and even then I think I made the effort just to keep them quiet, not from any sense of duty to educate these people. There was a young boy called Paul Delaney, skinny little thing, who I tried to help. Got me sacked in the end, no need to go over it now.'

'That must have been dreadful for you. I've heard of the Delaneys. They wouldn't thank a doctor if they were saved from blackwater fever.'

Delyth was descending down a slope. What on earth could I do to help?

'The children sometimes used bound notebooks, sometimes they used loose leaf paper. You know, the ones with two holes punched on the left-hand side so they can be kept neatly in a binder? To get a fresh piece of paper, the headmaster would drill into us teachers what he called "the procedure".'

'Procedure?' I enquired.

'He insisted pupils who wanted a fresh page had to come up to the teacher's desk at the front of the class, show the teacher that the page they were using was almost used up. Only then could I pass them a clean piece of paper. Save for the one time, just before I left. This boy came up, one of the problem kids, one who always had a point of view. Think his father was some local politician. He came up to my desk, showed his completed piece of paper, shoved it right up to my face, cheeky sod! I gave him a whole box of paper. I didn't look at him, I didn't say a word. His jaw almost touched the floor like those Tom and Jerry cartoon characters, and for once he didn't say anything. No smart comments, no backchat. He just ambled back to his desk with his treasure. Class didn't last much longer than that. We'd run out of paper.'

'You let the rest of the class down. All you had to do was to get the box of paper back. That wasn't difficult, was it?'

'This is Broken Hill, Daisy. It's the lucky and the strong who get the paper, everyone else suffers.'

'That's a European fantasy, Delyth.'

We always seemed to return to the same issue. Was it me or was it Delyth, reaching the same destination by different routes? I went over to the window and closed the curtains. I noticed that the panes needed cleaning again.

'Do you think Europeans are evil?' asked Delyth.

Here we went again.

'Not evil, just wrong, and they know it, but don't want to know it.'

'Another time, one of the parents, driving in their car, hit a little monkey, not sure of the type. Anyway the monkey was hit whilst the parent was taking their dear cherub to school. The monkey was still alive, just, and they brought it to class. They slapped it on a table and the headmaster started dissecting. There was blood and guts everywhere. I even think the monkey's heart was still beating. And then there was that poor bull frog.'

'What happened?'

'One of the kids brought in a live bull frog to school. His mama and papa were probably trying to impress the teachers. It was left in a big glass jar by the window. After a few days everyone lost interest in it. No one fed him, no one watered him, and he stopped croaking. The little thing became so emaciated, he was chloroformed, killed, dissected and thrown in the bin. I complained to the headmaster, Bennett his name was, whilst he was out supervising in the yard during lunch hour. I said it was cruel. He just looked back at me, smiled, told me not to worry, that he'd heard I hadn't actually been born here and therefore didn't know the ways of the country, that he'd run his school as he thought fit. Those original settlers are the worst, believe you me.'

I wasn't so sure of that.

'I don't know whether he was trying to impress me, but Headmaster Bennett called one of the pupils over, gave him a massive clout across his head, told the boy not to run around so much, said he was sweating a great deal and that sweating wasn't good for learning, wasn't what a good Christian would do.'

'I've always wondered why Christians are so cruel to everyone, including themselves, being you all supposed to love your fellow man,' I said.

'I resigned not long after that.'

'The headmaster could have been more supportive, don't you think?'

'Of course he could have. He caused me problems in more ways than one. He introduced me to one of his friends, an acquaintance, a travelling salesman from Livingstone. He dropped in on my life like a kestrel drops in on a field mouse. Constantly smoked a pipe, always a way with words. He made me happy, made me smile. A glance from him and, well, I know it sounds mushy, it felt like I'd be wafted elsewhere. He made me forget Africa. He even wrote me love letters. Me a thirty-year-old woman, receiving love letters. I cherished them, I read and re-read them. I've still got them. It was all so uncomplicated. If it wasn't for that Headmaster Bennett. I'm sure he turned Mrs Delaney against me. I don't think I was docile enough for Bennett. I wouldn't put it past that travelling salesman turning Bennett against me as well.'

This information unsettled me. I also knew of a pipe smoking salesman from Livingstone. But then again, there must have been dozens of salesmen from Livingstone hawking their wares up and around Broken Hill.

'If he made you happy, why did it all end?'

'He was married, and I... became pregnant when I was still teaching at the school. Please don't say anything to Gwyn. He'll be bitterly disappointed, I know he will.'

I was rather proud that Delyth had told me all this; after all, wasn't I only the housekeeper, and a Bemba housekeeper at that, and this was Northern Rhodesia. Delyth had no need to worry that I would gossip; after all, I was not a stranger to such events. Who was I to judge, who was I to disapprove? There was no need for Gwyn to know anything. What, I think, surprised me most was the way she said it: no histrionics, no tears. It was all so matter of fact.

XXIII

THE MORNING SUN SHONE on Kapiri Mposhi railway station, the morning clouds disappeared. Thomas was cutting a thick slice from a five-day old loaf of bread for his breakfast, hoping that not too many crumbs dropped to the floor; at dead of night, they attracted cockroaches and small rodents which were almost impossible to eliminate.

Thomas' first visitor of the day was Gwyn.

'Nice morning again, Thomas.'

'Sure is, Gwyn. I love bright mornings. See there's still no flags at half-mast for Kumar.'

'Ain't no masts on the Railways,' Gwyn replied.

Thomas could not allow Kumar's passing to go forgotten. He put aside his knife and the bread.

'Tea?'

'Yes, please.'

'Chibwe didn't come back on site this time,' Thomas enquired.' He was a good friend of Foreman Daniel, wasn't he?'

'Daniel tells me he's not feeling very well. Been losing a lot of weight. There wasn't a lot for him to lose anyway. All Chibwe's strength seems to be going. No good for the Railways.'

'Been happening to a few of Daniel's friends lately,' Thomas remarked. 'They lose weight quickly, most of them die soon after. No one knows the reason.'

'Strange, isn't it, but no need for us to grieve, didn't know Chibwe well. Where's the tea then?'

The daily sacrament before work, Gwyn's visit to Thomas, and a chance for Gwyn to catch Thomas on his own.

And then someone knocked respectfully, timidly, at the station door.

'Come in,' Thomas said. 'Ah, Chowdhury. I am sorry about Kumar.'

Chowdhury bowed his head slightly in acknowledgement.

'Morning, Chowdhury,' said Gwyn.

'Could I have a moment, Mr Bowen?'

'Of course, come in. Want some tea? It's the best Liptons north of the Limpopo, isn't that right, Thomas?'

'Sure is. Want a cup, Chowdhury?'

'No, thank you, Thomas.'

'I'll leave you two to it then.'

Thomas went back to cutting his bread, one hand on the knife, one hand on the loaf, two ears to concentrate on the conversation.

'Problem, Chowdhury?' asked Gwyn.

'It's one of the horses, sir. It's pretty bad, must have been bitten by a snake overnight, black mamba maybe. The horse, you should see it, don't know what to do.'

'OK, let's go, I've finished my tea anyway.'

Thomas was left to his breakfast, for now at least. He would have other visitors; he always did.

Chowdhury and Gwyn walked to the rear of the station, where the horse was tethered on its own, away from the other animals. Set low to the ground, strong limbed and heavy bodied, dun coloured. Gwyn smelled it before seeing it: rancid, rank, rotten, the misshapen head swollen to a monstrous size like an exhibit in a country fair freak show, saliva pouring in a permanent stream from its mouth, its left paw rubbing against the dusty ground.

Gwyn gave the beast a cursory look.

'No good to us in this condition. Get rid of it. Even the meat won't be fit to eat, got so much venom in it.'

'How shall I do that, Mr Bowen?'

'Go and see Thomas. He's got my Winchester, my rifle, that is, and he's got ammunition. A couple of shots in the head will do it. I'd do it myself, I've had plenty of practice, but got more important things to do. Make sure you take that nag well away from here. The stench will be bad enough, and besides, I don't want hyenas and such like getting too close to camp. I want my Winchester back in one piece, mind you, after you've finished the job. Hand the rifle back to Thomas. He'll give it a clean. I've shown him the ins and outs of that rifle enough times. It's easy to use. Any questions ask him.'

Chowdhury looked uncertain.

'Just ask Thomas. It'll be like giving the animal a painkiller, won't feel a thing.'

'I'll need someone to hold it, Mr Bowen, hold the horse when I do the shooting.'

'Take Desai, he ain't afraid of death, is he?'

'No, Mr Bowen. Thank you.'

'Well, off you go. Better get on with it, don't want the horse to die here and stink the whole place up. And by the way, sorry about Kumar.'

Thomas tightened the fore end screw for them, gave a three minute lesson on how to use the gun and passed it to Chowdhury with some cartridges. A few minutes later Thomas could see Choudhury, rifle over his right shoulder, Desai behind him, leading the fetid stinking horse away from the station northwards, out of sight.

The horse's eyes were almost completely closed with the swelling. Milky-coloured secretions discharged from its haunches, especially from the weals where it had been lashed on countless occasions. It was as if the horse was on fire inside.

They walked over a mica-strewn rocky incline, then on to horizon-ending grasslands, over which the breeze paddled in golden ripples. The uncomplicated land expanding before them uninterrupted, not a hint of humankind. The isolation became ideal, a hostile place to live, a perfect place to die.

'This bloody horse smells like rotting cheese,' said Desai.

'Let's be thankful for the breeze,' replied Chowdhury.

'Did you tell Bowen what happened to Kumar? What really happened to Kumar, what happened to me?'

Chowdhury didn't respond.

'You didn't, did you? We agreed you'd go and see him about this stupid horse and then have a chance to speak to him alone, that's what we agreed.'

'I know but—'

'But what?'

'The chance didn't really come up.'

'The chance didn't really come up? You were with him long enough!'

'What if I had spoken to him, what if I had told him, what do you think Bowen would have done? Taken Jabez and Daniel out into the bush, like us and this horse, and shoot them both in the head. I've told you before it doesn't work like that.'

'But we'd agreed! Kumar was our best friend, he was one of us. Jabez, Daniel, they've kept us too long in their twisted snaffle-bit, it's slashed our chops red.'

'Just shut up, just shut up, will you. We'll have to start this off on our own. I'll speak to some of the other boys. They don't like those two either. We'll all close the vice together, do everybody a favour. We need to put Daniel through the mill, but there ain't no mill big enough for Jabez. He deserves something more permanent.'

Chowdhury started singing a Bhajan to himself, about Gajendra Moksha, about how the god Vishnu came down to earth to protect Gajendra the elephant from the crocodile Makara, who then found Moksha, salvation from the cruel world.

'I thought you'd forgotten our songs?' said Desai.

'You should never forget the songs, Desai, not even in Africa. Let's stop here, we're far enough away. We can do it here. I don't think it can walk much further anyway. This animal smells like a shithouse.'

They had been walking in the heat for half an hour. The horse seemed to be frying from his innards. Its eyes were now completely closed, and all its body covered by the uncontrollable milky secretions, those and the stinking decay a magnet to hundreds upon hundreds of flies and mosquitoes.

The place of execution was under the branches of a dead rat tree, a baobab, some seventy feet tall and about half that in girth.

'This upside-down tree will do,' said Chowdhury. 'We'll be able to find it easy, just in case Daniel wants to know where we did the killing. He's bound to start getting nosy once he hears. Jabez won't give a hoot. We're just by the railway as well, we'll find this spot again no problem. How many flies can there be in this place?'

'They know a free meal when they smell one, and this one bloody smells. He's almost as smelly as you, cowboy.'

'Shut up, Desai.'

'Should we say anything before we do it. Pray to Vishnu or something? Or give him something to eat.'

'You don't feed a horse before a race,' said Chowdhury, scratching his bearded chin, his forehead. 'Come on, let's get this done.'

'What's its name?' asked Desai.

'What?'

'What's its name, what's the horse's name?'

'Bit late for crying now, ain't it?' said Chowdhury.

'It'd help to calm it down, you know, before you pull the trigger. What's its name?'

'Smiley, I think it's Smiley. But with all these flies in its ears it ain't going to hear much anyway.'

'Ain't that George's nickname?' asked Desai.

'George is called Smiler. Another one of those Bemba who said they didn't see anything when Jabez killed Kumar.'

'There, there, Smiley,' Desai whispered into the horse's ear, speaking soothing words in Gujurati. 'I can sense his fear. Even with his eyes as they are, he knows what's going to happen. If he could beg on his knees for mercy he would.'

'Quiet now, Desai. Hold his head down a bit, so I can get a good shot. One cartridge should do it.'

Desai drew the reins down as far as he could, lowering Smiley's head to make the shooting easier for Chowdhury, but also holding it as far away as the reins would allow, to avoid any contact with the horse's innards once the bullet was fired. Smiley's nostrils hardened.

Desai, Chowdhury and the horse were one, surrounded, hemmed in by the cloud of gnawing, nipping insects.

'Make sure you let go of the reins and step away quickly. Once this horse falls there'll be no holding him,' ordered Chowdhury.

Chowdhury placed the muzzle of the Winchester flush against Smiley's distended forehead, trying to remember Thomas' instructions as best he could.

'Ready, Desai?'

'Ready.'

Chowdhury squeezed the trigger, and with a loud bang the bullet discharged into Smiley's brain, killing it immediately.

The horse fell like a calving glacier, almost taking Desai with him. A heavy discharge of blood gushed from its nostrils, staining the savannah, drenching Desai and Chowdhury. Its legs twitched violently, just missing Desai, who screamed involuntarily at the carnage.

For a few moments both men stared down at the kill, waiting for the twitching, for the bleeding to stop.

'This is what we should do to Jabez and Daniel,' Desai breathed. 'Them two are no better than vermin, killing them would be godly.'

'Their time will come, don't you worry about that.'

They both looked at the carcass in its crimson pool, two executioners following orders. The insects kept up their irritation.

'We might as well stay in the shade for a while,' said Chowdhury eventually. 'No point going back to camp straight away, they'll only make us work in this heat.'

'Ok,' replied Desai. He watched Chowdhury rest the Winchester agains the trunk of the tree. 'Nice rifle, ain't it? Could come in handy.'

Leaning against the baobob they both dozed off for about twenty minutes, until their need for water took over. Tsetses followed, discovering Smiley's bits and pieces on them. The butchers walked back silently to the station without a backward glance, and before the shadows developed.

XXIV

LATER THAT AFTERNOON came the same respectful timid knocking on Thomas' door.

'Mr Bowen asked me to bring his rifle back and these four bullets. We only used the one.'

Chowdhury on his own, hands blood-soaked.

'The famous Winchester Model 70. Who did the deed, you or Desai?' Thomas guessed it would have been Chowdhury.

'We both did.'

'But who actually fired the shot?'

'That was me. Desai calmed the horse, held its head down and I fired the bullet.'

'Seen a horse shot before, ain't pretty. Lot of blood come out of his nose, did it, like a gushing mountain stream? Still, you did as you were told. After all, Mr Bowen's the boss, right?'

'Didn't want to see Smiley suffering no more. His time was coming, just come quicker that's all. That nag gave everything for the Railways, no one can complain.'

'A true servant, an honourable servant of the iron road. Virtuous beyond compare, no doubt. So who really killed dear old Smiley? You, Desai, Rhodesia Railways or a nasty African black mamba?'

'The snake killed him. If it weren't for the mamba he'd be alive today.'

'How many years of toil you think was left in him, Chowdhury?

The way upright settler folk like Mr Bowen and Mr Pugh treat their animals, use 'em up, and once they're done get someone else to kill 'em.'

'Smiley sure was beginning to show signs of slowing down a bit,' said Chowdhury, 'but he could have gone on, given more service. If Pugh had whipped him less, he could have gone on, but the mamba got him and that was that.'

'How long you going on for, Chowdhury, before a mamba or Mr Bowen or Mr Pugh gets you? Mr Pugh don't like your kind, does he? Strange that Kumar's dead, Desai's face slashed, and Mr Jabez Pugh in the middle of both events. I ain't saying he drove the QL into Kumar on purpose, just peculiar that's all.'

'Why does a Bemba talk to someone like me? None of your folk do. And why were you helping us with Kumar before the cremation?'

'We're one tribe, Chowdhury.'

'No, we clearly ain't. We don't look the same, we don't talk the same, we don't have the same gods, and we sure as hell don't eat the same, unless Mr Bowen has one of them stupid get togethers round the campfire.'

'You want to make a life for yourself in Africa, Chowdhury, you and your family?'

'Why not? Long way back over the ocean from here.'

'Then join us. One tribe, Indians and Bemba.'

'What about the Europeans, they in this as well?'

'They've got to make their own choice.'

'But they're used to giving the commands. If we're all one tribe, who becomes chief, who's going to give the order to kill Smiley? We going to have three kings: one Bemba, one Indian, one European. What if they can't agree? Do Chinamen count? They're human beings too, aren't they?'

'Of course,' said Thomas. 'Chinamen as well. Their civilization is as old as yours. Only saying there's room for us all, and one of us could be king. Fact you burn in the sun don't mean you a leader. Think on that, my friend. Talk to Desai. In fact, why don't you both come to see me. I can be your chai wallah for a few hours. We can all be in this as one, no need for Europeans.'

'The locomotive hurtling into a ravine drags all the carriages after it... Here's the rifle anyway. Needs a bit of a clean, what with the fouling from the horse and all.'

'Call again, Chowdhury. Bring Desai with you next time, let's do some more talking.'

'I'll think on that, Thomas, I surely will. I like your ideas, but maybe the cost of 'em is too high.'

As soon as Chowdhury left, Thomas pushed the aluminium base of the rifle stock into his right shoulder, closing his left eye, looking through the one piece telescopic mount, down the twenty-four inch barrel and out through the front office window into the bush outside. Jabez berating the navvies. Slipping the safety, finger on the trigger, feeling the amount of pressure required to make the trigger break, four pounds, six pounds. He squeezed and whispered quietly, 'Bang.'

From that time on, he would no longer walk around with his right thumb holding up his trousers by his back right-hand-side pocket. His leather belt would now do that work for him.

XXV

WORK FOR THE DAY had come and gone, and now Chowdhury and Desai were walking together, alone along the railway line, sharing a cigarette. The sun was disappearing. Twirring nightjars were rummaging for moths. Although he wasn't old, Chowdhury had the beginnings of a stoop; Desai walked upright. But both their hands were veined, calloused – working men's hands.

'How much you know about Thomas?' Chowdhury enquired of Desai.

'Thomas? He's just a ticket clerk, likes barmy music, drinks tea with Bowen. Probably licking his arse, best way to get promotion around here. What the hell do I want to know about him anyway? He's not a Buddhist, is he? Is that what you're getting at?'

'No, he ain't a Buddhist,' said Chowdhury smiling, 'but he's an interesting man for all that. The Winchester I took back to him, not to Bowen. That part I couldn't understand. Why does Bowen trust a Bemba with a rifle? It's his own gun, and those things are mighty dangerous. Could give someone a lot of power, could take a lot of people to the next life.'

'Could take a lot of Europeans to the next life.'

'True, true.'

'Thomas said we should both go to see him, talk about things,' said Chowdhury.

'What's his message? Politics, is that what you mean? What you and me know about politics? We got enough on our hands with Jabez.'

'Thomas says things could be different.'

'Yeah, President Chowdhury proclaiming new laws from Livingstone. More like King Thomas from his gold throne commanding us to work twice as hard for half the pay.'

'I think we should at least listen to him, see what he has to say. Could be a way to bring up Jabez in our discussions.'

'When we talk together, even when Kumar was alive, there was only three of us. We knew one another, fellow countrymen in this foreign place. There was trust. Once we bring in a foreigner, who knows who'll get to hear our dealings? Foreigners ain't us. They're different, they don't live by the same rules. They liable to knife you in the face or even kill you, just like that Jabez Pugh. Thomas, he's close to Bowen. Could be he's just a plain old fashioned snitch. We speak to him, it'd be as if we speaking to Bowen, and once he knows, then Jabez in on it too. Then we're both going Kumar's way.'

'If we do nothing, can the two of us get at Jabez, you think that's possible? Pugh thinks cruel. An evil scorpion, that's the way he is. But that Thomas got a way with him. He ain't some stupid navvy working his hands bare on the Railways. He looks to me as if he's got some of the answers.'

Through gritted teeth, Chowdhury took a last deep drag from the dying cigarette and flicked it away like playing marbles on a street corner.

'You only really met him once, when you took the rifle back. He hypnotized you or something. You be careful here, Chowdhury. Not like you to be swayed by a ticket clerk.'

'All men ain't the same. Just saying he's got something. Why do you think Bowen going in and out of that station office, like he buying train tickets all the time? He sees something in Thomas as well.'

'We all know why Bowen there, same reason he with Daniel. Why do they go on their long outings in that Land Rover? That settler's soft, he wants to be like Thomas and Daniel, wants to be taken for Bemba, wants to be seen as African. Except he ain't. And we ain't! More fool Bowen. Them Bemba laughing behind his back, you know that. Everyone hates Jabez but at least everyone respects him in a peculiar sort of way, respect him for being what he is, not like Bowen.'

'Forget Bowen. We got nothing to lose if we talk to Thomas. We ain't even got to talk to him, just listen what he got to say. We can act like two stupid Gujuratis.'

'Shouldn't be difficult, should it?' Desai said, smiling.

They both walked to Thomas' office, above them an endless ceiling of sparkling stars, the nightjars gone. A lion rumbled in the distance; they could also hear hyenas chuckling but too far away to worry. The darkness hushed them both.

The nights were cold in Kapiri Mposhi. Thomas was in his office, reading a book by the light of an oil lamp hanging from a joist above a potbelly cast iron stove, which, although small, produced enough heat for Thomas to be in his shirtsleeves. The smell of a recently fried rainbow bream hung in the air.

Chowdhury knocked on the door. Two quick raps, a pause, another rap.

'Come, Chowdhury, Desai, good evening,' coughed Thomas. 'What have I done to deserve the company of two illustrious sons of Gujurat? Tea? I've been lucky to get hold of some lovely jasmine tea from China. Forgive me for not having Indian tea, but I always think it's nice to experiment, to try something different, don't you think? To open one's eyes to new things, or in this case one's taste buds, so to speak. Jasmine tea for you both?'

'Yes, thanks, fine for both of us,' replied Chowdhury.

Jackdaw-eyed, seeing everything, Thomas smiled at them both.

'Good. Bring a couple of chairs over to the stove. It's one of those cold savannah nights tonight. Push them sleeper logs out of the way, only good thing about them is they burn well. Dead wood, creosote and fire, they best of chums.'

The floorboards were creaking again. Thomas made a note to himself to speak to young David in the morning, to help take care of the problem.

Thomas permanently kept a large black cast iron kettle on top of the stove, topping it up intermittently, ensuring that whenever he had visitors he would not have to wait unduly for hot water. His developing plans involved a lot of visitors, the more the better.

'I always maintain tea helps to oil the wheels. Nice to talk with something in one's hands, don't you agree?' said Thomas.

He walked over to his simple softwood cupboard and returned to the table with a Chinese white enamelled tea set, together with a small muslin bag containing the tea leaves, like a medieval monk carrying his meagre portion of vittels to table before evening prayer.

'Would you like to smell the tea, gentlemen? It's finest jasmine, the aromas are wonderful. Here, smell it.'

'Smells of flowers from a far off field,' replied Chowdhury.

'Absolutely correct, Chowdhury. Desai, do you agree?'

Desai peered briefly into the muslin bag like a young boar smelling for truffles, then passed it back to Thomas.

'Yes, flowery, it's flowery.'

Thomas placed some tea leaves into the teapot.

'Chinese friends call this "the black dragon enters the palace". Those Chinese they could teach us all a lot of things, don't you think?'

Holding the kettle at shoulder height above the teapot, he poured in the hot water, then, ostentatiously placed the lid on top, then poured more of the hot water onto the outside of the teapot, splashing water all over the table.

'I know it looks odd, but I'm told this is to make sure the temperature inside and outside the teapot are the same. As we're having genuine jasmine tea, we better brew it as it's supposed to be done. We're not fixed in our ways here in Kapiri Mposhi, are we? More we connect with different cultures the more we learn. Right, we need to wait a few minutes, my friends, for the tea to brew.'

'Can I ask you who taught you these Chinese methods? And all this paraphernalia, where did that come from?' asked Chowdhury.

'I have many friends, Chowdhury, across many continents. I receive gifts from them in return for my gifts to them, and I learn on the way.'

'What's wrong with our tea, masala chai?' retorted Desai. 'It's just as good, probably better than this jasmine stuff. Looks like piss to me!'

'Show some respect, Desai, we're guests here,' said Chowdhury, waving his right hand as if he was clipping a street urchin.

'No, that's fine Chowdhury. It's good that a man champions his own country. Patriotism is an honourable quality. Tell me about this masala chai. I presume this is the same chai as in chai wallah, is it not, Desai?'

'For masala chai you start with our tea, obviously. Stronger than this jasmine stuff. Because it's strong it retains its flavour. It'll survive for years long after the weaker teas lose all taste.'

'I see, Desai. Strong tea, that's a good start. What else?'

'The extra flavour comes from spices and herbs. We call them "karha", a mixture of cardamom, cinnamon, cloves, nutmeg and many other spices. A proper tea with proper flavour.'

'Not this Chinese concoction, is that what you mean? It is not so different to our refreshment this evening. The word "chai" itself is from Mandarin Chinese, their word for tea.'

Desai, he'd had enough already, and he started to bite his finger-nails for something to do. Chowdhury, however, was attentive, ready to accept learning from the ticket clerk.

'I think the tea has brewed enough. After all we are here to drink weak Chinese tea tonight. To leave it longer would strengthen the essence too much,' said Thomas.

He poured the brewed tea into a tea pitcher, the shape of a low, squat milk jug, and from this he filled three of the smallest enamel cups with tea. Always appraising, analysing the guests, his smile as sweet as ever.

'These small cups are called snifters, but we must not drink from these.'

Placing three slightly larger tea cups, of the same colour and design, on top of the snifter cups, Thomas continued, 'This part is supposed to bring prosperity and happiness to us.'

'More Chinese tricks! Why can't we just drink the stuff?'

'Desai!'

'Almost there, my friend.'

Using both hands, Thomas grasped both cups and smartly inverted them so that the tea in the smaller cup was now deposited into the larger cup. He did the same with the two other pairs.

'At last!'

'Not yet, Desai.'

Thomas threw the brewed tea from the three cups onto the station floor.

'How stupid is this? You spend so much time preparing the stuff and then you throw it on the floor. Chinamen are crazy,' huffed Desai.

'That part is the wishing us prosperity and happiness part,' replied Thomas.

Using the same original tea leaves, he poured more hot water into the teapot, again replacing the lid.

'One thing, Thomas, about the Chinese: you have to admire them for their patience,' said Chowdhury.

'They must have too much time on their hands. No wonder their country's in a mess!'

'We all have the same amount of time, Desai. It's what we do with it that's important.'

'Well, I don't want to be spending all my life making jasmine tea for hours every day,' said Desai. He had by now finished all the nail biting he could manage, some of his nails stinging and bleeding from his labours.

Thomas poured all the brewed tea from the teapot into the tea pitcher and from there into the tea snifter and finally from the snifter into the teacups.

'All done, comrades! It is traditional that one cradles the cup in both hands, smell the scent, then take three mouthfuls, one at a time to fully appreciate the experience. Prosperity and happiness to you both.'

'And to you,' answered Chowdhury.

Desai gulped the tea down in one.

'Not bad, not bad at all,' said Chowdhury, sipping exactly as he was told.

Thomas first sip was a small one, the second the largest sip, with his third he emptied the cup. Chowdhury did his best to emulate him, like a pet pupil in a classroom.

'That was a real pleasure, gentlemen, I'm sure you have a busy day tomorrow and will be wanting a good night's sleep, so may I bid you good night, and best wishes to you both always,' said Thomas brusquely.

Taken aback by Thomas' abruptness, Chowdhury and Desai said their goodnights and left.

'What was that all about?' snapped Desai as they walked back to their beds. 'You told me he was going to talk politics to us?'

'He's testing us, Desai,' replied Chowdhury. He's a wily old hyena. He's finding out about us, what we like, what we thinking inside. He's a man on the up, them types hide in the shadows, they never fully show themselves. Stronger he gets, more we'll see what he's really like, what he really wants. And the tea wasn't that bad either.'

'He makes me feel awkward, almost embarrassed. He's playing chess, watching us, ain't he, Chowdhury?'

'Correct. Let's make sure we ain't the pawns.'

'And the stink of that fish, bloody hell, almost made me puke!'

XXVI

THERE WERE USUALLY THREE FIRES in the camp at evening time, one for the Bemba another for the Gujurati and the Chinamen, and the third for Gwyn, Jabez and Daniel, together with Daniel's acolyte Chola. Chibwe was no longer fit enough for Railway work due to his illness. No one else was afforded favoured status.

The evening of Smiley's death saw only two campfires lit. Chowdhury, who had the responsibility for collecting firewood and preparing the campfires, had engineered the situation. Being so busy with Smiley's execution, he said he had not had enough time to collect the required amount of kindling and firewood for three campfires; two would have to suffice.

'You incompetent ruddy Indian,' Jabez had barked, 'what've you been doing all day? How many cartridges does it take to kill a nag? It was halfway dead from the mamba bite before you shot it, a few more hours it would have been finished. Never thought there was much work in you boys. Least there's one less of you thanks to the QL. Ephraim can join Gwyn, Daniel, Chola and me, rest of you will have to make do at the other campfire.'

The rules which dictated life on the Railways were applied as meticulously to the campfire: Gwyn, Jabez, Daniel together, opposite them Chola and Ephraim.

On the other campfire the rules were just as strict, save on this night Chowdhury ensured that he sat in a group with Kabwe, old man Mubanga, young David, and George. On the other side of the fire, Desai sat with the three Chinamen, Jimmy, Lee and John.

Fourteen phantoms, fire worshippers on a cold, dark African night. Save for the spitting sparks, the evening was unusually quiet, the savannah soporific, all the world asleep underneath the silent, secretive stars.

After eating, and after gaining permission, Daniel drifted over to the opposite side of the campfire to be with Chola and Ephraim.

At the other campfire, before sitting down in their company, Chowdhury addressed the Bemba with the only word he knew in their language. 'Muzuhile.' He looked at Kabwe. 'Pity about Smiley, wasn't it?'

'Smiley?'

'The horse, the dead horse shot today.'

Kabwe shrugged, lounging, all his weight on his right elbow, a man of confidence who bided his time, a man who looked people in the eye when he spoke.

'What are you doing sitting down with us, you should be over there,' Kabwe pointed to Desai and the Chinamen. 'David, pass me some more nkuku. Make sure there's chikasu with it as well before this foreigner takes the lot.'

'Yes, boss,' replied young David.

'What do you think of Daniel licking up to Bowen, getting all the easy jobs, the best food, the best pay, the quiet life?' asked Chowdhury, stroking his goatee. 'Doesn't seem fair, does it? I mean, we're all in this together, right? We're all equal save for Bowen and Jabez. We know they think they're more important.'

'Daniel does what Daniel wants 'cos of Bowen. He only got one hankering, and that's a hankering to be overseer, a pharaoh of the slaves. Fact he knifed your boy Desai, that's what's vexing you, ain't it? And stand down wind of me, Chowdhury, that horse's left half its guts on you.'

Chowdhury moved to one side and continued, 'That wasn't right, was it? And that devil Jabez could have been more careful in the QL, should have looked where he was going.'

'Probably did it on purpose,' replied Kabwe. 'Killing an Indian ain't nothing to him.'

'He shouldn't have lost his temper after the boomslang circus,' said Chowdhury.

'But we all had a good time there, didn't we? Mean to say a bit of sport with the drongos and the snake. Fact, I saw you whooping with the best of us.'

'Guess we've all got to die sometime, then we can all have a rest,' said Chowdhury.

'You been drinking too much chipumu. Who you be talking to? Evil snakes and wild birds or Daniel and Jabez over there? And when you going to take a bath?'

'You tell me, Kabwe. No one lives forever. Sooner or later we'll all be like Kumar, burnt to a crisp just like this campfire.'

'I never been no friend of Daniel, and as for Jabez, well, we all know about him. Then again, we all think we gonna live forever – that we can do whatever we want and get away with it.'

'But why can't we, Kabwe, why can't we get away with it? Accidents happen on the railway all the time.'

'Look at us, Chowdhury, look at us Bemba. How do you think we got to be working on the Railways? Pass a fancy exam or such like? Deputy High Commissioner chatting to us in some showy garden party down Livingstone. "Old boy, would you like to join Rhodesia Railways, hear they're looking for stout reliable chaps like you, be a valued contributor to that great institution..." Shit! It's Daniel, idiot, Daniel got me the job, he got all of us Bemba our jobs. Without him, I'd be brushing floors on some settler's verandah at half the pay I'm getting here. Daniel's the man, he in with Bowen. That's the price you pay. With arselicking comes power.'

'I hear you, but if Daniel goes, the king is dead, long live the king... They'd have to appoint someone else, that someone would have to be Bemba, and that someone would most probably be you, Kabwe. Bowen always puts you in command of the boys when Daniel isn't here. Think about it.'

'And Jabez?'

'He ain't immortal either. You want to play second fiddle all your life, Kabwe, or do you want to be Daniel?'

'Man, I don't want to be just Daniel. I want to be Jabez.'

Old man Mubanga, young David and George looked on and said nothing.

'Make no mistake, Kabwe, vengeance has no boundaries, and sure as shit has no time limits.'

'If you say so, Cowboy. Let's ask the Chinamen what they think. Hey Jimmy, what you think of Daniel, Jabez, Bowen?'

'Don't say nothing,' said Mubanga. 'You keep your thoughts to yourself. You Chinamen on the brink anyway. One push and you'll be falling headfirst into a deep hole and not coming back.'

'You ain't the prettiest are you, Jimmy?' Kabwe needled. 'How many holes you have in your face anyway. And that nose is as crooked as a lawyer's pen.'

'Leave him be, Kabwe,' said Mubanga. 'Hear you Chinamen good at telling stories, you got one for us, Jimmy?'

'Yeah, come on, a story for a cold night, what've you got Jimmy?' added young David.

'Come on, a yarn from the Orient for the boys to keep us amused,' ordered Kabwe.

Jimmy, crosslegged, looked at the fire, rubbed his hands and extended his arms to the warmth. 'John, put another piece of acacia on the fire for our friends. Nothing worse than being cold when listening to a tale.'

And then Jimmy started.

'Hundreds of years ago, during the Ming Dynasty, an old farmer named Xiang Shui Hu lived, as his venerable ancestors had done before him, in the mountains, just south of the Great Wall, one hundred miles north of Peking. Years of poverty were etched on his skin, his face like a stone on a riverbed, polished, rutted and worn away. Timeless. Religious disagreements, plague, plunderers and civil war had impoverished the people. The citizens had lost all hope, and even suicide had become commonplace. But Xiang Shui Hu never lost hope. He was a farmer, the rhythm of his existence a balm subduing all the madness about him. Every September he would leave his small

house and walk some two hours to the chestnut tree forest, ascending
a winding dirt track high up into the mountains. Carrying a jute sack,
a strong rope, a wooden ladder, a ten-foot bamboo pole and a small
roujiamo in his pocket for lunch.'

'What the hell's that word again?' Kabwe demanded.

'Roujiamo. It's like one of them Fray Bentos steak and kidney pies.
It's crusty but with lamb meat inside.'

'Then why don't you call it a lamb pastie, for Christ's sake?' said
Kabwe.

'OK, Kabwe, that's enough. Go on, Jimmy.'

'Thank you, Mubanga. Chestnuts were important to Xiang Shui
Hu, for he would take them to the local warlord, who, via his steward
would negotiate a price with Xiang Shui Hu for the harvest. The
money would help Xiang Shui Hu through the upcoming winter,
which was harsh in the mountainous region. Xiang Shui Hu was a
good man. He always ensured that his neighbour Zhu Yo Min
received a share of the chestnut bounty, as Zhu's household was
severely impoverished. Zhu's father had lost their farm, which had
been in the family for generations, when he'd wagered heavily, and
unluckily, on of all things his favourite fighting cricket. Each fight
consisted of five bouts. Zhu's father's cricket lost by three bouts to
two and with it their farm. Only one item was saved from the debt
collector, hidden away in the family ancestral tomb, and that was
the family ehru.'

Jimmy looked up quickly at Kabwe.

'That's a traditional Chinese two-stringed upright fiddle, Kabwe,
made of wood and python skin. An instrument which, after years of
practice, Zhu had become extremely proficient at playing.'

'Come on, get on with the story, for God's sake.'

'Sorry, sorry, Kabwe, not long to go now. Anyway, Xiang Shui Hu's
bamboo pole was as old as himself. The ladder, replaced and repaired
over the years, was made of ash. At the lower end there were two
triangular pieces about three feet in length. Strapped to the top of the
triangle was a vertical branch of ash about six feet in length. Horizon-
tal pieces of wood were nailed on the vertical branch and used as
steps.'

Jimmy, with the use of an acacia twig, drew a helpful diagram of the ladder on the dried earth, so that the men, and especially Kabwe, could picture what he was describing.

'The chestnut trees swept high into the sky. Xiang Shui Hu, placing the ladder against a tree, would climb to the top of his ash ladder, and then climb higher still, as far as the branches of the chestnut tree could support his weight, strapping himself with the stout rope to the nearest substantial branch. He knew how dangerous the work was. A fatality occurred every three or four years, a harvester falling from the high branches.

'Sharp blows from his bamboo would propel the chestnuts to the woodland floor below. Although tethered to the edge of extinction, the forest of chestnut trees, timeless and inexhaustible, sustained Xiang Shui Hu.

'Having eaten his roujiamo, filled his jute sack, contented but tired, he started the return hike down the mountain to his house, proposing to proceed without delay to commence negotiations with the steward. Hopefully another winter would pass, if not in plenty, certainly not in beggary.

'A mile or so before reaching his house he met his neighbour, Zhu Yo Min, walking purposefully up towards him.'

'You appear to be in a hurry, Zhu. There's been a fine harvest this year, come and look. Xiang Shui Hu, glad of the respite, placed the jute sack, heavy with chestnuts, on the ground.

'Look at all these fine chestnuts. I'll make sure, as in the years past, that you'll get an ample share of the profits. Once I've concluded my bargaining with the steward, it will be a good winter for us all.

'Zhu Yo Min did not answer, he did not speak. A dim ray, a mixture of slyness and zeal, shimmered in his dark narrowing eyes. Pulling a dao, a sword, Kabwe, a small sword, hidden behind his jacket, he stabbed Xiang Shui Hu twice through the heart. The old man fell sideways, dead before he collapsed, onto the jute sack, overturning the bag and disgorging the chestnuts in their hundreds onto the mountain path.

'After painstakingly collecting the last chestnuts and placing them carefully back into the sack, Zhu Yo Min half-kicked half-pushed the old man off the track, and Xiang Shui Hu tumbled and tumbled and tumbled down the mountainside into the torrent below. Only Xiang Shui Hu's blood and a few unfound chestnuts attested his passing. Using the bamboo pole, Zhu Yo Min tried to conceal the blood stains with the dust from the mountain path. As if asking for forgiveness from the gods, Zhu could only whisper, "I'm sorry, old man."

'But a share of the old man's labour was not sufficient for Zhu. He had to have all of it. Zhu threw the rope, the ash ladder and bamboo pole down the ravine, uniting them with their dead master. Zhu had no use for them, gruelling perilous honest labour was not for him.

'Zhu Yo Min was sure the chestnuts would fetch a good price from the steward, for the harvest had been plentiful, the quality superb.'

The tale ended, the listeners were quiet save for Chowdhury.

'See, Kabwe, it's always been dog eat dog, it's not just Africa.'

The gold sovereign sun had dropped into someone's pocket hours earlier, and just before he fell asleep old man Mubanga thought he heard, somewhere in the distance, the periodic barking squawk of a night heron, together with the haunting sound of Zhu Yo Min playing his ehru next to the family's fighting cricket.

XVII

GWYN AND JABEZ were hunched around the other campfire. The crackling and popping somehow always encouraged discussion. The bright light made it impossible to see anything more than a few feet away; the stars, however, were crystal clear.

'Jabez, I didn't like the way you shouted at Chowdhury this evening. He had to get rid of that horse on my orders. He can't do everything.'

'You give in to these people too much, Gwyn, you give them too much slack. You're forever telling me the Railway runs on discipline, rules and regulations and all that. If you have rules, you have sanctions; if you're out of line you get punished. If we couldn't punish these navvies, make them fear us, people like you and me wouldn't be here for long, and I don't mean on the Railways.'

'It's not the way I do things. The men respect me for that.'

'Respect? You think they give you respect because they like you? They respect you because they fear you, or more precisely they fear that boss boy of yours, Daniel over there with his good-looking boys. I've marked he's without one of them, that bloke Chibwe. Got some disease, I hear. Sure as hell his other mucker, Chola, has his eyes on some new ones. You be careful of Daniel. He's got the makings of a bad 'un, got talons on our jobs. I can see it, way he carries himself, way he talks to the men. And then there's that jumped up ticket clerk Thomas. He's got ideas above his station. Only saving grace is he likes music, hear it when I pass his shed sometimes.'

'That's something you have in common then,' said Gwyn, smiling.

'Gwyn,' sneered Jabez, 'the man with all the answers, the son of prophecy, come here to darkest Africa, to lead the Bemba out of oppression to the promised land. You're just a sinner at the gates of heaven like the rest of us, an outsider, as much an oppressor as I am, and I suggest you don't forget that. My kin, your kin, fought for this place. Wasn't given to us. Only Bemba will free the Bemba. You think you're Jesus Christ out here? We all know what happened to him. You'll end up like that prehistoric skull that Swiss prospector found in the mines outside Broken Hill.'

'Wasn't there a Bemba miner with him as well?'

'That ain't important.'

'It's called Homo Rhodesiensis.'

'Homo shlomo. Rhodesia Man! Rhodesia Man it's been called for thousands of years, now they want to call it Kabwe Man! What's this place coming to? That's what happens when you cut these people too much slack, they want to take over.'

'Shipped it to a museum in London, haven't they?'

'Of course, that's where it should be.'

'But it's from here, it's not from London. Ali Baba would be amazed at some of the stuff in those places.'

'I'm going for a piss,' yawned Jabez. He rose to a standing position, arched and stretched his back and walked into the darkness some twenty yards from the fire. He had a troublesome bladder. Through the murk, over and above his own noise, he could hear the snorting of a herd of zebras and the yapping of wild dogs, but apart from that there was silence. There was a faint smell of something rotting closeby, a dead animal probably, but this was of no interest to him - his bladder came first.

'I despair of you sometimes, Gwyn,' said Jabez, as he returned to the campfire, poking a finger into his ear, trying to inconvenience an irritation. The close-set heat and compact light a comfort to him, he sat down on his haunches and leaned back on an elbow. Gwyn made no acknowledgement, looking into the fire, sitting upright, clasping his legs together with his arms, his hands intertwined.

'Time is on their side, Jab. My old man left Wales, couldn't have been more than eighteen years of age to come out here. Said it was his duty to help the Empire. Like a lapdog at his master's table, eager to please, waiting for some morsel to be thrown his way. Help them push the Beira and Mashonaland Railway north of the Zambesi, those were his very words. Through all obstacles. He called it the spearhead of civilization. And here I am adding a new episode, additions to a previous chapter. I've alighted in his story, that's the way the track was put down.'

'Philosopher Gwyn! It's just a job, that's all. Only good part is that we get to give the orders.'

'Dad told me we were an outpost of Empire. He told me about cuttings and embankments, gradients and earthworks, tracks and tunnels, rails and sleepers and ballast, ballast, ballast. We'd discuss whether a Class 16A Garratt was superior to a Class 9B, were the Zambezi Railways locos better maintained than the Rhodesia Railways locos. That was my childhood. If I'm lucky enough to have a son he'll be a Railwayman too. Picking perfect oranges directly from the trees, on a small patch of land, the land of a free railwayman. Drinking freshly ground coffee, clothes individually laundered...'

'And Murphy's, don't forget Murphy's. It caters for a mighty powerful craving. No one on God's earth can defeat that craving. It's inside everybody, no one created it. Maybe God did, if you want, but now it's just there. Couldn't get Murphy's at home. Chapels would soon close that place down. Preacher told me once, "Mr Pugh, Mr Pugh," he says, "the venom of the flesh leads directly to the soul of satan himself." That was chapel talk. Only good thing about them chapels was the singing. That's where I learnt to read my part and sing with Auntie Maisie. She brought me up on singing. We used to sing duets together. She had a fine voice. Mine ain't bad but it wasn't a patch on hers. She even suggested I go in for the ministry, go to Theology College back home. That way I'd have more of a chance of practicing music. Can you imagine that? Minister Jabez Pugh! Got a nice ring to it, ain't it? Doling out communion once a month, services three times of a Sunday. Devil got hold of me, but he let me keep my singing voice, that's good enough for me, everything else is just, well, bullshit.'

'Were your family railway people, Jab?' Gwyn lifted the collar on his tan flannel jacket, old military issue. He folded his arms together for warmth.

'Farmers mostly. My grandfather was a cattle drover, taking steers over the Cambrian Mountains to lowland markets over the border. Ain't an ounce of railways in me. We're from a small country, you and me. Still, more than enough jealousy to go around.'

'Dad was proud that he worked for Northern Rhodesia Railways, proud of Broken Hill.'

'That shithole built in a bloody hollow in the bush?'

'He drilled distances into me. He'd say, Gwyn, Broken Hill is the headquarters of the mighty Northern Rhodesia Railways, stretching one hundred and thirty miles northwards to the Belgian Congo, and two hundred and thirty miles southwards to the Zambesi River.'

'Not the kind of information that'd help you with them farm girls, I don't suppose. No wonder you never got far in that specialism.'

'I'd hear stories of the old country from Dad and Mam. They had a small library of books.'

'Don't tell me, railway books.' Jabez looked down on his hobnailed boots, dusty, worn, needing repairing.

'We had some of those. Mostly they were about lords and ladies, stately homes, kings and queens, nobles and aristocrats, immeasurable wealth and antique blood lines. Their window on home. We also used to get music sheets for piano and harp in old notation, and some traditional folk song books. They'd be in sol ffa.'

'Sound like a pretty narrow window to me, bar them music pieces.'

'And of course the Bible in the language.'

'You ever been to the old country, Gwyn? We ain't nobles and aristocrats. We don't all live in stately homes. Cold sleet-soaked winters are a mystery to you, ain't they? And here we are being told what to do by the chumocracy of big wigs, necking champagne in some so called gentlemen's club in London. They give us their boot now and again to lick, ram their podgy arses into our gobs. Their clout's held sway over these parts for a long time. Only thing they're interested in is taking as much loot out of this place as possible, and in as quick a time as possible. They ain't interested in anything, and I mean anything else.'

'Long time ain't forever, Jab. We had a distant cousin at home, on Mam's side. Didn't know what her name was. Every few months Mam would receive a bundle of magazines and newspapers from her. Ancient news from the ancient land. Even as a young boy I knew that package arriving day was an important one. Brown papered, sello-taped, white stringed, multiheaded stamped, emblazoned with post office officialdom. A day when the whole family sat around the kitchen table to see Dad, never Mam, perform the ritual opening. Cutting the white string with his knife, carefully scissoring away the brown paper. They kept the string and the paper, everything would be put to use sooner or later. And always the kitchen table, never on the verandah.

'The last parcel arrived in the summer of 1932. I never knew why the parcels stopped, don't think I ever asked. I was more interested in railways, crocodiles, spotted hyenas and lions, not in magazines from over the sea. They were glorious days. Glittering sunshine, late afternoon trips to the river, wild beasts and sunsets. Avocados ripening, strawberries reddening, bananas if we were lucky. Rocking chair lounging days, happy African days. Dinners of minced venison, Fray Bentos steak pies and corned beef. Brown Windsor soup, beef, potatoes, gravy and then plum duff with custard. Dad having a Woodbine on the verandah.

'The Railways have been good to us Jab, the pay, the climate allowance, the holidays...'

'No more than we deserve. This job ain't a picnic. We're bloody prisoners of the railway. I don't mind admitting I'm a Railwayman, that's my work, but I'm a Murphy's man when I don't work.' Jabez cupped his hands and blew into them. 'We better throw some more wood on this fire, else we'll freeze to death.'

'You speak much Bemba?' Gwyn asked.

'No need to, all of 'em speak English. Those missionaries brain-washed Africans good and proper, pushing religion down their gullets and all. Stole their way of living good and proper. Speak a few swear words though, that's enough.'

'Dad was the same. Enough to tell off and to praise. That's all the Bemba you need, that's what he told me.'

'Sounds like good advice. You've got to speak to 'em on our terms, keep 'em at arm's length. They get too close to you, then you're finished.'

'Some of their youngsters have almost forgotten the old ways. Speaking English all the time, ignoring their old language.'

'Means were doing something right out here then, doesn't it? Anyway, what language are we speaking now, oh Bard of Cambria? Same things happened to us. This ain't our language.'

'What's become of us, Jab?'

Jabez crossed his legs and pulled two fat cigars from his breast pocket.

'We've got to make the most of where we are, Gwyn. Here, been saving these.'

'For a rainy day?'

'It'll be a while till the rainy season. They'll have lost their flavour by then. Come on, have one. A present from one Welshman to another.'

'Diolch, Jab.'

Eyes reflecting the glow from the campfire and their cigars, unprompted, Jabez pitched a song from his family's hearth, a song Gwyn knew well.

'*I am dreaming of the mountains of my home,*
Of the mountains where in childhood I would roam.
I have dwelt 'neath Southern skies
Where the summer never dies,
But my heart is in the mountains of my home.

I can see the little homestead on the hill,
I can hear the magic music of the rill.
There is nothing to compare
With the love that once was there
In that lovely little homestead on the hill.

I can see the quiet churchyard down below
Where the mountain breezes wander to and fro,
And when God my soul to keep,
It is where I want to sleep
With those dear old folks who loved me long ago.'

Gwyn thought he saw his friend's eyes moisten. But it might have been the shadows from the flames.

'We're definitely the musical Celts, Jab.'

'Or Italians in the rain!'

'Remember when we used to sing that song in Welsh?'

'Long time ago, Gwyn, long time ago. Does it bring back old memories? They've forgotten all about us at home, I'm sure.'

'Do you ever have regrets, Jab? Things you've done in the past.'

'Regrets, yeah, I regret letting Schillacci get up from the floor in Murphy's. Should've sticked him dead like a wild pig, before he gave me this memento on my face. Now everyone sees the scar, no one sees Jabez. I am the scar. I am not Jabez. And if it's the scar the world sees, it's the scar the world's going to get. Don't want to disappoint no one.'

They both fell silent, puffing away, a chunky gordo each for company and solace.

XXVIII

THOMAS WAS ALONE with young David in his office.

'You know what to you have to do, David,' said Thomas.

Thomas wanted to make the task sound easy. He would speak calmly. But he knew so many things could go wrong.

'Yes, yes I do, Thomas,' replied David, doing his best to hide his stammer.

'When that train stops we've got to work fast. The loco driver is only going to stop the train for a few minutes in case it gets shunted from the passenger train heading up from Broken Hill.'

'How do we know the driver's going to stop?'

'Leave that to me. There are many of us in this war and he's one of them. He'll stop.'

'How do we know which cab will have the payroll money?'

'Should be only two carriages on the loco. The first will be empty, the second will have the wages.'

'Any guards? Who's looking after the money?'

'This ain't the Wild West, boy, ain't no town sheriff riding shotgun. This just the usual, quiet, ordinary Rhodesia Railways train from Livingstone to the Congo. Only this particular one happens to be carrying British South Africa Company wages for their boys in the Copperbelt.'

'If we take the money, our people won't be paid.'

'Course they'll be paid. What's one month's wages to BSAC? They got plenty of cash. Hold all the Copperbelt mining rights, it'll be a drop in the ocean for 'em. Probably got insurance anyhow. They just like the government, everyone steals from them, don't they? They'll be whistling up another shipment, another train with money in no time. But their money will help us. We need guns, that means we need cash. You sure you all right with this?'

'Long as no Bemba gets hurt. We supposed to free our people, not kill 'em.'

'Fine. One more time. I stop the train.'

'And you sure you can do that?'

'Told you before, driver and the stoker, they one of us. All you have to do is open the door on the second carriage and walk in. There'll be nothing in there save four mail sacks which will be tied at the top. Might even be open. Ignore them. With these sacks will be a mail pouch, slightly smaller, made of thick canvas, more substantial looking than the mail sacks. It'll have a drawstring or maybe staples at the top and be clearly marked BSAC, British South Africa Company. That's where the money will be. All you have to do is grab it. Once I see you get out of the carriage, I shake hands with the driver and the stoker, and I spend the money with some friends who've popped over from the Congo.'

'What's the driver and the stoker gonna say when they turn up at the main station in Kitwe without the BSAC wages?'

'They prepared for that.'

'Whatever they say, Railways, the police, ain't going to believe them. They going to jail, ain't they? They going to jail for a long time.'

Thomas was impressed by young David's questioning. This was promising. Revolution was a thinking man's game; dullards were not required.

'They might get away with it, they might not. The less time the train stops, easier it'll be for them to make up time and arrive at Kitwe station on schedule. If the train arrives on time, how they supposed to have stolen the money? The driver can't drive the train, the stoker can't shove coal into the fire box and at the same time walk back to the carriage and steal the money. That'd be a physical impossible thing to do.'

'What've you told 'em, Thomas? Do they know the risks to them here? Two of us can run into the bush with the money, no one will see you and me, but the driver and the stoker, they on the frontline.'

'We all on the frontline now, David. You in or not? Once you make the decision, ain't no turning back. I know this, driver and stoker know this. Ain't no innocents on this venture. This is the test we've been set.'

It was a moonlit night over the Kafue River bridge a few miles south of the mining town of Kitwe, near the border with the Congo, the base of the British South Africa Company. Thomas and David hid in the bush, below the level of the track on the north side, the Kitwe side of the bridge. Stung and chewed by unceasing insects, they squatted, silent, staring south into the blackness, listening for the train. David felt sick. Thomas told him to puke quietly, willing the train into view, unsure whether David's resolve would hold. The Kafwe river below them, gliding on its muddy cradle.

'How long now, Thomas?'

'Don't be jumpy, not long to go. Rhodesia Railways always run on time. Reckon we've got less than ten minutes before that loco plods up the incline and slows down to a crawl to get over this rickety old bridge.'

'What you got hidden in that blanket, Thomas? Been meaning to ask.'

'A little provision in case of unlikely eventualities.'

'What the hell you talking about? Let me see.'

Thomas handed the blanket to David. Inside was Gwyn's Winchester Model 70 rifle, the oiled stock glistening in the moonlight.

'What the hell did you bring this for? You said all I got to do is walk into the carriage, pick up the BSAC bag and walk away. Don't need a cannon for that!'

'It's just a precaution. Thought it might give you a bit of courage, that's all.'

'Don't need a gun to give me courage.'

'I know that. Take it anyway. Spent a load of time cleaning and shining the thing the other day. Only three bullets in it anyhow. Look, as long as you've got the safety where it is, it'll be as harmless as a caged drongo. Come on, take it.'

As agreed, the driver sounded the high-pitched whistle as the train started its climb from the valley up the hill towards the bridge.

Thomas had filled his Rhodesia Railways lantern three-quarters full with lamp oil, and screwed down the wick by turning the key on the side of the lantern. The wick had been saturated for a good half hour, turning darker as the oil became fully absorbed. As soon as Thomas heard the train whistle, he turned the lantern key to move the wick an inch above the burner tube.

'Right, David, get your matches out, light this thing.'

'Didn't you bring any? You're the one making the rules! You're the tobacco farmer!'

'You young ones always smoking something. Come on, light the wick.'

Fumbling in his breast pocket, David, his hands shaking, took out a packet of Swan Vestas. Removing one match from the box he dragged it against the side, breaking the match in two. Thomas stayed silent. The second match lit but the white phosphorus flame vanished in the breeze. Thomas had seen enough.

'Give the box to me, donkey.'

Thomas's first attempt was successful, and cupping the flame in his left hand, he lit the wick and closed the lantern, which started to emit a thick black smoke.

'Get the wick down, quick!' he hissed at David.

David turned the lantern key to lower the wick, but in his panic he lowered the wick too far and extinguished the flame. Thomas pushed David's hand roughly away, turned the key gently, lifting the wick, reigniting the flame.

'Right, David, this is it. Good luck, and take this with you. A rifle gives everybody courage!'

Thomas scrambled up the embankment and on to the bridge, waving the lantern left to right, right to left. The locomotive driver had clearly applied the brakes on the ascent to the bridge, and the train came to a complete halt just short of the southern side of the river.

He ran across the bridge with David behind him.

'Come on, David, this got to be quick.'

Within two minutes they'd crossed the bridge and reached the other side. Thomas quickly climbed the steps to the cab. David ran to the foremost door of the second carriage. The door being three feet above ground level, it opened before David could reach the trackside lever. A startled shout came from the inside.

'What's going on here? Why have we stopped?'

'Get back, get back from the door, get back inside!' shouted David.

'Who the hell are you?'

'Get back or I'll shoot.'

'Ok, ok, easy, I didn't mean nothing, don't shoot!'

The guard retreated. David slung the rifle over his shoulder and clambered into the carriage. Once inside David pushed the Winchester at the guard.

'Where's the BSAC money bag, where is it? And don't give me any bull!'

'Over there, boss.'

'Where?'

'In the corner over there.'

'Show me!'

The two of them scuttled to the far end of the carriage past the mail sacks, the guard first, David behind, poking the rifle barrel into the guard's back.

'Here they are, these two bags here.'

'Two! Should be only one.'

'Last month's wages weren't paid 'cos of the strike. Company decided to pay this month's wages and last month in one payment.'

'Come on, pick 'em up, bring 'em to the door.'

'Sure, boss, sure, only don't shoot!'

The railway guard brought the two bags to the carriage door.

'Put them down, let me have a look.'

Putting the rifle on his shoulder, David tore open the staples on top of one of the BSAC canvas bag, peered inside, and saw hundreds upon hundreds of freshly minted, cellophane-bound one pound and ten shilling notes. Transfixed by so much wealth,

David was shoved harshly to the carriage floor by the guard, who then jumped out of the cab, falling awkwardly on to the track and spraining his ankle. Within seconds Thomas was standing by the same door.

'What's going on?' shouted Thomas. 'I could hear the commotion from up front! Have you got the money, have you got the money?'

'There's two bags, not one!' replied David.

'Get down here, for Christ's sake, get down here! We've got to get rid of the guard! He saw you! We've got to get rid of him!'

David took aim at the guard, hobbling away, now forty yards distant. He squeezed the trigger.

'The safety, you idiot, take the safety off! He's getting away!' Thomas screeched.

David, floundering, did as he was told, then squeezed the trigger. The bullet missed the guard, who looked back briefly and kept on hobbling as fast as his injured ankle would allow.

'Again, try again! Move the bolt, move the bloody bolt! Need to get another cartridge into the chamber! He's getting away!'

'How do you do that? How do you do it?'

Thomas grabbed the rifle from him, and as calmly as he could, he lifted and rotated the bolt, engaging another bullet into the chamber. Wrapping the rifle strap around his left arm, he took aim and fired. The bullet hit the guard squarely in the back, and he fell face down on to the ground.

'Get the bags, get both of them,' Thomas ordered coldy, then ran to the front of the train, shouting, 'Go! Go!'

The pistons opened, the wheels slowly turned, moving the train sluggishly towards the bridge and onwards to the town of Kitwe.

Thomas shouted to David, as much in anger as to be heard above the noise from the train.

'We've got to get rid of the body. Leave the bags here. We'll throw him into the river, crocodiles will get him. Come on!'

As they reached the downed guard, they could both hear his muffled groans.

'He's alive, he's still alive!' shrieked David.

'Shoot him,' Thomas ordered, offering the rifle to David.

'He's Bemba, he's one of us!'

Without debating the matter further, Thomas lifted and rotated the bolt on the Winchester.

He shot the guard just below the nape of his neck, killing him instantly.

'He's the one we supposed to be liberating!'

Thomas had no time for philosophers that evening. 'Shut up, just shut up!' he barked. 'Help me to pick him up, we'll throw him over the bridge.'

David felt muddled, agitated, tiny. Thomas triumphant.

XXIX

IT WAS COLD in the town of Kitwe, the comforting sun still many hours away.

'Come in, my friends, welcome to Kitwe on this cold night,' Thomas greeted his visitors, who emerged out of the pitch-dark street. Thomas needed to sound in control, secure. It was very late; he was always in bed at this time. He was chilly. The two callers had condescending eyes and noiseless, narrow grins. Thomas found it difficult to take their measure.

He ushered the visitors to the back of the room furthest from the main door, pointed to some shaky chairs around a compact wooden table, and tugged closed a long, blue woollen curtain, boxing the three of them into a small, private, candlelit scullery. The uneven walls were covered by old flock wallpaper which stunk of dampness, and behind which various spiders, cockroaches and other insects were going about their business.

'Can I offer you some refreshments, gentlemen? My home is humble but you will find my hospitality second to none. Something to drink, munkoyo perhaps, recently brewed? Or something stronger, some chipumu?'

'Thank you, no, we are both fine, save as you can see I have a heavy cold.'

The man pulled out a sodden white handkerchief from his trouser pocket and blew the contents of his nose into it. He was young, early to mid- twenties like Thomas, hungry-looking, lanky, with a week's growth of beard. An attempt, Thomas suspected, of hiding his cratered face – probably chicken pox as a child, he thought. His companion was older, also long and lean, perhaps the same family even, both with a noticeable gap between their large front teeth. Clean shaven, with a clever face, the older man could have easily passed for a university professor, but of course he couldn't possibly have been one; those days had not yet arrived. Thomas hoped the results of their meeting would help to bring that day forward. Surely even the Congo would change one day.

'As you wish,' Thomas replied.

The room was silent, soundless seconds passing before the younger man spoke.

'Sakania, although in the Belgian Congo, is not that far away, and we have been well fed and refreshed. I am told that I am to call you Thomas. My own name is Augustin. My friend speaks no English, although he speaks French excellently. Is French a language known to you?'

'Afraid he has an advantage over me on that score,' Thomas said.

'You will therefore need to speak to me only, and please forgive me if I speak in French to my comrade if the need arises.'

Thomas's tactic was a subtle watchfulness, as if approaching a stray dog who might or might not be rabid.

'And your comrade, what is his name?'

'That need not concern you. He is a man of business. An excellent chess player. Indeed, he taught me the beautiful game. A man of honour and I can vouch for him, as your friends vouched for you.'

Augustin smiled, nodded slightly, bidding Thomas to carry on the conversation.

'Well then, we know why we're here. I am in the market for weapons.'

'Ah, weapons, Thomas, those most cheerless of instruments. I admit that my English is not the best, so tell me, what do you mean by weapons? Revolvers, hand grenades, machine guns, rifles? Or even the modest chicote? That also has a way of inflicting pain.'

Augustin, hands clasped gently on the table, looking priest-like.
'A chicote?'

'A simple whip. Helps the Force Publique maintain order in
Sakania, indeed throughout Katanga and all of the Congo. Very useful
and very cheap. As you know, we are all monstrous devils in the
Congo.'

'I was thinking of rifles. Do you have any of those to sell?'

'Anything you want to buy, we can sell. We trade in all things,
coffee, copper, uranium, women, or boys if you are so inclined. We
make no judgement, we are merely here to supply what the customer
desires. We are uncomplicated men, our business is commerce, pure
and simple. We let the priests and the politicians do the judging. After
all, they have far more wisdom than we do.'

Augustin lifted his eyebrows as if to say, 'Is it not so?'

'Rifles, all I want is rifles and ammunition, nothing else.'

'My friend, you have come to the correct bazaar. We are experts
in that field. The Mauser Model 1935 bolt action rifle, standard issue
for the Belgian army and the Force Publique. Four point three kilo-
grammes weight, one thousand one hundred millimeters in length,
seven-point-six-five calibre cartridges, five round box magazine.
Excellent hunting weapon, good for buffalo and zebra. Are you a
hunter, my friend?'

'I am a hunter of sorts. How many rifles do you have and how
much do they cost?' Thomas shifted in his chair to hide his impa-
tience and stroked his petite beard.

'Ah, you people from the lowlands, always hotter in spirit than us
slower, cooler folks from the hills. Do you know that Sakania is almost
thirteen hundred metres above sea level? Forgive me, how much is
that for you? Over four thousand feet, is it not? A long way up from
the hot plains, a cold place in the winter, a place where you have time
to think, to consider matters over a hot bowl of broth. A place that
gives you influenza.'

Augustin examined his handkerchief, looking for a suitable dry
spot and blew into it again.

'You were told I wanted rifles,' Thomas said.

'Yes, that is true, Thomas.'

'Are those... what did you call them?'

'Mauser Model 1935.'

'Are these Mausers any good?'

'They have a proud history of killing from Europe to our Cites Indigenes. Oh, forgive me again, the native neighbourhoods in my country. Our colonial officers and our local askari soldiers speak highly of them and use them with pride. The Mauser knows how to deal death to animal or human, it discriminates against no one. After all, killing is such an uncomplicated event.'

'Are they as good as this?'

Augustin whistled aloud as Thomas produced Gwyn's rifle from under a blanket.

'A Winchester rifle, if I am not mistaken. Do not flaunt luxury before a jealous man.'

'Model 70, the best,' boasted Thomas, as if displaying a prize heifer at a county show.

'My friend, if you can lay your hands on such a trophy, why the need to come to my unworthy marketplace?'

'Need to show you I know what I'm talking about when it comes to rifles, save any confusion between us. Wouldn't want nothing to get muddled up between the four point three kilogramme weight, the one thousand one hundred millimetre length, the seven-point-six-five calibre cartridges and the five round box magazine.'

'Touché, my friend! It looks as if we are all experts in this field of work.'

'How many can you deliver, how long will it take?'

No Congolese middleman was going to get the better of Thomas, rabid dog or no rabid dog. The coughing general grade ticket clerk was schooling himself in the tones of the Congolese middleman. He would not be humbled by anyone.

'We must agree a price first, mon amie.'

'In winter the temperature here in my hometown of Kitwe, although not cold, is cool enough for thought. How many rifles can you deliver and how long will it take?'

'Bravo again! For such important questions I will need to confer with my business associate. Such a pity that so many different

European countries invaded our continent. If it had only been one we could all have been speaking the same tongue, but c'est la vie.'

Augustin ignored Thomas completely and turned to his partner, speaking mostly French, interspersed with Swahili, some words of which Thomas understood as they were similar to the Bemba language. But the rapidity of the discussion, and the fact that both merchants held their hands close to their mouths, made it impossible for Thomas to fully understand what was being said.

'My business partner wishes to know how many rifles you wish to buy. Are we talking about hunting one zebra or a herd of zebra, a hunting party of two or three, or a hunting party of say a hundred? Before you answer, remember the devil has no standing in our universe.'

'It will be a large hunting party,' Thomas replied. 'Say three hundred. There are very many zebras in Africa.'

'To bring the hunt to a successful conclusion you will therefore need many rifles and many bullets, for every bullet has a place and every bullet should bring a conclusion. But remember, killing is hideous, habit forming. Once you start, you will have to do it again and again. But if that is your wish we will supply all your needs.'

'Good news indeed. We can discuss payment once I see the numbers and quality of the merchandise. You know of my funding arrangements, but let that not overegg your ambitions when we come to negotiate prices.'

'I see you are a true negotiator. You will find us more than reasonable. You will receive full value from us for your payment. We will see ourselves out, thank you.'

'Good night then.'

'And good night to you.'

The two Congolese bowed their heads slightly, drew open the woollen curtain, closed it, and passed into the ebony street outside, disappearing like molten ingots in a furnace. It had started to snow, shavings from above vanishing once they alighted.

Thomas was pleased with himself, and with the evening's work. If only they could see him now in Kapiri Mposhi. He heard a barking dog, but the sound was soon swallowed by the night.

XXX

DELYTH WAS CHANGING, I could see that. Northern Rhodesia does that to settlers; they don't stay hundred per cent Europeans for long. They can't help it. Dare I say it, they're moulded into Africans. But that would be going too far, wouldn't it? Some turn into buffoons, some turn out wiser, some turn out dead.

'Looking back, Daisy, I thought it was too good to be true,' said Delyth. 'That travelling salesman never really wanted to know me. I meant only one thing to him. I should have asked who was this man, who was he really? Who were his family? Did he have any money? Did he have any past? I didn't ask any questions, but then again why would I? It was my body, it was my decision. But does love always come with misery and punishment?'

'Shush now,' I said, 'forget about that man. You've got Gwyn now, you've got me, and most importantly, you've got the baby. We're all here for one another. We'll be together forever whatever happens.'

I had no desire to probe any further into Delyth's past. It would help no one. After all, who can say that they are truly happy?

'One of the boys in my class actually slipped on a banana, on a bloody banana! Fell smack on his face, broke his nose, blood every-where. Headmaster Bennett said it was my fault. I should have shown more application, he said, should have kept the classroom clear and safe for children. More application! In a place which didn't think twice about being dripped in monkey guts and suffocating a live bullfrog to death!'

'It's all done now, all in the past. You've got so much to look forward to, you'll never change what's gone,' I replied.

Delyth started crying again.

'But why should I be the victim, Daisy? Because I'm a woman? Is it God? God seeking revenge because I didn't hold Mam's hand tighter? Is it something my family's done?'

I was scrambling for an answer. 'We're all passengers, Delyth, on a journey. If we travelled forever, the same experiences would in the end occur to all of us. Good things, bad things...'

'And you're saying I'm in the bad things phase, and that good things are sure to happen. How long do you have to wait for that to happen? That's Moriah Congregational Chapel talk.'

'I'm no prophet. Leave that to the religious people. No one's life can be all rotten. Remember the fun we had when we went swimming?'

'And then I had bilharzia. That sums it up, doesn't it?'

'I'm sorry, I didn't think,' I said. 'I shouldn't have brought that up. Gwyn will be back on leave in a few days. I'm sure he can't wait to see you. He makes you happy, he makes us both happy.'

'Ever since they discovered zinc and lead this place hasn't been the same. All those ruffians employed by that mining company... What's it called again, it's got a grand name.'

'The Rhodesia Broken Hill Development Company?'

'Those miners spend their money in that horrible Murphy's, pay their money to those indecent women, no need for polite conversation or long-term commitment... This travelling salesman I met, he was in the farm implement business, puffing on that showy calabash pipe. Always going on about his calabash pipe, the meerschaum bowl, his disgusting breath, his disgusting little jokes. I should have known. The thing is, I wasn't used to failing with men. I never used to drift meekly into disasters.'

'You lost both your parents at a young age, Delyth. You had no one to guide you.'

What could I do to help? I wasn't her judge, I wasn't her saviour either.

'He had a sideline, he bought Virginia flue-cured tobacco from a farmer in Fort Jameson, Eastern province, and then sold it retail to whoever he could persuade to purchase. Everyone said it was top quality stuff, he told me he sold agricultural equipment for his employer, but the tobacco he sold for himself. He had great plans for his tobacco business and he wanted me to be part of it.'

'And you believed him?' I asked.

'I believed him.'

XXXI

RHODESIA RAILWAYS had sent up from Livingstone one of their new track laying machines, with the capacity of laying a section of fourteen connected sleepers into place as one block. This would be the first time any of the men had used it.

'This is the end for us, boss,' said Kabwe, staring at Daniel. 'That there can do the work of fourteen men easy. What'll be left for us to do?'

'There'll be plenty left for them that keep ahead of the game, Kabwe,' replied Daniel. 'Granted things don't stay the same on the Railways forever, same as this country, but as long as you see which way the wind is blowing, you go with that and you'll be all right. It's them that don't go with the wind will do the suffering.'

'Look at us, look at young David, even Ephraim. Staring at the new machine. They're like kids seeing snow for the first time. This contraption's going to make them all poor. How you gonna pick and choose, boss? Who's gonna get work, who's gonna be idle when Bowen asks you for less men. Who you gonna disappoint, who you gonna make happy?'

'I'll make you happy, Kabwe, don't you worry. Ain't no problem there, as long as you keep that hair on your head in line. You ever cut it, boy? Need to fix you a meeting with my scissor-man, that's for sure. As for the others, let that be my problem.

Always opportunities in problems, and I'm good with problems. Bemba'll be ok.'

'It's those Indians and Chinamen, should go back where they belong, right?' asked Kabwe.

Daniel stayed silent, didn't look at Kabwe but down at his own feet, gave a slight smile which Kabwe took to be his agreement.

'This is some machine, Jabez. It's going to save time and money for the Railways.'

'Looks good, Gwyn. We won't need half as many men from now on if we can get our hands on this. You ok for Daniel to supervise the work? Think he's up to it?'

'Daniel'll be fine. I'll leave you to it, Mr Pugh. He'll be on the crane and I'll be back in the station with Thomas. Any problems give a shout. Don't see any issues here, work is all pretty straightforward.'

There were six rail sections to lay, comprised of fourteen sleepers each. Jabez, operating a small crane from the back of a flatbed rail truck, would lift one section at a time. Once hoisted off the truck, the crane would position the section in front of and in line with the track already in place, then manoeuvre the piece on to the sleepers with the help of the navvies positioned either side of the section; finally, the navvies would lever the section into its precise resting place.

'It's up to us today, boys,' said Jabez,' the Railways is trying out this new equipment on us, to see if we're up to it. We're on the frontline. There'll be no Mr Bowen, so let's get on with this nice and easy. We'll lay the first three then have a break. Once we get the hang of it, should be easy. Daniel, choose your men, equal strength on both sides. Don't want the section falling lopsided.'

'Right,' said Daniel, 'Desai, Cowboy Chowdhury, you'll get the chance to do some real work today.' He grabbed Chowdhury roughly by the arm, leading him to the railway line. Chowdhury hobbled after, his stoop accentuated by Daniel's pulling. Desai followed behind, still biting his nails, still with retribution on his mind.

'Ready!' shouted Jabez. 'All you boys ready?'

'Ready, Mr Pugh, we're all ready here.'

Carefully manipulating the levers on the crane, Jabez lifted the first section off the flatbed, steering it as close as possible to the completed track on the ground.

Even though it was a windless day, there was still movement once the track was airborne, swinging above the navvies' heads. Numerous arms were raised to stabilise its motion before it reached the ground, to be connected with the waiting section of track.

'Slow down a bit, Mr Pugh, just a bit, need to get our hands on the track.'

'OK, Dan, OK.'

Twenty-eight upstretched hands attached themselves to the hovering track – first Daniel, the tallest, and finally John, the shortest. A danse macabre on the veldt, an adagio pirouette, clasped in a dependent, smelly, blaspheming bond.

'Gently, boys, gently. Stop, Mr Pugh, stop! It's down.'

David disconnected the crane mechanism from the track.

'Kabwe, Ephraim, Smiler, get the crowbars. Let's slide her into place.'

Kabwe didn't like Daniel's tone. Ephraim spat on the savannah. George thought about the women he knew.

'Quit gobbin', will ya, keep your mind on them crowbars,' shouted Daniel.

After some effort, the first section was successfully laid. After a further two sections were in place, Jabez descended from the crane, shouting, 'Brew up, boys, time for a cup of Lipton's. We're too far away from the station to get some hot water, we'll use the water from the loco.'

A tremor of disappointment went round the experienced navvies.

'What's the problem, Mubanga,' asked David. 'We've worked hard enough this morning. We've earned a tea break.'

'It's the water, David, the boiled water from the loco to make the tea. The train boys gotta put some charcoal into the boiler to stop it rusting, makes the water smack of piss, and no amount of tea leaves takes that away. Jabez, he too testy to send someone back to the station for clean water. He just wants to see us suffer. Bowen'll be on the good stuff with Thomas, and we'll be on the swill.'

'But so will Jabez.'

'Jabez don't care, he'll drink anything.'

As predicted by old man Mubanga, the tea did taste like piss –
buffalo, zebra or rhino no one could agree, but definitely piss. Jabez
took his tea alone in the cab of the small crane. Everyone was glad of
that.

'Hey, John, what's that dribble coming out of your nose?' asked
Jimmy.

'What do you mean?' John replied.

'You've got a nosebleed. Work too hard for you, heat too much?
Make sure you hide that before Daniel sees it. Any excuse with him
and you'll get us all sacked.'

John tore a piece of frayed cotton from his shirt, stuffed it up his
nostril, making sure that none of it was in sight. The day was hot.
Chowdhury was sweating; they were all sweating, droplets descending, criss crossing over foreheads, down necks, down backs. Some of
the men blew upwards at their noses, dislodging the drizzle; others
used their forearms; others did nothing. Shirts were discoloured,
glued to backs, flies were swept away constantly, but the flies
endured, steady, unrelenting, and many more in reserve.

Twenty minutes later, they were back at it. Jabez in the crane,
fourteen navvies piloting the section into place. Two further sections
down, one to go.

'All the boys can stand down,' shouted Daniel. 'Cowboy, Desai,
John and me will be on the crowbars for this last one. Let's see if you
get a sweat up, Indians. You two stay on one side. And, John, keep
working those yellow hands with me till I tell you to stop. You boys
need to do some work for the Rhodesian Railways shilling.'

Chowdhury and Desai looked over at Daniel and John from the
opposite side of the track, small pellets of sweat dribbling down their
noses.

'Getting the hang of it now, Cowboy,' cried Daniel. 'Never seen
you work so hard. Might be a place for you people on the Railways
after all, long as you know your place. Ain't that right, Desai?'

'Want me to take over from John?' offered Chola. 'Ain't much of
him. Needs two strong 'uns both sides with these crowbars.'

Chola had always been in Chibwe's shadow, but no longer, now that Chibwe was unfit for work. Chola had no enemies, no vanity; he was probably the only one of the navvies who enjoyed the work, being out in the bush. All the others were being ground down, peppercorns between pestle and mortar. But Chola was glad of the escape of labour. His family life had never been of any worth, his mother overbearing, his three brothers no friends of his, his father dead. Labouring in heat, outdoor work, ingesting insects, with people to talk to, a pay packet, food... Could there be anything better?

'No problem,' answered Daniel. 'Chola, me and John here will be more than enough to keep the rail up against those two Asians, you'll see. All the hard work's done by the crane, John and me will have it easy.

'Bring it down, Mr Pugh. Easy, easy, that's good,' Daniel called up to the crane. 'Right, my Indian friends, it's you two now against me and John. You know what to do. We've almost got a good fit here anyway. Ready, lift! Lift it, you Indian bastards, put your backs into it!'

Any animal with a nose for miles around could have sniffed out the sweaty navvies, raising their arms into the air as one.

'Let me help them, boss,' Chola offered again. 'They're looking all in.'

'Tired, Chola? They've done nothing all morning. I've been keeping an eye on those two idiots. They've been resting on those crowbars, bunch of lazy slackers, letting all the others do the work. John, you can stand down. Two Indians to one Bemba, seems about right to me. Use the same crowbar, start working like proper navvies!'

'You sure you're ok, boss? Let me help you. Two men on one crowbar and you the only one on the other. Don't want the track to be out of balance.'

'Shut up, Chola, shut up!' Daniel's eyes bulged like a bullfrog, whether from the strain of taking the weight of the rail or his unwelcome appeals, Chola wasn't sure. 'Those two might as well do some work now, 'cos I'll make sure they won't get hired on the next job! You hear that, Chowd, Desai? You won't be on this railway long, won't be able to pay your rent, won't be able to eat! Right, one, two, three, lift! One, two, three, *lift!*'

By this time all the navvies had thronged around Daniel's side of the track. Jabez, still in the crane about to light a cigarette, unconcerned, was daydreaming of Murphy's.

'He should calm down, the boss should calm down. Tell him, Kabwe!' said Chola.

'No use,' replied Kabwe. 'He's gone, no one can get to him when he's in this mood.'

'One, two, three, *lift!* That's better almost there. One, two, three, *lift!*'

Chowdhury felt a small nudge on his shoulder from Desai, just enough for him to glance over to him. Desai, although holding the crowbar with both hands, was not exerting any downward force. All the weight on their side was now being carried by Chowdhury.'

'Come on, move it, you bastards, move it over!' shouted Daniel.

'I can't carry the weight, boss, we just can't carry the weight!' shrieked Chowdhury.

'Shut up, she's almost in place, come on!' replied Daniel, his neck one chunk of taught muscle.

'I've got to let go! Move back, boss, move back from the section!'

'Don't even bloody think of it!' retorted Daniel.

Chowdhury's arms burned with the effort. He felt the crowbar slip. His side of the section dropped sharply to the ground, causing the opposite side, Daniel's side, to ricochet backwards, hitting Daniel's right leg violently, breaking the tibia instantly like an unboiled bantam egg, crushing the metatarsals in his foot.

Screaming in Bemba, then in English, 'Help me, help me! Get it off!'

Daniel's dislocated ankle at a right angle to his broken leg. The men stepping back, pushing against the others like a breaking wave.

'Chola,' Kabwe shouted, 'George, help me with the crowbar! Let's get the rail off him!'

Hearing Daniel's screams, Jabez jumped down from the crane.

'What's happened, what's happened here?'

His voice barely audible over Daniel's cries.

'It's those bloody Indians, Chowdhury and Desai! Couldn't hold

the weight, couldn't hold the weight of their side of the track!'
shouted Kabwe.

'What, the two of them, the two of them couldn't hold it? Why
were they there? They're not our strongest? And why was Daniel on
his own on his side? Someone should've been with him. Move him,
move him to one side. Chola, run back to the station, tell Mr Bowen.
Get back here on the Pump Trolley. Get some splints and morphine.

'Ok, Dan, ok, we're getting help. You'll be okay.' Jabez looking
down on the screaming, shattered human being.

Daniel's shrieks subsided to sobbing tears – not the tears of pain,
but the tears of knowing that his working days on the Rhodesian
Railways were over. His right leg, his right foot, bloody, moist and
warm.

'Come on, men, let's get the section spannered on before Mr
Bowen gets here. Mubanga, you stay with Daniel,' said Jabez.

None of the navvies demurred. Jabez started the crane, lifting the
section, bringing it back down, four men on four separate crowbars
either side of the track, the last segment laid within yards of Daniel's
wretched, mangled body.

Shortly after the incident with Daniel, Gwyn decided to go back home
for a few days leave. The incident had troubled him. To outsiders he
hoped that his relationship with Daniel was perceived as that of a
trusted colleague, but for all the secrets he kept from the world, this
was one he could not keep from himself.

Gwyn found it very difficult to share his emotions with anyone.
Perhaps the accident had happened at an opportune time; the injuries, although life changing, were not life threatening. Accidents
always happened on the Railways, all the men knew this. Gwyn, in
the presence of the other navvies, wished Daniel well and did his best
to hide his emotions. He left the minimal repatriation duties to Jabez.
There wouldn't be much in that. And as for the paperwork, Jabez
would do the right thing. Gwyn and Jabez had had plenty of practice
over the years. If Gwyn didn't take his leave he would lose the
entitlement; besides, he was curious as to how Daisy and Delyth were
getting on under the same roof.

Daniel would become a statistic, would go back to living in his village. Gwyn would not visit him. That particular relationship, for Gwyn, had run its course. His relationships were always short, always brief; he'd always covered his tracks well. Lying was a necessity in Northern Rhodesia.

Gwyn would soon discover that brown Windsor soup, beef, potatoes and gravy, and most of all plum duff, were becoming something of a rarity in the Bowen household.

XXXII

DELYTH AND I were talking again of events gone by.

'That bloody travelling salesman lodged at the Great Northern Hotel when he was in town,' she said. 'He'd visit that bully headmaster Bennett, wearing his purveyor-of-top-quality-Virginia-flue-cured tobacco hat. That's when I first met him. He was very polite, called me Miss Jenkins to begin with. Looking back he must have thought I was an idiot. One of the new settler families, on her own, no parents, wet behind the ears. I'd only known him for three weeks, said he had some paperwork to do and could we meet after school in his hotel room? It all happened in that room. There wasn't much to it really. Fumblings and sweaty touches. Nothing. I don't think we even kissed! No forging of mouths for us, not even a bloody encirclement! I hadn't been with one single man before that, ever – well, not properly. The conception, such as it was, lasted seconds. So nothing, it was nothing at all.'

'But you're carrying something precious inside you now. I can see that, all the world sees that,' I said.

'I stayed the night, I don't think he even asked me if I wanted to stay, probably wanted me to go home. Afterwards, after the event, I asked him for a cup of tea. He said the hotel didn't do room service. He got up early the following morning, said he had to catch the six thirty train north to Sakania on the border with the Belgian Congo. I asked him when we could meet again, and that's when he told me.'

'You don't need to tell me all this, Delyth. I can see it's upsetting you, and it's none of my business.'

Oh, I felt so sorry for her. Better to not to have loved, and not to have lost, than to love at all. And I have to say I felt as embarrassed in the listening as I think Delyth felt in the telling. There was no need for her to hurt herself like this.

'I want to, Daisy. I've got no one else to talk to. You're my mother now.'

I wondered whether Gwyn was her father. He would never make a husband. I'd met men like Gwyn before, in my working days, men who didn't want to admit what they were, that had lied so much and so long, that had buried themselves in their work or in desires without emotion. But Gwyn had love in him, I hoped, for me. But as for Delyth I wasn't too sure, or so I told myself.

'He'd actually opened the door to go. He had to hold it open with his foot so that he could get his case and bloody catalogue books out of the room. That's when he told me, told me he was married, that he had two children whom he loved dearly, that he couldn't leave them, that he'd be lost without them.'

'What did you say, Delyth?' It wasn't meant to be prying; I don't really know why I even asked the question.

'I don't know. I started crying. I pulled the sheets tightly up to my chin. I was naked in that bed and I *felt* naked. Alone again. He said he'd miss his train, said he was terribly sorry. That was the last I ever saw of him.'

'I'm so sorry, Delyth, so so sorry.' I had seen the smoking settler salesman sort so many times before: a skirt, half a smile, these were enough for them. But I had thought this only happened to Bemba women.

'I didn't go to school for a few days, told them I had a cold and a sore throat. I was on my own, I had time to think, and that's where Moriah Congregational Chapel came to my aid.'

'You found God, did you, Delyth?'

'Not quite. Both my parents were zealous chapel people. Nothing wrong with that. I'm sure it helped them a lot, gave them comfort. After all, they had more than enough worries to go round.

Do you know Moriah, Daisy? It's built on a small hill just south of town.'

'I think I know where it is.' I knew it; in fact, I knew quite a few of the congregation – the male ones, their drinking habits and their other preferences too.

'Three times every Sunday. Morning service at ten, Sunday School two thirty, time for the women to wash up after Sunday lunch, evening service at six. There was also a bimonthly prayer meeting every other Wednesday at seven in the evening. But fair play to my parents, I wasn't forced to attend if I didn't want to. How I disliked Sundays. Thank my lucky stars my presence at prayer meetings was even more infrequent. They clashed with my piano lessons with Miss Frost, you see.

'Once that bastard had left me, I was determined to find someone, anyone within reason, who could provide marriage and respectability, not for me but for my baby. I had no doubt I'd be a mother, and a single mother in this place hasn't got a chance. Getting rid of the child was clearly out of the question; after all, I'm a Christian. Between bouts of crying and feeling sorry for myself, I was rummaging through my handbag looking for a handkerchief, and I found an old shopping list. I'd normally discard that scrap of paper. What's the use of an old shopping list? But I wrote down on that paper the names of all those boys of around my own age who were with me in Sunday School. I thought of listing my government school classmates as well, but they were from a medley of religions, some of them far too exotic for me. And besides, I didn't want to disrespect my dead parents. Moriah Congregational Chapel Sunday School attendees would meet the bill.'

'The bill?'

'Potential husbands. That shopping list wasn't a long one. I'd done my big shop a few days earlier, I'd thrown that list anyway. My roll call of husbands would have to be succinct and pertinent. I didn't want to spread the net too widely, so to speak. I was in enough of a pickle as it was. In fact, after taking into account the shortcomings of my memory, social mobility, marriages, total unsuitability, death... there was only one name left on that shopping list.'

'Gwyn?'

'I'm afraid so.'

'It's one thing to have a name, it's another thing to do something about it.'

'I knew Gwyn worked on the Railways. After all, most male settlers are either railwaymen, farmers or miners.'

'Or travelling salesmen.'

'Very funny, Daisy. My travelling salesmen days were over. Their trade value, as you may have guessed, was somewhat tarnished. The scalded palm is the finest schoolteacher. I made enquiries of acquaintances at Moriah and discovered, as I'd suspected, that Gwyn wasn't married.'

It wasn't just me, then, who understood what Gwyn was like. Before Delyth, and after a number of months in his household, Gwyn and I had lived a close life – understanding each other's needs, when I wanted to be on my own, when he wanted company. I couldn't say we were exactly husband and wife, but we were as close as two people could be; we shared the same bed, we shared companionship – but not passion. That can be coarse and pitiless. And of course in public we shared nothing. We could never be seen walking the streets of Broken Hill together. I think I'd call it love. I'm not sure what Gwyn would call it.

'You know him well. Does he look the marrying type to you? He'd only marry if hunted. Or trapped. If he got a girl into trouble or the like. I was told he was very often upcountry with his work, but that when on leave in Broken Hill on a Saturday morning he would invariably go shopping at Patel's Grocery on Broadway at nine o'clock sharp. Some of the parishioners told me that Gwyn and Mr Patel were good friends, but I dismissed this as nasty gossip. Clearly that couldn't be true. Europeans and Indians, you know...'

'No, clearly not, Delyth.'

'We met next to the paraffin-powered refrigerator. Romantic isn't it? The smell from that paraffin was horrendous. I was about to put some venison mince in my basket, and I made sure my arm brushed his as I tried to get past him through those narrow aisles they have at Patel's.

' "Gwyn, isn't it? Gwyn from Moriah Chapel? I haven't seen you since, I don't know, since poor old Tom Fletcher's funeral." I was a ticking clock. It wasn't a time for meekness.'

'Gwyn's not very relaxed in the company of women,' I said. 'He probably wanted to disappear back to the bush rather than make small talk.'

'I knew it was my parents' fault. I wished they'd sent me to social skills classes every Sunday. "How to Entrap a Potential Husband in an Indian Grocery Store." Instead of the usual Sunday farce on the superiority of Protestant Nonconformism and loving your fellow man!

'It was as if I was looking for ripe grapes in the middle of a snowstorm. It would soon have been, "Nice to have met you, goodbye..." Project Shopping List on the verge of wipe out. But my guardian angel must have been watching. Fray Bentos came to my rescue!

' "I see you like venison mince," Gwyn said, "but I have to say, Fray Bentos steak and kidney pie is my favourite." And with that, slowly, very slowly we were up and running. Or should I say, up and stumbling forward.

'We saw quite a lot of one another over the next few days. Some days I was quietly hopeful, other days grimly anxious. I was finding it difficult to hide my fears, not to mention trying to hide the physical changes which were happening to me.

' "What about going for Sunday lunch to the Great Northern Hotel?" Gwyn suggested. "It's the best hotel in town; they say the roast beef's excellent there..." If only he'd known.'

' "No, no thanks," I replied, "I've never much liked the place."

' "Oh, I'm sorry," he said. "I only want to show how much you mean to me."

' "And you mean so much to me, Gwyn," I said. "We don't have to go to some posh hotel to have a lovely time together. I've heard stories about that hotel anyway."

' "What kind of stories?"

' "You know, stories of married men taking their strumpet girlfriends there. Meals delivered to the room, promises made and broken. We don't want that for us, do we?"

'Gwyn said, "I'm not like that, Delyth. I've never been like that."
So it continued, and we got married. And they say that the best things
in a marriage happen in the beginning.'

Oh, poor Delyth, I thought. She would never become drunk with
life. For her heaven was hidden.

'So you got what you wanted?' I asked.

'At long last I wasn't holding a losing hand, but as you can see,
misfortune is never far away from the Jenkins family, is it, Daisy?
You can tell Gwyn the whole story if you want. It'll be just another
problem I've got to face. You would have thought that I'd be used to
them by now.'

'Why did you even tell me, Delyth? It's as if you're trying to hurt
yourself. Is that what it is? We all love you, we're all here for one
another. No one is out to hurt you. You must try and believe that. Lean
on us, lean on me and Gwyn.'

'Thanks, Daisy, but I think I'll go to bed now. Confessions are very
tiring. Will you excuse me?'

Now I was confused as well. Delyth had descended into my life; I
hadn't asked for her. Maybe there was a devil in me wishing she'd
disappear and leave Gwyn to me as we were before. But I couldn't
stop myself from feeling sorry for her. We were all trapped, the three
of us, one way or another. I could close my eyes and concoct a
different scenario, but that was, of course, just dreaming. I didn't have
an answer, but I wasn't daunted by the situation. Why should there
be answers for everything? Couldn't someone be loyal to two lovers?

But who was the devil and who was the saint? What if there aren't
any devils and there aren't any saints? I was not going to torment
myself over this.

In any event, a baby is blameless.

XXXIII

THE NEXT MORNING I was sitting outside on the verandah reading the *Bulawayo Chronicle*.

'Morning, Daisy,' said Delyth.

'Morning. Sleep well? I notice you haven't washed the dishes for a couple of days now, Delyth. We did agree. I'd cook and you'd do the cleaning up.'

'I know, I know, it's just...'

'And you get up later and later every day. Is everything ok?'

'Anything in that today,' said Delyth, nodding to the newspaper on my lap. 'I thought only Europeans read the *Chronicle*.'

'I usually read the *Northern News* but found this lying about,' I replied. 'I keep a pile of old newspapers, gives me something to read now and again. It caters for the settlers all right. Only time you read about people like me is if we've thieved cattle from a poor white widow, or if there's been a fight between Bantus or such like. Gwyn and I can't stand the rag, but it's always good to know what the opposition think. Last month they had a story about a European woman who wanted to paint pictures of wildebeest on the veldt. She was out all day with her housemaid and died a few days later from heatstroke. Paper said it was all the housemaid's fault for not insisting the wretched white woman wear a hat.'

'It's those nasty Europeans again, isn't it?' said Delyth.

'This country is yours now. It doesn't belong to the Bemba any-more. You used to aim guns at us, now you aim lawyers' fancy fountain pens and bulky Bibles. The result is just the same. Gwyn offered to take me last year – me, mind you, his Bemba housekeeper – to a square-dancing evening at some white folks' farm miles outside town. I thought he'd lost his mind, got a fever or something. Europeans always want some hustle and bustle taking place. Far too busy to stand still. Almost as bad as when he bought me a mango in the market last year. I pretended that he'd bought it as part of my monthly allowance.'

'So it didn't make the *Chronicle* then?'

'No, it didn't, but Gwyn should have been more careful. Things can happen here very suddenly, and not always for the best.'

'My parents always read the *Chronicle* when we moved out here. Said we should become like the locals, read the same newspaper, not stand out like some newly arrived immigrants. Go to chapel, keep our heads down, dissolve into colonial society. They even thought about changing my Christian name, said "Delyth" was too different, too foreign. In the end they didn't have the heart to change it, knew it would upset me too much. They just shortened it to Del.'

'Do you know what my name is, Delyth?'

'Of course I do. It's Daisy, what are you talking about?'

'No, no – my real name.'

'Which isn't Daisy, right?'

'You people gave me a name, Daisy. I am not that name. My Bemba name, my real name, is Kalinda. I had this very conversation with Gwyn once. Quick as a flash, he said, "That's 'watcher' in Bemba.'

'Is that right?'

'Yes, it is. I am the watcher. We all of us have more than one name, Delyth, different names for different circumstances, names to hide behind. Names give everyone a mask, the identity we want to present at any particular time to any particular set of people.'

'Or the mask someone wants to give to you. Housemaid, house-keeper, lover? Which mask do you prefer?'

'Which one do you want me to take?'

'I have no say in the matter, I don't think I ever had. Is it only

Gwyn who does the deciding, or do you both chip in? A sort of name-giving committee? I wonder what you do in the event of a tie, who has the casting vote? Or do you just draw lots?'

'We don't always use the name as we were given at birth. Why, you people have changed the names of entire countries. Changed the name of this country too, stolen it away and called the place Northern Rhodesia.'

I'd finally decided to speak to Delyth from the same pedestal.

'Blame Cecil Rhodes for that. Or are we all Cecil Rhodes to you, seeing as you see everything?'

'Gwyn says I only see the things I want to see, but I do think that I can enter the minds of most women. I know what they think.'

'And men, do you know what they think?'

'They usually think of one thing, except for Gwyn.'

'Good old Gwyn, he gets everything right. He has the answers to all the questions,' said Delyth.

'You mentioned Murphy's last night,' I said.

'That awful place near the Great Northern, where all the men go in through the back door with their collars turned up and their hats pulled down? Disgusting factory of sin.'

'It was in that disgusting factory of sin that I met Gwyn for the first time.'

'You worked there?'

'Yes, I did.'

'But, Daisy, how could you? As for Gwyn, I don't know what to say, I'd have expected more of him. I thought he'd be better than that. Didn't you know what it was like before going?'

'Both my parents were dead, I needed the money. It was catch a passing mouse and eat it for me. I was also very naïve. I had a boyfriend, William, he wasn't much older than I was. About sixteen, that's what he told me. I loved him, and I thought he loved me. He told me there was an opening as a laundry maid and dishwasher in Murphy's. Found out later from the owner that he'd paid William two shillings for what the boss man at Murphy's called my "future cooperation in the companionship services that his establishment had to offer."

'To begin with, everything was as I'd expected. I'd clean up the rooms after they'd been used by the girls and their customers. Usually only a bed in the room anyway. Did some darning, washed some dishes... got into a routine. Saw things I'd never seen before. Saw things I'd never dreamt of before. Then the call came. Two of the girls got sick. Hookworm, I think they said. Anyways, they were short on staff, and I don't mean the housekeeping type. Boss man told me to take their place, said he'd double my wages or he'd send me home, the choice was mine.'

'What about William, where was he?'

'Pretty much soon as I started at Murphy's, he was gone. I never saw him again. I had no home, no money, no nothing, so I became a working girl. Boss man called them clients, not customers. Said that's what I should call them, said it sounded more professional. Well, some of them clients, especially the older ones, preferred the younger variety, and all them clients were white, Delyth. Only Bemba allowed in that place were the girls and Joe the barman. I hear these days there's some white girls working there as well, not in my day though. That's progress, I suppose. Seen some of those clients walking with their family. Lot of them live in their windows, heads held high, all dressed up going to Sunday meeting at Moriah, and all them other Christian places in town. Bloody hypocrites! Some of the other clients, copper miners mostly, couldn't count very well. Guzzled enough whisky though, and got through more than enough tricks to help 'em count to a hundred! Only one thing boss man wanted, quick turnover, get the job done, on to the next one. The quicker the better. All men are the same; they don't want love, they ain't interested in feelings. Only feelings they want is what's between our legs. Five minutes of humping and that's them done. Still, that suited boss man down to the ground. A bed in Murphy's is no different to a bed anywhere else.

'First time I was crying, shaking like a leaf, sitting by the bar, waiting for that tap on the shoulder, and always the same question, "Can I buy you a drink?" Heck I hadn't even drunk alcohol before. Apart from water, I'd only tasted one glass of lemonade ever. Boss man told me what to do. Ask for the most expensive whisky in the house, a double, always a double. Joe would give the client his drink and then he'd give me mine. It was coloured water, bigger profit margin. We'd talk by the bar, client then haggles with boss man on the price.'

'What, in front of you?'

'Yeah. On those first few occasions, boss man said he needed to test market conditions, me being a new commodity and all. Soon as a new girl been there a few weeks, word gets round the place, price becomes set. It can stay the same, might even go up, once a girl becomes popular. But one thing's for sure, it always, and I mean always, goes down in the end. Wear and tear, boss man called it.'

'How could you allow yourself to go through this? It's barbaric, like those animals at the train station.'

This is a white settler woman talking, I thought.

'I told you, I had no family, no money. William was gone, I was totally alone. I couldn't go back to my village. If they found out I was working at Murphy's, all the men in the village would look at me in a different way, and all their women would loathe me. There was no future for me there. I couldn't go back.'

'So you worked there? I mean *worked* there?'

'Yeah, I worked there. On my back, on my knees, on most other places you can think of, and on some places you probably would never even think of. Boss man called them afternoon marriages. Then they turned into morning marriages, evening marriages... so many marriages.'

'Horrendous! Couldn't you run away?'

'Where precisely would I have run away to? The Sisters of Mercy Mission in Ndola? Anyways, going back to the story. Once they agree the rate we'd go upstairs. I knew all the rooms. Cleared them enough times. Save now it was my turn. I started crying again. The client, he ain't interested in none of that. Tells me to take my clothes off, but I couldn't, I just couldn't. He starts shouting, says he's paid good money to have me, and he ain't taking no for an answer. He don't want his money back, he wants me. I can't stop crying, my fingers won't work, I try to undo my buttons but my hands ain't listening. He loses his temper again, slaps me around the face. Calls me things, pushes me onto the bed, and the rest... well, the rest just happened. It was painful, it was the first time.

'It was easier after that. I wasn't going to cry over no client from then on. And besides, after a while some of the clients were prepared to pay me extra for, what can I say, their unique or unusual requirements. Requirements they weren't prepared to even discuss with the boss man himself in the privacy of his office. Everything had a price, and everything was for sale. They received full value from me for their cash, there were no complaints.'

'Oh you poor thing... But still you didn't escape?'

'No one escapes from Murphy's. Boss man kept reminding us girls of someone who tried to escape before. She ended up dead and no one cared. He said the place closed for a few days, that's all. It soon opened for business again. Murphy's would have closed down years ago if you settlers had wanted. Reason it hasn't is because of you. Your men folk tell you one thing in your kitchen, they talking a totally different lingo in Murphy's.'

'And Gwyn was a customer?'

'Yes, he was. I'd been working for seven months. Doesn't sound much, but it was a lifetime. Clients arrived and left. You lose count, you don't remember faces. You don't remember the other parts neither, unless...'

'Unless what, Daisy?'

'That don't matter. What you do remember is their smell. They all smell differently. They all smell of sweat, but different types of sweat. And by the way, we don't call them clients, the girls I mean, we call them Johns. Just like they were some kind of machine, 'cos that's what they were. I suppose we were as well. No feelings, only a mechanical activity. Things took their normal course, got pregnant, had no idea who the father would have been. I wasn't keeping count, or remembering too many faces. Had an abortion, and back to work.'

'What!' gasped Delyth. I thought she was consuming my tale rather too voraciously.

'Then I had a second one.'

'My God!'

'Don't judge me, Delyth. Boss man, he was a good businessman. His wife would check us every month, make sure we were on time.

He said clients didn't like seeing pregnant girls around the establishment, made them feel guilty. Bad for business. If we were off for two months running, his wife would perform the procedure on us. Didn't take long, and in a few days we'd be back at work. But that second time took me a while to get back up to speed.

'Been with Gwyn occasionally before – might even have been his child, who knows. Never sure if Gwyn liked what he was doing there. Us girls talked. Probably only there because there aren't many places to go to in Broken Hill...

'Then I heard from the boss man that Gwyn had been asking for me. Boss man told me to get better, get out of my sick bed, that I was costing him money, that I needed to start working again. I came back too soon. I was with Gwyn and I collapsed. Had a fever, some kind of infection. Gwyn told me later he took me to hospital, the white folks' hospital, not the native one. Took some negotiating to get me in. Some reasoning. Money, more like. But I slowly got better. Doctors told me I could never have children again. That would have been music to the ears for the boss man.'

'Did you go back to Murphy's?'

'No, I didn't. Gwyn offered me a position in his house. As housekeeper. Nothing more, Delyth.'

'What about the boss man, he couldn't have been happy?'

'He surely wasn't. Wasn't happy with his wife for botching up my abortion, putting me out of service for longer than he'd planned. Wasn't happy about me going to the settler hospital neither. Said I might have come across some of his clients, didn't want them embarrassed. Didn't want the publicity neither.'

'But he let you go?'

'Gwyn smoothed things over.'

'How did he do that?'

'How is anything smoothed over? Love does a bit, but money does everything. Don't know how much it cost, but enough for boss man to grant me my freedom. Expect he soon came across some other William who'd sell a girl to him for two shillings to take my place.'

'Oh, Daisy, I'm so, so sorry, I truly am.'

'So you see, I owe everything to Gwyn. Without him I'd still be at Murphy's sitting by the bar, waiting for the next tap on the shoulder.'

After a while, Delyth said. 'I wish I had the same faith in men as you do, Daisy, I really do.'

XXXIV

THAT EVENING DELYTH trudged off to her bedroom. She had decided to write a letter to her aunt at home, to tell her the news about the impending baby. She sat at the Davenport desk, which contained all the necessary writing materials, writing paper, blotting paper, envelopes, stamps. Daisy kept a good supply of everything, and she ensured that everything was in its proper place and in its proper order.

The Davenport had been in the Bowen family for generations, the only thing close to an heirloom that Gwyn possessed – save, of course, for the Bowen name itself. It was a type of small oak desk with a sloping top, a row of working drawers down one side, with a row of false drawers on the opposite side. Small front drawers, cubby holes and compartments.

Lifting the top, Delyth pulled out some paper, opened the Parker 51 fountain pen, Gwyn's favourite, and tried to write. But her thoughts left not a blemish on the paper, the Parker 51 inkless. Searching for a bottle of Quink, she opened the right-hand drawers. Pencils, paperclips, staples, pencil sharpeners, erasers... but no ink. Half-rummaging, half-ransacking, still inkless. Trying the left-hand drawers would be useless; they were all false fronted. She'd go shopping tomorrow, ink would be top of her list.

Replacing the writing paper neatly where it was found, she

discarded the Parker 51, half-throwing it into an available compartment. She heard a slight click: a further pigeonhole involuntarily opening.

Opening the wooden box fully, she found no ink, just an old letter addressed to Gwyn. For the ill-starred Delyth, it was in a hand with which she was disappointingly familiar.

LIVINGSTONE

Annwyl Gwyn,

My dear brother, it is with a heavy heart that I write this letter to you.

I know that we have never been close and you think I have never attained the expectations that either Mam nor Dad, nor indeed yourself, wished for me as the eldest son. I have tried, you will never know how hard, to meet those expectations, but I know, we all know I have failed, and I continue to fail.

My life in business as agricultural implement salesman sounds grand, but is in fact a series of cap-doffing exercises in front of colonial peasant farmers who have reached far above their station. However, I would say I am fulfilled when exercising my tobacco duties. And this now brings me to the burden of my letter. It was while utilising my capabilities in that department, to whit the selling of tobacco, that I came across a certain lady called Delyth Jenkins, only daughter of the late Mr and Mrs Gwilym Jenkins, who I am sure you will remember. Miss Jenkins would have been about your age and certainly in your Sunday School class at Moriah. Regrettably and through no fault of Miss Jenkins, the Devil took me, advantage was taken and I would imagine that she will be with child in the coming months. My child. I have told Miss Jenkins that I am already married and cannot in all conscience leave Margaret and the children, Mary and Elizabeth. I would stress that my marital status was not previously divulged to Miss Jenkins prior to our liaison.

Would you be an old sport and throw a lifeline to the poor girl? I know your fondness for Daisy and that you will be keen to seek her advice but this could be an avenue to respectability both for you and for Miss Jenkins. I'm sure you've heard the gossip, the misgivings of our people in Broken Hill regarding your unnatural closeness to non-Europeans and to Daisy in particular.

Could you do your best for me, old chum? Who knows, the child might be male, a chance for the Bowen name to live on. I think Miss Jenkins deserves some happiness. Needless to say, Margaret knows nothing of my predicament and I will rely on your discretion to keep it that way.

Yours in brotherly love,
Emrys.

P.S. Excuse the brown staining on the writing paper, too much tobacco in the Meerschaum.

P.P.S. Please do your best.

Delyth rested her forehead on her right hand and started to cry, salted tears on tobacco. She tried to read the letter again. 'Throw a lifeline... the poor Miss Jenkins...' The Bowens, the bastards, the bastard Bowens! Her first instinct was to tear the letter into shreds, line by knavish line. But still crying, she folded the letter along its original crease, placing it roughly in its envelope and back into the secret compartment where it had been hidden. Then, rising, exhausted, from the Davenport chair, she plodded sobbing to her bedroom.

Of course, I'd known about the letter, not that Gwyn had told me. I kept a clean house. Spick and span, that's me. That Davenport was always a bugger to clean; it seemed to collect household dust like a rabid dog collects fleas. And those ink stains, they never came out, as hard as I tried. As secretive as Gwyn was, it wasn't hard to come across that hidden compartment. I don't think I was even shocked when I read the letter. Such was the calibre of most men I had been familiar with, and knowing Gwyn, the Bowen family honour and all that, he would do as his brother asked. So much for my value to him. But I knew we could still carry on together; I still felt we both loved one another in our own way, and that was something precious. And if that made me seem weak, well, that was settler talk.

XXXV

GWYN NEVER TOLD ME in advance the time or day when he'd be returning from the bush. He would just turn up. On his arrival this time, I prepared a simple meal for Delyth, Gwyn and me, nothing special.

'Here you are, Gwyn, some chikanda and nshima, I know you'll like it. Del is getting used to my cooking now, aren't you, dear?'

I had laid three plates on the table. The darkness outside partnered well with the room, which was poorly lit.

'I didn't know you liked Bantu sausage and porridge, Delyth,' said Gwyn.

'I don't mind really, Gwyn. Daisy's good with the cooking and she helps me out no end.'

'Have to say, orchid tubers and compounded maize meal isn't usually my meal of choice,' remarked Gwyn.

'Chikanda and nshima is our standard fare these days, Gwyn,' I said. 'Isn't that right, Del?'

Eating quietly round the table, none of us peeped up from our food. Very little was said. I was the first to finish.

'I'll leave you two to it, don't want to get in the way of the newly-weds.'

I was hoping that they would have lots to talk about. I left the dining room, closing the door behind me.

'How have things been, Delyth? Been getting on with Daisy?'

'Like a house on fire. Save for a dead squirrel consumed by maggots in the kitchen, a plague of fish and frogs falling out of the sky, and young lambs torturing their mothers, things have been great.'

'Sounds more exciting here than out in the bush. There's talk, Delyth, from the chief engineer himself, that head office is extremely pleased with my work, and there may be a pay rise in the offing.'

'Gwyn, so many other things have happened since you've been away, so many, many things. Why do you need to be away so much? Get a steady job here in town. I'm sure there's a desk job at the Development Company for a good engineer. You could come home for lunch every day. We could be together. You could help me survive. I've heard so many bad things about the Railways. Wild animals, the men, the heavy machinery...'

'It's in my blood, Delyth. My father was an engineer on the Railways. It's in our family. It's who we are.'

'How do you know what's in your blood? Only God knows that.'

'And which God might that be?'

'The God you were born with, the God both of us were born with, the Moriah Congregational Chapel God!' Delyth grappled with the arms of her chair as if in an act of strangulation.

Gwyn scoffed slightly, avoiding eye contact with Delyth. Delyth, undeviating, stared straight at him.

'I'm not as partial to the Cross as you are, Delyth.'

'I've read the letter.'

'Read what letter?'

'The one from your brother, Emrys. I found it by mistake in the Davenport. You married me out of pity, didn't you? To throw a lifeline to the poor Miss Jenkins! Our marriage, God, a Bowen conspiracy! Why didn't you tell me? You've cheated me to help that bastard brother of yours! Does Daisy know? And I thought I was the clever one. I was the one supposed to trap you. The bloody Great Northern Hotel! The best hotel in Broken Hill, that's what you called it, wasn't it? The best roast beef around. We should have gone there when you suggested. I could have showed you where it happened, where the Bowen family had their sport! Room twenty-seven, that's where it was, right at the back on the second floor, overlooking the industrial buildings. Your brother chose it personally. I'm sure he'd used it many times before. And now I'm pregnant because of it! One son gets me into trouble, and the other son clears up the mess, is that the way the Bowens do it? I'm some kind of social experiment for the Bowen brothers, that's what I am. Get your older brother to make me pregnant and then the younger brother takes it from there! When's the joint PhD coming out? "How to destroy and resurrect a human being by Bowen and Bowen!"'

'I was going to tell you, Delyth. At some point I would have told you.'

'You think I should be grateful, don't you!' Delyth exhaled like a pricked soufflé.

'The result was the same, we just came at it from different angles, that's all. You wanted me to marry you, that was the plan, right? Marry the mug Gwyn Bowen, the lover of Bemba, women and men. Respectability, a father to your baby readily to hand. Who knows, he might be another engineer. It's in the child's blood, after all. You can't question that, can you? You're trapping yourself, Delyth, like a lawyer traps others with words.'

'But it wasn't my victory, it wasn't my choice! You made the choice for me. And I should be grateful? I know you think I should be grateful, but I'm not. I'm not! The bull's eye should have been mine, but you got there before me!'

'He's my brother. He's weak, does things, doesn't think, just smokes that pipe of his and does things.'

'I've got to be the first? Please tell me I am. Tell me I'm at least the only one of his women you've helped.'

Gwyn looked down at his unfinished meal. He sighed a gill-sized sigh.

'I'm *not*? I can't believe it. How many others have there been, how many other "*Annwyl Gwyn*" letters? What did you do with those poor girls? This is the family business, is it? Emrys creates the crap, and Gwyn, good old dependable Gwyn, clears it all up. The Great Gwyn, the Noble Gwyn, the Salvager of Fallen Women Gwyn. And then there's Daisy. Don't tell me you rescued her from Murphy's from the goodness of your heart. Men only want one thing from women. You're just as depraved as your brother. You're two sides of the same coin.'

'But this is what *you* wanted.'

'But I wanted to be the smug one, the one who won for a change. I wanted to be the keeper of the secret. I wanted my dignity, my *dignity*, Gwyn, not Bowen pity! And something else, as we're laying bare our souls. I've contracted bilharzia. It was all Daisy's fault... We went swimming, we both went swimming, we both went swimming and I picked this sickness up. But not Daisy, oh not her, nothing bad ever happens to Daisy. Saint Daisy of Broken Hill! So your new wife, your pregnant new wife, carrying the next of the Bowen generation, is also carrying a disease which may ruin the young engineer! But at least when it's born it'll have a family resemblance to you, Gwyn. You haven't got to worry about that.'

'Have you seen Dr Cosgrove?'

'What do you care? You're never here anyway.'

Both speakers were cut off from one another, two icebergs floating in different directions.

'Why should I be sorry, why should I be made to feel guilty? You were the one in trouble, you were the one who was pregnant.'

'No, no, it was the Bowen family that was in trouble, and I just happened to be part of it, a casualty of the chaos caused by your flesh and blood. Why don't you go back where you came from, go back to the bush and your navvies? That's your home, isn't it? That's who you really love. That's where you feel most comfortable. And that bloody letter'll become a Bowen family heirloom, another ancestral treasure to be cherished and handed down the centuries. Daisy will keep me company, she know's what's what. She rules this place anyway, the princess regent! We all know where we stand in this little congregation. I suggest you sleep over there, on the sofa, tonight!'

And with that Delyth left the room, and the two unfinished plates of cold chikanda and nshima.

Gwyn woke early the next morning. Rhodesia Railways his salvation as always. The house asleep, save for the cat, three-legged, one-eyed Shani, stretching and preening herself on the verandah, before another day of hunting began, the dawn sun shimmering flecks of gold over her ebony fur.

Although I had left the room, and let them to it, Delyth told me what happened later that morning. The more she talked, the more she plummeted into the depths of her shame. She repeated herself, more than once, the comments becoming more and more irrational. From what she was telling me, Gwyn's responses were no better. They had both been self-indulgent; they were both, in my opinion, talking twaddle.

Why couldn't they both have been open with one another from the beginning, told the truth? Or was that the European way? Just more and more lies, every lie bigger to cover the previous one.

I didn't offer any view one way or the other, but this subject was not going away. They were both being pummelled, and I wanted to rescue them, but how? Perhaps if I showed Delyth more affection, that would help; it seemed to me she hadn't experienced much love throughout her life. But I was afraid to approach her, to touch her. What if she rejected me? That might make her even more unhappy. Wasn't love, possibly even physical love, a way to soothe her?

XXXVI

JOE AND JABEZ knew that they were at a key juncture. They both had to trust one another and that was not something that came easily to them. They were both only, and lonely, children. It was one thing being pals in Murphy's, drinking whisky, telling dirty jokes, but to even discuss a robbery, and a violent one at that, left them each defenceless if the circle of trust was broken by the other.

'The boss man's bank is Barclays, ain't it?' asked Jabez.

'Barclays in town,' answered Joe. 'We finish the doings mid-morning usually. Boss man leaves the wages in the safe in his office till I return, and off I trot to the bank. He don't want all that money hanging around.'

'How long does it take you?' Jabez bending forward slightly, turning his head a few degrees, his right ear awaiting an answer.

'About fifteen minutes, maybe twenty if I go via Buntungwa Street. Nicer walk that way, means I pass that dainty Hindu temple and the Presbyterian Church. They got a fine cemetery. It's peace-ful there, quiet. Maybe one god or another might bring me to the light.'

'Two religions in fifteen minutes. Not many people can achieve that. I know the cemetery fairly well. Seems like a good place for an ambush; it's one of the biggest graveyards around these parts.'

'Them settlers dying like flies at times when blackwater fever gets hold of them.'

'Do you make an appointment at the bank when you deposit the money?'

'Appointment? What do I need that for?'

'So they ain't expecting you at a particular time? They wouldn't raise the alarm if you were late? That's all I'm asking.'

'Mid to late morning, early afternoon, nothing more exact than that. They all know I'm coming .'

'Good. That means someone at the bank could have tipped off your attacker.'

'Don't want no innocent at the bank being blamed for this, our sinfulness is ours alone.'

'We'll leave all that to the local constabulary, shall we, Joe. Do you ever come across anyone in the cemetery on your way to the bank?'

'It's usually pretty quiet. Unless there's a funeral, then its quieter still, even the birds don't sing. Might see some gravediggers, normally two Bemba who do the digging. And a settler, don't know what he does. He's more on the administration side of things, I think. They do the digging a full day before the burying. And then there's Gideon.'

'Who the hell is he?'

'Silly Boy Gideon. He simple, he ain't right in the head.'

'Settler or native?'

'He pure white. Church elders allow him to live in the cemetery. Cuts the grass, keeps the graves tidy, sleeps in a shed in the far corner so as not to upset the mourners. Me and him get along well. Then again, might not see him for weeks, when he's off on his wanderings, that is. Could be up country, out in the bush, then he just re-appears once he gets hungry. Some people say he catches fish with his teeth, eats them raw, guts and all. Me, I don't believe that. Them Presbyterians look after him best they can.'

'Well they are Christians, after all,' replied Jabez, looking at Joe with half a smile. 'What if he's there and sees what happens?'

'No worries on that account. Gideon don't speak. His father always in a savage humour, never took to him, and once he saw the kid wasn't right in the head, he had it in for the boy. Came home drunk one night, lost a lot of money on cards, got a pair of industrial pliers and tore his son's tongue out. Now Gideon couldn't say who his kin was. Too much of an embarrassment to his family. This a long time ago, mind. Last I heard, his old man done a bunk straight after, frightened the police would get him, throw him in jail. I hear he up somewhere in the Belgian Congo, maybe even further north, maybe even dead, who knows.'

'You're saying the only witness could be some halfwit who can't talk?'

'That's ain't the way I think of him. We're chums. I bring some stale bread from the kitchen, or a half-eaten pie, some John couldn't stomach, just in case he's around. That boy won't be no trouble. He been good to me and I been good to him.'

'This is what we'll do next Friday.'

'Friday, you want to do it Friday?'

'What's the point of waiting? Money's there just asking to be commandeered.'

'I need more time to think about this. Why don't we leave it for a month? My number ain't that bad here in Murphy's.'

'Leave it? How do you know boss man is still going to trust you in a month's time? He might change his mind and carry the takings to the bank himself. He's crazy leaving you to do it now. That wife of his might bring him to his senses. Tell him not to trust a Bemba with all his money. Seems to me he's displaying some decidedly unsettler sensitivities. No, we've got to do this now. If we don't, anything could happen. Do you want to be your own master or not? Do you have ambition, Joe? Do you want to better yourself?'

'The split ain't fair though! Should be seventy-thirty, not fifty-fifty.'

'You're a tough one, Joe. Sixty-forty.'

'That's sixty to me, right?'

'That'd be sixty to you, Joe.'

Joe was being turned by Jabez. Why was he allowing it, he thought, letting himself turn bad? He was honest, leastways most of the time. He was loyal. But that Murphy money was bad money anyway – mining money, farming money, government money, settler money. He felt as if Jabez had asked him to taste an unusual fruit which he'd never seen before; the first taste was bitter but the more he chewed, the sweeter it grew. Joe was becoming hooked, but hooked of his own volition. Ambition always had a price. And he would also have a comrade in his ambition. A partner. He wouldn't be just the barman holding the towel anymore.

'Come on then,' Joe said. 'How do we do it?'

'I'll wait for you in the cemetery. The path kind of zig zags in between the graves. Them Prebyterians would be no good on the Railways. There's a massive mausoleum-type grave more or less in the centre. You know the one?'

'Yeah, some relation to the land grabber in chief himself.'

'Who's that?'

'One of your heroes, I'm sure, Cecil bloody Rhodes.'

'Very apt. That's where it's going to happen, the ambush. I'll have to make this look good, Joe. I'll hit you on the back of the head twice, make sure you're unconscious. Few punches to the face. Bruises and a bust nose, couple of black eyes will make you look the part. The virtuous victim of a heartless robber, the conscientious and faithful retainer who was only going about his master's business.'

'Don't want no punches to the face! That'll mean I would have seen you. The whole point is that I didn't see you coming, you got me from behind. The story is I didn't see no one.'

'You're right, Joe. Don't worry, you'll be up on your feet in a few minutes. But stay down, give me some fifteen minutes to disappear.'

'That's the word I don't like to hear.'

'What do you mean?'

'You disappearing. What happens to the money?' There was no amazement or annoyance in Joe's voice; just that he didn't want any settler snobbery setting into the discussion.

'Like I said, we share it sixty-forty. I'll come and see you in your sick bed at home, look in on the patient as it were. Boss man knows I'm a good customer. Just a John wanting to know how Barman Joe is getting on after his beating. I'll bring your share with me, it'll be easy. But don't go spending it on chopsy women or hard liquor. You're a businessman now and you got to act like one. You'll become a civilized trader in whisky, soulmates and paramours.'

'All sounds tickety boo. Means you do the hurting and you got the money, that sound fair to you?'

'There's no other way. Who else can you trust to pull this off? This is your chance for a fresh start, a bright future, a prosperous future. You're smart enough to take it, I know you are. Don't just be another man of sweat.'

'Just remember, partner, you double cross me, it don't matter how long I'm in jail, how far you go... I'll get you. That little knock on your door, could be a friendly neighbour asking you to go to Sunday meeting, or it could be me. And I won't care if you've spent all the takings, or you a frail old man. I won't be wanting money, it'll be your guts I be wanting. And you won't die slow either. Clear to you, Mr Pugh?'

Joe spoke without theatricality; there would have been more expression in his voice if he had been explaining to a John the different types of hard liquor for sale on the shelves in Murphy's.

Joe carried the monthly Murphy arisings in a light brown, muslin shopping bag, wide gusseted, double handled, with a floral cretonne lining. Roomy enough for all the takings, and as Joe's whim would take him, big enough for a mouldy corned beef sandwich or some cold buttered toast for Gideon.

Jabez was already at the mausoleum before Joe arrived. The Bemba passed quickly between the gravestones attesting to all the dead saints buried thereunder. As we all know, according to funerary rites, every departed soul is flawless, without sin.

'Ready, Joe?'

'Just be careful, that's all.'

'Turn around then, as agreed. Once from behind.'

'One blow, then no more,' said Joe. He tensed his body, his mouth dry from the treble whisky straight he'd downed in Murphy's before departing.

Jabez pulled out a teak cudgel from his belt, about eighteen inches long, and hit Joe as hard as he could on the back of his head. Joe groaned and fell face-first against the ground, breaking his nose in the process. But he was still conscious, blood oozing down his chin.

'You don't look hurt enough to me. This has to look good or it won't work.'

'No more, that's it,' groaned Joe, spitting blood from a cut somewhere in his mouth.

Jabez lifted the cudgel a second time, ready to strike, then felt a heavy, rancid-smelling weight on his back. It was Gideon, who, walking back to his shed, had seen his friend being attacked by a stranger. He scratched at Jabez's face, putting his fingers into his enemy's eyes.

'Get off me, you bastard, get the fuck off me!'

'Gideon, no, leave him alone! Gideon, leave him!' moaned Joe, on all fours, too battered to get up on his feet.

Jabez, still holding the cudgel, grabbed one of Gideon's hands and smashed back against the mausoleum railings. But Gideon still hung on, scratching at Jabez's face.

'Get him off me! Get the bastard off me! Jesus Christ!' screamed Jabez, showering spittle with his venom.

Joe, bloodied from his head and nose, pulled at one of Gideon's legs, bringing both Gideon and Jabez crashing to the concrete floor around the mausoleum, thereby dislodging Gideon from Jabez's back. Seeing Gideon dazed on the ground, Jabez, in his rage, struck three heavy blows against his face with the cudgel.

'Stop it! Stop it! That's enough! You'll kill him!'

Jabez pushed Joe aside with such force that Joe lost his balance and fell awkwardly, striking his head on the concrete plinth of the mausoleum. Still in a wild frenzy, Jabez kept hitting and hitting Gideon until the boy's face was crushed beyond recognition. He only stopped when he didn't have the strength to raise the cudgel anymore.

Looking over his shoulder at Joe. He didn't move to help him. He watched Joe's frame, unmoving, entirely unmoving, for long enough to know.

Then Jabez picked up the shopping bag.

'You ruddy idiot, you poor ruddy idiot! I would have given you your share. We're all ruddy idiots!'

Wiping his hands with the muslin bag, Jabez surveyed the graveyard to ensure that he was alone. Leaving the cemetery to the dead, his task was to get home unseen, to wash, to change, and then to settle a debt with Ballard.

XXXVII

GETTING HOME UNSEEN did not prove difficult. Once through the back door, he undressed completely, placing all his bloodied clothes in a colourless plastic sack from Imperial Chemical Industries, formerly containing ammonium sulphate, the contents of which he'd used as fertilizer on his alkaline garden. There were still some fine traces of the chemical left towards the bottom of the sack, and these particles might help to ingest some of the blood. Jabez gave no more thought to this for the moment; there were other tasks requiring his attention.

There was rarely any hot water in the house unless Jabez boiled some on his gas stove, the process being far too laborious and time consuming, considering the amounts required for a proper bath. He therefore had to wash himself as best he could, as he had done many times before, in the kitchen, in an old portable cast iron sink with a bar of Wright's Traditional Coal Tar soap. The combination of cold water and the orange-coloured soap proved surprisingly effective, save that he found the deep cleaning of his labourer's worn fingernails problematic, deeply ingrained as they were with portions of flesh from Gideon's face.

His main emotion was one of relief. He had completed his task and he had not been caught. The pity he felt for his erstwhile partner was not long lived; the dead would have to look after themselves. Their bodies were already in a cemetery, after all. His duty to Auntie Maisie trumped all else. He did notice, however, that both his hands and his whole body were shaking, as if caught out on a mountain in winter without sufficient shelter. Jabez went to his kitchen cabinet, pulled the cork on a half-empty bottle of whisky and took two, but only two, large gulps then put the bottle back. Whisky always conquered tremors.

Drying himself briskly with an old tea towel, Jabez, completely naked, sat at the kitchen table with the Murphy's bag by his side, the holdall displaying the effects of the battering it had endured during the incident in the graveyard.

'Right, let's count the money,' he said to himself.

Opening the bag was a disappointment. Due to the bloodshed of the murderous skirmish, a large part of the money in the holdall had become soiled and would not pass muster with Ballard as payment of Auntie Maisie's fees; as for the cretonne lining it was spattered and streaked beyond purging. The loose change in the bag was clearly insufficient to discharge the arrears of debt and the additional four weeks in advance which that bloodsucker bursar had requested. There was only one thing Jabez could do, and that was to clean each and every note, every fiver, every sovereign and every ten shilling note. But how to do so without ruining the paper currency itself?

Jabez was not the domesticated type, but he did remember how Auntie Maisie had used to wash his bloodstained shirts when he came back from school after brawling with his classmates. Before washing each shirt by hand, she would place some dishwashing soap into an empty basin that was normally used to set jelly, then pour lukewarm water into it, stir it vigourously and create a lather. She would then dip a sponge into the solution and wipe the blood as best she could from the shirt, then give the shirt a good wash on the scrubbing board in the normal manner. This usually did the trick. If it was good enough for his blood it would surely be good enough for Joe and Gideon's.

Working coolly and methodically, Jabez created the concoction just as his Auntie Maisie had done those many years ago, save that this time the receptacle wasn't a jelly bowl, but a small saucepan he used to boil his eggs. Choosing the lowest denomination note first, the ten bob, Jabez started the cleaning process. He dipped a sponge in the soapy water, pressing some of the water from the sponge before using it, and wiped the note from the top to the bottom. Immediately, due to a combination of an excess of water and the clumsy oafishness of his hands, the note became torn in the direction of travel, from top to bottom. But the blood did come off.

Choosing another ten shilling note, Jabez repeated the process, this time using a slightly drier sponge, wiping not vertically but laterally from one side to the other. The results were certainly better: the note had not been torn, although the edges were still slightly smudged. Feeling more confident, he selected a particularly bloody five pound note. Changing his tactics he lightly wiped the note, again laterally, but this time from the middle of the note, as close to the word 'pay' as he could to the edge, ending with the serial number, and then again from the middle of the note to the other edge. These 'white fivers' were never any good at hiding dirt, but the result this time was perfect. Yet, as he picked up the note to clean the reverse side, the saturated fiver tore on the wooden table. Jabez was furious. And then someone knocked on the front door.

He tiptoed into his front lounge, still naked, cursing under his breath, peered slightly past the chintz fabric curtains adorned with garden flowers – European blossoms, of course, not African – and through the white linen, transluscent blinds. That gap-toothed Miss Jacobs from the care home was loitering outside. Must be another letter, he thought; the buggers would get their money in short order. If only they knew what he was doing; their disturbing of his endeavours was only delaying matters. He tiptoed silently back to his task. Miss Jacobs knocked a few more times and then left.

On this occasion Jabez singled out another ten shilling note; another experiment with a fiver was too risky. Instead of placing the note directly on wooden table, he cut a piece of the strong plastic from a cast-off portion which he'd used as a window in the main bedroom when the glass pane had broke, due to age and neglect and the result of a heavy thunderstorm of hail. He had for many years meant to replace the window and had indeed purchased a box of putty for that purpose from Cornelius the ironmonger's in town. Months after the purchase, he had got round to buying the glass itself, but due to his tardiness the putty had completely solidified into a dry block, as hard as rock, rendering it totally unusable. The glass pane was still unused, on its side in the rear hallway. He would use the robust plastic as a base for his laundering, in the hope that the notes would stay intact when turned, and not tear as previously.

This third time the whole process went smoothly. There were no lacerations; the ten bob note looked brand new. But now how to dry it?

Jabez thought of hanging the sodden currency on the outside washing line but gave that over as a bad idea straightaway. If he couldn't take the money to the washing line, the washing line would have to come to the money. At least that was one benefit of living in a hot climate: the notes would dry in no time. There was one thing about Jabez: he was never afraid of hard work. He rigged nine separate drying lines, five in the kitchen near his place of work and five in the back dining room; the other rooms were problematical as there was a chance, albeit only a small one, that they could be overlooked.

Jabez had been working for over two hours when he heard the front door being knocked again. Once more he sidled up to the front lounge window, still completely naked, subconsciously pleased to have a break from his exertions, which were now proving akin to drudgery. Peering through the blinds, he was surprised to see the whole of the care home secretariat, both Miss Jacobs and Mrs Harrison, looking like two pecking hens. Mrs Harrison knocked furiously at the front door; she even looked through the letter box. Jabez noticed that no envelope was deposited on the raffia mat in the hallway. 'Cheeky bitch,' Jabez said to himself.

'Well, Mr Ballard can't say we haven't tried,' he heard one of them say. 'Come on, let's go.'

Back Jabez went and continued with his work. By this time the first of his cleaned items were dry but severely creased; again these wouldn't pass muster with Ballard. The notes not only had to be clear of blood but uncreased, looking like normal paper currency, albeit clean ones. Still naked, far too engrossed in his labours to dress, Jabez walked upstairs to the box room, retrieving from underneath the single bed two heavy leather bound books, books which had been in Auntie Maisie's family for generations, *Y Beibl Cysygredig*, that being the Holy Bible, and *Taith y Pererin*, that being *Pilgrim's Progress*. Unopened since at least Uncle John's death, they would both now come in handy as heavy presses to uncrease the crumpled notes.

Jabez worked through the night, the final fiver cleaned, dried and pressed, ready for inspection, by eight o'clock that morning. Tired but elated, Jabez deposited the fees in a plain manila envelope; his plans, his industry, had triumphed. To mark the solemnity of his accomplishments he put on his woollen three piece suit, which he had last worn at his uncle's funeral. It was now slightly careworn but, in Jabez's eyes at least, perfectly wearable. He also found the white cotton shirt and black tie to match; the shirt itself was severely wrinkled and, if truth be told, needed a good wash and a flat press ironing. Jabez attempted to smooth the wrinkles in the shirt using the Holy Bible and *Pilgrims Progress*, as he had done for the lucre. As a final touch, he found the two red dragon cufflinks that Uncle John had brought from the old country, and inserted these into the appropriate holes in the shirtsleeves. Here was a proud man, an industrious man, swaggering, if not dressed to kill, certainly ready to do business with Ballard. Auntie Maisie would surely be very impressed to see him dressed in such finery. Jabez wanted so much to impress her, almost to the point of aching – to repay the limitless love and care which she had shown him.

Now that he had a few moments after his industry, he thought of Joe and the boy Gideon. They had entered the cemetery alive but the dead had claimed them, snatched them for their communion. But he had no room for doubts, for God or the Devil. The price of whisky and a Murphy's woman, and now Auntie Maisie: these were his concerns.

The morning was a glorious sunny sub-tropical day – a great day to settle old debts, for clean sheets, to no longer need to worry about Auntie Maisie's welfare. Jabez was so pleased with himself that, before going to see Ballard, he took a detour, heading to buy a bouquet of fresh roses at Quinnell's in the market to present to Auntie Maisie. What would an extra hour here or there matter? All debts would be paid today. Ballard would be off his back, Auntie Maisie could steer clear of the Government Hospital. Who should he thank for a cemetery and a teak cudgel?

Walking purposefully into the care home Jabez knocked rhythmically on Ballard's outer office door, two quick taps in succession, followed by a slight pause and then another two quick taps.

'Come in,' came a voice through the door. It was either Mrs Harrison or Miss Jacobs, he could not be sure. In he went.

'What's wrong with you two? Ballard been working you too hard? You look as if you've seen a blizzard in high summer. Ain't you seen a gentleman in his best Sunday go-to-meeting clothes before? Go on, tell Ballard I'm here with the money. Rather see my auntie than waste my time with that bloodsucker. Go on!'

Mrs Harrison was the first to react.

'Mr Pugh, my gosh, Mr Pugh!' she spluttered half-incoherently.

'I've come to see Ballard. I've brought him his money like I promised, and the extra four weeks in advance which the bugger demanded n'all. And before you ask, these flowers ain't for him, they're for my auntie.'

The two secretaries looked at Jabez open-mouthed.

Mrs Harrison knocked once on the bursar's door, stepped into his office, mumbled something to him and returned.

'He'll see you now.'

Jabez strode into Ballard's office, almost shoulder-charging Mrs Harrison in his eagerness to see his soon-to-be former creditor.

'Mr Pugh, please come in.'

'What's with the mister? It's usually no better than a snobby look-down-your-nose "Pugh" I get round here. Can't be the suit? Your gal's told you I've brought the money, ain't she? Well, she's right. It's all here in this bloody envelope and the four weeks in advance.'

'My dear Mr Pugh, please sit down.'

'Ain't got no time for ceremony, Ballard. I'm going to see Auntie Maisie straight after we've completed our business, so get on with it. Expect you'll want to count the stuff.'

'I'm not sure how to say this, Mr Pugh. Please brace yourself for some terrible news. I'm afraid Mrs Evans is dead. She passed away no more than thirty minutes ago. We tried to contact you... She'd picked up a chest infection late yesterday morning, I sent Miss Jacob's to your house to tell you. Patient's your aunt's age can go downhill fast. Your aunt worsened as the day wore on. I sent both the ladies to see if they could get hold of you at home, but again there was no answer. We all thought you were away with work. She died peacefully in her sleep, rest assured. Matron tells me she would not have been in any pain. The appropriate end of life morphine doses were administered in full compliance with Department of Health Government guidelines.'

Jabez dropped the flowers and the envelope to the carpeted floor and left the room holding his face in both hands, crying uncontrollably.

'Mrs Harrison, Miss Jacobs, come in here immediately!' shouted Ballard, slurring slightly, smelling of sweat and sherry.

As his secretaries gathered, Ballard examined the manila envelope that Jabez had left. It was the sole business at hand, Ballard's desk surprisingly clear for such a busy man.

The dearly departed's body was at that very moment on a trolley, being pushed by two of the care home porters towards the institution's morgue at the rear of the main building. Lamentably there had been three other deaths within the last five days, and the bodies patiently awaited burial, or such other means of disposal as would be determined by family members, and their respective financial capabilities. Unpaid fees being a live issue with at least one of the cadavers, possibly two, their sojourn in the morgue might be an indeterminate one.

The morgue capacity was a comfortable two, a crowded three, and Mrs Evans would therefore have to remain ensconced on her trolley outside the morgue, covered with dignity in one of the home's standard issue sheets. Matron promulgated that something had to be done sharpish with the dearly departed, as the refrigeration system was somewhat temperamental. The deceased in question, an eighty-five-year-old man of wiry disposition, was, as a result of tumescence caused by the equation of heat multiplied by time, enlarging hourly. Sutton the Death had a phrase for it: the pungency of degeneration.

'Pugh always was an ungrateful ruffian!' Ballard remarked to his hovering assistants. 'Heaven knows how one inch of track is ever laid over this country of ours if Rhodesia Railways have to depend on scoundrels like him!

'And by the way, Miss Jacobs, may I remind you yet again of the well-known grammatical aphorism, "I before E except after C". There have been far too many slip ups recently. This institution has standards to uphold. And please ensure that my debt letters regarding the morgue's present incumbents get sent in the first class post tonight. Pretty soon we'll be able to smell them from here!'

Miss Jacobs left the room, fuming and deflated.

'Check the door, would you, Mrs Harrison. Make sure that Miss Jacobs has closed it properly. There's no time like the present. Let's check this envelope. This establishment doesn't run on thin air. Bring that chair up to my desk. You can act as auditor to my count. Remember the Care Home Trust policy. There must always be a signatory and a counter signatory where cash is involved.'

Opening the envelope, removing the contents, Ballard relished the moment: to put on airs, to be alone with both cash money and the silk-stockinged Mrs Harrison...

'I must say these notes look incredibly clean,' he remarked

'They look mint condition to me, Mr Ballard.'

'Pugh must have taken my advice, been a sensible chap for once, and gone to see Wilson, the manager at the Standard Bank of South Africa, to get some sort of a loan. God knows what collateral he could stump up. Wilson must be getting soft. These notes must be straight from the bank vaults.'

'You mean they're freshly issued, Mr Ballard?'

'Precisely. No one can pull a fast one on this bursar, can they, Mrs Harrison?'

'Absolutely right, Mr Ballard.'

The counting came to a swift conclusion.

'According to my mathematics, everything is in order. All the monies are here. If you care to sign on the dotted line, Ms Harrison. Care Home Trust policy and all that.'

'Pardon me for asking, but Mr Pugh has paid one month's fees in advance, and as Mrs Evans passed away today...'

'How silly of me. Of course you're right. I'll personally make sure that Mr Pugh gets the overpayment. I'll take the money to him myself, once things settle down. He won't want to be burdened by tedious fiscal matters at this delicate time, with so much on his mind. Well, thank you, Mrs Harrison, I think that's all.'

'Mr Ballard?'

'Yes?'

'I've got one more query.'

'Yes, what is it? Come come!'

'According to my additions, there's been a ten-pound overpayment. See here, both our calculations match.'

'Bravo, Mrs Harrison! Well I never, well spotted! Can I suggest you take this sum and place it in the voluntary contributions box in the main foyer – a gift, as it were, from Pugh in memory of his dearly departed and much-loved aunt. I'll clear it with Pugh, don't you worry. I've always thought that robust donations to the contributions box reflect what a civilised society we are.'

'Of course, Mr Ballard, how very true that is.'

'Here's the pen then, Mrs Harrison. Don't mind using a fountain pen, do you? Sign just here. We can then close Mrs Evans' account, all done and dusted. Close the door on the way out, would you, and run along straight away to the contributions box with the money.'

'Thank you, Mr Ballard, right away, sir.'

XXXVIII

BROKEN HILL HAD SEEN NOTHING like it: exactly a week after Auntie Maisie's death, four Belgian blue-black stallions, chosen for their supremely tranquil temperament and noble aspect, brought down from the Congo no less, dyed black, original ostrich-plume feathers tied to their heads, pulling the glass paned landau carriage containing the mortal remains of Mrs Maisie Evans. The stallions went unfed and unwatered for twelve hours prior to the ceremony to avoid prejudicing the decorum and solemnity of the occasion. The teak casket, draped in shimmering black velvet, was unadorned save for one white rose. Notwithstanding the paucity of this floral tribute, the landau did have integral access from the anterior as well as the posterior sections to assist with ease of passage for any sizable floral or other tributes. Large floral tributes were a speciality of the funeral director's second cousin, who took great pride in his craft and always provided a generous financial discount to his cousin, Mr Sutton, or Sutton the Death as he was known to the local citizenry of the Nonconformist faith. The other funeral directors in Broken Hill naturally paid full price. The discount rarely if ever found its way from Sutton the Death to the family of the deceased. Although Sutton was honoured to be the recipient of such a prestigious instruction from the deceased's nephew, financial imperatives clearly had to take precedence.

The carriage was made of the finest mahogany, overlaid with intricate carvings of flowers, scrolls, cherubs and doves, the collared harness artfully constructed out of premium Italian patent leather, and specifically made to measure by professional artisans from Livingstone itself.

Unsurprisingly Mr Ballard had not been invited to the funeral. It would, in any event, have been difficult for him to attend. Two days after Auntie Maisie's demise, Ballard's peerless secretary, Mrs Harrison, on delivering his usual nine thirty morning cup of tea, one sugar, hint of sterilised milk, two chocolate biscuits, had found Mr Ballard hanging from a ceiling spar, next to his desk, the rope sprucely tied to his neck and neatly looped up and over one of the splendid mahogany roof beams.

In her state of shock Mrs Harrison hadn't noticed that the considerate Mr Ballard, so as not to tarnish the polished top of his desk, had removed both his shoes before ascending the scaffold. Second witness Miss Jacobs did notice however that Mr Ballard's big toe, on his right foot – large, dirty-nailed – protruded through his grey socks. A lack of prudent and timely darning, Miss Jacobs surmised. The feet also ponged a bit, but from what she could see were ivory white.

Disappointingly Mr Ballard would not now have the pleasure of being introduced to the new auditors of the care home, Messrs James, Young, Masterman and Lloyd, replacements to the well respected Messrs Ballard, John, Austin, and Davies, who had served the care home nobly for decades.

On discovering the body, Secretary Mrs Harrison and Secretary Miss Jacobs were inconsolable. On the same day, a few hours thereafter, they both tendered their written resignations, leaving them in two separate sealed envelopes, marked 'to whom it may concern', on the scaffold itself. Their respective places of worship and the Broken Hill Women's Guild were the poorer for it, as both eyewitnesses and their families promptly left Broken Hill, Mrs Harrison to Johannesburg and Miss Jacobs to Durban.

Jabez had given strict instructions for the funeral ceremony. No third party was invited, not even Gwyn Bowen. A lead walker from the undertakers, Sutton himself, would pace in front of the hearse, dressed in matching top hat and tails, with pinstripe trousers, cravat and gloves. The coachman was similarly attired. A groom was also recommended by Sutton, but to his surprise his services were declined, as was Sutton's suggestion that his company's name and logo, a pair of trumpeting angels, be tastefully displayed on the side of the hearse.

Sutton, carrying his top hat in his left hand, black cane in his right, was to walk at a dignified pace at a constant distance of ten yards or so from the lead pairing of stallions. Sutton, coachman, horses and landau had partaken in a dry run the previous day, to avoid any embarrassing events occurring during the funeral itself. The coachman had over twenty years driving experience, mostly church weddings. He couldn't rightly remember when he'd last partaken in a horse-drawn funeral. He had, in fact, never previously done so, an insignificant detail that Sutton the Death felt need not concern Jabez. In any event, this fact and others were glossed over during the financial negotiations over costings, etc, Sutton perceiving Jabez's desolation over his aunt's demise as meaning there would be no arduous bargaining over such squalid matters as money. In fact, once the ceremony was over and immediate payment made, Sutton kicked himself for not asking for a higher emolument.

The only mourner was to be Jabez himself, once again dressed in the same suit as he'd worn at his late uncle's funeral and that dreadful last meeting with Ballard. On this occasion, and upon Sutton's suggestion, the suit and shirt were taken to the Chinese dry cleaners in Broken Hill. The deep clean revealed a certain weathering on both knees of the trousers and on both elbows of the suit jacket. However, these were neatly concealed by some dexterous stitching from the dry cleaner's proprietor, an accomplished tailor, for a small extra charge. Naturally, Sutton the Death added a management fee for himself. The final result, a set of steam-pressed garments were a joy to behold. The white shirt, alas, was beyond redemption, Sutton the Death advising Jabez to invest in a brand new Egyptian white cotton affair from a colleague, Jeremiah Owen, who ran a gentlemen's outfitters and haberdashery in Ndola. The insignificant discount he negotiated with the outfitters being too trifling to pass on, Sutton entered the cotton shirt in the final invoice under the heading of 'miscellaneous sundries', management fee included. Owen also did a fine line in bespoke luggage, made from zebra skins, Gwyn a frequent visitor, delivering the raw materials, compensation negotiable.

'And one more thing, Sutton.'

'And what would that be, Mr Pugh?'

'This!' Jabez thrust a folded piece of A3 paper torn from a Rhodesia Railways notebook into Sutton's hands. 'That's what I want carved on the headstone.

'MAISIE SIÂN EVANS 1870-1955

BORN TŶ GWYN FARM, CYNHEIDRE, CYMRU.

DIED BROKEN HILL.

CARES CAUSED BY LIFE'S FAULTS AND SINS, I NEVER SAW,
THEREFORE DO NOT WEEP.
BEREFT FROM ALL SUFFERING
IN MY GRAVE, I AM FREE.'

XXXIX

THE ILL-DOINGS IN THE CEMETERY were one of the most shocking things that I, and probably all of Broken Hill, had heard of. Poor Joe, he wasn't everyone's cup of tea, granted; I knew that he had taken advantage of the girls behind boss man's back, especially the new ones, but still... And in a cemetery! It was a short cut I'd used hundreds of times, although I'd never liked the place. Full of dead hypocrites. Even so, who on earth would do that to him? But that Murphy's attracted all kinds of clientele – 'the cream of settler society', or so they called themselves.

That other wretch who was killed, Gideon, I'd seen him now and again, on my way through there – slow witted but harmless enough.

I'd spoken to comrades and they assured me that the deaths had nothing to do with the struggle. But they had no idea who'd committed the killings. There was talk that Joe had been carrying Murphy's takings at the time, but I didn't hear more of that. As for the police, there was as much chance of them untangling the riddle as a zebra going to the moon. Nobody important had died. Whoever had done it was wicked, they didn't deserve compassion, but they'd get away with it, I was in no doubt of that.

I don't think Delyth even knew anything had happened. More and more she kept herself to her room, never read any papers, never saw anyone, save for me and Gwyn when he was about. If I'd told her that Cecil Rhodes had been resurrected, I think she would have shown more interest in a ticking clock.

I tried to get her out of the house to see Jabez's aunt's funeral. I've forgotten her name now, but it was a hell of a show. I'd never seen such a send off. Most of Broken Hill was out on the streets that day. We should have had more of those occasions, to bring us all together. But when I suggested it to Delyth, she looked right through me, and retreated back to her room.

XL

'COULDN'T KEEP AWAY, EH, GWYN? How's them two grass widows of yours, Delyth and Daisy?'

'They're both fine, doing well. Going to be a father.'

'Christ, you don't mess around. Where did you get the time?'

Gwyn forced a smile. 'That was some funeral you had for your aunt. All of Broken Hill was out watching. My condolences to you. I know you were very close.'

'She was like a mother to me. For all purposes she *was* my mother. I ain't the sentimental type, but her dying knocked me for six, it really did. Still don't think I'm over losing her. Tell you the truth, don't think I ever will be.'

'You gave her a great send off, that's for sure.'

'Yeah, went to Murphy's afterwards, got plastered.'

'I take it they've found a new barman then. Sleepy old Broken Hill... By the way, how did you get those cuts on your face? Been in a fight again?'

'They ain't nothing, just a little misunderstanding with another of the clientele, that's all. We're blood brothers now.'

'I'm sure you are. Wouldn't have looked good at the funeral though. I mean that face of yours ain't a picture at the best of times.'

'My face was a picture at Auntie Maisie's burial, don't you worry.

That Sutton thought of everything. He plastered me in some woman powder, made me look almost normal.'

'Sutton the Death? Woman powder, is that what he called it? Embalming fluid more like!'

'Who cares, it's all done. I've done my duty by Auntie Maisie. Daisy'll be a great help now, Gwyn, good thing you kept her on. Most young wives would be jealous. She'll be able to help with all the other things that'll require doing. You know, mother things. You'll love them both forever, but I still ain't sure whether you'll be content in their company.'

'Right, Jab, enough milling air. Now that we've lost Daniel, I'm going to appoint Kabwe foreman. He seems sensible enough. He's strong, speaks English well, has the respect of the others. How is Daniel, by the way?'

'He's back with his folks. Don't think he'll be able to walk proper ever again. He won't work on the Railways again either, that's for sure.'

'Pity, sorry to lose him.'

'Always thought you two were close, friends even,' proffered Jabez.

Gwyn hesitated. He had been able to hide things between him and Daniel, between him and the others before Daniel. Their times together were now memories, and he preferred very much to keep them as memories. New memories could always be created, even in Northern Rhodesia. Perceptions were crucial to Gwyn; there were no circumstances where he could be open and disclose the truth. It was not just that such friendships were illegal and taboo; it was just the man he was, a private man. He preferred not to be noticed – more than that, to throw people off the scent, away from the trail that might lead them to who he truly was. Because of this, many people thought of him as a bit of a cold fish.

'I was fond of poor Daniel, but he's gone now. Nothing we can do about it. All we can do is give him our sympathy.'

'Behind that polished mask of yours, Gwyn, there's a pretty heartless streak.'

'It's the Railways. They don't run on pity.'

'Why Kabwe? Why not one of the others, someone less ambitious, like old Mubanga?'

'Well, fella's got to be Bemba, for one thing. It's their country after all. They think I'd be gloating at Daniel's bad luck if I appointed anyone other than a Bemba. And Mubanga's canny, but he's too old. It's just an accidental union of occurrences, that's all.'

'Accidental union of occurrences, is that what you call it? Spoken like a head office memorandum, written by some Livingstone pen pusher! We all know there was no love lost between the Indians and Daniel. Can't say I'm too keen on them myself. And as for the Bemba, never been able to work them out, even after all these years. The Chinamen, no one understands them.'

'No point in us looking into the matter too deeply, nor into any of the other happenings out here, else the whole railway system would collapse. This is Bemba country and I'll respect that.'

'We'll soon be finished with this shithole anyway. Kapiri Mposhi can kiss my arse. Most of the work's been done, then you can go home to your ladies and I'll go back to mine in Murphy's.'

'You've never liked Africa, have you, Jab? You were born here and you still don't like it.'

'I like Broken Hill better than you do, and that's a fact. It's got Murphy's, and that's all I need to call it home,' said Jabez.

'I've got my home there, my books, and soon, God willing, I'll have a son.'

'The Good Lord told you, did he? "Gwyn Bowen, I shall give you a son for being a good man." Another case of immaculate conception. You believe you're so close to the Almighty, he'll do you a favour and grant you a boy, another Railwayman!?'

'First born of every new Bowen generation has been a strapping boy, that's a fact, Jab. Ten, twelve pounds, all strong healthy boys.'

'Granted, I ain't much of a professor in the birthing business. All I know nothing is guaranteed in that game. You better call that to mind when the time comes.' Jabez took out a tin of chewing tobacco from his side trouser pocket, grabbed a piece and offered it to Gwyn; the offer was declined.

'Best we send a Spanner up the track today,' said Gwyn. 'We've got to find some work for the men to do. We've broken the back of most of the stuff. Thomas told me there were some loose bolts few miles from here.'

'We may as well send two,' suggested Jabez. 'Send old man Mubanga out.'

'He's getting on, it'll be a few miles walk.'

'Why'd you take him on if he ain't fit for the work?'

'Took Daniel's say so. Wanted to give him one last job. I've known Mubanga longer than all the Bemba, even longer than Daniel. He's crafty all right, but dependable. Need someone we can trust will do the work when it comes to the spanners. We don't want a derailment on our watch. Send out one of the young ones with him as well.'

'What about David?'

'He'll do.'

Kabwe got the order from Jabez.

'Mubanga, David! Mr Bowen wants you to be Spanners today, get a couple from stores and some skoff from the canteen, don't want to see you back here till night time. Mubanga, you know what to do. Speak to Thomas, he'll tell you where to go. Go on, see you tonight,' ordered Kabwe.

All this was new to David. Each rail was sixty feet long and bolted together by a two-foot long smooth piece of steel called a fish plate. The regular motion of rolling stock over the fish plates caused slackening of the bolts, which meant they had to be periodically tightened.

Old man Mubanga, by far the eldest of the crew, still carried the semblance of a smirk. But these days, his face also had the hint of a death mask, slightly drawn, a face untouched by soap and razor for a number of days. Old man Mubanga had already outlived two of his children, but in strength he was not elderly, able to hold his own with the rest. In quieter moments, when he was alone, he would sometimes weep silently, knowing that his toughness was trickling out of him. Like a hushed murmuring from a stethoscope, he prayed that he was the only one that could hear it.

'Good job for us today. Easy pickings, no Jabez looking over our shoulders...' said Mubanga.

'And no Daniel either,' David chipped in.

'Never had much to do with him, save on the hiring. He left me fend for myself out here, no interference. Didn't see what happened neither. Thought he was strong enough by hisself on the crowbar against those two Indians.'

'Those Indians never been the same since their kin died, that man Kumar—'

'Happened to be in the wrong place at the wrong time, could've been any one of us,' said Mubanga.

'Yeah, that was funny.'

'What was?'

'It's usually the Chinaman, the boss Chinaman,' said David.

'Who, Jimmy?'

'Yeah, him. He usually the one goes back with them Jerry cans to fetch the water, he being a sort of cook and all. Saw him talk to Kumar. Think he gave him something. Money probably, so Kumar could do the water burden for him. Might be wrong though.'

Mubanga did not show much interest. 'Makes no difference now. Kumar plain dead. Listen, Thomas says there's a slack about three miles yonder, some engine driver reported it to him in the station, but we to check all them joints as we see fit.'

'How the hell we gonna find the slack on the savannah, old man? This railway just goes on forever.'

'Says it's near some big baobab tree, says we can't miss it. And we better not miss it, young David. If that bolt kicks out, we might be another Kumar and Daniel. And something else, whoever does the tightening, other man does the looking, you hear me? These railway bends so sharp, you never know what's coming at you till it's too late. Trains don't stop for no Bemba, even genuine homegrown, blue-blooded Rhodesia Railways Bemba.'

'We'll be the saviours of Kapiri Mposhi, they'll be writing stories about us. David and Mubanga, Mubanga and David, Protectors of the Fish Plates, Saviours of the Savannah,' laughed David.

'What you talking about, just keep an eye out. Should've asked Thomas for the timetable. We need to know when those machines come down the line.'

'Kabwe should have given us a pump trolley, get to that dead rat tree quicker,' suggested David.

'Glad he didn't. There's some steep inclines and fierce keen bends on this track. We come across a train all of a sudden steaming towards us, then how we gonna get away? Outspeed the loco in a pump trolley? Lift it off the track, just the two of us? Stupid!'

'Thought you'd agree. Pump trolleys for old men like yourself, Mubanga. Daniel paid the price for that. Wasn't strong enough to hold up his side. That's what happens when you get old.'

'Remember the story of the hare Kalulu and the lion? You must have heard it from your mother. Not sure if you knew your father!'

'You be careful what you say, old fella.'

'Calm down, calm down. You know the tale, the big lion, king of the animals, made a decree, a big decision, that all old animals should be killed, on account of old animals being weak and still eating a goodly supply of food, leaving less for the young, fit animals. And that's what happened. All the old ones were killed save for an old hare called Kalulu, who'd hidden deep in a cave. One day, king lion, he asleep with his mouth wide open when a big long snake mistakes the lion's mouth for a cavern. In he goes, right into the lion's throat, so the lion loses his roar, and every time the snake move, the lion hurt bad. Using sign language, the lion say whoever get the snake out of his mouth would be granted whatever he wanted.'

'How long this going on for Mubanga, and where's that tree?'

'Shush, sievehead! A long line of young sassy animals come to see the lion. They full of themselves just like you, boy, trying to get the snake out, but that snake, he don't budge from his warm and cosy new home. Old Kalulu's son, we'll call him young Kalulu, seeing his chance, goes up to the lion and tells him he knows of a wise man living in a cave who could get rid of the snake. "Get him here," whispers the lion, who by this time is thin and weak on account he ain't eaten for so long. The young Kalulu rushes to see his father and explains the situation to him. Kalulu the old disguises himself as a magnificent magician, singing spells and suchlike in front of the lion, whilst at the same time placing a mouse stuck in a mousetrap just outside the lion's open mouth. 'Fore long, the snake, he smells the mouse, and it slithers out of the lion's mouth to investigate. Immediately old Kalulu grabbed that snake and threw it into the bush. "Oh thank you, great magician, what is your wish so that I may grant it to you?" says king lion. Old Kalulu replies, 'I ask nothing for myself save that you allow all the old animals to live their lives in peace and not be killed. Because in your time of need, none of the young animals could help you and only the wisdom of an old hare like myself freed you from your burden.' The lion realized his mistake and granted the wish of old Kalulu. After that, all the old animals were allowed to live out their lives in harmony and happiness. So you be careful when you talk bad about us older folk. Remember the story now, David, remember it?'

'Sort of. But this ain't the time for stories, old man. Let's keep an eye out for them trains, and any passing peckish beasts. Tsetses bad today, this dark blue shirt like a magnet. And why do all the tales say the old are wise when they can't even go twenty minutes without needing to piss? And why do you old folk look back all the time? Remember this, remember that all you talk about...'

They'd walked some two miles and rested just off the tracks.

'Water?' offered David.

'Thanks. Ain't it good out here? We got water, a full skoff box, no Jabez, bit of shade... Must be what our Lord's life is like. We're monarchs of the universe.'

They saw a flash of lightning far off but could hear no thunder.

'Your mind's failing you, Mubanga, we ain't no monarchs of the universe. We ain't even monarchs of this scrap of spinney. Time you put all your tools on the bar and take to your bed. And try to remember all your long agos through your antique eyes, pretty girls, their hips... They all memories to you now, ain't they. Bet you don't remember the half of it.'

'Shut up! You'll understand more when you get older, boy. All of us living away from home for months at a time, we forget the old ways, the traditions we've had for as long as we can recall. Living in men-only camps, only going home once or twice a year, that ain't right.'

'Think you could go back to the old way of living? Would old Kalulu be there? Even the villages change.'

'True.'

'You got me muddled now, old man. What plan you advancin' here?'

'Get an education, David, don't waste your life on the Railways. You've seen what happens. The Indian's dead, Daniel might as well be. Get an education, get out of the Railways. This work kills you in the end.'

'Hang on, old man, *you* still alive, *you* still healthy, save you a little light in the head. You been a Railwayman for longer than anyone, how do you answer that?'

'Luck, boy, luck plain and simple.'

'Well I could be lucky too.'

'Talk to Thomas, the ticket master, he'll have more answers for you. He the future.'

'Why you so close to him, old man?'

'We kin. He's learning to poke his head out, get to see what's really going on around here. He wants to change things, he ain't just a ticket clerk.'

'Don't change bring calamity? That's what your friend Kalulu would say, ain't it?' asked David.

'We can't stay small all our lives, David.'

David grimaced to himself, recalling the Kafwe river bridge holdup. That railway guard was dead, and he and Thomas had killed him. The knowledge, the horror, never really went away. He could still see, sniff, taste, sense that night, from the insects to the steam to the blood, and not only in his nightmares.

A zephyr zigzagged gently about the bush, picking up bits of loose dirt. A drop of spittle slobbered out of the side of Mubanga's lips. He juiced up some more and spat it out onto the waterless veldt.

'What you think of Kabwe? He going to turn out to be Daniel?' David was slowly spinning into a politician, and he wanted to know what old man Mubanga knew. But Mubanga was no hollow reed or tinkling cymbal.

'Yep, I do. Seen plenty of Daniels, and he'll turn out one of them,' replied Mubanga.

'You, me, would we be no different? Give us command and we be Daniel?' asked David.

'You tell me. Traitors betray, that's what they do. Pay men a farthing they won't do nothing, pay them a fiver, they'll do anything,' said Mubanga.

'You'd refuse the top job on account of what you might turn into? You afraid of yourself, old man? We haven't all gotta become a Daniel.'

'Is that so? Well, you missed your chance to prove me wrong, boy. There's a vacancy at the moment with him being invalided out, but Kabwe first in line,' retorted Mubanga.

'There's always happenings on the Railways. There'll always be vacancies. What was it like here before the Railways? You should know, you been here forever. Must have looked clean, untouched,' said David.

'Sedition, that's sedition talk, boy!' said Mubanga, raising his voice like a circus master. 'That's what the settlers would say. Before the Railways, before the types of Jabez and Bowen? Hell, I ain't that old. All I do know is you're on your own hereabouts. No one helps you out, you're just trying to find the path from this world to the next. And no priests passing round the communion wine out here, to help you on your way. What with Jabez bitchin' you, Bowen, Kabwe scoring points—'

'How do we get to the next world, Mubanga?'

'You got to die first, son, and you've come to the right place for that.'

'Least you know where you are with Jabez, that's true, ain't it? Not like Bowen. He wants to be like one of us, he don't know his place. Hell, them settlers even trying to cart off our language to a museum, the very words we speak. Kabwe was right, wasn't he, about that bloke Konkola? We should be giving the orders.'

'Our lingo already lost. Changed no end since they arrived. We're voiceless. Don't care for that, don't care for none of it. It's like we're being nipped by midges all the time. One thing, one thing only you need to keep in mind when you dealing with them Europeans: they'll always treat you as a savage. Never, ever forget that,' said Mubanga.

'Then they won't mind if we act like savages,' replied David.

'Out here in the bush, it's humans that give you the most pain, don't matter what colour they are. And yeah, Kabwe was right, we should be giving the orders. It's our country after all. Come on, find me that baobab tree, your eyes are much better than mine,' said Mubanga.

'Maybe my eyes are stronger, old man, but yours see things better.'

XLI

THERE WAS NO LIGHT in my bedroom. A tap, tap, tap on the window woke me. A persistent tapping, like a winter wind-blown branch against glass, uniform, unflagging. Undeterred by my lack of response, the tap, tap, tapping continued. Going to the window like a frightened impala at a shrinking water hole, I whispered, 'Who's there?'

'Open up, open up, it's me! Quick, open the back door!'

I recognized the voice at once. It was Thomas. I put on my nightgown and opened the rear door, the door which led directly out into the garden. Numberless stars punctured the dark evening sky.

'What you doing here at this time of night, what on earth do you want?' I asked, my voice barely above a murmur.

'We want your help.'

'Help for what?'

'Need you to look after some goods for us. For a few days, that's all.'

'You're lucky Gwyn isn't here.'

'Don't fret, we know he's not here. We keep an eye on things.'

'What goods you talking about?'

'Don't need to concern you about that, all we need is somewhere safe for a few days. Three crates, three wooden crates and one smaller one. Where can we put them?'

'Follow me.'

The struggle wasn't academic anymore. I was in it. And I suddenly felt afraid. I led Thomas and a group of eight or nine men and women, I wasn't sure how many, through the garden towards the unfinished swimming pool, my seesawing lantern sending its shafts of light hugger mugger through the darkness. I prayed that Delyth wouldn't be disturbed.

'See that tarpaulin in the pool?' I said. 'Gwyn uses it to cover the cement mixer and equipment he's using. Only I never know when he'll be back from site. He just sort of turns up when he turns up, so you better hurry.'

'We know when he'll be here. We've got friends in the Railways too.'

A torch flashed down into the dry floor of the unfinished pool.

'That'll be good. Get the crates, comrades. Bring them over here, make sure the merchandise is safely stowed.'

'Be quiet!' I hissed as loudly as I dared. 'I'm not the only one in the house.'

'I'm sure Delyth is a sound sleeper. Being pregnant must be very tiring.'

'You seem to know a lot about us, Thomas.'

'It's our business to know. We're never far from where you are, Daisy. Look over your shoulder now and again, you might see us. Then again, delusions might be catching. Your visits to Dr Cosgrove, your swimming lessons... I can hold my breath in the water for a long time as well, and I also am partial to Welsh cakes.'

'You've been spying on me?'

'Better mistrust undeserved than secrets disclosed. Each one of us is watched. After all, that is your name, isn't it, Kalinda? You watch as well.'

'I was told no one would be hurt.'

'And you believed that? I don't think so. Squeamishness does not befit you, Daisy. Don't fool us, don't fool yourself. You may have been a simple country girl once, but not any longer. You worked at Murphy's long enough, you've seen how the world works.'

'How dare you!'

'Leave your dramatics for the eyes of others, they'll be more appreciative. We need your help now. This is your test, Kalinda. Prove to us that you're truly on our side. We are all watching.'

'Be quick about it then.'

The night people carried the wooden boxes, the large ones around four feet in length by two feet, the smaller box close to three feet square. The boxes had left their Belgian factory many years ago, their journey towards me circuitous, someone profiting each step of the way.

'Right under the tarpaulin, they'll be safe here till we need them. Make sure you cover them good, don't want anyone discovering our little treasure.'

I could see that Thomas was in charge. He didn't want to be one of the cattle, he wanted to be the drover. Four to each long box and two to the smaller box. The crates stored and hidden within twenty minutes.

I did not think of myself as especially courageous that evening. It was a duty that had to be fulfilled. I looked on as the packages were brought across the garden and down the swimming pool steps. The light was not good but I could make out writing branded on the boxes, but the language was unknown to me.

'They're guns, aren't they?'

'Don't turn delicate. We're not going to debate the Europeans out of our country, they'll only pay off our politicians. Not so easy to pay off a man with a gun, and anyways death is only painful for the living.'

'When will you pick them up?'

'I told you, a few days, no more than a few days. I'll knock your little window again when we come to collect, something for you to look forward to. Farewell, Kalinda, until the next time.'

With that they were gone, bleached into the shadows, the night noiseless and total. I returned to my bedroom as silently as I could.

'Delyth! What are you doing here, can't you sleep?'

Delyth, her lanterned face furrowed and gaunt. 'Who were those men, what were they doing here this time of night?'

I was flustered.

'Just some workmen bringing more cement for the swimming pool. Been trying to get them here for ages. Wanted to surprise

Gwyn and get the pool finished before he comes home from leave next.'

'Oh, Daisy, I'm a fool in your eyes, aren't I? Ignorant little settler lass gets pregnant, gets herself into trouble in this bad, bad world of Africa, needs to be kept quiet, needs to hear lies to keep her sane.'

'I'm not like that, Delyth. I'm concerned. I want to see you get better. I am not one to lie.'

'You know, I don't really care anymore. I've had enough. Of Gwyn, of you, of this country… I've had enough. I'm just so tired of all of it. There could be all the diamonds in Kimberley in those boxes and I wouldn't give a tinker's cuss. Do what you want, Daisy. You and Gwyn, do what you want. I'm used up, tired of all the happenings in this horrid place. These lodgings are no longer for me.'

'There isn't a different world elsewhere, Delyth. I'm sorry, I should have told you the workmen were coming, but I thought you'd be asleep. Didn't want to wake you. Please. Come here.'

Delyth's face hadn't seen the sun for some time. She looked pale, she'd lost weight, even though she was carrying a child.

I lifted my right hand, opened my palm, beckoning Delyth to me. She didn't move. I advanced three steps to her and placed my hand on her shoulder. I kissed her. Delyth did not recoil, but stood there like a shop window mannequin waiting to be undressed.

XLII

THE SUN SHONE through the curtains. A mixture of colours and patterns, turquoise-printed lillies on a cream background, scalloped, held up by plastic rings on a white-painted wooden pole.

Even though I had closed the curtains tight the evening gone, the dawn still shimmered through. The light and the last musings of a nightjar mixed, and the beginnings of the song of a rufous ant thrush stirred me from sleep. Delyth, beside me, was already awake.

'I always thought that it would come to this, Daisy. From the first time I met you. I'm not sure what it was. Maybe my need for love, my need for love from someone... anyone.'

'And that anyone was me?' I replied.

'I'm not a greedy person. It's just... Everyone I meet is "hail fellow, well met", but it's a sham isn't it?'

'You have to find contentment, Delyth. It doesn't come to you, it doesn't pass you in the street and tap you on the shoulder.'

'Things are changing, aren't they, Daisy? Everything is turning topsy-turvy.'

I thought about getting up and making us both a cup of tea.

'You began to tell me queer things last night. Or was I dreaming, Daisy? The things you did to me last night, have you done them before? To other women? Have you done them to Gwyn? When I'm with Gwyn we never touch. He never reaches for me like you did last night.'

'I learnt many things in Murphy's, Delyth. Some I regret, some I don't.

'And did you change? Did Satan's backyard change you?'

'I grew up. I had a friend there, she was my age. Called Jane. Started work a few months before I arrived. Pretty girl, the prettiest there. All the johns wanted to be with her. Boss man could charge a higher rate for her and hire her out for a shorter time. Even the drinks she ordered at the bar cost them more. Boss man could have charged more again and they still would have paid. She working constantly, hour after hour after hour. Boss man always told Joe the barman to give coloured water to the girls, still charge whisky rates, but with Jane it was different. Boss man could see she flagging, she suffering. He didn't mind though. As long as she working, them tenners and tenners and tenners would keep flowing in. Told Joe to put whisky in her glass, none of that coloured water, and always doubles, sometimes even trebles. Whatever time she on shift, ten in the morning or ten in the evening just the same, big slug of whisky every glass.'

'She was so special, johns only allowed twenty minutes with her, thirty minutes cost double. Every time she'd finished with one, she'd be back down the bar holding a whisky from Joe, always someone ready to buy. Some johns wanted to talk with her a while before going upstairs, that meant more drink. Times were she so drunk, she'd be holding on to them bannisters to save herself from falling over.

'One night towards the end of her obligations, one of her regulars came in. I seen him plenty. Big, fat, balding... Early sixties I'd say. European obviously. Anyways she was drunk with johns, so many of them, and she was drunk with whisky. Off they go upstairs.

'All us girls knew this john was different, had peculiar tastes, unusual practices. It wasn't long after that bedroom door closed that we heard wild shouts and screams coming out of there. Me, Joe the barman and the boss man ran upstairs. Boss man didn't even knock on the door, used his passkey to get in, and me and Joe followed. Jane there in the bed, crunched up like some frightened porcupine, pulled up the bedclothes right up to her neck, shaking like a miombo tree in a storm. The john, he on the floor, shaking too.

' "She likes it, I know she does… We've done this thing before, there's been no problem… The bitch said she didn't like it this time. Don't know what's got into her. You been paying her too much, giving her too much slack, she's getting too high and mighty. I had to teach her a lesson. Few cuffs, that's all… Show her she needs to respect the client more, show her who's the boss."

' "You're absolutely right, Mr Thompson. You can rest assured that I'll deal with her in the severest manner. Joe, pick up Mr Thompson's clothes, take him next door, get him dressed and freshened up. No need to fret, sir, we'll clear all this up. Joe will wash that blood clean away from your hands and face. Apologies again for the girl not treating you right. Next time it'll be on the house. I'm expecting some young fresh ones in any day."

' "You need to keep these girls in line, they need to know their place. I know all the right people in this town, they could make things very difficult for you."

' "Of course, Mr Thompson, I couldn't agree with you more. We'll sort you out, make sure you get home safely. Don't want Mrs Thompson and the kids worrying about you. No need to brood over this girl neither. She has no family, no one will be troubled. We'll keep this amongst ourselves. The entire situation will turn out fine."

' "I don't want to see that slut ever again, is that clear? This place will get a bad reputation if you're not careful!"

'Perfectly clear, sir. The good name of Murphy's is close to all our hearts. Joe is here to help. He'll see you safely home. We all hope to see you soon. And remember, it'll be on the house."

'Joe took Thompson away, poor Jane still in the bed shaking.

' "What's happened here girl, what the hell did you do to upset the client?"

' "He punched me, he punched me, he kept punching me!"

' "What you talking about, girl? There ain't a mark on your face!"

'Jane's face is twisted with tears. "It wasn't my face he punched!" she says.

' "Oh no," I shout out. "Shut up, Daisy," boss man says. "If you can't shut up, get out of here.

' "Let me see, Jane let me see..." Boss man had to tug real hard at them cotton sheets, only way he could get them out of Jane's trembling hands. Finally he lifts those sheets, she naked as the day she born. Blood everywhere. The bed, her legs drenched in red, soaked through... If that john had still been in that room I would have scratched his eyes out and that would have been just the start. The piece of shit!'

'What happened to Jane?' asked Delyth.

'Boss man got some tame medical man in. He a john too, not a real doctor, he something to do with horses, cattle and the like.'

'You mean a vet?' suggested Delyth.

'Possibly, I don't know. We washed her and she was stitched up, and me and this quack more like half-carried, half-walked Jane home. Boss man insistent she be taken off the premises double quick. Plenty more johns waiting to use the room.

'Jane never worked at Murphy's again. Boss man said she bad for business. Works street corners now. Needs the money for whisky and whatever else she can lay her hands on to make her forget. The john, Thompson, he came back a few weeks later. None of 'em can keep away. No longer pays premium rates, no one left in Murphy's as good as Jane. Boss man told me he sad to see her go, but Murphy's not the place for drunks and ruined articles.

'When we got her home the quack left straight away. Me and Jane, we cried a long time. Maybe I should have helped her more, maybe I should have schooled her better... Maybe, I don't know.'

'Are you going to tell Gwyn about last night?' asked Delyth.

I was still at Murphy's, with Thompson and Jane. I'd forgotten about Delyth.

'Not unless you want me to.'

'I'd prefer if you didn't. You know all the truths, Daisy, and you know when, and when not, to tell them.'

'Your choice, Delyth.'

'I have choices? I don't need choices, I need help. I'm worried for my baby, I'm worried for my sanity. This tic, I've got this tic in my eye, comes now and again. Can't stop it, keeps coming back and back. I think it's getting worse. Sometimes I can't move my arms. They're stuck, as if they've been glued to the floor. I have dreams again, dreams of two snakes suckling at my breasts, and everything is so dark. What's happening to me! I cry when I should be laughing and laugh when I should be crying. I think I've got feelings for Dr Cosgrove. He comes to me in my dreams at night.'

'Don't be so silly, you hardly know him!'

'I think he also has feelings for me. I've seen his eyes, the way he looks at me. I know I'm right. I've started having dreams about him.'

'Oh, come on, Delyth! Why don't you try and have different dreams?'

'Don't you dream?' Delyth started to cry, lifting herself from a prone position so that her back was at right angles to the bed.

'Of course I do! I must. I'm human too. But I can't remember half of them. Dreams aren't important, Del. It's what we do when were awake that's the thing.'

Delyth plumped up her pillows for more support.

'I dream of his surgery, of his consulting room… I dream of being alone with him. He touches me and I let him. I encourage him, just like with you last night. But I touch him back.'

'Don't fall in love with a dream. You've got to put them to one side, forget about them. There's no future there. You can't live inside your mind. Think about the future, the baby. Think about getting better. There's so much for you to look forward to.'

I felt she was falling away from me, like a woman slowly drowning, but there were no flailing arms, no screams, just a quiet descent like a tiny pebble disappearing into the bottom of a lake. I hope I'd done the right thing, showing her physical love, a tender love. Had I been granted the ability to save people? I knew that couldn't be true. How could I be a saviour of someone else and her worries? Enjoyment can't be the answer every time. Pleasure alone can't save. But surely it must help.

'I see things as well. When I'm awake I see things. Do you believe me?'

'If you tell me you see things, then I believe you,' I said.

'A lot of them are to do with you.'

'With me?'

'Did you give me that egg with the embryo in it? Did you buy those dozen eggs? Did they all have embryos in them? You put them there to frighten me, didn't you?'

'No, of course not.'

Delyth was looking straight ahead to the hanging clock opposite my bed, her staccato voice beating a tempo with the ticking of the second hand. *Tick tock, tick tock.*

'You took me swimming in the river, didn't you? You gave me bilharzia. Are you poisoning me, Daisy? You and Gwyn, are you both conspiring to poison me? I should ask Dr Cosgrove. I'm sure he loves me. I'll have to go and see him more often, I'll have to show him my feelings, that they're the same as his for me. And you and Gwyn better stop trying to poison me, or I'll tell Dr Cosgrove about you. He'll come over here and protect me, I know he will. I'll need to get rid of this tic before I see him again. He won't want me to see me like that. I'll need to look my best when I go to see him. Do you know where he lives, Daisy? I'd like to see what he does with himself when he's not in the surgery. If I follow him around, I'll know how to accidentally bump into him, like I did with Gwyn. I'd like to talk to him on his own when the surgery staff aren't about. He'll be more relaxed then.'

I tried to calm her down. I saw weakness and fear in front of me. Was she becoming her mother? It seemed to me she had too many notions in her head; the more she thought the worse she became. I had no idea how to help her.

'Delyth, you must rest.'

'You didn't give me much rest last night, did you? Did I come up to your expectations? Did I pass the Murphy's entrance exam? Could I become one of the girls by the bar? Man and woman couldn't have created last night, only woman and woman.'

'Let me bring you some breakfast. Some hot tea and toast will do you the world of good.'

'No more tea from you, no more food from you, all of it's poisoned! I'll be making my own from now on. I want to look my best for Dr Cosgrove. I'm going to have his baby.'

XLIII

'ALL THEM SLACKS been tightened, boys?' enquired Kabwe as Mubanga and David arrived back from their humble safari.

'All done, boss,' enthused David having already forgotten both the young Kalulu and the old Kalulu. 'Found the big kick, out by that massive baobab. Lucky we did, that bolt almost loosened clean off. Our noses got to the bolt before our eyes.'

'What's he talking about, Mubanga?' asked Kabwe. 'Can you make sense of the boy?'

'The stench, boss. Had to hold our noses for a while. Vultures and such like feasting on some dead animal next to the tree. We got used to it right enough, tightened them bolts up and off we went, left them vultures to it.'

'Last day at camp today, boys,' said Kabwe. 'Jabez says he's gonna lay out some entertainment for us.'

'Railway wages don't stretch to payin' women, do they?' asked David.

'I know that chump Mubanga knows that. The longer you work on the Railways, you'll know it as well. We all to go over where the rest of the boys are. You two only just made the party. Jabez, Pugh, don't wait for no spanners.'

'You coming, Mubanga? Lot of noise over there.'

'Yeah, I'm coming. Sounds like they've got another boomslang.'

*

Whilst Mubanga and David had been on their spanner travels, Jabez had taken George into the bush on a search for vervet monkeys.

'Notice you mighty fussy with your rig out, George, keeping 'em spruce like a preening peacock.'

'Aim to find me a wife some day soon, need to look the part, Mr Pugh.'

'I can highly recommend dry cleaners in Broken Hill. Partook of them for my Auntie Maisie's funeral, save they're a tad expensive. Then again, you pay peanuts you get monkeys, which is where we're going today.'

'What we looking for, Mr Pugh?'

'Targets. Targets in Thomas' tobacco field.'

'What kind of targets?'

'Vervet monkeys. The ones that move and the ones we can catch alive. We'll wing 'em, then we can catch em.'

'With that fancy rifle you're holding? Will it do that? You gotta be some marksman, boss, if you can shoot a monkey just to wing it,' said George.

'This is a very fancy rifle, George. This contraption's called a tranquiliser gun. It's like those air rifles I've seen Bemba kids play with. Shoots these darts here, full of poison. Not the poison that kills, the poison that brings sleep not death.'

'How much poison do you use? These vervets ain't no rhino or buffalo. How much to bring sleep, how much to bring death?'

'The magic ain't the putting to sleep, the magic is making sure they wake up. We'll work that out as we go along. Makes no mind if there's a few dead ones on the way. They're animals, and they don't count. We're on the cutting edge of science here. You and me, George, expanding the range of human knowledge, scientists of the bush. I'll start off big with the poison, see how we get along, and reduce the dose accordingly.'

'Why not start the other way? Start with small poison. Less them monkeys have to suffer, less of 'em die. Seems to me we expanding science by killing monkeys one at a time.'

'Start with too little poison they'd just run away. Kill first and then reduce. They're only monkeys. They don't go to heaven – come to that, hell neither. We'll just be providing carcasses for fellow scavengers. I'll shoot, you run to check if the monkey's alive or dead. I'll drop the dose till I get it right. That's how proper scientists work: trial and error.'

'But if the monkey's dead, we'll have an afterlife of insects around our heads.'

'Just do as you're told, George. I've got a lot of different strengths for these darts, one of them is bound to do the trick.'

'We not going to eat them, are we? They don't taste so good.'

'I'm going to shoot, you're going to catch. We'll take the ones ain't dead back to camp. The boys deserve some fun before we all go our seperate ways.'

'Pardon me asking, Mr Pugh, this affair don't sound like something Mr Bowen would approve.'

'Don't you worry about Mr Bowen, you leave him to me.'

'I got no problems with huntin', killin', we all got to eat, but killin' for killin's sake. Don't seem right to me.'

'It's a European thing, George. And besides, the boys enjoyed the boomslang circus, didn't they? Hope I ain't come across the only Bemba who doesn't like a bit of sport.'

'We ain't all the same, boss. You Europeans always seem to forget that.'

Jabez lifted his bush hat and wiped his forehead with a polkadot handkerchief, then pulled the hat down his forehead as far as he could. The day was hot even for him, and it wouldn't have looked good for a railwayman to get heatstroke. That only happened to townspeople who lived their lives indoors.

Stealthy as spies in their adversaries' barracks, the two men crossed due west behind the station to the field of tobacco plants cultivated by Thomas, a magnet for vervets. The lupine-gaited George followed behind Jabez. The monkeys usually arrived early afternoon, in separate family groups of about fifteen or so.

'We'll hide near the acacias. We'll be downwind of 'em, see what happens. We're a little early from Thomas' accounts. It'll give us time to let things settle down a mite.'

George pulled out a packet of Star cigarettes, offered one to Jabez, which he accepted. The smoke helped on the insect front. A small group of three, possibly four southern ground hornbill, red-throated, black-feathered foraged on the savannah not far from the tobacco field.

'Them hornbills ain't no friends of vervet monkeys either. When we get those monkeys, what we gonna do with them?'

'It's a secret going away party, and if I tell you it won't be a secret, will it, George? Look, do as you're told. Think of it as a scientific experiment. Even better, think of it as helping your fellow Bemba. Mr T in the ticket station office, getting rid of a plague of pests lunching on his tobacco plants.'

The first vervet to appear was the lead alpha male, about twelve pounds in weight and about a foot and a half in length, excluding the tail. More soon followed, a female cradling a baby with some juveniles in her wake.

'Let them start eating first. Make for easier targets when they're not moving,' said Jabez.

'Can't we find some other sport for the boys. These vervets are delicate, dainty. They were around long before tobacco.'

'They're eating Thomas' profits. We'll be doing him a favour, he's Bemba too. These monkeys ain't saints. I've seen 'em destroy tobacco plants just to stop other vervets having a meal. No need to feel sorry for 'em, they're wild animals. You're a Christian, ain't you?'

'Yes, I am,' replied George.

'Good Book says we Christians have dominion over the earth and everything on it. We been put here to dominate the land. No need to pay no heed to brainless animals. They're just here for our pleasure,' said Jabez.

'That's what the Almighty said?' asked George.

'That's what He said, sure enough. Ain't that what them Bible-bashing missionaries told you?'

'Queer thing, the Almighty,' said George, as he looked up at a black-cheeked parrot in a nearby mopone tree. 'He's made everything but He's made us blind. We can't see the whole beauty of the savannah, we only see the monkeys we want to kill.'

'Tranquilise, George, tranquilise. Leastways that's the start of proceedings. Hey up, here comes the first candidate for our experiment. See that big buck over there? He'll be our first volunteer.'

The two men crouched ready for an ambush, the vervet contentedly nibbling away at the tobacco plants, black-faced, edged with a fringing of white hair, the rest of the body a grimy grey.

'How much you think he weighs?' asked Jabez.

'A good fifteen pounds,' replied George. 'He the chief,'

Jabez lifted the tranquiliser gun and pushed it tightly into his right shoulder. 'Got to piss ice when you go hunting.' He looked through the scope and gently squeezed.

The vervet collapsed instantly. High pitched screaming followed from his petrified family, who ran in all directions, leaving the tobacco field empty save for the downed target. Crested guinea fowl cackled, blue quail whistled, and ten to fifteen speckled pigeons flew into the air like reversed confetti.

'Get over there, George, quick. See if he's alive, go on!'

Rushing over to the quarry, George, elbows out, shouting back, 'He's dead, boss, he's dead. Too much death, not enough sleep.'

'Bring it back, bring the dart back, and don't leave that dead meat out there, it'll scare away the others. Another pack'll turn up, give it a while. These apes just love tobacco.'

Tossing the body into the bush near their hide, George, carefully and with some solemnity, handed the dart back to Jabez.

'I'll reduce the dose a tad. We'll soon find the sweet spot. There's more than enough monkeys to go round,' said Jabez.

Another thirty minutes passed, Jabez and George continually sweeping away the mounting collection of flies.

'Look, look! Over there! See the male nibbling?'

'Spotted, George. Bit too far away. Let him settle, he'll bring the others in. Let them feel at home, have a nice time. Don't want to disturb their picnic too soon, do we? Bit closer now... Got to be patient when it comes to shooting.'

A female vervet, nursing an infant in her arms, came within what Jabez thought to be appropriate distance. He squeezed the trigger again. The dart pierced the mid-neck section of the female's head, her chin falling like a drawbridge against her chest. Again the vervet alarm shrieks discharged over the tobacco crop, together with avian squawking, piping and clucking. Off glided George.

'Dead, she's dead,' he reported back. 'The young one's alive though.'

'Bring 'em back, bring 'em both back, and make sure you bring the dart.'

George threw the second victim on top of the first.

'What shall we do with the cub? Is this any good for us?' asked George.

'Yeah, he'll do. Tie him up, give it a bang on the head. Knock it out. Don't want it squealin' and warning the rest of its kind. Got to start working fast on these darts before those dead uns start attracting too many flies. Once these monkeys start smelling their dead, they'll be gone.'

And so the process continued. The sun throbbed. Sweat-soaked skin sucked cotton like a baby at its mother's breast. Within a few more hours the slaughter meadow vomited two more dead vervets. Then Jabez got the hang of things, adjusting the potency of his missiles. The afternoon ebbed and a half light entangled the tobacco plants. By dusk George had four adults roped together: two males, two females and three young. Two of the adults were now conscious but groggy from the anaesthesia, the other two comatose but alive. The three youngsters shivered with fear, clinging to the adults. The hide buzzing with flies feasting on dead monkey flesh. George would have a job tonight to clean his clothes.

'I think that's enough,' Jabez declared. 'I'd shoot some more, getting the hang of it now, but the light's fading and these flies are vexing me. There'll be bigger game around soon, looking for something to eat. Drag the two snooze monkeys back to camp and I'll bring the lively brigade.'

'What about the little ones? Sure are dainty. Bring them back as well?' asked George.

'Nah, four is enough for what I've got in mind for the boys. Four is more than enough. Go on, you start back to camp with the two who can move, I'll sort the rest out. Two of these are sleeping pretty heavy, don't want them giving up and perishing after all this experimenting we've done.'

George walked off hand in hand with the two responsive vervets, like a teacher dragging wayward pupils off to see the headmaster.

Shattering the skulls of the three babies with his rifle butt, Jabez pulled down the zip on his trousers, relieved himself over their dead bodies, then walked triumphantly back to the station, carrying his sleeping quarry slung over his shoulders. As he walked, he sang a childhood lullaby under his voice, followed by 'Do Not Forsake Me, O My Darlin' ' from the film *High Noon*, which he had just seen on release a few months earlier in the Lyric Cinema in Livingstone.

Things were looking up for Jabez. The hunt had been successful, the last night party was about to begin, he'd get his pay tomorrow and Joe and Gideon's deaths no longer made even the middle pages of the *Northern News*. He'd never thought much of the constabulary. How many brawls had he been involved in over the years and not even a ticking off from the peelers? There had, initially, been a bit of a fuss over the cemetery killings, especially from the Moriah Chapel sisterhood, but that had soon died down. Too many of their husbands were customers at Murphy's; no need to stir up anything to do with that establishment. The police were johns as well; they wanted to bury the incident as much as anyone. Boss man at Murphy's, he was upset, sure, but he knew the more fuss he made, the fewer customers he'd have. And as for poor Gideon, he had no one – no family, no one to love him. So it all went away.

A lot of people didn't like Jabez; in fact, most people didn't like Jabez. A lot of people called him an animal, and many other things besides. But he would have shared those takings with Joe the barman – shared them, as he'd promised, sixty to Joe and forty to himself. His word was not unimportant to him.

XLIV

BACK AT CAMP, whilst the hunting was going on, Kabwe was meticulously discharging his duties as given to him by Jabez, roping in old man Mubanga, Chola and Ephraim. Two six-foot-long railway sleepers, hewed sharp on one end, were to be hammered into the ground, six feet apart, and a large stack of wooden railway detritus was to be heaped together to create a structure some five feet high and the same wide. The mound was to be six feet away from the two sleepers but parallel and behind them.

'Got to be careful with these measurements, boys. Don't want to mess with Jabez, this being our last day and all. We want to be leaving this site in one piece. We been here long enough to leave our mark, don't want to leave anything more of us here,' said Kabwe.

'Been to these last night railway shindigs before, Kabwe. Things can get out of hand, boys letting their hair down,' dribbled Ephraim.

'You fret too much. The boys deserve a good sending off. Need to pay our respects to Daniel and that Indian fella who died – what was his name now?'

'Kumar, boss, Kumar.'

'Yeah, him.'

'Should be beer and whisky as well, ain't that right? That's the routine.'

'That's the routine all right, Ephraim, you've got it.' Kabwe smiled, displaying his Transylvanian canines as if ready for a human sacrifice.

Towards the end of the afternoon, first George then Jabez arrived with their quarry. Jabez's two were still slumbering, but George's were squealing, chafing in fear and pain from the twine which now bound their necks, pulling it with their fingers, snared in their own homeland.

Once the preparations were concluded, posts and bonfire in place, Gwyn walked towards the navvies, huddled for the final ceremony to conclude their sojourn at Kapiri Mposhi. The sun was beginning to make its escape for the day, an orange-red departure over the horizon.

'Men, gather round, men,' shouted Gwyn. 'Most important thing first, you can pick up your pay tomorrow at the office in Broken Hill!'

A loud cheer went up.

'We're all Rhodesia Railwaymen here tonight. We all know the boundaries and we all know the trust and reliance we place on one another as comrades in the great work we're undertaking.'

'Did Mr Bowen say comrades there, Mubanga?' whispered Chola. 'He a communist? Didn't know that.'

'Not sure if Mr Bowen knows hisself what he is,' replied Mubanga.

'And it is great work. And not without its difficulties. We lost Kumar, and thank you, Chowdhury, or should I say Cowboy, for conducting the funeral ceremony. Didn't have much to do with him personally, but he was a family man, and his family, I have no doubt, will still be grieving, as I'm sure are Chowdhury and Desai. But sometimes a price has to be paid for our endeavours, for forging the Iron Road through this great continent.'

'Yeah, so that Europeans can feast in them high price, outta bounds, first class carriages, puffing on their pipes and cigars, lording it over the rest of us,' muttered Desai, touching his thorn bush face, feeling the mark of Jabez.

'I know all of us express our sadness at Kumar's passing. His cremation ceremony was a glorious one, a fitting send off, now a piece of holy ground, another memorial to a man who died so that the

Railway could live. And poor Chibwe, let's not forget him. We don't know what illness he picked up, but I'm told he's as thin as one of Jimmy's crickets; can't be much time left for him.'

Jimmy looked on and said nothing.

'And then there's Daniel... A man, a Bemba, a noble Bemba, who I was proud to call a friend. A terrible accident. His days on the Railway are also sadly over. We will all miss him. I've heard he wants to go into politics. Always had plenty to say for himself. I'm sure he'll make a fist of it, but don't want him to become too successful, do we, Mr Pugh?'

There was no acknowledgment from Jabez, who was occupied trying to control the four vervets, now completely awake, straining against their leashes, shrieking with terror.

'Enjoy the evening and the revelry which Mr Pugh has lined up. Hope to see you all again on our next project. Good night to you all!'

Gwyn approached the distracted Jabez. 'What's your plan with these vervets, Jabez?' he enquired. 'Don't like the look of things. These creatures look out of their minds. They ain't going to come to no harm now, are they? I don't want another boomslang incident, is that clear?'

'Thought I'd give the boys some fun. Like a coconut shy at a fair. You hit the coconut, you get a prize.'

'And what's the prize?'

'A slug of whisky. Got a few bottles with me for the occasion.'

'What's going to be thrown at the monkeys?'

'Well we ain't got no tennis balls round here, have we, Gwyn? Guess it'll have to be some stones.'

'What?'

'Don't worry, the boys will be so drunk they won't be able to hit a Garratt loco from five yards. Once they've had their fun, I'll cut these creatures loose. After all, don't want the boys drinking all my whisky.'

'You be careful now. I'll hold you responsible that events don't get out of hand.'

'It's their last night, Gwyn, they deserve some entertainment.'

'Just be careful, that's all. I'm off to see Thomas. See you in the morning.'

Gwyn set his course for Thomas's shed, ill at ease with what the evening would bring. The shouting of the navvies, the screams of the vervets fading with every one of his steps towards Thomas. He'd had his chance to change things, but he hadn't taken it.

'Jimmy, Lee, Joe, Chinamen, bring up those cardboard containers. Boys there's two dozen ten ounce cans of the finest Welsh pale ale in each of these boxes, a taste of home! We've got twelve boxes in all, should be enough to go round. David, David, come over here! You're the youngest, you can light up, light up the bonfire. Are we all aboard, men?'

'All aboard, boss!' returned the united shout.

'Come on then, let's get to it,' cried Jabez.

David went to the bonfire as ordered; all the others went for the boxes, ripping them apart, spilling cans like used artillery shells all over the parched earth.

'What's this stuff, Mubanga?' asked Ephraim.

'It's beer, man, and cut down on that drizzle coming from your mouth, would you!'

'I know it's beer. What's it say though? I was never much at reading their language.'

'Let me see, some kind of flying dragon. It say F-E-L-I-N- F-O-E-L...'

'What?'

'That's what it says,' said Mubanga. 'Drink it. Free, ain't it? That's all that matters.'

'I'll drink to the health of Daniel and to politicians everywhere,' said Ephraim. 'He'll start a war somewhere, I'm sure. That's what they usually do.'

'I bet he will, then blame someone else. Politicians don't do the dying, rest of us do,' replied Mubanga.

XLV

'GEORGE, GIVE ME A HAND with these!' yelled Jabez. The racket from the men was growing louder as the alcohol stocks got lower.

'What's the plan?' asked George.

'We'll tie two to each of the two stakes. Give themselves some company. I ain't a cruel man. I want the ropes round the monkeys to be about five feet long. That'll give them enough to scamper round a bit, it'll give them a fighting chance.'

Jimmy, Lee and John bunched within their own flock, distinct shapes created by the blaze, cans of Felinfoel beer stacked neatly to the side.

'Be careful with these, beer is for fools,' said Lee.

They watched the revelry of their fellow Railwaymen, their faces in the intense orb of the fire soiled and stinking. Swindlers and swindled, water, work and wood their only necessities, a comrade killed, a master maimed, a friend disfigured, assaulted by dead horse stench of the savannah... Most would be back. That's the way it was.

'You going to stay out here, Jimmy, look for more work on the Railways?' asked John.

'What else is there, what's there to go back to? Collecting chestnuts for the winter like Xiang Shui Hu, only to be knifed by a neighbour?'

'But that was only a story, Jimmy, from hundreds of years ago, you said so yourself,' said John.

'One of my other names is Zhu Yo Min. I was the old farmer's neighbour. It was my father who foolishly lost the farm wagering on crickets. On bloody crickets! I can't go back. You and Lee, do what you want. Do what you want with this information as well. I don't expect anyone will believe you. No one here believes anything which comes out of the mouths of people like us.'

'You killed the old farmer?' shouted John. 'You heartless bastard! How can we trust the word of a murderer? Did you kill Kumar as well? Our bet's void! You made a fool of me, Jimmy!'

'What of it, John? The bet was a fair one. No one said how the dying was to come about. Kumar died first, didn't he? That was the bet!'

'That's trickery, that's wrong. What you say, Lee?' yelled John.

'I told you, Jimmy always wins.'

'But he killed a man to win a bet.'

'Except he didn't kill him, Jabez did. Or more precisely the QL did,' replied Lee.

'Ain't you the QL mechanic, Jimmy?' asked John.

'What of it?'

'Ain't you supposed to make sure it's ok?'

'All I did was even the odds. I gave Kumar your farthing, Lee, the one you lost to me in our three gods bet. Gave him the farthing so he would go fetch the water and not me. How did I know that Jabez would hit him on the way?' said Jimmy.

'Hell was following Jabez that morning, he could have hurt any-one.'

'Exactly, Lee. Your wages are mine, John, fair and square. We're the outsiders, outcasts in this place. No one cares about us, no one protects us. I'll be on your shoulder when you collect your pay from the Railway office in town. I'll bring my dao with me for company, in case you need persuading. You'll give me your wages, so fuck you and fuck all Chinamen!'

'Chuck some more firewood on the stack, Chola, don't want this night to end,' ordered Kabwe.

Kabwe with his entourage, George and newfound friend Chola, sometimes standing, sometimes sitting.

'You're in with Bowen now, ain't you, boss? You're his new Daniel. Guess that makes you better than the rest of us.'

'Sure does, George, and don't you forget that. Now get me another beer. No, get me two,' said Kabwe.

'Right away, boss.'

'You missing Chibwe?' Kabwe asked Chola. 'You two and Daniel were always close.'

'He's dying man, nothing to be done about it. He just wasting away, day by day,' answered Chola.

In another group, a few yards away, sat Mubanga, Ephraim and David.

'Look over there, Mubanga,' said Ephraim. 'Look at George running his master's errands. That crippled politician Daniel would be proud of the next in line. Must've been giving Kabwe secret lessons.'

'Save that Daniel got no say in the choosing, that was handed down from above. Bullshit always baffles brains, my friend,' replied Mubanga.

'True enough,' said young David. 'Nothing ever changes, do it? Someone's always jerking the chain. Travel forever through centuries of time, the same happenings would repeat themselves. There's a Daniel, a Kabwe, a Bowen in every slice of eternity. And a Jabez, will there be a Jabez in eternity?'

'There's always a Jabez,' said Mubanga. 'No one gang wins in this game. Just that one gang gets destroyed at a different speed. We all lose in the end. All you got to do is drink when the drink is there, 'specially if it free.'

Chowdhury and Desai were not drinkers of alcohol.

'What we going to do with him?' asked Desai.

'Now who might you be talking about?' replied Chowdhury.

'You know who I mean. That bastard Jabez. It's our last night, we might never see him again. With all these drunks around us, anything could happen. Accident, fire... We could blame Kabwe, he needs taking down a step or two. Or blame one of those stupid Chinamen.

Nobody cares about them anyway, their lives even lower down the pecking order than we are.'

'Stay calm, Desai. Tonight's our opening, but not yet,' replied Chowdhury, scratching his goatee, scragging some midges. 'There'll be so much mayhem and pissed up railwaymen here soon, that Jabez will have roped himself up, tied his own flax necktie. Then all we got to do is pull the lever that opens the trap door. I've looked at Jabez closely, I've studied him, like a butterfly collector. He knows he's pursued – by others, even by himself. He tires of this, he craves for the end.'

'Or craves for comradeship?' asked Desai.

'The scar on his face allows for no comradeship, it throws back all attempts at friendship. My dear Desai, the scar only wishes the chase to conclude.'

Above the burning, cackling bonfire, the noiseless dotted stars were too numerous to consider, a roof of sprinkled icing.

'Boys, boys! Here's your chance to win a slug of whisky, on the house, to go with the beer!' slurred Jabez above the hubbub. 'Quiet! Listen to this.' Jabez slowly and deliberately lifted the cork from the whisky bottle, which made a muted popping sound.

'Ah, the greatest sound in the world, the opening of a whisky bottle. The sound of paradise! That'll be your prize, boys. No one in his right mind can resist that. Anyone who doesn't like the grog shouldn't be working on these Railways! This balm will go to your vocal cords like quicksilver. It'll make you all top tenors one minute, and bass baritones the next! What's not to like about that! Come on, come on! My friend George, the cleanest navvy in Christendom, been good enough to collect some sharp nasty-looking shale pebbles. That'd be shale throwing pebbles. And see those vervets? They've been wanting to entertain us all night. Can't say it'll be as good as the entertainment you'd get at Murphy's, but don't worry, boys, because you ain't allowed in there anyhow!'

Jabez, waving the bottle, stumbled to the ground. His brain was spinning like a dervish, whirling in and out of consciousness. His fine white Egyptian cotton shirt, as worn at Auntie Maisie's funeral, was now dirty, torn; Jeremiah Owen, gentleman's outfitter and haberdasher of Ndola, would not have been happy, but had been paid for his product, so that was that.

'Help me up, George, for Christ's sake, help me up. Well, who's first, who's first on stage for the Jabez Pugh extravaganza? Who will grace the game? Who'll sit the game out? Are you all aboard!'

'That settler's mad, Kabwe, he plain mad,' said Chola.

'Drunk, drunk and mad,' replied Kabwe.

'Wouldn't mind some whisky though.' Chola was drunk but not drunk enough to look for a fight, or to make a fool of himself. He strode forward.

'Me, boss!'

'Ah, my friend Chola, that's the ticket. George, pray give your colleague Mr Chola three of your best and sharpest pebbles.' Jabez gave out one prolonged burp which not even the crackling fire could obscure.

Jabez then lurched to the gap between the two stakes. The four monkeys, tied to the stakes, cowered and screamed as far away from the flames as their leashes would allow.

'Ten paces, Chola. I'll count them out, draw a line in the dirt, and you throw from there. Any hits you land with them pebbles, don't matter where, don't matter which monkey, a slug of whisky's yours.

'Quiet, please. *Quiet!* Give our first contestant the best of order, there's a lot of drinkin' at stake.

'What kind of men are we, Mubanga? Maim a monkey, get a slurp of whisky, this what European civilization is?'

'You ain't required to look if you don't want to, Ephraim.'

'That ain't the point and you know it. We got to stop this.'

'Ephraim's right,' agreed David.

'Remember what I told you, young David,' said Mubanga. 'Europeans always treat us as savages. That's what Daniel learnt. Took him a while but he learnt it. For all Bowen's fake friendship, Kabwe's about to learn it as well,' said Mubanga.

'So there's nothing we can do then? Just look and watch them lording it over us.' Ephraim spat on the sand, the wrinkles on his face one long line of contempt.

'Well, we could wait for a priest to start handing out the wafers, 'cos these Europeans sure are good Christians.' Mubanga gave a wry smile. 'Don't think our nights of defeat are numbered quite yet.'

'Quiet!' Jabez half belched, half shouted.

The vervets, by moving as far away as they could from the heat of the fire, had put themselves in greater harm's way; they were now only some seven paces away from Chola and his pebbles.

Sinewy, rangy, with a good eye, although now dimmed by alcohol, Chola let loose his first missile. Nothing happened – not a thing, not even a squeal of pain from the vervets. He threw another pebble. Nothing.

'Come on, Chola,' shouted Jabez. 'For God's sake, you some animal lover or something? Throw one in memory of your pretty boyfriend, Chibwe!'

Chola threw a third time, and the female vervet tied to the left-hand post squealed in agony. The jagged shale pebble smashed into the monkey's forearm, breaking both radius and ulna. The three other monkeys screamed as well.

'Got her, got her!' yelped Chola. 'Got her, Mr Pugh!'

'Well done that man. Prize for Mr Chola.'

Pouring a good measure of whisky into a Railway issue mug, Jabez threw the cork to the ground and handed the prize over to Chola, who devoured the contents voraciously, like a thirsty suckling calf drinking sweetened milk out of a bucket.

A waning gibbous moon, its right side lit, rose in the sky.

XLVI

THE SUN WAS BRISKLY SETTING over the horizon, its diagonal shafts of light illuminating Thomas' office. Gwyn could see a lamp flickering in the shed.

Thomas was reading quietly in the station office and thinking back on the death of the railway guard. He had replayed the events of the ambush many, many times over, but the outcome was of course always the same. Money, guns, fighting, freedom. The goal had to become everything. He had therefore to love the goal, throw himself at it, be consumed by it... There was no return journey for him from that moonlit night on the Kafwe river bridge. His logic had always been impeccable. The time to kow-tow to the settlers was gone.

He heard a soft knocking on the door. Gwyn let himself in.

'Not taking part in the last night party, Gwyn?' asked Thomas.

'I'm too old for parties. Just hope things don't turn into too much of a rumpus. There's beer and whisky on the menu.'

'You can guarantee ructions. Alcohol and railwaymen have never mixed. I've just boiled some water, one last cup of tea before you go back home. And by the way, thank you for giving me time off to see my mother in Kitwe.'

'How is she now?'

'Still very ill. We'll have to see. That's all we can do now. There is little by way of medical facilities up there, and none for natives.'

'Sorry to hear that. Is she able to travel down to Broken Hill? She'd have a better chance here. I could ask my own doctor to see her.'

'Old folk, you know what they're like. Don't want to leave their own surroundings. And besides, she's too ill to travel anymore. But thank you for the kind offer.'

Only mugs were honest.

'How was young David on the trip north?'

'He is a fine boy. His country should be very proud of him. It's more of his type we want.'

With the aid of the Congolese middleman, Augustin, Thomas had purchased a few items for his office; there was more than enough British South Africa Company wages to go around. Nothing too luxurious, a few lanterns and a mirror in a carved mahogany frame. He had asked Augustin to source some gramophone records for him but it seemed it was easier to track down Mauser Model 1935 bolt action rifles than 78rpm shellacs.

'Heard there were some shenanigans on a train whilst you and David were up there. BSAC wages stolen and a guard got killed in a robbery. Nasty business.'

'We heard the story up there. Never knew what BSAC meant though. What's it mean, Gwyn, do you know?' Thomas started to stroke his neatly shaven beard.

'British South Africa Company. You should know that, you read enough. Much police activity there? Expect they rounded up the usual suspects. Bet they never brought anyone to book though, you can almost guarantee that.'

'Didn't take much heed of the story. Had more important things on my mind, what with my mother and all.'

The police had arrested the train driver and stoker, beat them up pretty badly in the station, but they hadn't talked, save to say that they were bushwacked on the Kafwe river bridge by unknown assailants. No one believed them, of course, and both were immediately sacked. The stoker's wounds turned septic, and his nailless fingers started to stink, especially on his right hand, so much so that it had to be amputated. The driver got off better; he only had to contend with a limp for the rest of his life, on account of a smashed patella.

Thomas knew all about this, of course, but the main thing was that they had kept their traps shut; that's all that was important. He held back the intelligence on the beatings from David. They all operated in standalone cells anyway, and Thomas was three cells removed from the driver and stoker. Even if they'd coughed up the truth, the risk to Thomas and David was manageable enough for it not to be a worry. The point was coming, though, when all would be out in the open, and there would be no need for secrecy.

Thomas felt his time on the railways was coming to an end. He knew he had a higher calling: to be a soldier, to make life and death decisions. Gwyn had certainly been an influence on him: his books, their discussions... But Thomas, from his covert talks with Daniel, knew that Gwyn had not been open with him on all matters, and Thomas, of course, was not an open book for Gwyn. Thomas refused to be Gwyn's good and faithful servant anymore, and the last night on site was probably the right time to let him know.

'I let him go because you wanted some company going up there,' said Gwyn. 'What did he have to say for himself? Must have been a first-rate travel companion.'

'First rate, yes, that's what David was. Ready to listen, ready to learn.'

'Where did you get the mirror from? It's new, isn't it? It's a fine-looking item.'

'It's from my mother's house. She didn't want it, was going to throw it in fact, so here it is with me.'

'Tell me, how've you been getting on with the books I sent over? You did get them, I hope. There's truth in books.'

'But they're just stories, ain't they? Stories someone made up, full of make believe and lies,' replied Thomas.

'Truth is often buried in lies. You've just got to look hard enough,' said Gwyn.

'Most of these books written by Europeans. How does an African like me find my truth in their lies? Even if I find the truth in their lies, it will be their truth and not mine.'

'Books make life worth living, Thomas. They take you away from where you are, take you away from reality, the suffering...'

'Got them books all right. Finished one already, *The Picture of Dorian Gray.*'

'I've read that book so many times had to buy a second copy. That's the one I gave you to read. My first one's at home, pretty dogeared now. What did you think of it?'

'Dorian thinks that beauty is everything, doesn't he?'

'Well, there's one thing you can say about Africa. It's beautiful.'

'No question about that. But the beauty here ain't tranquil. There's always a bite, a fang or a tooth or a stone, a dark soul to it,' Thomas replied.

'Just like Dorian Gray then,' said Gwyn.

'Beauty in Africa is different. Does beauty attract you, Gwyn? Is Delyth beautiful? I've never met her. Does she ever cross your mind when you're out here, when you went on your long rides with Daniel for hours, far away from the rest of the men? Did you think that Daniel was beautiful? He can't be now, can he? What with his mutilated leg. He's probably limping around on crutches, being a nuisance to his wife, if he has one. Getting in the way of her household chores, sitting around all day whilst she wants to do the tidying up. Probably drinking himself into the grave, feeling sorry for himself, crying over his bad luck. I know Chola doesn't think much of him in his condition, and as for Chibwe, he's out of the game too. What did Jabez call 'em, the pretty boys? Well Daniel ain't pretty anymore, and Chibwe's counting down the days. I hear they've given him another name in his village. Do you want to hear it?'

'Come on then,' prompted Gwyn.

'Slim, they call him Slim.'

'Slim?'

'Chibwe's lost so much weight he's down to about seven stones. He's skin and bones, that's all that's left of him.'

'Some kind of cancer, is it? That's a vicious ailment.'

'More like a disease, wastes a healthy man away.'

'Sorry to hear that. Glad it isn't happening to you or me.'

Thomas looked at himself in his new mahogany-framed mirror, taunting himself to say what he really wanted to say, not just to Gwyn but to everyone. Thomas a sincere man, a genuine man, a leader, a saviour, a man who murdered, a monster; there should be gratitude for him, there should be respect, there should be fear.

'Hear Kabwe's your new man now. Is he beautiful? Can he replace Daniel in your life? Will he now be the one to light your candle? Something will happen to him, I'm sure, just like Daniel. Young men don't last long out here. They don't remain untouched, they always get spoiled. Once he gets blemished there'll be another willing Dorian ready to be corrupted, ready to pay the price. We all get corrupted out here, one way or another.'

Gwyn was taken aback, not just by Thomas' gall. Was it only Thomas who was making these type of presumptions or were there others? His authority and standing were shaken; he didn't wish to appear weak, as then his Railway life, his only real life, would come to an end. He felt frightened; he'd thought Thomas was his friend.

'But we have options,' Thomas insisted. 'We can pick and choose, can't we?'

'I don't think so. Nothing to do with picking and choosing. It's all to do with luck. Good luck, bad luck... Your good luck is that you're a ticket clerk. There's order in the station office, no QL can kill you here. Someone like Mubanga, one of the brightest I've come across, should be much more than he is, but he's just a navvy. His bad luck to be born when and where he was. People like him should be running this country, not people like Jabez and me.'

'I'm lucky to be a ticket clerk? I suppose you think I'm lucky to be given this book to read!'

Thomas had had enough; he held the book in his rigid arms upwards towards Gwyn's head.

'Why should I have to read about lord this or lady that? I am not European! These are not my people. Where is the book about my people, about Bemba? You shout in our ears, pour lies into our minds, steal our thoughts, enfeeble our courage... But I have escaped. And more will follow!'

'It wasn't my intention to offend you, Thomas, I just thought...'

'Just thought what? Teach the ticket clerk some manners, to crawl behind you like a cudgeled dog? Teach him something about civil society, European aristocracy, how they behave? Get him to wear a three-piece suit, white shirt and tie? Sing your stupid anthem? You ram your culture down our throats without thinking! Your arrogance oozes out, drips on everything, drenches us all with your conceit... Here, take the bloody book back, I've read it! I understand it!'

'I'm sorry, Thomas, I truly am. I'm just a ruffian of a Railwayman. I only wanted to show you that I consider you as an equal, as a friend, I do not wish to offend you or your country. All I want is for us to be equals.'

'How can we be? I know where I am in this gutter, and it's about time you knew where you are as well! And those two locations aren't the same; they never will be unless everything changes! Do you understand that? Do you?'

'Yes, I do understand that, Thomas. Truth be told, me and Jabez and Dorian Gray, all of us, I'm ashamed of all of us. I've lied all my life. To you, to Daisy, to Delyth, to everybody. Even to myself, thinking that we can all be equals.'

'That can only happen once the sunburnt leave the country and only return on our terms!' Thomas shouted.

Gwyn picked up the discarded book from the station floor. He didn't look up, simply turned around and left, trying his best to close the one hinged corrugated iron door as softly as he could behind him.

XLVII

'HERE, HAVE SOME of this water,' I proffered.

Delyth was trying to breathe as normally as she could. Over the last few weeks the number and severity of her contractions had increased from barely noticeable, irregular periods of aching, to intense pains accompanied by acute soreness in her back.

I had decided that the time had come. I was now to become Daisy the midwife. Removing all Delyth's clothes, I gently raised her arms and placed a long, white, loose-fitting cotton nightdress over her, pulling the folds down over her head and shoulders.

'Come on, Del, let's get you into bed.'

I held her by the elbow, guiding her to bed. She was my age but she had become old with the baby. Thank God I would never be in her position. Delyth took robot steps, one small step then another. She sat on the edge of the bed and I lifted her legs up and over and guided her head back on to the pillow. I looked down on her, she looked up at me. Poor, poor Delyth. How was she going to cope? How was I going to perform?

'I don't think I can go through with this, Daisy. I really can't. I don't feel I'm strong enough, brave enough. How do we get hold of Gwyn? Should he be here?'

'No need for men for what we're about to do. All they're needed for is the easy part. It's up to us women now. We always have the hard parts to perform. I'll be with you all the time. Gwyn's commitment to you is strong, Del, no concerns about that. He keeps his promises.'

'What about a doctor. Doctor Cosgrove. Do I need a doctor, Daisy?'

'No need for one of those, don't worry. I'll be with you all the time, you'll be fine.'

I hadn't done anything like this before, save for helping boss man's wife in Murphy's a few times with her gruesome work.

'It's like I'm cramping up. I'm afraid, Daisy. Is this the price you pay for being with a man in the Great Northern?'

I could see that the pain was returning, her body convulsing, Delyth looked worn out. I put my hand on her stomach, judging the strength of the contractions as best I could. I wished someone was there to help me.

'Follow me, Del. Big deep breath in, that's it, and then big deep breath out. Once again, deep breath in, deep breath out, and then push, come on now.'

Delyth rose up from the bed, sat on the edge for a moment, stood up, stooped on the edge, holding the sidepost with her right hand as if crushing an over-ripe pear.

Face contorted, staring towards the floor, eyes bloodshot, lips cracked and dry.

'I feel like I want to go to the toilet, Daisy. I'm supposed to be producing a baby, not going for a number two! How funny is that?'

'Please, Del, back on the bed. Please lie back on the bed.'

'It's so hot in here.'

'I'll open the window.'

I lifted the sash. A small group of brightly coloured, green and yellow bee eaters flew past, their squeaking songs filling the air. Delyth, I'm sure, heard nothing, only the noises from the pain she was suffering.

'I feel sick, Daisy. Help me, I feel sick!'

'You'll be all right. It'll all be worth it. I'm here, deep breaths now.'

'I've been a nuisance to everyone, haven't I?'

'Just deep breaths, that's all. Deep, deep breaths. Once the baby's born you'll forget all about this. You'll forget all of the past, you and Gwyn will be proud as Punch, I know you will.'

I gently pushed Delyth's legs further apart. I was as scared as she was.

'We need to do some pushing now, Delyth. You'll know when. Push when your body tells you to push, push as much as you can. Big deep breaths and push! Come on now, that's it. It's coming, Delyth. The baby's coming, I can see it. Push now, come on push!'

The baby emerged like a heavy raindrop falling from a leaf of a miombo tree, plopping into my hands, wet, slimy, screaming. I immediately placed the baby on to Delyth's stomach who probably thought it more akin to a flayed hare than a human being.

'It's a boy, Del. A beautiful boy! Congratulations! Gwyn will be over the moon!'

I cut the umbilical cord and placed the son in a tightly bound cotton blanket, before handing the quiet package back to Delyth. By now she was crying, as I was.

'This is all my fault. Oh what did I do! I didn't want to be a burden to anyone. It was supposed to be so easy.'

'You're all right. Everything will now be all right.'

Delyth glanced at her baby and looked at me.

'Could I have some water, please?'

'Of course. Let's get you tidied up a bit, Del. I'm sure you'll have visitors from Moriah soon. They'll all be glad to know that everything went well. You should be proud, be proud of everything you've done. Be proud of your son, be proud of Gwyn.'

Delyth, exhausted, said nothing, and gazed at her son as if contemplating a carving in a museum. The tears kept rolling silently down her face. I looked at the pretty little baby with happiness in my eyes. He looked a peach.

XLVIII

'WHO'S NEXT? WHO'S NEXT? Roll up now!' shouted Jabez. 'I'm gonna have a quick squeeze on my lemon whilst you boys decide.'

Jabez was still urinating in front of the navvies when Kabwe walked up to the mark.

'Mr Kabwe! The new Daniel, Mr Bowen's toothsome new sidekick. Watch out for Bowen in the Land Rover, eh, boys! Or is Mr Kabwe not of the same persuasion? Give him three, George.'

'No need for that, George, just give me one. That big jagged one will do,' said Kabwe.

'You hear that, people? Mr Kabwe only wants one projectile! The confidence of the heir to Daniel! That's why you natives will never win! You should always make sure you've got the best odds. Still, it's your call. Don't ever say this settler never gave you a chance!'

The vervet injured by Chola sat almost motionless, nursing her broken arm, whimpering. Kabwe closed one eye, aimed and threw. The pebble caught the monkey flush in the face, killing it immediately.

'Bullseye for Mr Kabwe, bullseye! First prize for Mr Kabwe!'

Jabez drained a few mouthfuls from the whisky bottle for himself, then watched Kabwe as he drank his prize from the Railway mug and looked out for the next candidate. The surviving vervets screeched with horror.

'We're getting pulled down into a swamp by these settlers, ain't we, Mubanga?' David murmured. 'Those vervets are delicate, dainty little things. Thomas would give no heed to them being shot, but tortured for our entertainment, that's another thing altogether. We should stop this suffering right now!' said David.

'Course we should, young David, but this ain't the right place nor the right time,' replied Mubanga.

'And when would that be? We're living in Eden here,' said David.

'But you want freedom, don't you?'

'Course I do, we all do, save some round here don't know it yet.'

Jabez swinging the whisky bottle like a flag bearer in a carnival. 'You know where this came from, George? Know where it comes from. It ain't bloody Scotch and it ain't bloody Irish, it came from my country! Yeah, that's right, my country! It's the best! We had whisky stills all over the place for centuries, every village had one til them black-draped, narrow-minded, Bible-bashing Christians came along, banned 'em all! Stopped us dancin', stopped us laughin', stopped us drinkin', stopped us being human beings! Only a few stills left now, out in the wilds, beyond the reach of them bloody zealots, and you've got the pleasure of drinkin' some tonight! It ain't just your way of living been wrecked by Christians and missionaries, it's mine as well!'

Jabez swung himself around, the bottle a satellite around a larger object. He could just about stay on his feet.

'Get rid of the dead chimp, George, cut it loose, throw it on the fire. It'll save on firewood. Who's next, who's next?'

Jabez ripped his shirt, Auntie Maisie's funeral shirt, buttons popping, and threw it on to the ground.

'Ah, Mr Desai, the shopkeeper's son, my Gujurati friend. Thought you Hindus, Buddists, whatever the hell you are, didn't like all this animal killing. Figure you can't keep away from the whisky, right? Three pebbles for Mr Desai. And what's this, Cowboy Mr Chowdhury, another co-worker from the great subcontinent. The sons of shop-keepers feel confident tonight! Step right up, form an orderly queue here, one participant at a time.'

Jabez slurped from the whisky bottle again, using his right thumb as a stopper.

'We were thinking, boss...' said Chowdhury.

'A thinking Indian, that's funny, ain't it? Those two words together don't sound right, like Mr Bowen and singing, or Kumar and the QL. Spit it out, man, what are you thinking!'

'What if I go for the monkey on the right and Desai goes for the one on the left. Whoever hits a monkey first gets double the prize.'

'Spoken like a European, always looking to improve the human condition via competition,' said Jabez.

'But, boss, there's two on the right. Means Chowdhury would have double the chance of winning,' said George.

'Good point, excellent point. Hey, I always thought, Chowds, always thought you were a sly bugger. You watch him, Desai, he's tying you up in knots. George, let one of the apes loose, give him... is it a him or a her? God, who gives a toss. Give it its freedom. That's what you Indians want, isn't it, that's what you Bemba want? Deliverance!'

Jabez shouted to the night sky, all the men, the drunken ones and the not so drunken ones, transfixed by the heartlessness of the situation: Jabez, the monkeys, the railways, the slogging, the sweating, the everything.

George ran up to the right-hand pole, knife in hand, the vervets screeching, their eyes saucers hateful, horror-crammed.

'Quiet now, quiet now, little monkey.'

Barely able to wangle the knife between the rope and the vervet's neck, George cut the noose. The tormented animal screeched away into the darkness, leaving two remaining screaming victims, contorting, zig-zagging on the fetid ground, soiled by their fear and torture.

'Good work, George! Pick your weapons, boys, from the clump over here. And stop gawping at me like that! I see you thinking. You ain't tricking no one. You going to say some prayers, ask your heathen gods for help, like you did when you buried Kumar. Dear, dear Kumar, poor poor Kumar...'

The devil himself was now in charge of Jabez, had skewered him and would not let go. The whisky wanted Jabez to do sinful things; Jabez wanted to do evil, to destroy life, any sentient life, to crush anyone with emotion, to enjoy their pain. Anyone: a monkey, a navvy, a Jabez...

'Mr Pugh...' said Chowdhury thoughtfully, like someone suggesting a different way to peel an orange.

'What is it, Cowboy? You Indians, you're like sounding brasses or tinkling cymbals, ain't yer? I suppose that means nothing to you, does it?'

'Mr Pugh, how we going to know which monkey gets hit first? Me and Desai will be throwing at the same time. There's got to be a referee here, someone's got to decide who the winner is.'

'I'll do it, boss. I'll go between the posts, see which monkey gets hit first,' said George.

'That's way above your station, boy! That's a settler's job, and as far as I can see I'm the only settler hereabouts. I'll be the referee, can't even allow Kabwe to do that job. Mr Bowen, he'd allow Kabwe to do the deciding, I'm sure, but I ain't no Mr Bowen! Needs a good eye, needs a man with authority. Don't want no bickering from these Indians as to who's won and lost.'

Jabez was beginning to hiccup. Taking another slug from the whisky bottle, Jabez staggered, fell, and staggered again, equidistant between the two stakes. A drunk, berserk, shirtless, scar-faced monster, gloating in ecstasy over the vervet quarry, devil-trapped, out of reach of all atonement.

'Look, Hindus, I'll make it easier for you!'

Grabbing hold of a vervet, Jabez forced it roughly against the wooden stake, winding the rope tightly around it, tying the animal rigidly to the post, like Odysseus to the masthead. He did the same to the other monkey, who in its terror bit Jabez's hand. Instinctively Jabez punched the vervet heavily on its jaw, rendering it unconscious, or so he first thought, but the ferocity of the blow had in fact killed it. After tying the second, dead, monkey to the stake, Jabez shouted back to Desai and Chowdhury.

'There you are, boys, I've wrapped both these stiffs tight as clams to the posts. Them wild animals ain't going nowhere. Even you Indians can't miss! On my count! And no cheating you Indian bastards, on my count, three, two, one! Come on, start throwing, start chucking them down and keep your faith in Jesus, boys, before I kill the chimps myself!'

Jabez, pie-eyed Jabez, hedged in by hatred and lethal scrutiny, clueless.

The first pebble whizzed past Jabez's head. Too drunk to notice. The second pebble caught him square on his lower left pectoral muscle near the heart. The next two pierced his torso, this time near his stomach, turning his head down and across to look at his midriff. The last thundered into the right side of his forehead. Jabez dropped on to his knees on the savannah floor, the whisky bottle falling away from his right hand, the contents gurgling away into the dirt. Jabez still on his knees, the upper torso involuntarily collapsing forward, the head falling gently to the floor, supporting the rest of the crumpled body.

All the men ran towards Jabez.

Desai got there before all of them, lifting Jabez's head, by his hair, from the savannah,

'He's dead, he's dead, the bastard's dead!' shouted Desai. Jabez groaned, tried to speak, his eyes half-open, half-closed against the blood trickling down from his forehead.

Chowdhury reached the body moments later. Unhurriedly, he removed a knife from his belt and took hold of Jabez's hair. He began to run the blade deeply and slowly across the devil's throat. Kabwe pushed himself through the throng and looked at Chowdhury,

'Give me the knife, I'll finish the job.'

Kabwe, in no hurry, like a florist methodically cutting the ends of individual rose stems, severed the head completely from the torso and handed the knife back to Chowdhury. With both hands, Kabwe lifted the bleeding, dripping head of Jabez high over his own head, a David to a Samson, and with all his strength cast the head into the flames. All the men shouted in all their different languages and continued their shouting, until their voices became hoarse, cheering, celebrating, drinking to the death of Jabez.

Mubanga did not cheer, instead he walked over to the sole remaining living vervet, who cowered at his advance, and cut its cords, allowing it to scamper, screeching and squealing away. He also cut the cords of the dead vervet and threw the body onto the bonfire next to Jabez's burning head.

XLIX

GWYN AND DELYTH decided to call the baby Delwyn, a solid combination Gwyn thought, of both their names. Translated it meant handsome and pure. The child's paternal grandfather, if he'd been alive, would surely have approved. Delyth wasn't fussed either way.

Gwyn saw much of me after the birth, but not so much of Delyth. Meals of chikanda and nshima became the norm. Delyth was permanently drained and would take to her bed early evening, at the latest, rarely having supper.

Gwyn and I ate together, our suppers extending long into the night. After our meals we shared Woodbines on the verandah and whispered.

'She's saying the strangest of things, Gwyn. You and me are supposed to be poisoning her. That I've got it in for her. She says she sees things, she says that Dr Cosgrove is the father, not Emrys,' I said.

'Once things settle down, Daisy, with the baby, I'm sure matters will balance out again. All her troubles will go away,' replied Gwyn.

'I wouldn't be so sure. And what about us, Gwyn? What's going to happen to us? Do we go back to the old makebelieve, the obedient and dutiful Bemba housekeeper tending to the needs of her settler master? Keep our little secrets from the decent folk of Broken Hill, let the gossips think what they want? Is that why you really married Delyth, respectability for you? The crusty Gwyn Bowen finally settled down, married a nice decent girl from Moriah Chapel, but you and me still meet in secret like we did in Murphy's. Only this time without payment for the whisky or the merchandise.'

'It's not like that, Daisy.'

'No? Tell me what it is like then.'

'Emrys was in a pickle. He's my brother. I had to help him.'

'So you saddled up your trusty steed of conscience, rode to the rescue, saved your brother and delivered a damsel in distress. This isn't medieval Europe, Gwyn, it's twentieth century Africa. You knew Delyth's family, didn't you?'

'Vaguely... What's that got to do with anything?'

'You knew both her parents had died. You knew about the mother's delusions. Who was to say that the same delusions wouldn't afflict luckless Delyth? You could get her sectioned, lock her away somewhere. Visit the mad woman every other Sunday. Or at least get your friend Cosgrove to inject her so full of sedatives that she'd be drugged out of it.'

'What's got into you, Daisy? I thought of all my relationships, you were the most permanent.'

'So why in the hell did you marry her instead of me?'

Was Gwyn throwing dust in my eyes? I could hear not that far away a spotted eagle owl, *whoo, whoo, whoowhoo* and then the shriller call of water dikkop. Gwyn was beginning to test me.

'It isn't that easy, the occasion didn't present itself,' he said.

'Didn't present itself! What the hell does that mean?'

'I had to help Emrys. We're the only Bowens left. Daisy, our time will come.'

'I don't know whether to believe you or not, I really don't. You had a choice, Gwyn, Delyth or me, and you didn't choose me.' I wanted to catch his eyes, see what he really meant, but he looked sideways – anywhere but at me.

'But I have, I've always chosen you, from the first time in Murphy's, to the time I got you out of there, to now. To forever. I'll always choose you.'

'Then prove it!' I leapt up from my chair and peered down on him like an admonishing mother.

'How can I? What more can I do? We must look after Delyth and the baby. They both need our help. Surely we can agree on that? We're not animals, are we?'

'For how long, Gwyn? Until we all grow old together? Which one of us will go first? You to your God or me to mine? And the baby, what's going to become of him?'

'Something will turn up. We'll get by.'

'Is that what your God promises his believers? Pray hard enough and every worry evaporates? All Emrys had to do was write a short letter to his stupid brother. He found redemption straight away.'

'We must be patient. All questions receive answers in the end.'

I'd had enough of undressing my heart for one night. I went straight to bed, alone. I couldn't stand any more Bowen man piety that evening.

It was about eleven months after the birth. Navvies still recounted their rememberances of Jabez's tragic drunken fall into the blazing fire, the brave, vain attempts at rescue, to any settler who asked. No one dissented; the verdict was unanimous. No one had left the scene for hours. Acacia upon acacia, brush upon brush had been thrown into the blaze, until only bones and ash were left, auntie Maisie's fine Egyptian cotton funeral shirt a memory, just like Jabez himself.

'You know the men, Daisy. They showed Jabez enormous respect during his funeral ceremony. I must say this surprised me somewhat. There wasn't much to bury, but he was given a decent Christian burial for all that. We even persuaded the Railway Company to contribute to the cost of a striking Celtic cross above his remains. Rhodesia teak is more than an adequate substitute for marble. The company sequestered a few tanners from each of the men's wages to help with payment. I'm sure the boys didn't mind. Only thing missing was a close harmony choir. Jab would have loved that. He had a wonderful voice. But it wasn't to be. I stepped into the breach, gave a solo of 'Calon Lan'. One of the navvies, Kabwe, joined in during the chorus. Couldn't sing the words obviously. Truth be told I was beginning to forget some of the words myself. Been away from the old country for so long, things tend to get forgotten.'

'I'm sure Jabez would have been very proud of you,' I said.

I had heard rumours of a different ending for Jabez, but I felt no need to share this with Gwyn. What was the point of saying everything about everything. There's no honour in always telling the truth. Why should people suffer if you can hide the truth from them?

'Don't know if Jabez was born bad, but that's one soul that's got perdition to look forward to, and that's no mistaking. Can't see him singing with the angels somehow. Still he's dead now. The Railways and Murphy's will miss him,' said Gwyn.

Gwyn had been away on his most recent secondment for three weeks, carrying out maintenance to the track in the copper mining district near Solwezi. In the time he'd been away, I'm sure he'd missed my food, my company. Brown Windsor soup a fading memory.

The meal on the evening of his return was fish, tilapia to me, which I served in a peanut sauce with green beans and mealie meal. I think Gwyn found the fare quite agreeable.

'Don't think it's wise to disturb Delyth tonight, she's still weak. Best to let her sleep. Both her and the baby need rest,' I said.

There was nothing at all unusual in this, and that was precisely why I was worried – about Delyth, and particularly about little Delwyn.

Gwyn, with the ear of the hunter, heard Delyth's bedroom door open. He heard her dragging herself along the corridor to the dining table. The baby was wrapped in the blue shawl which Moriah Chapel sisterhood had presented to her when news of her impending motherhood had become known.

Mrs Griffiths herself was nominated by the sisterhood to deliver the gift, such was the esteem with which the Jenkins family was held in Moriah. I believe Mrs Brady chose the best of the finest wool procurable from Rees' Emporium in Broken Hill. Mrs Francis performed the cutting and the squaring of the edges. That delightful Polish lady Mrs Kowalski had sewn the seams and trimmed the four corners. She even topstitched around all the edges to keep them in place. As a final touch, four Polish royal crowns were embroidered on each corner. Of course, the Moriah Chapel sisterhood all knew that Mrs Kowalski was a Roman Catholic, but that couldn't be helped.

They said she'd see the true light one day, they were sure, and in the meantime they all agreed her embroidery skills were second to none. As for me, Moriah Congregationalists, Roman Catholics, is there a difference?

Delyth had told me she had a hazy recollection of seeing similar shawls on sale at Yorath's Haberdashers in Ndola, when she had visited with Gwyn shortly after they'd married, but maybe she was wrong.

The light around my supper table was not that of the first class compartment in a dining car, but it was still good enough for Gwyn to see how much Delyth had aged since the birth. Ignoring me, Delyth held the baby in two hands away from her body, as if offering a sacrifice in a satanic ceremony. She looked directly at Gwyn,

'Do you think he looks all right?'

Delyth the carrier of worries, perceptive Delyth, ill Delyth, tortured Delyth.

'He never stirs from his cot, his eyes always fixed on the fig tree outside the bedroom window, or staring at a spider's web...'

Up to that point, I'm sure Gwyn had been enjoying my tilapia, but now Delyth entered the room my delightful peanut sauce, even the green beans, would have to be left to turn cold, and whatever pudding I had prepared would stay uneaten. Both Gwyn and I could see that there were issues to resolve. It was high time, I thought to myself.

'Daisy, would you leave us please? I need to discuss some private issues with my husband,' said Delyth, her face bony, wizened, dried rivulets everywhere. I could see her veins in her hands; they weren't her usual masculine hands, they were an old woman's hands. She was fizzling out, turning into nothingness.

Delyth was not surprised to see that I remained seated.

'Daisy's one of the family. She can stay,' said Gwyn.

'He doesn't look right,' said Delyth, flopping on the nearest chair, holding the baby like a small sack of potatoes which was beginning to turn mouldy.

'What do you mean, he doesn't look right? He's a Bowen isn't he? He might not be my son, but he's a new engineer for the world. His grandfather would be very happy.'

'His grandfather! Don't plan his life for him, no one knows his future, and I'll make damn sure that no one will know his past either. He'll write his own book and we may all be disappointed with what he comes up with. He looks... I don't know... Peculiar. He never looks me in the eye, even when I was feeding him. He still never looks me in the eye. When I point at things, like the cat or the sky, he's just not interested. A stampede of zebras could thunder by and he wouldn't show the slightest curiosity.'

'I'm sure you're overreacting. Daisy should take you and little Delwyn out more, visit the ladies from Moriah,' said Gwyn.

'What do you mean, overreacting? What would you know? You're hardly here. You're away half the time and the other half, you're stalking Daisy like some hyena looking for a kill. What do you want from me, Gwyn? Did you ever want anything at all from me? Did you ever love me? You didn't even have to love me, did you? That never came into it. Silly me. The Bowen honour trumped everything else.'

'Have I ever been violent to you? Have I asked you to do things you didn't want to do? Asked you to change? I think you should go back to your room, lie down, have a rest and leave the baby with Daisy tonight.'

'Leave the baby with Daisy? What can she do with him, how will Delwyn being with Daisy change his mind? I'm not even sure if he has a mind inside that head of his.'

'That's enough of that!' Gwyn snapped.

He rose from the table, left his meal, walked over to Delyth and the baby and tried to put his arms round them both.

Delyth cowered, retreated further into the chair, her eyes reddening.

'Keep away, stay away from me, from both of us! How on earth are we going to be able to look after him? I'm convinced it's because of the bilharzia. Remember that, Daisy? Your great suggestion we go swimming? It's all your fault.'

'But I thought Doctor Cosgrove sorted that all out.' I protested. 'He gave you all the injections, didn't he?'

'Doctor bloody Cosgrove. If there'd been proper medical facilities available it would never have come to this.'

'Come on now, Del, you can't say things like that.'

'Come on now, Del...' She was parroting me. 'Come on now, Del... It's easy for you to say, it's not you that's suffering! You're Bemba, you're immune to all these settler diseases. You'll live forever!'

'That's harsh, Delyth, very harsh,' I said.

'Gwyn,' Delyth persisted, ignoring me, 'the nearest proper doctor is Doctor Faulkener. He lives three hours' drive away and he's very highly spoken of, unlike the quack we've got here. The time has gone for sweet words. I feel like a bloody salmon caught in a net and thrown on the riverbank. Twisting and turning for air ready to be gaffed. Look, even if we take your precious railway, what with all the stops and transfers, it would be close to five hours. The only proper hospital, if you can call it that, is in Lusaka!'

'What exactly are you saying, Delyth?' implored Gwyn. 'You want to leave here? Is that it? And where exactly would we go? Ndola? The medical facilities aren't much better than here. Lusaka? Who do we know there?'

'And are you saying we know anyone here? We've lived here for most of our lives, but do we *know* anybody. Do we know anybody really?'

'What about your friends in Moriah, in the sisterhood? I'm sure you have friends there, don't you? After all they went to the effort of knitting that handsome shawl, must have taken them hours and hours to fashion that.'

'The one they bought in Yorath's in Ndola? And I'm not talking about going to Ndola, and I'm certainly not talking about Lusaka. I'm talking about going home.'

'What do you mean home? This is our home. Our life is here. I've lived here all my life, and you've lived here long enough by now. We know nothing else. This is our home.'

'Once he was born, and born the way he was...' Delyth nodding towards the child, 'the decision was made for me. And if it's important to you, which it clearly is, for *us* – for all four of us. We have to go back, his condition demands it. You can bring Daisy as well, if that's what you want, but we must go back.'

'His condition demands it? Delyth, just because you've convinced yourself he's not quite with it—'

'For heaven's sake, look at him!'

Struggling to undo the shawl, Delyth pushed the boy towards Gwyn. She sobbed as if she was suffocating. 'Look at him!'

Awkwardly Gwyn had no choice but to accept young Delwyn, fearing that Delyth would drop the child if he did not acquiesce. Once unburdened, she turned her back and left the room. The shawl trailed abandoned on the floor, royal Polish crowns indiscernible save for one, which in the poor light looked like an object the baby had disgorged after an indigestible evening meal.

'Give him to me, Gwyn,' I requested calmly.

Gwyn did not require a second supplication and handed the baby over. The child was dressed in a one-piece white cotton nightdress, with a matching bobble-headed hat that Gwyn thought was a hand-me-down from Mrs Brady's time as a young mother.

'Do you think Delyth is fit enough to bring up the baby?' asked Gwyn.

'Once you cut the umbilical cord, a baby can be brought up by any human being. Don't even have to be related. The most important thing is love. If the baby is loved, then that's the mother. The bringer of love is the mother.'

'And you want to be that mother, Daisy?'

'Well you wanted to be the father, didn't you?'

I cherished the little boy in my enfolding arms. The small, fine, clutching fingers, the closed eyes, the gentle breathing. Caressing him, softly singing a Bemba lullaby, I willed contentment and peace on the boy. The bobble hat, I didn't like. The bobble hat was a drizzly European winter; it didn't belong on the savannah. Gently removing it from the baby's head, I discarded it like a rotting avocado, on to Mrs Kowalski's shawl, the colours now fading into the murky dusk.

'I'll clean up tomorrow, Gwyn.'

I reversed my chair from the table, quietly chanting, cradling the baby in a way Delyth never did, never could, bearing the cherished bundle to my bedroom, a bedroom I knew would soon be occupied by another, as it had been occupied since shortly after the birth. I cradled Delwyn for a long while, speaking to him.

'How will you break free from your lot? They don't want you, nobody wants you. Even the cattle in the railway loading pens in town have more blood in them than most people around here. No one will take you but me, and you must therefore, little Delwyn, take me.'

L

BERNIE SPOONER was a man possessed of a sunny disposition. For him the glass was unceasingly half full. He had a loving wife and two contented, healthy children aged eleven and nine. No money problems to speak of, save that he had quite recently purchased a brand new Land Rover on hire purchase, but his secure employment and, who knew, possible promotion meant that, with prudent housekeeping, the payments were affordable. Both his parents were still alive, in early old age and in fine fettle, the usual aches and pains expected of retirees of that generation notwithstanding.

Most of all, Bernie enjoyed his work. He was the youngest loco driver in the whole of Rhodesia Railways, and the happiest. His schoolboy wish of being a train driver had come come true. Based in Livingstone with his supportive family around him, he drove the Garratts up the line to the Belgian Congo and back again three times a week. What could be better? Bernie took immense pride in being in charge of such gargantuan machines, gushing their huge quantities of soot and steam over the savannah. The steam locomotive towered over everything, a massive physical being under his sole control. He was at home with the smell of the fire box and boiler, at ease with the pungency of the lubricating oils which maintained the wheels' momentum; the cab was a warm place for the driver in winter, stifling in the summer, and a home away from home all year round.

'Remember to do your homework, you two, whilst I'm away, and do as your mother tells you.'

'Yes, Daddy.'

'Got to go, Bernard, or they'll be late for school. When can we expect you home?'

'Friday night. By the time I'll have finished the paperwork I should be back about seven. We can have the weekend together. What about taking the boys out on Saturday to the bush, have a picnic? We'll be safe in the Land Rover.'

'Lovely, they'd enjoy that. Got to run. Love you!'

'Love you too! I'll bring a present back from the Congo!'

Rushing out the door with the children: 'Wonderful, love, you, see you Friday!'

'Love you too! Bye, Daddy!'

'Bye, Philip! Bye, Chrissie!'

Rhodesia Railways prided itself on its punctuality. Gwyn always boasted that if ever there was a prize for railway punctuality, Rhodesia Railways would be there or thereabouts – if not first, certainly on the podium. It was an article of faith sworn to by the settlers, from all the religious denominations of Broken Hill. There was one thing they could agree on: you could set your watch by the 14.35 Garratt 9B (sometimes the 16A) steam locomotive, as it thundered majestically from Livingstone on the Zambesi in the far south, through Broken Hill and up to Sakania in the Belgian Congo, via the northern Copperbelt.

It was a normal, uneventful, cloudless Tuesday afternoon at exactly 14.24 when Delyth stepped between the three-foot six-inch gauge of the railway a mile or so south of Broken Hill. The Garratt 9B didn't even quiver, roaring onwards to the Congo.

A board of enquiry investigation into the death was convened some months later by the Railway company. A board of enquiry for a death on the Railway was an unusual event. The Moriah Chapel Sisterhood were puzzled as to why the late Mrs Delyth Bowen deserved such an honour, with three eminent members on the board as well. Gwyn was as surprised as anyone. He had no political influence. He would have much rathered if there had been no fuss, no digging up of old memories, to leave the event well alone.

Delyth was not an important person, just one of the many settlers whose life was, how shall we say, easily forgettable, and of no concern to anyone save for her immediate circle. But one person did remember her. The sandwiches, the school lunches, it seemed, had in the end nurtured gratitude – remorse not condemnation. Mrs Delaney, the mother of Delyth's pupil Paul, was indeed closely related to the high commissioner; she was, in fact, his sister. Grief, ambition and alcohol had sent brother and sister their separate ways many years previously, but a sister is still a sister, and the sister's request to get to the truth was granted, a valedictory gift from the brother on condition that they should never, ever meet again. The high commissioner had a quiet word with the chairman of the Railway company, something along the lines of, 'Could you do me a favour, old boy,' and the chairman devolved the matter to one of his middle-ranking executives. That is how the board of enquiry came to be created. The outside world knew nothing of the conception, but that's the way it has always been.

The board was chaired by Sir Michael Webb-Moore, a retired senior civil servant, assisted by Mr Maxwell Lunn, local luminary, and lastly Mr Royston Weeks, retired railway engineer. Known as the Webb-Moore Report, it absolved the driver, a Mr Bernard Peter Spooner, from all blame. The wordy report did note, however, that Mr Spooner was somewhat on the youthful side to be in charge of such a powerful locomotive, on what was the most prestigious line on the Rhodesia Railways network, namely the Livingstone to Sakania run.

The inspectors pronounced that the deceased must have stepped into the train's path a second or so before being hit, her propinquity leaving the driver little or, to all intents and purposes, no chance of circumventing the impact, unfortunate as it was. The inspectors held that, as Mr Spooner's reputation was unblemished, as he could not in all conscience have avoided the deceased, he should be allowed to remain in post with Rhodesia Railways. However, they further stated that the driver would be subject to demotion, with the concomitant reduction in salary until further notice. The appended reduction would be set at seventeen-and-one-half per cent, calculated on his initial pre-demotion salary, to reflect the seriousness with which Rhodesia Railways viewed the incident. Mr Spooner would also be transferred with immediate effect away from the Livingstone to Sakania run, and on to local, less demanding, district routes on the Copperbelt in the north. Mr Spooner was not represented at the board of enquiry hearings, which were all held in private session. Moreover there was no right of appeal, and the company did not concede the right of any trade union involvement. Future Rhodesia Railways history students and researchers of the Webb-Moore Report did note the numerous typographical errors to be found in the first edition and the regrettable spelling of the driver's name in some sections as Looner or Mooner. These errors were mostly corrected in the second edition.

Serendipitously, the inspectors remarked, no structural damage was suffered by the Garratt, save that the incident did require the diligence of three Bemba, supervised by a settler, over a whole morning, to give the loco a good wash and rinse.

Unable to live for weeks on end in Ndola, working in the northern Copperbelt whilst his wife, children and parents remained in Livingstone in the far south, Bernie resigned his dream post as traindriver with Rhodesia Railways and took up a position as clerk in the Railways office in Livingstone, at an even further reduced salary. Within four months of his office post commencing, the hire purchase company repossessed the Land Rover due to arrears with repayments. Bernie died a year or so later, some say of a broken heart, but officially of tuberculosis, brought on by failing health – too late to see the publishing of the second edition of the Webb-Moore Report a few years later.

Indeed, Sir Michael Webb-Moore had, prior to the second edition, also passed away, leaving Mr Maxwell Lunn and Mr Royston Weeks to proceed with the revised edition. The inspectors, in the foreword to the second edition, justified its publication as a mere tidying up process. What were termed miscellaneous inconsequential amendments were made to the first Edition, including the revision of their initial conclusion regarding Bernie's demotion. The inspectors stated that they had probably misdirected themselves and erred inadvertently in that Mr Spooner, on studied reflection, should have retained his post as train driver on the Livingstone to Sakania run and not been transferred to the Copperbelt. They absolved Bernie from all blame, imputed or otherwise, for the death of Mrs Bowen.

Taking this finding to its logical conclusion Bernie should also not have been subject to any salary reduction. There are reports that the unfortunate widow still awaits the arrears of pay to reach her bank account.

Most of the typographical errors in the first draft were corrected, save that many years later a diligent doctoral student from the Economic History department at the University of Zambia did notice Mooner and not Spooner in appendix eight, paragraph seven, sub paragraph three of the second edition.

Delyth's burial at Moriah Congregational Chapel was a dignified if rather small affair. Four lines of type, three sentences long, on page nine, even appeared in the Bulawayo Chronicle, that edition being woefully short of any decent stories, reflecting what had been a quiet news week.

Naturally, Gwyn was the chief mourner. Mrs Muriel Griffiths and Mrs Brenda Brady had performed their usual duties, two days prior to the funeral, of polishing all the chapel pews on the ground floor, and also on the balcony. Weed killer was also liberally applied to the paving accessing the main chapel entrance.

'Isn't it good to see Emrys here, Brenda, giving moral support to Gwyn. I'll have to remind him that pipe smoking isn't allowed within the chapel precincts. That Emrys always was a bit of a handful. He got up to all sorts of shenanigans as a boy. I'm sure he's calmed down by now, surely.'

'Don't think we needed to have bothered with the balcony, won't be much use for that today. Thought there would be more here,' replied Brenda.

'Can't see the young baby here, can you?'

'He's been sickly since birth. Expect that housekeeper is looking after him. She seems to have her claws in everything to do with the Bowens.'

Gwyn and Emrys sat in the front pew, just below the deacons, who sat in a half square above them, six feet below the minister in his pulpit. Emrys and Gwyn's family pew was two rows from the back on the right-hand side; sitting as they now did, so far forward, made them both feel uncomfortable – watched, examined.

'That byre was here for Mam and Dad's funerals,' remarked Emrys.

'It's mopani wood, lasts forever. It'll do you and me no doubt,' replied Gwyn.

'Always thought there were more deacons in Moriah, must be my memory. Apart from Mam and Dad's funerals, when were we last together in chapel?'

'You couldn't make it to the wedding obviously, so it must be when we were at Sunday school. Mam and Dad would be proud to see us side by side again, in the front pew, hymn books in our hands,' said Gwyn.

'These hymns haven't changed. Still the same old dirges.'

'Who fooled her the most Emrys, you or me?'

'We're all somebody's fool, but I don't quite know what you're getting at, old chum.'

Emrys felt for the calabash in his jacket pocket.

'Do any of us know what we're getting at. We were both playing games with her, weren't we? And we both knew it. We both gave her hope in our own way, Emrys.''

'Hope is for fairy tales, Gwyn,' replied Emrys. Hope is a fantasy.'

'Or a deception?' said Gwyn.

'Maybe. You've got to be religious to have hope, and neither one of us has. She's in the past now, old boy. We've got to make room for other items. We've made it through, that's the main thing. That's the only thing that's important. By the way, I wanted to tell you, haven't had the chance until now: Margaret and I have decided to emigrate to Australia. Give the girls a different future.'

'A better future, you mean, don't you?'

'Of course a better future. The way of life is changing here. And

Margaret never liked Africa, not like me. We're off to Perth. Been making arrangements for a while. Found a great job there as district manager of another farm implements business.'

'When are you going, Em?'

'Two weeks today. Travelling to Cape Town and then boarding a ship for Perth. You must come to visit us once we've settled in. The girls would love to see their favourite uncle. What about you, Gwyn, what are your plans?'

'Let's get today over with first. The future can wait until tomorrow.'

Delyth's casket was laid on the long shiny mopani byre in front of the deacons as they faced the pulpit, with their backs to the congregation. Two small posies, one of yellow daffodils and another of purple bougainvillea, were placed on top. Moriah's resident minister, Mr Cadwaladr Roberts, an unkempt mop of thinning red hair over a balding pate, ageless, walked slowly from the chapel entrance door up the right-hand aisle. Passing the seated Gwyn and Emrys on his left, he nodded his head in acknowledgement. Beyond them, he turned left up two carpeted steps to the deacon's' level, nodded to the coffin, then taking a further four carpeted steps up and two across to the left, he arrived at his pulpit. He sat down in his cushioned armchair, bent his head slightly, held the top of his nose, just below the forehead, in between his right thumb and right forefinger, and closed his eyes in silent prayer.

'Mr Roberts still here. He must be close to meeting his maker.'

'He's not far off eighty. One of the old school.'

'See he still does that, Gwyn, that praying stuff before the main event. Good to see some things never change. Helps the commodore up in the pulpit cope with the situation better, I dare say.'

'Does God hear our prayers, Emrys?'

'Prayers? God? These things are above me. You decide on your own answers because I sure as hell haven't got any.'

Mr Cadwaladr Roberts, deeming the time to be right, stood up and started.

'Mrs Delyth Bowen came from a well respected family. The Jenkinses were a family from the old country who tried to make a go of it in this new country of ours, symbolised by the wonderful flower arrangement atop her coffin today. The daffodil and the bougainvillea, Cambria and Africa entwined as one. The Jenkinses, a family touched by tragedy – fated, you might say. They are all together now, all of them, and in a better place. I remember Delyth as a young girl singing in Sunday School, lovely soprano voice, attending all our services morning and evening. If memory serves me right, she also joined us in our Wednesday bimonthly prayer meetings, the only one of our young people to do so. Mr and Mrs Jenkins did indeed give her a Christian upbringing, and I am sure she was the better for it, a true daughter of the Chapel. Oh that there were more of her type. She will be sadly missed. I also had the pleasure of officiating at Delyth's wedding with her dear husband, Gwyn. They were a very happy couple. As a chapel it was so pleasing to see the children of two families from our congregation uniting together in God. It was a joyous day for all of us, it surely was. Of even greater joy was when Gwyn and Delyth announced that Almighty God had blessed their union with a child. Gwyn, in this dark hour, the child will forever bring you comfort, I'm sure, a reminder of your deep love for your dear wife, a reminder that through the child she lives on. Our deepest condolences to you, Gwyn, and of course to your brother Emrys, who in his youth defined the word urchin for me and the elders of this chapel. Welcome Gwyn, welcome Emrys. *Croeso i'ch dau.*'

Mr Roberts continued his eulogy for another twenty minutes. Embroidered blue shawls, the sisterhood, bilharzia... Gwyn and Emrys had closed their minds to it all a long time earlier. Gwyn was in Kapiri Mposhi, Emrys in the Great Northern Hotel.

'Lovely send off, Brenda. We're all saints when we die,' said Mrs Muriel Griffiths.

'Certainly has a way with words, does Mr Roberts. We're fortunate to have him,' replied Mrs Brenda Brady.

'Talk about good fortune, Delyth was fortunate she renewed her dues a few weeks ago! She hadn't paid them for years. Else she wouldn't have a place in Moriah cemetery next to her parents. Some people have all the luck. The treasurer, Mr Davies, informs me that

Gwyn has done the same. His place will be safe for another few years too.

'Not many here though,' said Muriel.

'Just as we suspected. The Jenkins family was never really one of us,' said Brenda.

'True enough. Outsiders one and all. Can't but feel sorry for Delyth though. Even as a youngster she was never really happy, I always thought there was a deep sadness to her. Perhaps we could have done more, knowing what happened to her mother. That shawl wasn't enough. Where was our Christianity? If we can't lend a hand to one of our own, who can we help?'

'It can hardly be our fault that she did what she did. They didn't want to be helped, none of that family did. They were all closed off. They didn't know if they wanted to be here or be at home. As Mr Roberts said, they were fated.'

'I think she was looking around to be rescued.'

'But we didn't come to her aid, did we?'

'She was born to die like she did.'

'Don't you think his sermon was wonderful.'

'Aren't the flowers nice.'

I wasn't fussed whether I attended the funeral or not. Someone had to look after little Delwyn, and I'm not one for funerals anyway. What's the point of making a fuss over someone when they're dead? The dead won't know the difference anyhow. When you're dead, you're dead. Those settlers with their fancy funerals, the singing, the sermons, the show off, the talking big about the dead person in life... It's rubbish really, isn't it? But the Bowens had to go through with the process. Funny really: the two men who'd caused her death were the chief mourners. I just could never understand these settlers. Lying, it seemed to me, was a pillar of their culture.

LI

THEY WERE EIGHT, all armed with Mauser rifles from the Congo. All Bemba. One commander, Russell.

'You've all had long enough to learn how to use these rifles, they ain't difficult. Once the Land Rover stops by the roadblock, wait for my command to fire. No one do anything until I shout. We've got to be disciplined. We ain't bandits, we're an army. This ain't no free for all. We clear on that?'

'All clear, sir!'

'Any extra rounds you want, ask David. He'll be flitting around like a cichlid. Things bound to get a bit messy. There'll be confusion. Going to get noisy too, so you better shout for him as loud as you can. Without David and Thomas here, we wouldn't have these Mausers. He's played a big part in the logistics of this operation, haven't you, son?'

'Yes, sir,' replied young David.

'They set the chess board, we're the pieces, and the first move will be ours, because we've got the surprise on them. And we better make it count, or it'll be the worse for us. You two, get up on the bluff up there, aim for the Land Rover tyres, keep firing at 'em. Even if you think they're done, keep firing. I don't want to see that vehicle escaping either backwards or forwards. The five of us will use these trees for cover. David will be running with ammo between the two units. We'll go for the police inside, keep shooting till I shout cease fire, but pay heed to my commands. No one fires a cartridge until I say so. We've all got to be in control. This drama we're about to embark on will echo around the whole country and far beyond. We're expecting them about two o'clock this afternoon. They'll have eaten back at the station. I'll go for the driver first, he's got to be disposed of as soon as possible.'

'Shouldn't we have some riflemen on the other side of the road, sir?' asked one of the volunteers. 'We'll get them on both sides if we do.'

'Too much of a risk. That'd be a crossfire, we'd be shooting at each other. I'm not going to have my men shot by stray bullets from their comrades. They won't be expecting anything, just a nice peaceful jaunt on the savannah. A quiet amble from one station to another, admiring the buffalo, a zebra or two. But we'll give them a surprise, won't we, boys?'

'How many we bargain'll be in the Land Rover, sir?'

'Three, possibly four. Usually a gazetted officer, a sergeant and maybe two constables.'

'They going to be armed, ain't they?'

'They'll have steel riot helmets with wicker shields and tear gas stowed in the back.'

'And guns, sir? What kind of guns they carrying?'

'Point three o three Lee Enfields Number Fours Mark 1. We tried to steal some a few months back. Luck was against us. Like the rest of the equipment, the rifles will usually be stowed in the back of the vehicle. These boys ain't anticipating any problems on their outing. Officer usually in the front passenger seat. Will be carrying a point four five five Webley. Only got a range of fifty yards, so won't be troubling us none. All you have to do, men, is keep on firing into that Land Rover. These Mausers have proved themselves before, and remember, David will have more than enough ammo for all of us. Just shout out his name and he'll be there. Shoot till I say cease fire. They'll have no time to get their rifles. Four or five minutes the whole show will be over.'

'They all going to be settlers in that Land Rover, sir?'

'Settlers, Bemba, they're all police. Instruments of the colonial state. No colour bar with us when it comes to shooting. Northern Rhodesia police, that's who we'll be killing. No matter what colour, we got to show them we ain't taking it no more, time for them to go. Anyone who helps them settlers, they deserve the same, remember that. They're all police. Right, let's get this miombo down, block this track good.'

Unluckily for this particular miombo tree, it had been growing for a number of decades on the side of the bush track between two small ravines, a sanctuary for some animals, a place of ambush for others, welcome shade for all. Flat-topped, its crown spread like a pancake. Three men from the squad made the most of the last of this shade as, axes in hand, they cut through the rough greyish-brown bark in short order, ensuring the tree fell across the track, a perfect roadblock. The miombo felled, all voices slowly quietened. They became eavesdroppers, noiseless watchmen.

The dirt roadway, such as it was, followed a sandstone ridge before descending into a tree-lined valley via a number of sharp bends, then fording a small, murmuring pebbly stream and ascending again on the other side. Running each side of the stream for some thirty to forty yards were clumps of miombo trees. The particular tree felled a few yards short of the stream blocked all traffic in both directions. Due to the meandering nature of the road, any oncoming vehicle would not be within sight of the stream until thirty yards from the roadblock itself. In view of this, a ninth man, a scout, had been deployed on the sandstone ridge itself, tasked with signalling the approach of the police Land Rover. He would then traverse the ridge and direct fire on the Land Rover from the rear. He was also to ensure that any escapees from the Land Rover running back down the roadway were dealt with in the appropriate manner.

It was a dry savannah afternoon, a slight breeze. A troop of chacma baboons, some dark brown some grey, congregated near the stream, dipping their downward-sloping faces in and out of the water, unaware of their proximity to the ambushers, who were by now well hidden. A hyena screeched in the distance. A three-banded courser scuttled through the short grass.

The scout, crouched like a predator behind the grey, fissured bark of a Guinea palm tree, glinted his mirror against the sun.

'That's the signal, men. It's all about to start. Good luck to you all and do not open fire until you hear my command!'

The startled baboons screeched out of the river up into the miombo trees.

Travelling at a speed of twenty miles an hour, the dust-covered Land Rover, its windows peppered with dead flies and mosquitoes, had plenty of time to stop before coming into contact with the fallen tree.

'Fire, commence fire!' shouted Russell.

Seven bolt action Mausers opened up from the two locations. Lined up in Russell's sights the was the driver of the Land Rover, a sergeant. He was killed within seconds with a shot to the head that propelled his brains against the Land Rover cabin and splattered his fellow policemen. The tyres on the vehicle, visible to the ambushers on the bluff, were blasted to slivers of shredded rubber. The three remaining policemen tumbled out, two from the rear seats, taking cover on the blind side of the Land Rover. The third, a major, firing his Webley wildly, stumbled out of the passenger side. His long spindly legs making a speedy exit laborious, he provided a perfect target. Constant fire from the seven riflemen killed the major outright, his body buckling mechanically and collapsing into the dusty road. The two surviving policemen, both constables and both local Bemba, grabbed their weaponry from the vehicle and started to return fire from the cover of the Land Rover.

'More ammo, David, we need more ammo!' came the shout from the bluff.

Running up to the two shooters on the hillside, David dispensed twenty cartridges apiece.

'Down here, David, ammo down here!'

Off he went again.

One of the constables attached a rifle grenade launcher to his Lee Enfield and propelled a barrage of grenades towards their enemy. As David ran down to the second unit in the trees, a grenade landed a few yards away from him. Shrapnel pierced his abdomen, the ammunition box plunging down the bluff, disgorging the cartridges on the ground, blood spurting from his body, spreading over the savannah, the mangled stem of a miombo sticking out of his groin, his left foot in a nearby acacia tree.

'Help me, help me, someone help me!' young David screeched. He shouted for his mother, then said nothing, looking up at the perfect cloudless savannah sky, coughing up his own blood.

The firing continued, the grenades continued.

'Get back up there!' shouted Russell to one of his squad. 'Get the ammo box down here. Go, go on!'

'What about David?'

'Leave him for now. Get the ammo, go!'

The scout had by this time reached the battle from the rear, having ascended the sandstone ridge. Falling on his right knee, and with a clear view of both policemen, he shot the constable with the grenade launcher twice in the chest, mortally wounding him. Seeing his friend fall on his left-hand side, the lone remaining policeman opened the rear passenger door, providing some cover. The scout kept firing, unaware of a second police Land Rover stationary on the crown of the bend.

Two of the four occupants of this second Land Rover ran along the side of the road, towards their besieged colleague. Their four shots hit the scout in the back. He would die of his untended wounds less than an hour later. In a flanking movement, the two other policemen began ascending the bluff, one holding a standard Lee Enfield, the other a Bren light machine gun.

'You said there'd be only one Land Rover! Where the hell did the second one come from?'

'Intelligence said there would only be one. Aim for the two on the road, try and stop them before they reach the Land Rover! Keep your discipline, men!'

Prone to the ground, the Bren gunner sergeant rested the weapon on its bipod and opened fire. The lance corporal with him did the same with his rifle. The Bren, capable of firing at a rate of five hundred rounds per minute, exposed the flank of the ambush squad with terrible effect.

'We've got to retreat, sir. They've got us!'

The two policemen from the second Land Rover, unscathed, had now reached the lone survivor from the first. The ambushers scrambled for cover as the barrage of grenades resumed.

'We've got to leave, we've got to leave now, sir, or we'll all be killed!'

'We'll regroup on the bluff with the rest of the boys. Come on!'

Running up the escarpment, under constant fire from the police next to the Land Rover, they reached David. He was holding his stomach in a hopeless effort to stem the bleeding and to stop his innards collapsing out of his body. One of the men put his hand underneath David's shoulder to help to pull him up.

'Leave him! He can't be helped! You go ahead, I'll catch you up!

Russell placed his palm on David's forehead, looked at his stomach, then his eyes.

'I'm sorry,' Russell said.

Young David looked back at Russell and said nothing.

Thirty more metres up the slope, Russell and his men arrived at the vantage point of the two other commandos. One was dead, hit by a burst of fire from the Bren gun. The other was wounded but capable of walking with assistance.

'All of you go. You know the safe houses. Thomas, stay here with me, we'll cover the retreat. We'll see you all in a few days.'

Commander Russell and Thomas stood their ground discharging their Mausers at the advancing police. Three were coming up directly at them, the other two pinning them down with a mixture of Bren gun and Lee Enfield fire directed at their flank. The shooting continued for another thirty minutes. The grenades had by this time all been used up. Thomas, shrapnel wounds in his left leg and left shoulder, yelled above the din.

'The rifle's jammed, my bloody rifle's jammed!'

'Let's go, Thomas! We've given the boys a good start.'

'I can't move, sir, I'm done for. You go, leave me your Mauser. and the ammo. You go.'

'You sure, Thomas?'

'Go! I'm proud of what we've done today, sir. I'll die with honour. It's for others now to follow us. Now go, sir, please go.'

Russell ran as fast as he could over the veldt, stopping as long as he dared to look back at Thomas before disappearing over the hill. The last Russell saw, Thomas was still shooting, but within another ten minutes the second rifle had jammed. Thomas moved the bolt up and back, up and back to dislodge the blocking cartridge, one of the first things he'd learned in his rifle lesson with Gwyn, in a peaceful place a long time ago. A single advancing policeman, a captain, had a clear view of Thomas' head and pulled the trigger on his Lee Enfield.

The captain couldn't be sure whether his shot was successful, or whether there were others lying in ambush. It was therefore a further fifteen minutes before the police felt it prudent to advance to the top of the bluff. Crawling on all fours to the hideout, they could see at once there were no survivors; the left side of Thomas' face had been completely blown away.

'One of them's still alive, sir!' shouted one of the Bemba constables. 'Down here! The bugger's still with us. Shall I put a bullet in the bastard?' The constable stamped on David's hands and groin, causing David's guts to pour out on the savannah. The other policemen came running over.

'That's too good for the villain. Get a full jerry can and that empty pop bottle from our Land Rover. We'll roast this one.'

Carefully half filling a lemonade bottle with petrol, the officer tore at David's shirt, thereby dislodging David's hands, releasing his remaining intestines onto the grass. Shoving a piece of the shirt into the bottle, the officer walked some twenty paces back.

'Stand well back, men! We don't want to go up with the rebel. Here's some refreshing lemonade for you, you fucking shit!'

The captain lit the shirt and threw the Molotov cocktail at David, who burst into one ball of flame. All the policemen cheered.

The ensuing bushfire lasted several days, the insects and small mammals who managed to flee the flames providing a welcome feast for scavenging yellow billed kites.

LII

Waungron Road bus station was not the best bus station in the world. It wasn't even the best bus station in Cardiff. There wasn't much shelter when it rained. Shoppers came in and out of the adjacent convenience store, glancing at us as they went about their business.

'I'm not sure I've put on enough clothes this morning. It's colder than I thought. This drizzle gets everywhere,' said Gwyn.

'Don't worry, I can see the bus from here,' I replied.

Gwyn got on first and tried to sit next to the driver in his cab. He was only stopped from doing so by his inability to negotiate the handle to the cab door, plus the shouts from the driver himself.

'Keep a grip on him, missus. He's a liability. Shouldn't be allowed out, man in his state.'

I led Gwyn away to the two pop up seats, at the front of the bus, reserved for mothers with prams. Hopefully no one would make a fuss. People were usually pretty good.

'Come on, Gwyn, sit down here, there's a good fellow,' I said.

A stench of winter clamminess hung about the bus, misted windows dripping, obscuring the streets. Christmas decorations were already fluttering and quivering all along St Mary Street. In front of the castle, four larger than life reindeers turned fluorescent every night.

Sitting in the bus, Gwyn inspected his wallet, as he did nowadays with greater than ever frequency. He was checking that he still had the photograph, slightly dilapidated now – the photograph of himself as a younger man, with his new wife and baby son, their only child. Two outwardly contented, ruddy-cheeked settlers holding their destiny, doing their duty. Northern Europeans. Lords of the savannah. When I looked at it, I reflected on my actions, my inactions.

The photograph had been taken fortuitously by a peripatetic professional photographer called Mr Jones, who pursued his calling in and around the towns of Broken Hill, Ndola, and Solwezi and all villages, hamlets and homesteads in between. Mr Jones, as occasion demanded, also topped up his income as a water diviner, itinerant pig slaughterer and lay preacher for the not insignificant community of Dissenters in that area. It was during Mr Jones' attendance with a local farmer, Mr Hooper, dispatching farmer Hooper's fatted pigs, that his and Gwyn's paths had crossed. Farmer Hooper was good enough to introduce Gwyn to Mr Jones as a photographer, and also to endow him with a dozen thick sausages, one of the biproducts of the coupling of farmer Hooper's Large Whites and Mr Jones' substantial slaughterhouse knife. Both Gwyn and farmer Hooper commented fulsomely on Mr Jones' professional attitude to his duties, save for his water divining and lay preaching, for they had no experience of these.

'Must be all going shopping, Kalinda,' said Gwyn.

'Too late for them to be commuters. They're all at their desks now, in those glass towers in town. Don't forget your doctor's appointment tomorrow,' I replied.

'Doctor? What do I need to go to see a doctor for?' asked Gwyn.

'It's those melanomas on your face. I always told you to be careful in the sun. You should have worn your hat more often. But you knew better, didn't you?' I said.

'Did I? If you say so, I'm sure you're right. Not many zebra around today. I wonder where they've all gone. Must've gone to the river to drink. Can't see any buffalo either. They must be down at the river as well. The lions and crocs will have a feast.'

'Yeah, they'll all have a feast, Gwyn.'

'I wonder how Jabez is these days. Haven't seen him for a while.

He had a great singing voice, all the men respected him. Old Jab liked Murphy's all right. Did I tell you about Murphy's?'

'Don't think you did, Gwyn,' I said.

'Not much to say really. Can't remember where it was now. One day at a time, eh, Kalinda, that's the way to be. One day at a time. Do you remember my friend Jabez? Do you know what happened to Jabez? He was a good friend of mine, it'd be good to know that he's all right. He had a good voice, excellent really. Knew all our songs, all our songs from home. I'll go back there one day. Leave Africa and go back to the old country. Expect nothing will have changed. Chapels full to overflowing, people singing, people speaking the old language... One day at a time, that's what I say, one day at a time.'

We both stared out the bus window, cwtching together to keep out the damp and the cold as best we could.

'We need to get rid of the big tree in the garden, what's it called now?' asked Gwyn.

I struggled for a moment.

'Baobab, Gwyn, baobab,' I replied eventually.

'It's getting out of control. Too big, blocking out the sun. I do like the sun. You like the sun, don't you? I'd be lost without the sun. I'll buy a new sun hat when I'm in Ndola next. We can go there next week.'

A young lady came on to the bus at the Pencisely Road stop, pushing a pram.

'Don't you know these seats are reserved? Mothers with prams, they're reserved for mothers with prams. You old people think you can do whatever you want. Look, do your eyes work? There's plenty of room on this bus, over there, at the back, up those stairs. Why can't you go there? You look pretty fit to me.'

I didn't answer. What was the point? Gwyn started to sing 'Calon Lan', but soon forgot the words.

I wondered if I would ever go back. Gwyn was on his last legs, but then again so was I. At least I wouldn't forget my songs. My eyes began to fill up. I was becoming sentimental; this wouldn't do, would it? The ringing of the 'stop' bell ended my ponderings, though I knew they would soon come back.

'It's our stop next, Gwyn, the Caio Arms. Come on, old timer, I'll give you a hand.'

Tottering along the bus gangway, both of us careful not to lose our balance, handle to pole, pole to handle, from one support to the other.

'It's my cat, I'm so worried.'

'I've tried so hard to give up.'

'Lovely deep black colour.'

'I blame my granddad.'

'It was more of a house cat really.'

'Told me to have a drag.'

'My ex gave it to me.'

'What could I do?'

'He was great company.'

'Couldn't say no.'

'Tommy, his name was Tommy.'

'Since then I was hooked.'

'Opened the window, few months ago now.'

'I've tried everything.'

'To let some air in.'

'You name it, I've tried it.'

'He jumped out.'

'It's not as if I'm weak-willed.'

'I can see it now. Off he went.'

'You ask anybody. I'm a stubborn one.'

'I've waited and waited for Tommy to come back.'

'Suppose it's meant to be.'

'I've got no idea where he's to.'

'I'm off by here.'

'See you.'

'See you.'

'Good thing that they've improved the roads around here,' said Gwyn. 'Broken Hill was getting a bad name. These new tracks will stand up well now it's the rainy season. Can't see these disappearing in the floods. Do you remember my friend Jabez? Oh what was his surname now? He was a good friend. Excellent singing voice, bit of a rough diamond, a good friend for all that. He must be retired now in Ndola.'

'You can go and see him next week when you buy your new sun hat,' I replied.

'Sun hat? I need a new sun hat?'

'Next week in Ndola, when you buy your new sun hat.'

'One day at a time, that's what I say, one day at a time. Still here. One day at a time.'

We walked arm in arm, walking stick by walking stick the thirty yards or so from the bus stop to the entrance into Preswylfa, voted best care home in Cardiff.

We were met in the foyer by Mr Singh, the manager.

'Morning, Mr and Mrs Bowen. Cold and drizzly one, isn't it? Delwyn's been looking forward to seeing you. He's had a restful night. Can I offer you a cup of tea?'

And the sun shone on in Kapiri Mpòshi.